Tear Down Heaven: Book 5

Rachel Aaron

Series Info

Hell for Hire
Hell of a Witch
Hell to Pay
Hell Hath No Fury
Tear Down Heaven

Publishing and Copyright Info

Tear Down Heaven

Aaron Bach LLC
"Writing to Entertain and Inform."
Copyright © 2025 Rachel Aaron

ISBN Paperback: 978-1-952367-52-6

Cover Illustration by *Luisa Preissler*
Cover Design by *Rachel Aaron*
Editing provided by *Red Adept Editing*

Prologue

THE KING OF HEAVEN was disappointed.

Here he was, standing in his full regalia in the Desert of the Chains, surrounded by piles of perfected sin-iron ingots. He had a forge of Enki painstakingly reconstructed from the wreckage of the crafter god's main facility on the banks of the River Lethe. He had Enki's golden Hammer of Creation, the only tool the divine forge would accept, as well as the Crown of Anu, which gave him the authority to swing it.

Every element of his great work—possibly the *greatest* work ever attempted by man or god—was finally at his fingertips, but King Gilgamesh was not laboring at his forge. He was *not* firing the perfected sin iron the war demons had made for him. He was *not* swinging Enki's golden hammer to craft the solution that would save all mankind. No. He was standing in an otherwise unremarkable corner of the new workshop he'd built beneath the chained Wheel of Rebirth, staring down at the dented bronze disaster that had once been his Princess of War.

Such a disappointment.

"Please, greatest and most sacred king," she sobbed, splattering her ugly black blood all over his work floor as she prostrated herself at his feet. "Repair this broken body. Use Enki's hammer to make me whole again, and I *swear* I'll—"

"What's the point of that?" Gilgamesh interrupted with a cold look down his nose. "You were given a simple task, Dalanea: Kill a crownless, weaponless queen. You didn't even have to do it alone. You had an entire Hell's worth of war demons to assist you, and yet, somehow, you still failed."

The bloody queen began to shake. "I—"

"If you can't win a battle so heavily weighted in your favor, I don't see how it makes sense to give you another chance," Gilgamesh continued. "Would *you* show mercy to a subordinate who failed to produce a victory under such grossly advantageous circumstances?"

"No, Great King," the fallen Queen of War whispered, clenching her three remaining fists. "But, in my defense, this was not my idea. It was Crown Prince Alexander who sent me down there. He said he'd take full responsibility—"

"And what should I hold him responsible for?" Gilgamesh snapped. "Expecting the strongest Blade of Ishtar to triumph over a severely handicapped opponent? Believing that a general backed by her entire army would be capable of defeating a single foe? If I have any criticism of my son's judgement, it was that he was too cautious. He handed you the Coward Queen on a platter, and you *still* managed to drop her." The king shook his head. "This is your failing, Dalanea, and you know it. You were the one who shamelessly cried out for my help, so don't try to lay this at Alexander's feet."

"Forgive me," the queen whispered, pressing her corroded bronze forehead to the bloody ground. "The Eternal King's judgement is infallible. If you say it is my fault, then it must be so, but our enemy is not so weak as you describe. Even without her crown, sword, and name, the Bonfire of Wrath's fire was greater than I have ever seen. It infected my demons and turned them against their queen. That's the only reason Rebexa was able to best me, but I know the extent of her powers now. If you'd just restore my body one last time, I swear she will not triumph again. I'll fight to the death to—"

"Fight to the death?" Gilgamesh repeated with a scoff. "What a theatrical waste of time. If you couldn't achieve victory under the ideal conditions my son arranged for you, it's obvious you never will."

"Then make me better," the queen begged, lurching forward to wrap her bloody arms around the Eternal King's armored legs. "You're the one who improves the creations of the gods. If I am weak, use your skill to make me strong. Just *please*, my king, my savior, give me another chance! I swear by my name that I will never fail you again. I'll—"

Her desperate pleading cut off as King Gilgamesh reached down to lay his golden-gloved hand upon her hornless bronze head.

"Foolish Dalanea," he said sadly, "we both know that's not true. Ishtar created you perfect, but the trouble with divine perfection is that it can never exceed the static vision of the gods who created it. Perfect creations cannot grow. They cannot evolve or exceed their limitations. Even with all my brilliance, I was never able to do more than cover you up. No matter how beautiful I made you on the outside, your inner truth remained what you have always been: an insufficient bronze statue, howling in pain."

The Queen of War's grip loosened in shock as the king stepped out of her hold.

"That is why the gods fell in love with humanity in the first place," Gilgamesh explained as he walked back to his repaired forge. "Unlike you, we were *not* their creations and thus were able to exceed their stagnant imaginings. Even my betrayal was treated with wonder because it was a surprise. That's a rare and precious thing to immortals, but you have never possessed such talent, which is why I'm not going to waste my time repairing you again. No matter how many gifts I bestow, you will never change, never flourish or excel. I already know that you are incapable of surprising me, so I'm afraid this is as far as we go."

He finished with a benevolent smile, but the Queen of War's fists were already clenched. "No," she snarled, pushing off her knees. "You promised me. You *swore* that if I served you, I would never be cast aside again!"

"And you were not," Gilgamesh said. "I've known all of this since we met, and yet I tolerated your shortcomings for five thousand years. I made you my general, gave you dominion over your sisters. I even assigned my best son to be your prince. I have been infinitely patient, rained favor after favor upon your dented head, and still you let me down on the eve of my greatest victory." His blue-gray eyes narrowed. "That makes you the one who betrayed me, but unlike the gods, I find no novelty in that. I'm sorry, my dear, but this is the end."

"No!" she screamed, summoning her sacred sword. "You *promised*! You—"

Her voice cut off like a switch as Gilgamesh waved his hand, and what was left of War's scarred body dissolved into bronze pellets. They rattled like hail onto the stone platform the king had built to keep his golden boots out of the black desert's sin-iron dust before rolling into a neat pile around a woman's bronze-skinned hand with a black ring on its third finger. The king was bending over to pick the hand up when his eldest son finally huffed his way to the top of the steps that connected Gilgamesh's new workshop to the rest of his palace.

"Oh," Alexander said when he saw what his father was doing. "Looks like you already know."

"It was fairly obvious," Gilgamesh replied, tossing the severed hand to his son. "She doesn't yell for help when she's winning."

"Looks like she won't be yelling for anything anymore," Alexander said as he snatched the Queen of War's severed hand out of the air.

"Is that bitterness I hear?" Gilgamesh asked as he grabbed the forge bellows he would have been working all this time if a whining failure had not interrupted him. "I'm sorry, Alexander. Did I destroy your favorite?"

"Of course not," the Crown Prince replied. "The Princess of War has always been more burden than help. If I'm upset about anything, it's that you didn't save the eye I gave her. I was hoping to get that back someday."

"I'll make you a new one," his father promised. "A proper one crafted from flesh instead of gold. I should have ample time to master such arts now that I'm about to solve our greatest problem."

"About that," Alexander said, glancing nervously over his shoulder at the staircase to the lower levels.

"What do you want to do about the Coward Queen? I feel it's accurate to say that we've completely lost containment at this point."

"Don't worry about her," Gilgamesh replied dismissively, reaching up to tap the golden circlet of the Crown of Anu that he'd incorporated into his lion-headed helmet. "Even the Coward Queen can't threaten what she can't reach."

"I see," Alexander said, even though there was no way he could. Alexander had never truly understood anything about Gilgamesh's great work, but that was why the king trusted him. Clever, creative sons like Leander and Adrian had their uses, but a practical, unimaginative man who viewed the world in simple terms was the one you wanted watching your back. And speaking of trust...

"Come," the king said, letting go of the forge bellows to hold out a golden-gloved hand to his Crown Prince. "I owe you a gift for turning your sword into bronze pellets."

"I am blessed to receive anything you deign to offer, my king," Alexander replied with flawless politeness, though even his famous discipline couldn't completely eliminate the tremble from his voice. "If it's another princess, though, I don't think I can—"

"Not a princess," Gilgamesh assured him. "This is something I've never offered to anyone before. I wasn't planning on ever giving it away, but I think this is the right time, and you are definitely the right person."

"I am honored," Alexander said, sounding like he meant it this time. "What is it?"

Gilgamesh smiled wider and crooked his finger, beckoning his most competent prince to a reward that only the man who slew the gods could bestow.

Chapter 1

IT WAS COMPLETELY INAPPROPRIATE, but all Bex could think about as she and Adrian climbed the steps out of the Hells was the feel of his work-roughened hand where it wrapped around hers. Going up to scout the situation in Heaven had been her idea, but as they left the war demons' tower and started up the long, enclosed spiral staircase that led to the final door, her feet moved slower and slower. It wasn't that she was afraid—she was actually more convinced than ever that they could do this—it was just...

"Bex?"

She raised her head to see Adrian looking at her, his mirrored eyes glowing in the dim light like torches. That should've freaked her out, but not even Gilgamesh's prince eyes could make Adrian look like anything other than Adrian, and Bex's pace grew even slower. She was practically standing still when Adrian finally turned to face her with a huff.

"What's wrong?" he asked, placing a hand on Boston's arched back to keep his clearly impatient familiar from blurting out something insulting.

"Nothing's wrong," Bex replied, looking up the torchlit spiral stair behind him. "That's the problem. We still don't know what Gilgamesh is up to, but *I* know we're going to be neck-deep in trouble again the moment we step outside, and I..."

Her voice trailed off, but Adrian didn't say a word. He just stood there, watching her patiently as

Bex slumped against the sin-stained black stone wall with a sigh.

"I don't want to jump back into that mess again so soon, you know?" she admitted in a tiny voice. "We just freed all of demonkind from the Hells. This is the biggest victory I've ever won. The biggest *any* version of me has won, and it feels like we're blowing right by it."

That was the most selfish thing Bex could bring herself to say out loud, but it was only the tip of the iceberg. It'd been so easy to keep rolling when the thrill of beating the Queen of War was still pumping through her veins. Now that it was just her and Adrian on the stairs, though, Bex was discovering that the closer they got to Heaven, the less she wanted to let go of this moment. This rare, beautiful fragment in time when she wasn't fighting or burning or being stabbed. When no one was looking to her for orders or depending on her to save them.

It felt like something precious, a treasure to be savored, but Bex couldn't stop to enjoy it. The battle wasn't over. Everyone was still depending on her. She needed to stop being selfish and keep moving, but when she shoved herself off the wall to keep walking, Adrian reached out and pulled her into a hug.

"It's okay," he whispered, squeezing her close with his arms while his clever fingers worked her hair out of the wet, bedraggled ponytail she hadn't even realized was pulling on her head. "It's okay, Bex."

As always, he didn't say what was okay, and, as always, it didn't matter. Her subjects needed her to be strong, but Adrian wasn't a demon. He didn't need her to hold him up, which meant she was free to break down.

Bex did so with a sob so hard that even she jumped. The ugly sound was both mortifying and terribly timed, but Bex had nothing left to stop it. It'd been a long, hard push even before they'd left for the Hells, and she was so tired. Tired of fighting, tired of being responsible, tired of forcing herself to be brave. The moment they stepped into Heaven, she'd have to do it all again, but they weren't there yet. They were hidden in a dark stairwell where no one could see. Even Boston had hopped off his witch's shoulder to give them some privacy, which made it dangerously easy for Bex to pretend it was just her and Adrian.

That thin pretense was all her body needed. Her demons were just a few spirals down in the Hell of War, so she couldn't bawl like she really wanted to, but she was still a mess. Adrian had to be disgusted, but when Bex tried to move away, he pulled her back, pressing her face against his shoulder as she cried and cried and cried.

"Sorry," she whispered when the storm finally passed. "I'm always doing this to you."

"I'm glad," he insisted, petting her loose hair. "It makes me feel special to be the one you cry on."

"Well, I hate it," she muttered, scrubbing her puffy face. "What kind of queen cries after she wins?"

"One that's not a robot," he replied, bending down to press a kiss against the top of her forehead where her horns used to be. "Winning can be as hard as losing sometimes. Just because you came out on top doesn't mean the fight wasn't brutal, or that you didn't get hurt. You've been waging this war for your entire life. That's a lot of damage to carry, so I think it's a good sign that you can still cry. It means you're healthy."

Bex thought it meant she was a weepy embarrassment, but while her cheeks were burning with shame, she did feel a lot better.

"Okay," she said, pulling herself straight again. "Let's do this."

"Are you sure?" he asked. "We don't have to move just yet."

"I've already wasted enough of our advantage," Bex insisted, finger-combing her hair back into a fresh ponytail that she fixed in place with one of the spare hair ties she'd stashed in the back pocket of her black fatigues. "Gilgamesh is probably scrambling his troops as we speak. If we want to take a look at the battlefield before it gets swamped, we've got to go. Besides, if I cry anymore, I'll dehydrate myself."

Adrian's shoulder was damp enough already. Thank Ishtar he always wore black, or her ashy tears would've ruined his clothes. It was pathetic how much she liked knowing that she could cry on him without leaving a trace, but Bex was used to her heart being an idiot by this point, so she rolled with it, grabbing his hand so they could run together up the staircase's final spiral.

Boston was already waiting when they got there, pawing at the bottom of yet another set of massive sin-iron doors. It was the biggest, heaviest, most ornamented doorway Bex had seen yet, which she took as a sign that they were on the right track. Gilgamesh had always been a sucker for grandeur, and those *definitely* looked like the gates of Hell.

"*Finally*," Boston said, looking over his shoulder with a lash of his tail. "I'm not sure if the doors are locked or just heavy, but I can't get them to budge."

"Have you heard anything from outside?" Adrian asked as he crouched beside his cat.

"Not a peep," Boston reported, leaning down to push his nose against the perfectly fitted seam where the giant doors met the floor. "I haven't smelled anything, either, though that could be because the doors are so tightly sealed. They were meant to keep the Hells out of Heaven, after all."

"Let me give it a try," Bex said, pressing her hands flat against the cold, ornately carved metal. "Um, you might want to give me some distance."

Boston leaped out of the way at once, scrambling up the front of Adrian's coat to his damp shoulder like a fluffy black squirrel. When Bex was confident she wouldn't have to worry about singeing anyone's fur, she closed her eyes and called her fire.

As always since she'd reignited during her flight with the princess version of herself, the flames came over her in a rush. That was normally a good thing, but Bex was only a few minutes off the blinding-white, cutting-torch burn that had taken down the Queen of War. Her arms started shaking the moment the fire engulfed them, but she'd wasted too much time being weak already, so she forced herself to push through, silently reciting all the things Gilgamesh had done to her people to stoke the flames of her anger higher and higher, hotter and hotter. She was closing in on the sin-iron melting point when Adrian said, "Hit it here."

Bex turned in alarm to see him standing way too close. She was pretty good with her fire these days, but one mistake was all it would take to burn him to a crisp. Adrian had to know that, but either he was very good at hiding his nerves or he trusted her to an insane degree, because he'd planted his hands less than an inch away from her flaming ones without a trace of fear.

"There's a smaller door hidden inside the big ones," he explained, running his fingers over a crease in the sin iron that Bex had assumed was just part of the decoration. "I saw the war demons using it when I was here earlier. It might be easier to open."

Bex nodded but waited until Adrian stepped back to lean in for a look. Sure enough, when she got her face right next to the metal, she spotted a hidden seam exactly where Adrian had put his fingers. The rectangle it made was still pretty big for a door but much smaller than the rest of the massive gate and sealed only lightly with a few pins at the corners. It looked more like it'd been made to stop bad smells and noise than demons, which made a weird sort of sense when Bex thought about it. If a rebellion ever did get this far, Gilgamesh would stop it with an army, not a door. This gate was probably meant to be more of a logistical barrier than an actual security measure, a suspicion that was proven correct when all the pins snapped like cheap birthday candles the moment Bex's flames touched them.

She froze the moment they broke, smothering her fire so she could listen without the bonfire roaring in her ears. She didn't hear anything, though, which made no sense. After saving the Queen of War, Gilgamesh *had* to know they were coming. His army was probably just waiting for her to stick her head out so they could fill her face with arrows, so Bex led with her foot instead, easing the unlocked door open with the reinforced toe of her combat boot.

The first thing that came through was light. The moment the door cracked, blinding-white radiance burst into the smoky, torchlit staircase like water from a fire hose, along with the scent of something sweet. Bex had been down in the Hells for so long now, it took her several seconds to recognize the aroma as fresh air. It entered her nose like a shot of pure nostalgia, reminding Bex that this was home. No matter how much Gilgamesh had changed it, they were still in Paradise, the land she'd been made to protect, and the moment its cool, clean scent hit her brain, Bex yanked the door open with all her might.

The flash that followed whited out her vision. For several heartbeats, blinding light was all she could see. When she finally blinked the glare away, though, what her eyes saw next wasn't any more informative.

"Wait, what?" she said, shielding her face against Heaven's brilliance as she stepped through the black doorway into what appeared to be a completely empty square.

She was standing in the White City, where she'd fought the Queen of War only a week ago. Back then, the streets had been filled with golden war constructs. Now, though, there was nothing. The pale-blue sky was empty, the elegant white-stone buildings silent and still. Bex didn't even see any guards standing watch, which was almost scarier than finding an entire army.

"You're seeing this, too, right?" she whispered to Adrian, who was hovering directly behind her, staring over her shoulder. "Is there actually nothing there, or is this a trick?"

"It looks real to me," he whispered back before glancing at his feet. "Boston?"

Bex hadn't even heard the cat jump down, but Boston was suddenly standing between her boots, poking his nose out as far as he could reach without actually stepping over the threshold.

"I smell a lot of sorcery," he informed them after several seconds of intense sniffing. "But I don't think there are any spells active in our immediate vicinity. Nothing big enough to hide an army or blow us up when we step on it, anyway."

That was good to hear, but Bex still didn't step forward.

"What is going on?" she asked instead, crossing her arms over her chest. "We just took over all Nine Hells. Why is there no response? What is Gilgamesh doing?"

"I have no idea," Adrian confessed, pressing even closer as he tried to look around the door's corners without actually crossing the line into the city. "This place was full of people when I passed through a few hours ago."

"Well, they're not here now," Bex said, finally stepping through the gate into the apparently empty square.

She stopped the second she was through, but nothing happened. There was no wind, no sound, no blasts of sorcery or creak of armor from a hidden ambush. Her senses were admittedly duller since the loss of her horns, but so far as Bex could tell, they really were alone. She took a few more steps into the open, just to be sure, but no sniper shots came out of the silent buildings to hit her in the head, so she went ahead and motioned for Adrian and Boston to come out.

They did so in a rush, hurrying to join her in front of the Hells' gate, which, now that she was outside, Bex could see was shaped like a giant black cube. Its surface was carved all over with reliefs of suffering demons and, of course, a giant image of Gilgamesh guarding the doors. It looked just like the oversized hallway Lys had led them down when they'd first come here, but where that had been a tunnel through the ground, this was a monolith standing alone at the center of a huge, empty square.

The open space was clearly meant for staging troops, but the only security Bex saw at the moment were four white obelisks capped with Gilgamesh's creepy golden eyes. *Those* were watching them with the same intensity as the princesses, but Bex didn't hear any alarm bells. Just heavy, empty silence and the faint whine in her ears that always came when she knew she was walking into a trap.

"Okay, I officially hate this," Bex announced, circling around Adrian as she tried to keep an eye on every direction at once. "Where in the Hells is everybody? Where are the warlocks? The sorcerers? Where's the damn army?"

Rather than answering, Adrian pulled his broom off his back and hopped on. Bex sat down behind him a second later, followed by Boston, who took his usual position on the broom's tip. When they were all aboard, Adrian kicked them into the air like a popping cork. In the blink of an eye, they'd cleared the roofs of the white residential buildings that lined the empty square, and the Holy City came into view.

It looked just like Bex remembered: a perfect circle of elegant white buildings surrounded by a towering white wall. The melted carcasses of the lion cannons were still glimmering on top of the battlements, but everything else was gone. There were no construct soldiers, no white-robed warlocks, not even any demon slaves peeking through the curtained windows. The entire city looked like it had been emptied, but it wasn't until Bex's eyes made it over to the palace at Heaven's center that she saw why.

"Aw, crap."

Gilgamesh's entire multi-tower fortress was covered in a shimmering golden shield. It hadn't been visible down in the square, but now that she was above the rooftops, Bex could see that the glittering spell went all the way from the castle's white-paved courtyard to the tip of the tallest golden tower. It was the biggest barrier spell she'd ever seen on anything, but other than blocking access to the palace, it didn't seem to be a threat, which meant Bex was now very confused.

"Wait," she said, leaning so far over that Adrian had to stick his arm out to keep her from falling off the broom. "Is that a good thing or a bad thing?"

"Bad," Adrian replied at once. "The chains we need to get back to Earth are in there."

"That's a long-term problem," Bex argued. "Our biggest immediate worry was retaliation, but it seriously looks like Gilgamesh evacuated his city and retreated into his fortress." A smile spread across her face. "If he's in there and we're out here, does that mean we're safe?"

"I wouldn't go that far," Boston warned. "Just because he put up a barrier doesn't mean he can't take it down again."

"We're not safe until we're out," Adrian agreed, pulling his witch hat out of his coat and placing it back on his head to shield his eyes against Heaven's eternal glare. "Gilgamesh is absolutely not defeated. He probably just pulled back because a palace is easier to defend than an entire city, and because he knew we wouldn't be able to get in. It's a lot bigger this time, but that barrier looks exactly like the one I saw over the entrance to the chain back when I infiltrated the Boston Anchor. Malik claimed it could only be crossed by those in Gilgamesh's favor. That could've been another lie, of course, but I'm sure it won't be easy to break."

He glanced over his shoulder for Bex's reaction, but she just blinked at him.

"You infiltrated the Boston Anchor?"

"I did a lot of stupid things while we were apart," he confessed, turning back to the glittering palace. "That said, I think you're right in the short term. The barrier is cutting us off from the chains, but it also means that our biggest immediate worry is solved. If Gilgamesh has retreated into his fortress and the city really is as empty as it seems, then—"

"We can evacuate into it!" Bex finished with a grin, reaching up to tap the comm in her ear. "Lys? Iggs?"

"We're here," Lys's voice crackled over the connection. "Iggs is standing right next to me. What's the bad news?"

Bex's grin got wider. "Believe it or not, it's good news this time. Heaven is clear. Go ahead and start moving everyone up."

"Wait, did you say Heaven is clear?" Iggs demanded.

"Clear how?" Lys asked at the same time. "Did you already beat the army or—"

"There was no army," Bex interrupted, looking down at all the giant empty buildings with a new eye. "Gilgamesh has abandoned the city and retreated into his palace. I don't know if he'll stay in there, but for the time being at least, it looks like the whole place is ours."

"You're kidding," Iggs said excitedly. "That's great!"

"It's suspicious," Lys argued. "How do you know this isn't a trap?"

"I don't," Bex confessed, sliding her arm around Adrian's waist as he flew them back down to the ground. "If it is a trap, though, it hasn't gone off yet, and I don't intend to wait around until it does. Just come on up. Whatever Gilgamesh has in store for us, it's gotta be better than the Hells."

"That wouldn't be hard," Iggs muttered. "But if you say it's safe, that's good enough for me."

"We're on our way," Lys confirmed. "See you in a minute."

Bex nodded and released the button, leaping off the broom the moment it got within safe jumping distance of the ground to go meet her people.

It took a little over six hours to evacuate everyone out of the Hells. Part of that was because the former slaves were starved and exhausted, especially Bex's wrath demons. Mostly, though, it was simply a matter of throughput.

Even after Iggs and a bunch of war demons shoved the main doors wide open, only so many demons could go up the spiral staircase at a time. Once they got outside, there was another slowdown as everyone stopped to let their eyes adjust to the brightness of Heaven's day. It caused a backup every time, but Bex didn't have the heart to hurry them. Even if it was just Gilgamesh's sunless fake, this was the first time some of these demons had ever seen an open sky. Bex always let them stare as long as they wanted, though she did encourage them to step to the side so the demons behind them could keep moving.

At least there was no shortage of places to put people. Just as it had looked from the air, the White City really did seem to be completely abandoned. All the elegant apartment buildings surrounding the Hells had even been left unlocked, some with food still set out on the tables as if the residents had been in the middle of a meal when they got the order to flee.

That was great news for Bex, Adrian, Boston, and Leander. True to Heaven's reputation for excess, every apartment they checked had a modern, state-of-the-art kitchen stuffed to the rafters with food. It was all shelf-stable pantry items since the Anchor Markets—the only place where the Heavenly denizens could purchase fresh produce—had been closed for weeks, but the Holy City's emergency supplies were still gourmet. There were so many cocktail crackers, olives, summer sausages, packets of dried fruit, and bottles of wine that Bex could've survived for years off just what they found in the first apartment building alone. But while she was okay since Adrian had filled her with the fires of life, her demons were a different story.

Most, like Iggs, were happy to eat the party food along with anything else they could get their hands on, but that just filled their physical bellies. Their actual hunger could only be met by human emotion, and with no humans around aside from Adrian and Leander, that was a problem. They couldn't even scrape sins out of the flooded Hells since Gilgamesh had polluted the water. It wouldn't have been an emergency if everyone had started out healthy, but many of the former slaves and all of Bex's wrath demons had come out of the Hells on the verge of starvation. They needed *actual* food, not cocktail party fillers, which was why, the moment the last demon made it up the stairs from the Hells, Bex took over the rooftop deck of the apartment complex with the best view of Gilgamesh's tower and called a meeting.

It was a pretty motley affair. The evacuation from the Hells had been chaos, but now that everyone was settling into the empty buildings, leaders had started emerging to speak for their representative factions. The final coalition included Bex's crew, who seemed to be universally revered as trusted servants of the Bonfire Queen; Nemini, who was a queen in her own right; Desh, who'd been elected to represent all the escaped demons from the Founders' Tunnels plus the demons Bex had freed from the Lowest Hells; Captain Roga of the war demons; a variety pack of respected elders from all the various segments of the Middle Hells; and a tall pride demon who refused to look at Nemini or give his name.

None of the wrath demons were strong enough to sit through a meeting yet, so Iggs had volunteered to represent their interests. Leander had also refused to attend, since doing so would mean leaving Mara's side, but this wasn't his business anyway, so Bex let him be. Adrian was there, though he'd been forced to hover off the edge of the roof on his broom since his mirrored eyes freaked the other demons out. This arrangement left Bex alone in the middle, but it was a position she was used to now, so she didn't waste time fretting as she hopped up onto the marble-and-steel patio set the warlocks had placed up here for their deck parties and announced the obvious.

"We can't stay here."

"It's not a bad place," said one of the wizened elders from the Middle Hells. "Even abandoned, Heaven's luxuries abound. We have soft beds to sleep on, rooms for privacy, clothes to wear, and wine to drink. Truly, this city is a paradise compared to where we were."

"But we have no food," Bex reminded him stiffly. "The Rivers of Death don't flow up here, and there aren't enough humans to pull sins out of directly. If we don't get back to Earth or find something else to eat up here, we're going to lose even more people."

"Is there any way to clean the floodwaters?" asked Lys, who'd put on their neutral, genderless body for this meeting plus a big black coat to hide their still-bleeding shoulder. "That stuff's so packed with sin it's sludgy. There has to be some way to get it out."

"There isn't," Desh insisted from the side table where Streya was playing with the jewels she'd found in one of the bedrooms. "Not only did the flood protocol dump in poison at the start, the whole Middle Hells cavern was coated in eons of toxic ash and grit. The water's actually getting even more poisonous as it marinates." He shook his pale head. "There may be a way to clean it, but I don't know what it is, and we don't have time to figure it out. I'd much rather just abandon ship. This whole place is cursed so far as I'm concerned."

"I agree with that," Adrian said, moving his broom a little closer so he could join the conversation without yelling. "But getting out is going to be a challenge. While you were busy getting people out of the Hells, Boston and I flew over to take a look at the shield."

"And?" Bex asked.

"And it's impenetrable," he replied with a shrug. "But we knew that already."

"What my witch is trying to say is that the barrier is immune to sorcery," Boston explained with a swish of his tail. "I still maintain that a strong enough blow from a different magical source could crack it. If we were in the Blackwood, for example, I'm certain we could beat our way through."

"But we're not in the Blackwood," Adrian said in the exasperated voice of someone who'd already made that point many, *many* times. "We're not on real land. We're inside a magical construction where nothing grows, and I've still got a block inside my chest. I can't even reach my heart, never mind my forest, and if I go through you again for something that big, I'll kill you."

"There are many difficulties," Boston admitted. "But it's hardly *impenetrable*. We just haven't found the right mechanism yet."

"Then we'd better get to finding it," Bex said, interrupting Boston before he could draw Adrian into one of their hours-long technical arguments. "Just because nothing's come out of the palace to kill us yet doesn't mean we're in the clear. Until we've got everybody safely back on Earth, this is still an active war zone. I want everyone to stay together at all times and keep an eye on anybody more injured than yourselves. When our window comes, it'll probably come quick, so sleep in shifts and be ready to move at a moment's notice."

"What kind of window are you expecting?" Iggs asked.

"I don't know yet," Bex admitted. "But I'm going to find one. I didn't break Ishtar's children out of the Hells just so we could starve to death while Gilgamesh laughs at us from his palace. We're getting out of here, so stay close, stay safe, and stay together until I give the order to move."

Despite the direness of their situation, that seemed to raise the demons' spirits, especially the former slaves. The representatives from the Middle Hells all bowed at once and left to spread the queen's word to all the other demons sleeping in the apartment blocks that surrounded the entrance to the Hells. If they'd spread out, they probably could've filled the entire city, but the demons were afraid of Heaven and preferred staying together. They'd packed themselves into the luxury apartments ten to a room, for which Bex was very glad. Protecting people was a lot easier when they were clumped together. She couldn't protect them from their biggest threat, though, which was why, the moment everyone cleared off the roof except for her crew and Adrian, she called a huddle.

"Is there any way we can get to the chains that doesn't involve going into Gilgamesh's palace?" she asked as soon as they were all together.

"There's gotta be," Iggs said. "We saw the chains from the cliff where we got banished. If we can get to the edge of this place, I bet we could hop right off and walk our way down them to freedom."

"It's not going to be that easy," Lys warned, their androgynous face pinched and frighteningly pale from the wound Bex knew was still bleeding under their coat. "You can't see it right now because of the high walls, but the Holy City is famously surrounded by the Goddeath Wastes. In case you couldn't tell from the name, that's not exactly a place you can just walk across."

"I'd rather take my risks in a desert than starve here doing nothing," Iggs argued. "We also won't have to endure it for long. We saw the edge of Heaven above us when we landed in the Hells. It can't be *that* far away."

"That's where you're wrong," Adrian said in a grim voice. "The barrier wasn't the only thing Boston and I checked when we were flying around. We also went up on the walls to do a triangulation spell."

"Surveying magic," Boston explained at everyone's blank looks. "Normally used for mapmaking."

"It's used for a lot more than that," Adrian insisted. "The main Blackwood is huge and complicated. If you don't get good at triangulating distance, you spend a lot of time being lost. Fortunately, the same calculations work whether you're standing on a battlement or a tree. All we had to do was measure the height of the walls and apply some known distance charms to estimate roughly how far away the horizon was."

"Except it didn't work," Boston finished irritably. "No matter how many times we did the math, the numbers always came back different."

"How is that possible?" Bex asked.

"It's possible because this place makes no damn sense!" Boston snarled, glaring at Heaven's sunless blue sky. "I know everything up here's a magical construction, but it's not even internally consistent. So far as I can tell, this whole place is a patchwork of unrelated spatial architectures that have all been mashed together!"

"Okay," Bex said slowly. "Now explain that to me like I'm not a witch."

"It means we can't use one known distance to as a base to calculate others," Adrian translated. "Aside from the points where they connect, the Holy City, the Hells, and the Goddeath Wastes are all separate conjured spaces that operate according to their own rules. That's why the triangulation spell couldn't tell us the distance to the horizon, because this city is not actually part of the land it appears to sit on."

"That does explain how Gilgamesh was able to pilot his city through the void in order to bomb the Seattle Anchor," Bex said thoughtfully. "If we did manage to get into the desert, though, do you think we could walk to the edge?"

"I don't know," Adrian said, biting his lip. "I'm not even sure Heaven *has* edges now that we're inside it. Given the lengths Gilgamesh has gone to so that he can control access, I suspect this place is actually a self-contained bubble in the same way Limbo was."

"Which means we can't just jump out," Iggs finished with a heavy sigh. "Damn king thought of everything."

"No one thinks of everything," Adrian insisted. "Gilgamesh himself told me that even the gods were forced to build their creations around what was already there. He's made a lot of renovations, but ultimately this is still the same Paradise the gods attached to the Great Cycles like a bead on a string. So long as it's connected to the living world, we can find a way back. We just need to keep trying."

"Let's get to it, then," Bex said. "Where do you want to look first?"

That question was supposed to be for Adrian, but as she asked it, a wave of dizziness washed over her. That'd been happening a lot over the last hour, but she'd always been able to hide it. This time, though, nothing could stop her from listing into Iggs. She was still trying to get herself back upright when Lys grabbed her face and forced Bex to look at them.

"You need to sleep," they announced, staring hard into Bex's glowing eyes. "You've been going for fourteen hours straight with multiple battles, and that was after you worked a full day at the Blackwood's festival."

"I'm fine," Bex insisted, pushing them away. "It's just a little dizziness."

"If you don't lie down soon, your body will make the choice for you," Lys argued, getting right back in her face. "Do you want to faint in front of all the demons you just saved?"

Bex heaved a long, angry sigh. She knew Lys was right—Lys was *always* right—but that didn't make the truth any easier to swallow. They were still in the middle of their fight for freedom. She didn't have time to sleep, but her head was spinning nonstop now. She couldn't even tell who was pulling her in which direction until she found herself being carried in Iggs's arms as Lys directed him down the stairs like a drill sergeant.

Since this was the building with the best view of the enemy's palace, Bex's crew had commandeered the entire top floor as their operational headquarters. This apparently included a master bedroom suite for Bex herself, a luxury she didn't know she had until Iggs set her down on the bed. Lys was still removing her boots when Nemini appeared from nowhere to press something warm into Bex's hand.

"What's this?" Bex asked, wincing when she heard how slurred her voice sounded.

"Water," the other queen replied. "The sin in the rivers might be too polluted to eat, but the water's still drinkable if you run it through an evaporative still. There's a whole platoon of war demons using the forge fires to boil out enough water to keep us all from dying of thirst. I brought you one of the first mugs."

Bex grabbed the cup at once, pushing up on one elbow so she could gulp down the mug of lukewarm water without choking and spilling it. "Tell them thanks for me," she said when she finished. "That's a lifesaver."

"Ishtar's children are survivors," Nemini replied with quiet pride before she slipped back into her usual monotone. "Not that it matters, of course, since we're all going to die in the end no matter what we do."

"Well, it still tastes amazing right now," Bex insisted, falling back into the surprisingly soft bed with a sigh. "Do they have any more?"

"I'll go check," Nemini promised as Lys pulled the covers up to Bex's chin. "You rest. We'll wake you if there's an emergency."

"I'm not waking her unless Gilgamesh himself comes down," Lys grumped as they pulled the covers tight. "Now *go to sleep*. You're no good to us if you can't swing straight."

That felt a little harsh, but Bex was having a hard time keeping her eyes open, so it was difficult to argue. The room was still annoyingly bright, but Bex's body must have been even more exhausted than she'd realized, because the moment she decided it wouldn't hurt to take a little rest, she passed straight out, sinking into a deep sleep before she'd even figured out which of the bed's dozens of decorative pillows were actually supposed to be used for sleeping.

Bex woke up an unknown number of hours later feeling like a new demon. Her body was still weirdly heavy, and her head felt packed full of cotton, but she wasn't dizzy anymore, and there was a whole pitcher of water on the nightstand beside her.

She felt even better after she drained it and used the strange waterless toilet in the unknown warlock's fancy master bathroom. There was no sink or bathtub, but there was a large towel that seemed to be enchanted to always feel moist. Bex used that to wipe herself down. Someone had found her backpack as well and left it by the door, which meant she even had a fresh change of clothes.

It was just leggings and a T-shirt this time instead of combat fatigues and a knife-proof shirt, but Bex was so happy to be out of her filthy, sin-caked outfit that she didn't care. She used the enchanted towel to wipe the grime and blood off her leather jacket as well, though she didn't want to touch the warlock's hairbrush. She made do with finger-combing her black hair instead, leaving it loose around her shoulders to give her scalp a break as she headed out to see what had happened while she was asleep.

The answer seemed to be not a lot. Demons were still moving around the square by the Hells' gate when she looked out the window, but she must not have been the only one who was exhausted, because all the crowded apartment buildings were quiet and dark. There was no sign of violence or fear. Just demons taking a much-deserved rest. That was a miracle Bex was loath to interrupt, but now that she was awake, she needed to get back to work. She was creeping toward the stairs to go find someone for a status update when she spotted Adrian sitting in the apartment's lavish kitchen.

Like everything she'd seen in Heaven, the kitchen was white from floors to ceiling. Appliances that would've been stainless steel in any other luxury home were made from shiny white plastic in this one, making her feel like she was peering into some kind of minimalist spaceship. But while the rest of the room was oppressively modern, the table in the middle looked like a scene straight out of her best memories of Adrian's cottage.

"Welcome back," he said when she walked in, smiling at her over the piles of dried fruit, dried grains, dried nuts, and dried herbs he'd spread all over the gleaming white kitchen table. "Do you want something to eat?"

"Only if you're not using it," Bex said as she pulled up a stool, which was also made from polished white metal and ridiculously heavy. "What's all this?"

"False hopes, mostly," he replied with a sigh, running a hand through his curling black hair, something he'd been doing a lot, based on the way it was sticking up in all directions.

"Did you get any sleep?" Bex asked.

Adrian shook his head. "I tried, but I'm a bad sleeper under the best circumstances, which these are not. I tossed and turned for a while, but all I was doing was keeping Boston awake, so I came out here to spend my time on something more productive."

"Always a good move," Bex agreed, then she frowned. "Though from what you said earlier, I'm guessing it didn't work."

"It worked a little," he said, flashing her a sly smile as he waved his hands over the food-covered table. "Heaven has a prohibition against growing things, but the pantries here were still stocked with plenty of legumes, grains, and seeds. All of those have the potential to germinate, so I made an array of the most likely prospects to use as the base for a finding charm. My aim was to see what I could dig up in the immediate vicinity without actually having to go through a hundred apartments' worth of cupboards and pantries by hand."

"And?" Bex asked.

"And nothing," Adrian finished with a sigh. "My spell didn't turn up so much as a single sprouted head of garlic."

"Oh," Bex said, face falling. Then she scowled. "So why did you say 'it worked a little' then?"

"Because while I didn't find what I was looking for, the act of searching did give me a different idea," Adrian told her excitedly. "Specifically, I think I finally figured out what I'm supposed to do with this."

He nudged the piles of dried beans out of the way and placed something on the table between them with a soft *clack*. It sounded like a rock, but when Adrian removed his hand, Bex saw it was an acorn.

"Is that the one your aunt gave me?"

"The very same," he confirmed with a solemn nod. "I've been trying to figure out why she sent it to me ever since you handed it over, but things were so hectic in the Hells that I never got the chance to really think about it. Now, though, I've had tons of time, and while no can ever be *really* sure what the Witch of the Future has in store for them, I think I've solved it."

"That's great," Bex said with a grin. "What is it?"

Adrian dropped his silver eyes to the table. "That's the bad part," he confessed. "The spell I think she wants me to do is very dangerous. Even for a Soul Witch working within her own grove, there's a certain amount of unavoidable risk. Since I'm *not* a Soul Witch and I'm completely cut off from my forest at the moment, the threat to me is even greater. I'd never have even considered it if my aunt hadn't had you push the starting trigger into my hand. That's as close to a direct command as the Witch of the Future gets."

"That doesn't mean you have to follow it," Bex snapped. "You've complained since I met you that your aunts put the safety of the forest above everything else, including their own flesh and blood. I've seen how dedicated they are to the Blackwood with my own eyes now, and while I'll be forever grateful to them for saving us, I know now that you were right. The Old Wives of the Blackwood will do absolutely anything to secure their coven's future, including ordering you to perform a spell that will blow us all up along with Gilgamesh."

"It's not *that* bad," he insisted. "I mean, if the Old Wives could use me to blow up Gilgamesh, they absolutely would, but witchcraft doesn't work that way. We're trees, not volcanoes. The vine beats the stone wall by eroding the mortar, not by smashing it down. Think about it from that perspective, though, and the spell I'm considering actually fits perfectly."

Adrian looked at the acorn he'd placed on the table. "Acorns are the essence of the future. I was worried about that at first because I'm terrible at divining, but I am very good at growing trees. I've actually grown one here in Heaven already, so I know it can be done. I'm certain that's why my aunt chose to send me this seed in particular, because unless I'm grossly mistaken, that's an acorn from my mother's own heart tree. Not one of the big ones that could attract Gilgamesh's attention but still a piece of the Old Wife of the Present's connection to the Great Forest. The same connection she shared with me when she taught me how to be a witch."

His handsome face lit up with the warm, confident Adrian-smile that Bex loved best. "Connection and patience are the core of witchcraft," he said as he closed his long fingers around the little acorn. "My coven has already marked the path for me. I don't know where it will lead, but as a Witch of the Present, I don't need to. I don't need to worry about the future or the past. I just need to grow the tree I've been given and trust the Forest to do the rest. That's what I think my aunt is telling me."

"If you say so," Bex said nervously. "I'm not going to tell you how to do your witchcraft. If you say this is what you have to do, I'll support you in every way I can. What do you need from me?"

Adrian blinked like he was coming out of a trance, and then he flashed that smile again. This time, however, it was just for her.

"Nothing," he said, reaching across the table to touch her hand. "I didn't tell you this because I needed help. I just wanted to explain what I was doing before I ran off and did it because charging into danger without talking it through first is exactly the sort of bad behavior I'm trying to leave behind. I meant it with every fiber of my being when I said I wanted to be your partner, and part of being in a partnership is making decisions together. That's why I told you the spell was dangerous before I went and did it. I'm willing to take the risk, but I'm not the only one I have to worry about anymore. We're in this together, so I'm not moving forward on anything unless you say you're on board."

Bex stared at him in horror for a moment, and then she dropped her gaze to their joined hands as her heart began to pound. It wasn't that she wasn't used to being asked to make decisions—people asked her what to do all the time—but this wasn't a demon beseeching his queen. It was Adrian. *Adrian* was asking *her* if it was okay for him to do witchcraft, and that felt every kind of wrong.

"I don't think I'm qualified to make that call," she said at last, squeezing his hand hard as she struggled to find the exact right words. "Your witchcraft is yours. It's part of what I lov—what I admire about you so much. I understand where you're coming from, but leaving the decision to me doesn't feel right. You should be the one to make that choice. It's your magic."

"Let me put it another way, then," Adrian said, picking up her hand in both of his and pulling it across the table until Bex's fingers were cradled right above his chest where his heart used to be.

"Bex," he said solemnly, holding her gaze when she finally looked up and met his eyes. "Do you trust me?"

"Yes," she answered without a second's hesitation.

He looked gloriously happy at her quick reply, but he didn't stop. "Do you believe me if I say I can do this?"

"Yes," she said again just as quickly.

"Why?" he asked.

That was slightly more embarrassing to explain, but he'd made it clear just how important her opinion was to him, so Bex forced herself to be honest.

"Because I believe you can do anything," she replied as her face began to heat. "You brought me back from the ashes. You grew a tree that stopped a collapsing Anchor. You restored Nemini's horns. I trust you more than I trust myself at this point, so if you say you can do this, I believe you, even if I don't understand what 'this' is yet."

He chuckled at that last part before his face grew serious again. "Do you trust me with the lives of your demons?" he asked, squeezing her hand hard. "I'm going to be casting a dangerous spell well outside of its intended parameters. It could blow up in my face, or it could bring Gilgamesh down on top of us. There are so many ways this could go wrong that I don't even know them all, but if it goes *right*, it could be what gets us out alive."

"You should have led with that," Bex said, squeezing him back with a smile. "If you think this spell can free my people from this prison, then I don't just trust you. I'm counting on you. You're the reason we started winning in the first place, so if there's anyone I believe can take us over the finish line, it's you." She squeezed his hand even harder. "From the first day we met, it's always been you."

Adrian's face split into an enormous grin. "Then let's not waste any more time," he said, springing up from his seat. He swooped back down to kiss her next, pressing his lips to Bex's so quickly she would've fallen off her stool if he hadn't had his hands clamped around her shoulders. He kissed her lightly and sweetly, and then he was gone, running back to his room yelling for Boston while Bex sat in a daze at the kitchen table, wondering what in the Nine ruined Hells she'd just helped set in motion.

Chapter 2

"Explain it to me again," Boston demanded with a lash of his tail. "In a way that makes sense this time."

"What part don't you understand?" Adrian asked as he dumped yet another armful of dried herbs, fruit, meats, and crackers onto the waist-high pile of nonperishable organic material he'd already heaped in the middle of the street that connected the plaza of the Hells' Gate with the rest of the city. "I already told you twenty times: we're growing a tree."

"And I still haven't heard an acceptable answer to my question," his familiar insisted, moving to stand between his witch and the demons gawking at them from the plaza. "You keep saying 'We're growing a tree' like that's something we can do, but I fail to see how we're growing anything in the middle of a road in the land of *death* with no apparent soil and definitely no water table. I've been sniffing around since we arrived, and I haven't found so much as a mouse dropping. I don't think things even rot up here."

"They don't," Adrian confirmed. "But I've got that covered. Watch this."

He picked up the ornate glass fruit bowl one of Bex's demons had been kind enough to fill with water from the evaporation stills the war demons were running like a factory down in the Upper Hells. Protocol Three must've been designed not to interrupt sin iron production, because the toxic sludge-water had stopped rising the instant it reached the entrance to the forges. That was several hours ago, and the war demons had been hard at work converting the poison into potable water ever since. Being distilled, it was completely sterile, which wasn't ideal. It still got stuff wet, though, which was the attribute Adrian needed most.

Moving carefully so as not to waste a drop, Adrian poured the large bowl of water over the pile of dried food he'd brought out here from all the various pantries in the apartment building Bex had chosen as their headquarters. When everything was nice and soggy, he leaned over and spit on the top, adding his saliva—and all the bacteria and digestive enzymes that came with it—to the pile.

"That's your plan?" Boston asked scornfully when Adrian straightened up again. "Spit yourself dry and wait nine months for this heap of processed trash to compost into soil?"

"More or less," Adrian said as he took off his black coat and rolled up his shirt sleeves. "Except I don't intend to wait." He flashed his cat a grin. "What's the point of having magic if it can't speed things up?"

"What magic?" Boston snapped. "Even if Gilgamesh hadn't put a seal on your heart, there's no Blackwood to pull on up here, and the last I checked, sorcery can't grow trees."

"O ye of little faith," Adrian chided as he got down on his knees. "Just watch."

His familiar looked extremely skeptical, but he did as Adrian asked, hopping onto his witch's back to observe as Adrian plunged his bare hands into the soggy pile of wet crackers and powdered herbs. When he could feel the organic matter under all of his fingers, including the wooden one he'd carved to replace the pinky he'd sacrificed to the Morrigan, Adrian closed his eyes and started building the wish in his head.

It was a very simple one. Back when his father had called himself Malik and Adrian had hung on his every word, Gilgamesh had described sorcery as a prayer one granted to oneself. Since Adrian had never been the praying sort, that logic hadn't worked for him. He preferred to approach sorcery the same way he did woodworking or gardening or any other project he embarked upon: picture the end goal and then imagine how he was going to reach it.

For the pile beneath his fingers, the path was conveniently obvious. To grow a tree, he needed soil, but soil was just broken-down organic matter. Since nothing rotted in Heaven, he needed sorcery to fill in the gaps. Fortunately, as someone who'd spent his entire life inside forests, Adrian knew exactly how matter decomposed. All he had to do was lay the process out in his mind, pull some power out of his new white blood, and the sorcery responded just like it had when his father taught him how to teleport.

By the time Adrian opened his eyes again, the waist-high pile of water crackers, smoked meat, and bright-red cocktail cherries had been reduced to three cubic feet of warm, loamy compost. He was feeling hugely proud of himself when Boston jumped off his back and gave the pile a sniff.

"It's too salty."

"Is that all you have to say?" Adrian demanded. "I just pulled off a miracle, you know."

"I refuse to praise sorcery on principle," the cat informed him with a sniff. "And I've seen Leander create metal out of thin air. After that, a bit of high-speed composting is nothing, especially since you didn't even remove the excess sodium required to make all that food shelf-stable. How do you expect anything to grow in soil that's full of preservatives?"

"All right, Mr. Criticism," Adrian said, putting his fists on his hips. "What would you have used?"

Adrian's bet was excrement, which wasn't a bad call. As usual, though, his cat surprised him.

"Bed linens," Boston replied without missing a beat. "The denizens of Heaven are all horrific snobs. If there's a sheet in this place that isn't made from high-thread-count silk or organic Pima cotton, I'll eat your hat. They're all white too, which means they're not drenched in heavy synthetic dyes. The fibers are also carbon-rich, so we can mix them with the nitrogen-heavy compounds you already made to create a balanced fertilizer. If we can just find a way to remove the sodium, we should be good to go."

"Boston, you are *brilliant*," Adrian said, reaching down to pet his cat with a grin. "I'll get to work on the salt levels. Can you ask Iggs or someone to start pulling us some bedsheets?"

His familiar nodded and trotted back toward the square where the demons were milling with his nose held high. Adrian, meanwhile, wiped the mud off his fingers and headed into the closest abandoned building, in search of dried pasta, flours, cocoa powder, and any other pantry staples that weren't packed full of salt.

Two hours, thirty-seven apartment kitchens, sixty fruit bowls full of water, and twenty all-natural organic cotton bedsheets later, Adrian *finally* had fifty pounds of workable, sodium-balanced soil. It wasn't the rich, loamy black stuff he was used to working with back in his own forest, and there was a serious lack of earthworms, but he was ready to call it good enough.

Their work had amassed a large audience by this point. Even Bex had come down to watch. When he'd said goodbye to her in the kitchen, she'd told him she was going out to make the rounds, but either checking on a medium city's worth of demons took less time than Adrian realized or his work had been so bizarre that she'd changed her plans, because when he looked up from his final composting spell, Bex was hovering right beside him with a half-amazed, half-horrified look on her lovely face.

"Is that what you're growing the acorn in?" she asked, pointing at the now-knee-high pile of soil filling the middle of the street. "Not to question the expert, but it doesn't look big enough for an oak tree."

"That's because it's not," Adrian admitted. "The root system of a full-grown oak is generally three to seven times the size of the visible tree. I could compost every bit of organic matter in Heaven and still not have enough dirt to hold it all, and we haven't even gotten started on water needs. Add in the incredible number of antigrowth, antifungal, and antibacterial magics Gilgamesh uses to keep his white city pristine, and we're looking at an impossible situation.

Fortunately, doing the impossible is what sorcery is for."

Bex winced at the word "sorcery" but kept her obviously negative opinion to herself. Boston wasn't nearly so polite.

"Again, I don't understand why you think this is going to work," the cat announced with a lash of his tail. "Sorcery might be good at creating miracles, but it can't keep them going. Even if you command that acorn to grow into a tree, it won't stay alive with no soil and insufficient water, and let's not forget that this place has no actual sun. How do you expect oak leaves to photosynthesize under Gilgamesh's magical version of fluorescent lights?"

"I don't," Adrian said irritably. "But none of that matters because I'm not planning to support the tree using only what's here. I just need enough to get it started."

"And then?" Boston demanded.

"And then I'll put my faith in the Witch of the Future," Adrian replied as he picked his coat up off the street. "You're the one who's always telling me to trust the Old Wives, aren't you?"

Boston gave him a furious scowl, and Adrian reached out to rub his hand over his familiar's flattened ears.

"You worry too much," he chided. "Yes, there's risk involved, but it's like I told you when we got on the plane to go to Seattle: If I'm not willing to jump, I'll never get out of the hole."

"I'm still not convinced our move to Seattle was a good idea," Boston replied grumpily. "You've had more near-death disasters in the last six months than in all the rest of your life combined. As your familiar, it's my job to give you good advice, which I interpret as advice that will keep you *alive*." His ears pressed even flatter against his skull. "What am I going to do if you die?"

"If I don't pull this off, there's a good chance we'll all die," Adrian reminded him, pulling his hand back. "I'm not stepping off this cliff for no reason, Boston. We've all put our lives on the line to get here. *You* put your fur in the fire when you came to the Hells to rescue me. Now it's my turn to return the favor, and while I know our position looks weak at the moment, Aunt Muriel wouldn't have sent me that acorn if she didn't think I could do it."

"I don't think someone as bad at divination as yourself should be trying to predict the Witch of the Future's motives," his cat pointed out. "But it is a familiar's duty to support his witch, so if this is *really* what you want to do…"

He looked up at Adrian with pleading green eyes. When Adrian didn't cave, the familiar heaved a long sigh.

"Let's get it over with, then," Boston said, trotting over to the edge of the dirt pile. "I presume you'll need me to reach the Blackwood again, since Gilgamesh's seal is still over your heart?"

Adrian shook his head. "I can't. This isn't a little corpse-finding charm. The amount of magic I'm planning on moving this time will kill you. Don't worry, though. I've got it covered."

Boston looked *critically* worried. It was a familiar's job to fret, though, so Adrian didn't tell him to stop. He just scooped him off the ground and handed him to Bex, who also looked anxious enough to have a heart attack.

"I'll be *fine*," he insisted as he deposited the cat in her arms. "Just keep the road clear and make sure no one interrupts me after I start. That's the most important part. Whatever happens, whatever I do, don't let anybody touch me until I'm finished, okay?"

"Okay," Bex whispered, squeezing Boston to her chest. "Be careful."

"I'll do my best," Adrian promised, giving Boston one last pet before he turned on his heel and strode up to the pile of soil he'd just spent the last hour making.

"All right," he said as he got down on his knees again. "Let's do some gardening."

Before he could lose his nerve, Adrian reached into his jacket pocket and took out the acorn his aunt had sent to him through Bex. He rubbed it briefly between his palms to get a feel for the seed inside the hard shell, and then he stuck it into the dirt he'd made.

When the acorn was buried nice and deep, Adrian placed the little wooden cat he'd used to locate Nemini on top of it. The finding charm was long spent, but the cat-hair-covered statuette was still the closest link he had to the Blackwood that didn't involve Boston or Bran. It was also something he'd made in the past, a critical element for any witchcraft. Finally, Adrian reached into his pocket and pulled out the golden woodworking knife he'd stolen from the workshop where his father had locked him up. The ostentatious tool was nothing like the comfortable, practical blades he used at home, but it got the job done, slicing his finger just enough to let five drops of his new white blood fall on top of the pile.

That last element was the most critical of all. Even though it was basically pure quintessence now, his blood was still his blood. Just as his spit had been the catalyst for turning crackers and bedsheets into soil, blood was also a transformative element. By adding a piece of himself to the pile, Adrian changed what was otherwise an unremarkable mound of improvised dirt into flesh of his flesh.

That was how he thought of it, anyway. There was no visible reaction, but as Gilgamesh had told him back when Adrian still trusted him enough to listen, sorcery was all about perspective and creativity. Because Adrian was a Witch of the Flesh, his magic was innately biological. Gilgamesh had built his Heaven to be a sterile prison, but so long as his city was home to living humans who ran on human biology, life was inescapable. It was in the food they ate and the bacteria they carried inside their bodies, in the clothes they wore and the microbes that lived on their hair. Even the sheets he'd composted had been taken from beds, not closets, specifically to preserve the skin cells and oils trapped in the fibers.

Every one of those biological elements was vulnerability. By bringing his human army into the Land of the Dead, Gilgamesh had undermined his own defenses. Even when the gaps were too small to be seen with the naked eye, they were there. It was the flaw in Heaven's perfection, the chink in the Holy City's white armor, and Adrian wedged his magic into it like a crowbar, throwing all the quintessence his father had dumped over his unconscious body into a single, simple wish.

"Grow."

He spoke the command in a whisper, but it came out in a roar, shaking through the ground like an earthquake as the demons in the square behind him cried out in fear. This was the biggest act of sorcery he'd ever attempted, but Adrian wasn't cocky enough to think he could actually break Heaven. Quintessence sorcery was Gilgamesh's invention. No matter how good Adrian got at it, he'd never be able to beat his father, which was why he didn't try. He didn't push against the white walls or fight the overwhelming command that constantly told all life here to shrivel and stop. He didn't bother with any of that. Instead, Adrian focused all of his magic on the pile of soil *he* had made. The cauldron of decomposition he'd created to hold a spell from his past, blood from his present, and the acorn that would become his future.

"You are no longer a part of Gilgamesh's Heaven," he whispered as he dug his bare hands deep into the hot, humid soil. "You are not white or stone or dead. You are the living body of the Great Blackwood, a grove bound to me by flesh, bones, and soul. By the decay that created you and the roots you will nurture, I ask you to grow. Grow and return us both to our rightful place in the Great Cycle that connects all living things."

The words were a variation of the spell he'd spoken the very first time he'd dug out his heart and buried it beneath the forest for the ceremony that had bound him as a witch of the Blackwood Coven. But while his request this time was slightly different, the feeling was exactly the same, because even though his father had replaced his blood, blocked his heart, and removed his body from the land of the living, Adrian had never stopped being a witch. That title was something that could never be stolen, because it had never belonged to Adrian in the first place. He belonged to the Blackwood, not the other way around. That was the entire point of the coven initiation, and the moment Adrian pulled on that connection, the acorn that represented the future—his future, his aunt's future, the future of all witches who offered their hearts, bones, and souls to the Great Blackwood—burst out of the mounded dirt.

Adrian had grown more trees in his life than he could count. They'd always sprouted quickly, but even the hundred-foot hardwoods he'd grown in an hour to test his new blend of sorcery and witchcraft hadn't grown this fast. The seedling shot out of the soil like a spear, but not toward Heaven's sunless sky. This sapling grew straight up the arms Adrian had pressed in the soil, using his limbs like guide poles to stab him in the chest.

Adrian jerked with a silent gasp, his voice choked by the white blood that was suddenly bubbling out of his mouth. That wasn't what he'd expected to happen. He'd thought the tree would explode into the air and break though Heaven's protective shell, not break though *him*. From the amount of white blood pouring onto the sapling's roots, though, Adrian was starting to worry that he'd grossly misread the situation. Maybe Bex had been right all along. Maybe this *was* actually a plan to use his quintessence blood as fuel for a Heaven-destroying bomb.

It wouldn't be the first time his family had traded his life for the forest's safety. Given how high a wall they were all up against, though, Adrian couldn't bring himself to be mad. He was far more worried about Bex and the others getting caught in the blast. But just as he'd made peace with the idea that his family had used him to enact a properly witchy vengeance on Gilgamesh by turning the son he'd stolen into the tool of his own destruction, Adrian realized he wasn't dying.

That couldn't be right. A tree was growing straight through his chest. Even with the copious amount of magic involved, there should be no way he could survive, and yet here he was. He wasn't even in that much pain, because aside from the initial entry wound, the sapling wasn't digging into his flesh. It was digging into his father's seal—the hard, lion-toothed wall of magic that Gilgamesh had placed over his heart to block Adrian's connection to the Blackwood.

The moment he realized that, Adrian's entire demeanor changed. He stopped waiting for death and lurched forward, stabbing his fingers into his chest to widen the wound so the sapling would have more room to work. Just like every time he'd tried to break it himself, the lion-headed magic roared and fought back. It shredded the sapling with its claws and teeth, filling Adrian's chest cavity with splintered greenwood, but the shoot of the Blackwood didn't give up. Every time Gilgamesh's lion tore the young tree apart, it grew back and tried a different direction, attacking the seal with a thousand little tendrils, until, like an ancient citadel consumed by the forest, the lump of hardened sorcery fell apart, shaken to pieces by the thunder of Adrian's own heartbeat.

It was the first time he'd felt his pulse as anything more than a distant echo since Gilgamesh had brought him here. Each contraction hurt so much it brought tears to his eyes, but Adrian had never been so happy to be in pain. The sapling's supple branches were still lodged inside his chest, but he didn't bother trying to dig them out. He pushed his own hands deeper instead, reaching through his rib cage into the empty hole left by the organ he'd surrendered the night he first became a witch.

Just like that first time under the moonlight in the coven circle, he dug his hands as deep as they would go, reaching through his body into the forest that lived at his core. The beloved, familiar forest he could finally feel again. Adrian had barely opened his fingers in request when the Blackwood responded, digging out its own roots and placing them in the cup of Adrian's palms.

When he finally removed his white-bloody hands from his chest, Adrian was holding a piece of two worlds: a human heart wrapped in roots and fungus, the living proof that the heart of a witch was the forest, and the heart of the forest was a witch. He'd never realized the old adage could be so macabrely literal, but witchcraft was an ancient magic born from the cycles of life itself, and life was never clean. It was bloody, dirty, and beautifully biological, the exact opposite of everything Gilgamesh had made his Heaven to be, and it was with great satisfaction that Adrian Blackwood took his filthy, blood-smeared, root-infested heart and buried it in the ground. He buried it deep, tucking the vital organ he shared with his forest around his aunt's acorn, the symbol of all their futures. When it was all bound together in a bloodsoaked mess, he bent his head lower still, pressing his face into the damp earth he'd crafted to whisper his wish once more.

"*Grow.*"

The tremor that followed the word this time put everything before it to shame, because Adrian was no longer speaking sorcery. This was something new and uniquely his, a hybrid just like Adrian himself. Every time the heart he shared with his forest beat, more white blood poured out of him, but Adrian no longer cared. He could finally see the whole picture, the reason all of this had to happen. For the first time in his entire life, he understood the shape of the plan his coven had been nurturing for centuries. He could even feel them reaching back, a thousand generations of witches all speaking with him in one voice as Adrian shouted the most forbidden word in Heaven at the top of his lungs.

"Grow!" he bellowed, tilting his sundered chest so that the liquid quintessence Gilgamesh had poured into him would flow down his arms to water the seed Adrian's coven had bet everything on. "*Grow!*"

His Blackwood heart thundered in response. The oak sapling was already shriveling, crushed under Heaven's oppressive aura of stillness and death, but Adrian's heart was different. Gilgamesh had already filled it with the power he'd stolen from the gods. The same quintessence that made Adrian a prince also allowed his heart to flourish here, and the tree that grew out of it wasn't white or sickly or even an oak.

It was a Douglas fir, a beautiful deep-green offshoot of his original heart tree. It burst out of the dirt he'd made like an exploding bomb, shattering the road Adrian was kneeling on along with the buildings beside it. It broke everything it touched, leaving the orderly White City in ruins as the Great Blackwood, the oldest forest that connected all forests, crashed its way into Gilgamesh's Heaven.

The rest of the woodland followed right behind. Within seconds, the empty white plaza surrounding the black cube that marked the entrance to the Hells was covered with bright-green flowering grass. Streams of clear water filled with fish and frog spawn poured from the windows of the root-tilted apartment blocks and pooled in the new cracks on the ground. Trees of every sort—conifers, hardwoods, softwoods, and evergreens—sprouted wherever their roots found purchase, transforming the dry, blindingly white City of Heaven into a wet and shady grotto filled with singing birds.

It was the most beautiful thing Adrian had ever seen. Sadly, it was probably also the last thing he was ever going to see. His aunt's acorn had gotten it started, but this forest was a Blackwood grown directly from his heart and fueled by his white blood. Considering how many barrels of quintessence Gilgamesh had dumped into him, Adrian thought he'd never run dry, but by the time the new trees' roots were deep enough to hold the trunk upright, his reservoir was tapped. He didn't even have enough strength left to push back when the roots of his new tree pulled him into the mound where he'd buried his heart.

It was what his forest always did when he was wounded, but Adrian didn't think he'd be digging himself back out this time. He couldn't bring himself to regret it, though. He'd just grown a witch's forest in the center of Heaven itself! Not even the Old Wives could have managed that. And since he'd grown them out of his own heart, the new trees counted as an official grove of the Blackwood, which meant the rest of his coven could connect to them through the main forest and give Bex's demons a way out.

That was the best outcome he could've hoped for. Adrian would still rather have done it without killing himself, but if everyone else got out alive, he wasn't going to complain. He just wished he could've seen Bex and Boston one last time to say goodbye. He was probing his new heart tree to see if he couldn't leave them a letter on a leaf or something when three strong hands reached up through the roots to grab him.

"*Not yet!*" cried a voice that was actually three voices blended into one. "*You're not done yet!*"

Adrian begged to differ. The only reason he was still conscious was because he shared a soul with his forest. He'd used up every drop of his white blood to pull this off. No human, not even a prince, could survive total exsanguination. His physical body was already starting to break down. But just as Adrian was about to pass into the grove of his ancestors, the huge force of witchcraft he'd felt rising to meet him when he told the forest to grow hit him again, knocking him out of death and into something that felt like a boiling cauldron.

Chapter 3

Five minutes earlier.

BEX STOOD AT THE EDGE OF THE SQUARE, clutching Boston like a lifeline. She could hear a crowd of curious demons gathering behind them, but for once, Bex's people were not her first concern. The demons were fine, or at least not in immediate danger, but she couldn't say the same for Adrian. He didn't seem to be doing anything but kneeling in front of a pile of dirt with his eyes closed, but she could feel sorcery rising like a knife in the air.

The hairs on the back of her neck rose at the same time. She tried reminding herself that it was Adrian's sorcery and he was using it to save them, but five thousand years of threat response wasn't something that could be overcome with logic. Bex might not remember her previous one hundred and ninety-eight lives, but she knew she'd fought sorcerers in all of them. It was a good thing Drox was still asleep on her finger, because the urge to pull her sword and start swinging was overwhelming. She was keeping her eyes on Adrian and telling herself to just breathe through it when the acorn he'd buried suddenly shot out of the dirt to stab him through the chest.

No logic or breathing could stop her after that. Bex dropped Boston and charged, hand already stretching out to yank Adrian off the spear his father's faithless magic had turned on him. She was less than a foot away when something grabbed her leg and yanked her back.

Bex stumbled with a gasp and looked down to see Boston in his big form with his teeth wrapped around her calf and his claws digging into the white-paved road. He knocked her off balance next, taking advantage of her shock to fling her to the ground and leap on top of her, pinning her with his huge furry paws as Bex flailed beneath his weight.

"What are you doing?" she screamed.

"What Adrian told me to!" Boston snarled back, his growling voice terrified but resolute. "He ordered us not to touch him for any reason!"

"But he's *dying*!" Bex cried, whipping her head back to Adrian, who was now covered in the prince's unnatural white blood. The overwhelming scent of it filled her with so much fear that Bex couldn't have called her fire if she'd tried. She didn't know what had gone wrong, if his witchcraft had failed or if Gilgamesh had deliberately turned his sorcery against him, but his face was blank with shock and pain.

That wasn't the face Adrian made when things were going right. She *had* to get to him, but Boston was putting up a surprisingly good fight. If she'd still had her old strength, she would've tossed him into the sky, but while Bex's fire was back, she was still hornless and weakened. It wasn't much, but between her fear, her faded strength, and her reluctance to hurt Adrian's cat, Boston had the edge he needed to stay on top.

"Would you *stop it*?" he yelled, slamming a paw the size of a dinner plate onto Bex's back to shove her down.

"*Bex!*" a different voice shouted at the same time right before Iggs ran up beside her. Her demon was still looking frantically between Boston and his queen when Adrian's familiar lost what was left of his patience.

"I know it's not your strong suit, but I need all of you to calm down and act rationally," he ordered, keeping his full weight on Bex while his green eyes glared at Iggs and the small army of demons who'd run over to defend their queen that were standing behind him. "I know things look bad right now, but that's exactly why Adrian warned us ahead of time not to touch him. Great acts of witchcraft always require sacrifice. Have you forgotten everything you saw in his grove?"

"This is different!" Bex yelled as she squirmed against the hard, spotlessly clean white pavement. "We're not in Adrian's forest, and that is *not* his magic!"

Bex was no witch, but that was a hill she would die on. Adrian's magic smelled like a summer forest. It was warm and rich and beautiful, and while it could definitely be scary, it still always felt like him. This didn't. The white blood pouring out of his sundered chest smelled like dust and death. It was the same overwhelming scent she remembered from Enki's tomb, and while the look on Adrian's face had gone from shock to intensely focused concentration, that could just be him trying to save his life. Nothing good came from Gilgamesh's magic, but when she tried again to grab him, Boston slammed the full weight of his now lion-sized body down on top of her.

"*Please*," he begged, retracting his claws so he could grip her shoulders without hurting her. "I don't know what's going on either, but I'm certain that Adrian's the only one who can fix it now. I might not always agree with my witch's risk assessment, but I trust his skill with my life. More importantly, I trust it with *his* life. He knows what he's doing, but he can't succeed if you're pulling him down!"

Boston turned his giant furry head back toward Adrian, who now seemed to be helping the tree dig into his chest. "Just let him work," he said, the words rumbling through his chest into Bex's. "You trusted my witch enough to let him start this. Trust him to finish it."

She did. Bex trusted Adrian's witchcraft to a near-religious degree at this point, but it was still so *hard* to lie there and watch him die. The whole mound was soaked with his white blood now, and his face was a frightening shade of gray. If the expression on it hadn't been so determined, nothing could have kept Bex away, but Boston seemed to be right. Adrian did look like he knew exactly what he was doing as he reached his bloody hands into his chest and pulled out his heart.

At least, Bex thought it was his heart. The root-covered lump pumping in his white-dripping hands looked nothing like the healthy red organ she'd watched him bury the day he'd arrived in Bainbridge. That had been a mythical, magical experience. This was a ghastly spectacle as Adrian ripped the bloody, root-riddled heart from his own sundered chest and buried it shakily in the white-drenched ground.

She held her breath the entire time, praying frantically to Ishtar that the hole in his chest would start closing now that he'd retrieved his heart, but it didn't. If anything, he seemed to be bleeding out even faster as he curled over the dirt and whispered something she couldn't hear. It looked like just one word, but the moment he said it, the ground began to shake.

The street cracked a second later. Bex hadn't felt anything change, but the whole road was suddenly breaking apart like an ice sheet in spring. The destruction hit the apartment blocks next, sending the demons inside fleeing for their lives as the buildings' foundations began tilting like something was pushing them up from below. Bex's first thought was that it was a monster coming up from the Hells, but that turned out to be totally wrong. This was no retaliatory weapon or creature of Gilgamesh. It was a tree. An enormous Douglas fir that exploded out of the broken pavement like a rocket to send both Bex and Boston flying.

By the time they landed much farther down the road, the whole city looked different. What had once been a pristine white square lined with identical apartment buildings was now carpeted in the softest, greenest grass Bex had ever seen outside of Adrian's forest. The Douglas fir that had thrown her into the air was still going up like a skyscraper, but other trees were coming in as well now. They were all varieties Bex remembered from Bainbridge, but much, *much* bigger. Adrian always said it took time to grow a forest, but the new trees were climbing taller than the White City's apartment blocks as she watched with no sign of slowing down.

It wasn't just plants either. The new greenery filling the plaza that surrounded the gates to the Hells was being crisscrossed with burbling streams before her eyes. The formerly bone-dry air of Heaven was suddenly thick with humidity and loud with the drone of insects. Birds darted among the growing branches, and fresh mud oozed through the cracks in the street.

In the space of less than a minute, the entire eight-square-block portion of the Holy City surrounding the entrance to the Hells was transformed from a cold mausoleum to a verdant forest teeming with life. Bex couldn't even see the white stone anymore. It was all vibrant green leaves and craggy brown bark, colorful insects and flashing birds, darting chipmunks and lazing lizards, splashing fish and swarming tadpoles. Everywhere she looked, life was blooming. Every life, that was, except Adrian's.

"Where is he?" Bex demanded, beating back the chest-high undergrowth that was suddenly between her and the massive trunk of Adrian's new tree. "Where did he go?"

"I think he was carried up," Boston said, shrinking back to his house-cat size as he leaped onto her shoulder. "Let's go! Hurry!"

Bex didn't bother asking why the familiar had switched from holding her down to telling her to hurry up. She just launched herself into the air, using her fire to blast them both up onto the lowest branch of the skyscraper-sized fir tree that now dominated the Holy City's skyline.

Just like the inside of Adrian's heart tree back in Seattle, the inside of the tree was incredibly thick. Heaven's white light vanished in seconds, blocked out by a wall of shaggy fir needles and thick limbs covered in dark, scaly bark. Bex's hands were instantly covered in sticky sap, but that just helped her hold on tighter as she leaped from branch to branch like a squirrel.

The fir was so tall at this point it felt like she was scaling a mountain, but even when the needles got so thick that no light at all could sneak through, Bex didn't slow down. She just kept climbing, using her fire to blast them higher and higher through the pine-scented dark. She was wondering if the tree would keep going up forever when Boston's claws suddenly dug through her T-shirt into the skin of her shoulder.

"Over there!"

Bex whirled around, smothering her flames so she could see past her own glare only to discover she needn't have bothered. Boston was pointing at a light that was even brighter than her fire. It shimmered like a star that had gotten caught in the fir tree's thick branches, but it wasn't until she got closer that Bex realized it was a house.

Not just any house. It was balanced in the branches like a birdhouse, but Bex would know that well-built log cabin anywhere. Its tall roof, open skylights, fieldstone fireplace, and roomy front porch with steps that were perfect for sitting on were as near and dear to Bex as her own RV. That was Adrian's house lit up like a lantern in the dark, and standing in the doorway like she'd been waiting for them to arrive was his mother.

"Hello, Boston," the Witch of the Present said, giving the cat a dazzling smile.

"Lady Agatha!" Boston cried, coiling his body to leap off Bex's shoulder into the Old Wife's arms, but he never got the chance. Before he could even finish his crouch, Bex had landed on Adrian's front porch like a flaming comet, her hands already shooting out to grab the smiling witch by the collar of her perfectly stitched black linen dress.

"*Where is he?*"

"There's no need for that," the Witch of the Present chided, sliding out of Bex's grip with surprising deftness to point through the open cabin door. "Adrian's right over—"

Bex blew past her in a burst of fire only to stop again the moment she got inside. The interior of the cabin looked *exactly* like she remembered. The carefully organized jars of ingredients on the built-in shelves, the greenhouse full of plants through the back door, the bundles of herbs drying in the kitchen, the fire crackling under the giant cauldron in the fieldstone hearth, they were all right where they should be. There were even still mugs of half-drunk tea left out on the table, like Adrian had simply forgotten to put them away. It was all perfect, like she'd stepped back in time, but the one element Bex didn't see was Adrian himself.

She was about to go out and check the greenhouse, since that was where Adrian always stuck her when she was injured, when Boston galloped past her toward the big iron cauldron hanging above the fire. He clambered up the rocky fireplace like a pro and trotted out onto the wooden mantel, where he could see down into the bubbling pot. It wasn't until Bex followed him to see what could possibly be so important that it could distract him from finding Adrian that she realized what was happening.

Adrian was in the cauldron. His body was lying at the bottom of the giant pot like a dumpling, curled up in a fetal position under a boiling version of the same herbal soup that he always dunked Bex in when she was injured. That should've been an enormous relief, but the cauldron was so hot that even she couldn't touch it. It looked like he was being boiled alive, but when Bex turned desperately to his mother for an explanation, the Old Wife of the Flesh was smiling just like her son did when he'd pulled off something especially clever.

"Don't worry," she said as she joined Bex beside the cauldron. "He can take the heat. You could even say he needs it. Adrian poured out every drop of his blood making an entrance for us. If we hadn't treated him immediately and aggressively, his body would not have survived."

She grinned at Bex, clearly expecting her to be grateful, and she was. Bex was *so* grateful that Adrian wasn't dead, it was physically painful, but she also couldn't ignore how perfect his mother's timing was. How she must have been waiting in this cabin with the water already boiling for the moment Adrian reached out.

"You knew."

"Of course I knew," Agatha said. "My little sister sees the future."

She laughed as she said that, smiling like this whole situation was just another clever move, and Bex's hands curled into fists.

"You did this to him on purpose," she snarled, whirling on Adrian's mother with all the pent-up rage and fear she'd been swallowing since she'd first realized Adrian was gone. "You knew that Gilgamesh would steal him. Knew that *all* of this would happen!"

When the witch didn't deny it, Bex's fire spread over her body with a *whoosh*. "You used us!" she roared. "Used me and my demons, used your own son to strike back at Gilgamesh!"

"Naturally," Agatha replied, her voice no longer motherly or laughing but as hard and sharp as the pain of the present. "Using what's around you is the foundation of all witchcraft. The moment I saw Adrian grow his first seedling as a child, I knew I'd finally found the thing Gilgamesh desired most. The fact that Adrian also wanted to become a witch made things easier, but I don't deny what I did. I used Adrian the same way as I've used every son I've had with Gilgamesh: as a weapon to preserve the Blackwood and a step toward his eventual demise."

She said all of this openly and honestly, but the fact that she didn't seem the least bit remorseful sent Bex's fire roaring up to Adrian's beautifully carved rafters.

"How could you?" she demanded. "He was your son, your *child*, and you turned him into a weapon!"

"I could say the same about you," Agatha replied, staring into Bex's flames with blue eyes that were as calm as a frozen lake. "You've been a child nearly two hundred times now, and every one of those little girls was forged into a Blade of Ishtar."

"That's different," Bex insisted. "I chose to fight!"

The witch shook her head. "Duty isn't the same as choice. This isn't the first time our paths have crossed, Bex of the Bonfire. I've met many of your lives over the years, and in every one of them, you were fighting for your people because there was no one else who could. That makes you noble, but it does not make you free."

She stepped closer to the bubbling cauldron. "We've all done what was necessary to save the things we care about, and our sacrifices were not in vain. You were absolutely right when you accused me of setting this up, but you and Adrian were still the ones making the decisions. *You* fought the battles *you* chose to fight. All Muriel and I did was nudge you toward the choices that had the best outcomes."

"Best outcome for who?" Bex snarled.

"All of us," the witch replied, her ageless face lighting up with a lovely smile. "You especially should rejoice at our foresight. If my baby sister hadn't known this day was coming two hundred years ago, we would not have started working on the spell Adrian just brought to fruition. Had things been even a hair out of place, my son, your beloved, would not have survived."

Bex supposed she had to give her that one. She'd seen how much blood Adrian had spilled on the ground. If his coven hadn't been ready to catch him, he definitely would have died today. That didn't excuse the way his family had used him his entire life, but knowing he would live calmed Bex's anger enough that she could finally pay attention to other things.

"What do you mean you've been planning this day for two hundred years?"

"Exactly what it sounds like," Agatha replied, waving her hand at the cabin windows that looked as dark as midnight thanks to the pitch-black interior of the fir tree. "Do you really think one prince's worth of quintessence was enough to do all of this? Absolutely not. My sisters and I started growing these trees centuries ago in preparation for the day Heaven's defenses cracked."

She nodded at the pot her son was still stewing in. "One of the reasons I hid Adrian from Gilgamesh as long as I did was to make sure the forest was well rooted in his heart before his father took him. I'm sure Gilgamesh saw the risk the moment Adrian showed him his forest, but by that point it was already too late. Gilgamesh has always been a greedy, egotistical king. If he sees something he wants, he always tries to take it. That said, he's also a bit of a coward. He never makes a move unless he's certain he has an overwhelming advantage, which is why we went to Adrian's forest to stop him even though we knew perfectly well it was already too late. We had to make sure Gilgamesh believed he was stealing Adrian away from us."

"I get it," Bex said, leaning against the fire-warmed hearthstones. "You played him."

"Men are always weakest in their moment of victory," Agatha agreed with a smile. "Gilgamesh was so confident he was about to get everything he wanted that he left Adrian to his own devices, and we all know how dangerous *that* can be." Her grin got wider. "In many ways, the King of Uruk is the cleverest man I've ever met, but in this one aspect, he has always been a fool. Despite centering his life around his hatred of the gods, he constantly repeats their mistakes. He sincerely believes that if he just gets enough power, he can control the uncontrollable. That with the right leverage, he could bring a wild thistle into his garden and turn it into a daisy."

The witch cackled. "How foolish! How *kingly*! There are no reins on the Great Cycles, and there is no controlling a witch. My sisters and I have always understood that, which is why we only gave Adrian commands when we wanted him to disobey. We trusted him to follow his own headstrong, rebellious nature, and when my son did what he always does, we made sure we were waiting with an arsenal full of the one weapon Gilgamesh has no defense against."

"Trees?" Bex guessed.

"Life," Agatha replied, adding another log to the fire that was burning merrily under Adrian's cauldron. "Paradise has always been an artificial construct, because life and death were never meant to be separate things." She snorted. "Gilgamesh knows that perfectly well. He's the one who's always going on about the illusion of separation, but he only listens to his own wisdom when it suits him. The moment he has to admit that the same logic means his own goals are flawed, suddenly we're all ignorant heathens."

Bex gave the witch a flat look. "Sounds like you know him well."

"I have borne him nearly a hundred children," Agatha reminded her. "It's hard not to know a man after that." She chuckled for a moment, and then her face fell. "There was a time once when I thought I could bring him around. He was actually quite open-minded when we first met, but his resolve and frustration hardened as he got older, and eventually there were no paths left but this."

She waved at the boiling cauldron, but Bex didn't understand.

"Resolve to do what?" she asked. "What is Gilgamesh working on in there?"

"The same thing he's been working on since the original Rebexa slew his best friend at Ishtar's behest," Agatha replied. "Complete and total conquest. His tactics have changed, but Gilgamesh is still fighting the same war he's been waging for five thousand years. That's why we had to wait so long to do this. It wasn't until the end was in sight that he finally did something reckless enough to give us an opening."

"So what do we do with it?" Bex demanded. "Don't get me wrong, I'm super happy you had a forest ready to save Adrian, but trees aren't going to break the shield around Gilgamesh's palace. I'm assuming this is just the first stage of your plan, so what comes next? Do you have a big spell or a final curse or something that will take him out?"

She *really* hoped it was a curse. Bex could think of nothing more satisfying than Gilgamesh rolling around on the ground in agony from the same magic Adrian had used to finish off the Spider. It probably wouldn't be that easy, but she was sure the witches had to have *something*, which was why she was so confused when Agatha shook her head.

"If the Blackwood had magic that could kill Gilgamesh, we would have used it eons ago. Unfortunately, since we're his oldest and most respected enemy, the Eternal King has invested a great deal of effort into countering our witchcraft. He's immune to even more poisons than Adrian at this point, but there is one weapon he's always dismissed, and thanks to the excellent planning of the Witch of the Future, she's standing right in front of me."

Agatha finished with a dazzling smile, but Bex dropped her eyes.

"If you're counting on me to kill Gilgamesh, I'm afraid your sister's plans didn't work out so well," she grumbled. "I might've gotten my bonfire back, but my horns are still locked inside the palace. I'm pretty sure Drox could cut the barrier—he can cut anything—but I can't draw him without my name, and Nemini's sword is broken, so that won't work, either. There's a chance one of my other sisters could do it, but none of them have woken up yet."

Her spirits sank lower with every word. Bex had been pushing so hard to keep ahead of the ax that she hadn't allowed herself to stop and take stock of how much had already been chopped off. She finally had another queen to help her, but it was Nemini, who didn't want the job and didn't have a sword. She'd finally rescued her sisters, but they were all lost in their own minds and didn't have swords either.

It felt like every win she'd scored recently came with a loss. At this point, Bex was ready to settle for getting her people out alive. She was about to ask Agatha if the refugees from the Hells could use the new forest to escape back to Earth without the chains when the witch said, "There's another way."

Bex's head shot back up. "Another way to what?"

"There's another way to break the barrier and attack Gilgamesh without retrieving your crown," Agatha clarified. "I'm not the one most fit to explain it, though. My expertise is witchcraft, the magic of the living world. But despite the fires of life my son poured into you, you are still a queen of Paradise, Ishtar's divine creation. To address your situation, you need a god."

"I don't know," Bex said skeptically. "The last god I met wasn't very helpful."

"This one will be," Agatha promised as she took Bex's arm and started pulling her away from Adrian's cauldron toward the cabin's front door. "Despite starting out on different sides, the two of you have been working toward the same goal for a long time now. I think you'll find you have a lot in common once you start talking. We even took the liberty of paying for her ticket."

Before Bex could ask what in the Hells that meant, the Witch of the Present held out her hand to show Bex the freshly healed stump where her right pinky finger once was.

"Adrian isn't the only one who paid for this day," she explained when Bex gaped. "My sisters and I all sacrificed, but it's up to you to make it count."

"Make what count?" Bex demanded. "What do you want me to—"

Before she could finish, Agatha used her four-fingered hand to shove Bex out the door. That shouldn't have been possible for a human, but the witch was a lot stronger than she looked, and Bex had been caught by surprise. She still only stumbled a few feet, but before she could yell at Adrian's mother for pushing her, a giant black talon shot out of the fir tree's shadows and wrapped around Bex's waist.

"Well, well, well," a croaking, inhuman voice chuffed above her. "If it isn't my son's remorseless murderess. This should be rich."

Bex barely had time to cock her head back to see the absolutely *gigantic* crow perched on the cabin's roof before the bird flicked its giant claw and threw her off the porch, sending her plummeting down the center of Adrian's enormous new heart tree.

Chapter 4

BY THE TIME BEX GOT HER BEARINGS, she'd already hurtled out of the fir tree's thicker upper branches and was now falling through the open air beside its skyscraper-sized trunk. She was so high up, her eyes had trouble making out the canopies of the smaller—but still gigantic—trees she was falling into. She had no problem seeing the shadow of the giant raven diving after her, though.

"Ho, ho, ho," the bird croaked in a smug, rasping voice. "Didn't Ishtar teach you to catch yourself? It's a good thing my precious witchlings vouched for you. You'd be eaten in a second if you came into my forest with such sloppy moves."

Bex's reply to that was to slam her hands toward the ground. Flames blasted out of her palms a second later, creating enough opposite thrust to turn her fall into a hover. She was still trying to get the balance right when the giant talons closed around her body once more, stopping her flight and flipping her over before bringing Bex face-to-face with the most monstrous bird she'd ever seen.

It was similar to a crow with jet-black feathers and a sharp black beak, but no mortal bird had ever had such a delightedly bloodthirsty gleam in its beady eyes. The thing looked like it was getting ready to pick every bit of flesh off Bex's bones, but when she swung her burning hands up to grab it, the bird smacked her fists away with a flick of its beak.

"There's no call for that," it croaked, spreading its giant wings to check their fall. "Your mother and I never could cross paths without trying to tear each other's eyes out, but the two of us have a shared enemy. That makes us allies of a sort, so I will overlook your participation in the callous murder of my son and greet you, youngest daughter of the fool known as Ishtar."

Bex lowered her burning hands cautiously. The giant bird's arrogance certainly matched the other gods she'd spoken to. But while she didn't appreciate being talked down to, Bex *really* didn't want to get into an aerial battle with an opponent who was clearly better equipped for it. She also didn't want to waste her energy fighting anyone who wasn't Gilgamesh or his sons if she could help it, but that didn't mean she was going to roll over and take this.

"Who are you?" she demanded, leaning against the crow's talons to show she wasn't afraid.

"Some humility would serve you well," the crow scolded, turning its enormous head to look at Bex with each of its giant beady black eyes in turn. "But I know better than to expect manners from a child of Paradise, so I won't waste my breath except to say that you may call me the Morrigan."

Bex had thought so. The Morrigan was the crow goddess Adrian had told her about, the one who'd eaten the crazy prince Leander had sent to kill him. She'd also eaten Adrian's finger, but saving his life and their attack on the Anchor balanced that out, and Bex wasn't exactly in a position to hold a grudge right now.

"Okay, 'the Morrigan,'" she said, crossing her arms over her chest. "What do you want, and what does it have to do with throwing me off a tree?"

"I threw you because you were distracting my sweet Agatha," the goddess replied, tucking Bex closer to her feathered belly as she swooped in a spiral around the fir tree's giant trunk. "She needs all of her attention to save the life of her delicious son, whose flesh I very much look forward to sampling again."

Bex's scowl deepened.

"As for what I want, that's easy," the Morrigan continued, turning her sharp beak toward the golden palace hidden behind the glittering shield. "I want Gilgamesh to die in agony for the harm he's heaped upon my forest and my witches."

That was a plan Bex could get behind, but she still didn't understand. "Are you the goddess of witches?"

"Never," the crow snapped. "Those who belong to the Blackwood need no gods. I'm more of a benevolent neighbor. I help the witches in return for payment and the advancement of our mutual interests, which include you at the moment."

"Why didn't you help me before I lost my horns, then?" Bex asked bitterly. "It's a little too late now."

"Now is the perfect time," the goddess promised. "My sweet Muriel is never wrong about these things. Helping you earlier would have tipped our hand, but losing your crown, sword, and name was what caused Gilgamesh to ignore you long enough to allow your incursion into the Hells and their subsequent destruction. That's heaps more than any of the idiot Rebexas before you ever managed, so clearly, your horns aren't as important as you think."

"Not as important?" Bex squawked. "I can't draw my sword!"

"Why not?" the Morrigan asked, tilting her head like an actual curious crow. "Isn't it yours?"

"No," Bex said with a wince. "It's Rebexa's, and I'm not her anymore. That's my whole problem. I can't pull my sword without the royal name bestowed upon me by my horns, and I can't get my horns back without my sword."

It was an obviously hopeless situation, but the Morrigan just gave Bex a frustrated shake.

"And here I thought Ishtar's daughters were supposed to be clever," she croaked in disgust. "If you need your name to get your sword and your sword to get your name, then there's only two solutions. You must either get a new sword—"

"*No!*" Bex shrieked, clutching her black ring to her chest. "Drox is my family!"

"Would you let me finish?" the crow snapped, striking Bex painfully on the head with the sharp tip of her beak. "As I was saying, you must *either* get a new sword or get a new name."

Bex stopped rubbing her smarting head to stare at the goddess in wonder. "A new name?" she repeated in a trembling voice. "Could you give me one?"

"I didn't mean from me," the Morrigan said, crushing Bex's newborn hope before it could finish rising. "I was never part of the Paradise fiasco, which is why I'm still alive."

Bex scowled. "Then what are you—"

"I am still a wise and powerful goddess, however," the Morrigan went on, speaking over her. "And as someone *so* much older and cleverer than Ishtar's clumsy creations could ever hope to be, I will benevolently remind you of *them*."

She tilted her wings as she spoke. They'd been gliding slowly down this whole time, but the Morrigan must've planned this from the start, because the moment she said "them," they came back around the giant tree, and the square by the Hells' Gate came back into view.

The sight made Bex go still. The newly plant-covered section of the White City was overflowing with a shocking number of demons. The sheer size of the crowd staring up at her was almost more than Bex's brain could handle. She'd been told how many demons they'd saved from the Hells several times, but she'd never actually seen them all together in one place before this moment. They'd always been scattered between buildings or moving in smaller groups. Now, though, the sudden appearance of the Blackwood had brought the entire population of Gilgamesh's former slaves out into the open.

There were *so* many demons crowded into the square that even standing shoulder to shoulder, they still filled the entire plaza surrounding the entrance to the Hells. Still more had packed themselves into the tree-filled side streets while others leaned over the balconies of the listing apartment buildings. There were winged demons perching in the trees and war demons pouring out of the Hells' Gate from the drinking-water distillery in former sin-iron forges to see what the commotion was about. More demons than she'd ever realized existed were pointing up at them right now, but while the Morrigan was smirking like that was the answer to everything, Bex still didn't understand.

"I don't get it," she said, clinging to the Morrigan's talons as she stared at the sea of demons below them. "What do my people have to do with my name?"

"That's the question, isn't it?" the crow replied with a chuckle. "But unlike some gods, I don't believe in giving answers away for free, so here's a question of my own instead. What makes a queen a queen?"

Bex thought about that for a moment. "Power?"

"But where does that power come from?" the Morrigan pressed. "Obviously it was Ishtar initially, but she's been dust for eons. If she was still strong enough to swing a sword at Gilgamesh, she'd be out here doing it herself, but she's not. Instead, she's relying on you."

The crow tilted her huge beak to look straight down at Bex. "Why do you think that is? If your crown and name are truly the source of your power, but the goddess who gave them to you is so weak that she can't even talk to you unless you die, how are you a queen? Where does the power to name demons come from if not Ishtar?"

Bex had no idea. She hated riddles, and she *hated* wasting time. Her loyal wrath demons had already suffered long enough. She needed to be down there evacuating them through the Blackwood back to Earth, where they could get food, not stuck up here playing guessing games with—

She stopped, glowing eyes flying wide. "It's my demons."

"Your demons, you say?" The Morrigan flashed her a smile, which was how Bex learned that her beak was full of razor-sharp teeth. "And what makes you think that?"

"Because they're the only ones who could be doing it," Bex said, talking faster as her brain began to whirl. "Every time I speak a demon's true name, it takes effort. Back when my fire was super low, I could barely do it at all. Even after Adrian and the Blackwood rebuilt my bonfire, though, I could only name large groups if I got really fired up. I thought I was having trouble because my rebirths had ground me down, but that was never the problem. It *always* takes power to speak a demon's name because our names have power in and of themselves."

Now that she'd said it out loud, the truth felt face-smackingly obvious. She'd actually witnessed this exact phenomenon in action just a few hours ago with the Queen of War. Even though she'd surrendered her horns to Gilgamesh, Dalanea still had her name.

If being queen was truly a divine right tied to being Ishtar's daughter, then War should've been able to stomp her rebelling demons into submission, horns or no horns. That hadn't happened, though, because War *didn't* have enough power to name them on her own. Bex wasn't sure if *she* could have quelled an entire tower full of rebelling demons who hated her guts even with her horns and her fire blazing. There simply wasn't enough power now that Ishtar was no longer around to back her daughters up. But when those same demons had acknowledged Bex and offered their wrath to her of their own free will, she'd blazed brighter than ever before.

Bex had always assumed her ability to consume her demons' fury was due to her nature as the Bonfire of Wrath, but what if turning into a sky-filling storm of fire every time the kick demons bowed to her in Limbo didn't happen only because of their anger? What if Bex's people—her loyal demons who'd never bowed to anyone else and never stopped believing that their queen would return to save them—had *actually* been empowering her the same way drinking vials of deathly water used to?

"Now you're starting to get it," the Morrigan said, nodding down at the crowd. "I can't give you a name because you don't belong to me, but you do belong to *them*. As an extension of Ishtar's power, you should have withered and died with your goddess five thousand years ago, but your people's need for a champion kept you alive. Ishtar wasn't the one who brought you back when you died. All she did was catch your soul. I'm sure she would've kept it if she could, but you were always born again because your people still needed a rescuer. You were *their* sword, not Ishtar's. *That* is what makes you Queen of Wrath, so if you need a new royal name, I suggest starting there."

The Morrigan dipped her beak toward the throngs of demons watching below, and Bex swallowed.

"How?" she asked around the lump in her throat. "We're talking about meddling with the magic of Ishtar herself. Even if you're right, how do I get them to—"

"The same way you get anything," the Morrigan interrupted. "You ask."

"But—"

"Good luck," the goddess said as she opened her talons, dropping the hornless queen like a discarded kill.

Bex fell with a scream. She tumbled in free fall for several seconds, too shocked to do anything except windmill her arms. Then her survival instincts kicked in and she blasted her fire, catching herself seconds before she crashed into the canopy of Adrian's huge new forest.

The moment she was certain she wouldn't plummet to her death, Bex changed the fire's direction, rocketing over the crowd like a comet to land on top of the giant black cube of the Hells' Gate, the only building left in this part of the city that hadn't been swallowed by forest. She kept her fire blazing even after she set down, covering her body in the brilliant flames of Wrath as she straightened up to face her people.

And realized her mistake.

The plaza surrounding the entrance to the Hells was so packed with demons that she couldn't see the end of them. The crowd surrounded her on all sides like a sea. A silent, terrified sea of faces all looking at her in desperation. No one cheered. No one yelled. They didn't even bow. They all just stood there, holding their breath as they waited for Ishtar's last queen to work a miracle, but Bex didn't know what to say. Even if she had known, she couldn't possibly yell loud enough to reach so many people with the mortal voice she had now.

That realization hurt even more than she'd expected. This was the moment when she most needed to be a queen, but Bex wasn't larger than life anymore.

Other than the fire burning on her skin, she was exactly as she appeared: a short, hornless, scrawny girl who didn't even have a sword. Even if Drox had been in her hand, Bex had no idea how to explain what she needed. How in the world did you ask a crowd of hundreds of thousands of starving, terrified refugees to give you a new name? She was still struggling to think of where to start when the Morrigan suddenly landed beside her.

The goddess came down like a feathered meteor, blowing the demons standing in the front rows to the ground. The moment her talons settled on the black gate, though, she changed her shape, transforming from an aircraft-sized raven into a tall, pale woman wearing bloody leather armor, a cape of black wings, and a crown of human bones. She looked absolutely terrifying, but that was nothing compared to the *feel* of her. Even Bex had to fight the urge to flee before the force of nature the Morrigan had revealed herself to be. She was forcing herself to stay still and not make a fool of herself in front of everyone when the great and terrible goddess turned and spoke in a voice pitched for her ears alone.

"Good show, eh?"

Bex blinked in surprise, and the Morrigan's blood-red lips curled into a smirk.

"I didn't break my rule about never entering Paradise just to be informative," she whispered as her eyes, which were still beady and black like a crow's, darted over the terrified crowd. "My three favorite witchlings cut off their fingers to bring me here. A half-hearted display would shame their offering, so I expect you to do your part as well. Follow my lead, daughter of Ishtar, and together we shall see what your people really think of you."

She spoke those words like a threat, but Bex just nodded and pushed her fear-dampened flames back to their normal roaring height. When she was burning bright again, the goddess lifted her arms and spoke in a ringing voice that thundered to every corner of Gilgamesh's Heaven.

"Hear me, creations of my foolish sister!" she boomed. "I am the Morrigan, Triple-Faced Goddess of Prophecy, the Phantom Queen and the Battle Crow. I was the only god who did not join in the folly that was the creation of Paradise and thus was the only god who escaped its fall when Gilgamesh arrived to slay the rest of my kind. I swore ages ago that I would never set foot in the graveyard of my kin's mistakes, but I have broken that oath and come here today to bear witness to the birth of a new age."

She extended one sharp-taloned hand toward Bex.

"This is the Bonfire of Wrath," she announced. "Ishtar's Sword. For five thousand years, she has fought to free the children of Paradise from their enslavement. Many thought such a thing was impossible. *I* thought it was impossible, but even after her treacherous sister tore the horns from her head, the Queen of Wrath did not abandon her fight. Together with her loyal retainers, she outwitted the Eternal King and tore down the Nine Hells of Gilgamesh. Because of her, the people of the Riverlands walk free upon the face of Paradise for the first time in fifty centuries!"

Her hand came down like an axe to clap Bex on the shoulder. "Such actions have made her worthy in my divine sight!" the Morrigan cried. "In honor of this victory, I have decided to grant her a boon. Speak, daughter of Ishtar, and if it is within my divine power, it shall be so."

The promise cracked like lightning over the dead-silent square. Every demon in Paradise seemed to be holding their breath, including Bex herself. She hadn't expected any of that, but the Morrigan was scowling at her like she was flubbing her line. That sent Bex into a panic for a second because she didn't *know* her line. Then the goddess flicked her black eyes pointedly toward the watching crowd, and suddenly, Bex understood.

"Great Morrigan," she said in a voice she hoped was loud enough to carry to the buildings at the edge of the square, "I humbly ask that you restore my name."

"Your name?" the goddess repeated in theatrical surprise. "How did you lose it?"

"It was stolen," Bex replied, getting into the swing of things. "Gilgamesh took it when the traitorous Queen of War ripped my horns from my head. He has stolen all the queens' names because he knows that we are his defeat. If I had my name, I could call the Blade of Wrath to cut open Heaven's defenses. I could cut the slave bands from every demon's neck and set Ishtar's children truly free! Gilgamesh stole my name precisely to keep me from doing these things. I cannot defeat him without it, so for my boon, this is what I ask." She bowed her hornless head. "Please, great Morrigan, sister of my sacred mother, make me whole again."

Her chest was heaving by the end. It took a crazy amount of breath to say all that so loudly. Bex had never realized how much she relied on the queen's supernaturally booming voice until she lost it. She thought she'd done a good job at matching the goddess's grand style at least, but she still didn't know where this performance was going. The Morrigan had already told her she couldn't replace Rebexa's name, and sure enough, the goddess shook her head.

"I cannot."

She'd known it was coming, but the rejection still felt like a slap. Everyone else must've felt the same way, because the crowd that had been watching in terrified silence up to this point suddenly gasped. Standing at the center with her bonfire roaring, Bex could feel their shock and dismay like a sword in her guts, filling her with real anger as she yelled back.

"Why can't you?" she demanded. "I thought you were a goddess!"

"I am," the Morrigan replied. "The problem is I'm not *your* goddess."

That must've been the point she was aiming for this whole time, because the moment she said it, the Morrigan seemed to forget that Bex existed. She focused the entirety of her divine attention on the crowd instead, turning in a slow circle so that every corner of the packed square could see her terrifying face.

"Ishtar created her children for her own purposes," she told them in a measured, calculating voice. "Were you creatures of the wilds, your names would be mine, but I cannot give you what does not belong to me. But just because *I* cannot restore the Bonfire Queen's name doesn't mean it's lost forever."

It didn't take any acting for Bex's voice to fill with hope. "How do I get it back?"

"You can't," the Morrigan said. "But *they* can."

She swept her hand over the crowd, which stepped back in alarm. The goddess's black eyes narrowed when she saw it, and she bared her sharp teeth in fury.

"Do you think the queen should fight alone?" she roared at the demons. "You are *all* Ishtar's creations! A fraction of her divine power still resides in each of you. If it didn't, you'd all be dust just like the rest of Paradise. The reason you were permitted to survive is because Gilgamesh needed that power to make his sin iron, but his greed shall be his downfall!"

She whirled in a circle, sweeping her sharp-taloned hands over the crowd that surrounded her and Bex on all sides.

"You want freedom, Children of Ishtar? You want Heaven to fall and this war to end? Then you, too, must act! Don't waste your prayers on a dead goddess who can no longer help. Offer them to the living queen who is fighting for you here and now! Bow your horns before the only daughter of Ishtar who ever gave a damn about whether you lived or died. Offer your names to the Bonfire, and she shall burn Gilgamesh and all his creations *to the ground*!"

Her voice reverberated like thunder through the forest this part of Heaven had become, but no one shouted back. Even Bex was shocked speechless, because those words were blasphemy. A new name was one thing, but offering prayers? Honoring Bex instead of Ishtar? That was too far. It was sacrilege. It was—

"Bonfire."

Bex raised her glowing eyes to see the Morrigan staring down at her. She was still in her human form, but the goddess looked much bigger now than she had before. She towered like a giant over Bex's five-foot-two frame, her black wings blotting out even the light of Heaven as she asked, "Did Ishtar order you to storm the Hells?"

Bex flinched away, but everyone was staring at her, so she answered the question truthfully.

"No."

The Morrigan looked pleased. "Did she tell you to attack the Anchor in Seattle and free the slaves that were kept in bondage there?"

"No," Bex said again.

"Has she *ever* interceded on her people's behalf?" the goddess demanded. "Do you remember even one instance when Ishtar blessed you with her power or helped you directly?"

"She brought me back to life when I died," Bex offered.

"No, she didn't," the Morrigan spat. "I saw everything through the forest's eyes when Adrian Blackwood worked with the Great Forest to rekindle the fire Ishtar had allowed to die. *You* were the one who chose to return to the fight. All the 'Merciful Mother of the Riverlands' did was fuse the new fire with the old, and the only reason she was able to do that much was because of all the deathly water you kept pouring down your gullet. If you hadn't been watering her like a houseplant for five thousand years, Ishtar wouldn't have had enough strength to meet you inside your own head. She's nothing but a parasite riding in your body, a critic watching and judging and doing nothing while *you* fought the war *she* lost."

"That's not true," Bex said angrily. "She's my mother, my goddess!"

"She *was* your goddess," the Morrigan corrected. "But a god who demands worship while providing nothing in return is no better than a king who demands tribute and then sits idle on his throne while invaders slaughter his people. Such useless monarchs were beheaded in ancient times, but you lot keep brainlessly defending yours like Ishtar hasn't neglected all of you for the last five thousand years." The goddess's black eyes narrowed. "Such mindless obedience sickens me. Are you sure your people don't deserve to be slaves?"

Bex opened her mouth to object, but the crowd beat her to it. The throng of demons who'd been silent all this time was suddenly screaming at the Morrigan in fury. Rather than being angry back, though, the goddess threw out her arms in welcome, grinning from ear to ear like the insults were hymns in her honor.

"*That's it!*" she cried, waving for them to give her more. "Howl like the hit dogs you are! It's a vast improvement over the quivering sheep I saw when I came down, but all that wrath is still meaningless if you don't use it." She reached down and grabbed Bex by the arm, yanking her up beside her.

"You want to end your suffering?" the goddess yelled at the demons. "Then stop being good little slaves and seize your freedom!"

She yanked Bex's arm higher, forcing her to stand as tall as possible or be lifted off her feet.

"This is *your* queen!" the Morrigan bellowed. "In five thousand years of slavery, Wrath is the only ruler who never surrendered you to Gilgamesh. Even Ishtar gave up and accepted defeat before his sword, but the Bonfire Queen has fought, died, and been reborn *one hundred and ninety-eight times* for your sake! That tenacity is her strength. Not even I could defeat Gilgamesh in his present state, but she can. She's the *only* one left who can end this, but only if *you* give her the power she needs to do it."

The Morrigan's smile grew wicked. "This is how you win your own freedom, demons of the Hells. *This* is how you destroy the man who killed the gods! The Blade of Ishtar is your sword now, so give her your names. Feed the Bonfire with *your* wrath, and she shall tear all Heaven *down*!"

The goddess finished with a flourish, but even her booming voice was lost in the crowd's answering roar. The wave of wrath that came with it was strong enough to knock Bex off her feet. She would've gone down if the Morrigan hadn't been holding her arm in a death grip, but while the enormous power of her people's fury was shoving itself down her throat, Bex didn't want it.

She understood why they were mad. It was impossible not to resent being the victim of a war that had started five thousand years before you were born. She'd felt the same way several times, but unlike her people, Bex didn't have the luxury of indulging in such feelings because she was a daughter of Ishtar. Her entire existence was framed by being her mother's sword. She was the Wrath of Ishtar, the ever-loyal blade. Betraying her mother was the one thing she absolutely could not do, but the anger of her people was too strong to escape.

Just like when the demons of War had shoved their traitorous queen away, the demons in the square had Bex in a chokehold. Her bonfire was already flaming to the sky with the intensity of their wrath. Wrath at Gilgamesh for doing this to them but also wrath at Ishtar for not saving them despite years of loyal worship.

The anger wasn't new, either. The Morrigan must've known exactly what she was doing. Her words had tapped into a well of resentment so ancient and deep that it seemed to have no bottom, because the Morrigan wasn't wrong. Ishtar *hadn't* helped them. She and the other gods were supposed to be all-powerful, but the demons were slaves because the infallible gods had *lost*. Lost and never recovered, never risen again or returned in glory to fight for their creations.

Bex knew that was because Gilgamesh had chained the Wheel of Reincarnation, but the demons in the square knew no such thing. In their eyes, the gods had abandoned them, and now that the Morrigan had stirred the pot, they were furious about it. Not normal levels of furious, either. This was a toxic, simmering resentment born from generations of humiliation and powerlessness. For centuries, it had grown like a headless monster, but the moment the

Morrigan painted Bex as the solution, all of that formless anger slammed straight into her.

Even for the queen who'd been born to eat this specific sin, it was too much. If the Morrigan hadn't been holding her up, the tidal wave of toxic, bitter rage would have sent Bex to her knees. She was still struggling not to pass out when the Morrigan grabbed her face.

"None of that," the goddess scolded, forcing Bex to look her in the eyes. "You wanted to be a full queen again, didn't you?"

"Not like this," Bex choked as her flaming hands dug into the Morrigan's clawed ones. "I thought you were going to ask them to give me a new name. Why did you turn them against Ishtar?"

The Morrigan's smile grew cruel. "Because Gilgamesh isn't the only one who hates the gods," she whispered, holding the queen close as the raging fire of wrath began consuming Bex's body. "Ishtar killed my beloved son out of petty jealousy. All the gods were like that: shallow, spoiled monsters who cared for nothing but their own enjoyment. You've already killed Enki, so don't pretend you don't know what I mean."

"Ishtar is different," Bex insisted. "She's merciful. She—"

A wave of pain cut her off before she could finish. She writhed in the Morrigan's grasp, fighting off flames that were suddenly bigger than she was. This wasn't the wrath she was used to. This bonfire was fueled by resentment of Ishtar herself, and it was bigger than anything Bex had ever produced. If she couldn't control it, the resulting firestorm would destroy Ishtar's children as easily as it consumed everything else. Her own people's anger would turn them all to ash if she let it, so Bex held on tight, clutching the toxic fire to her chest even as it burned her alive.

"Good," the Morrigan's voice said from somewhere above her. "That's the reaction I was hoping for. I knew you would put your people first, Bex of the Bonfire. Remember that when she comes for you."

When who comes? Bex wanted to ask, but she couldn't get the words past the char that blocked her throat. Every bit of her was on fire now, filling her vision with so many flames that she didn't even see the skeletal hands reaching up to grab her until they snatched her by the throat, dragging Bex out of her burning body and into a world of ash.

Chapter 5

WHEN BEX OPENED HER EYES AGAIN, she was on her knees in a dry riverbed. The silt was so soft and powdery that she could barely feel it beneath her fingers. If there'd been any wind, the whole bank would've blown away in a single gust, but there wasn't. There was no wind, no sound, no movement or life of any sort. Just dust and ash and the shadow of a faint, ghostly figure hanging like a pall in front of her.

What do you think you are doing?

Bex flinched. That was Ishtar's voice. She'd know it anywhere, but it was so faint. The goddess's words were as weightless as the dust that flew into the air just from the puff of Bex's breathing. The anger that burned inside them, however, was as hot as the bonfire's flames.

What do you think you are doing? the ghostly image of Ishtar demanded again. *You are* my *sword,* my *weapon! You swing at* my *pleasure!*

The shadow turned her head sharply, causing her towering crown of six tall horns to flicker like an old film.

I thought you understood that, she whispered, covering her once-beautiful face with her hands. *You were so loyal, so good. Rebexa would never betray me. That's what I always thought, but what do I see now? My faithful daughter, telling my demons to swear to her.* The dead goddess ripped her hands back down to reveal a terrifying visage of rage. *You stole my worshipers!*

"I didn't steal them!" Bex cried, putting up her own hands. "It was the Morrigan who riled them up!

The children of the Riverlands are loyal. The only reason the Morrigan's attack got through is because your people are suffering. They're hurt and terrified, desperate for salvation. If you'd just speak to them—"

Why should I? Ishtar snarled. *I don't care how they feel. I'm the reason they exist! They should be grateful.*

"They *are* grateful," Bex insisted, looking up at her mother. "But all the demons you originally created are gone. These are their children's children, who know you only as a story. They want to believe, but no matter how faithfully they pray to you, it never works, because you're dead."

You think I wanted to be dead? Ishtar snapped.

"Of course not," Bex said quickly. "I'm just asking you to look at things from their perspective. Their lives have been terrible under Gilgamesh, and their goddess can't do anything to help them."

I gave them you, Ishtar argued. *I didn't have to keep catching you every time you died. I could have let you fall into the void, but you act like your rebirths are all your doing. You seek to steal my place.* Her ghostly eyes narrowed. *You're as faithless as War.*

Bex's jaw ticked. "Maybe War wouldn't have been so faithless if you hadn't thrown her in a pit."

You only say that because you've forgotten what she used to sound like, Ishtar said dismissively. *She was an embarrassment—howling like an animal, cursing my name. She ruined the peace of our divine Paradise. Of course she was punished.*

"War only howled because the job you made her do left her in constant pain," Bex retorted. "You're her mother. Why didn't you try to ease her suffering instead of locking her up?"

Because her suffering was not my problem, Ishtar's ghost snapped. *Paradise was a joint project, the gods' great work. If I let your sister slack off, the sin of War would not be cleansed, and we'd fall behind schedule.*

Bex couldn't believe her ears. "And that was worth your daughter?"

Don't let her manipulate you, Ishtar warned. *You all suffered for humanity's sins, but while the rest of you bore it gladly, War was weak. She screamed at pain the rest of you endured without complaint, so I put her in that hole to toughen her up. I took no joy in it, but it had to be done. After all, a queen who cannot do her job is worthless.*

She said this as if she couldn't understand why anyone would be upset by it, but Bex was staring at her mother like she'd never seen her before.

"Is that all we were to you?" she whispered at last. "Was Gilgamesh right? Did you only ever see us as your tools?"

Oh, darling, no, Ishtar said, reaching down to stroke her daughter's hair. *It's true I made you for a purpose, but that's what makes you divine. You were all part of our great and important work: the perfection of humanity. When we were done, there would be no more war or wrath, no pride, greed, sorrow, lust, hate, fear, or envy. All of humanity's demons would be vanquished, and the entire species would know nothing but peace, solace, and tranquility. They would worship us forever in deathless bliss. Isn't that a Paradise worth suffering for?*

Her ghostly hand kept petting her daughter's hair the entire time she spoke, but Bex pulled away.

"What about us?" she asked, looking up at her divine mother. "What about your demons?"

Your work would be finished as well, the goddess assured her. *When humanity had no more sins to scrub clean, I would reclaim the divine spark of power I placed inside each of you and take you all back into myself. As you came from me, so would you return to become part of my divine happiness forever.*

Again, she said this as if it were the only sensible conclusion, but Bex had never been more horrified in her life.

"What about *our* happiness?" she demanded, shooting to her feet. "We were the ones doing all the work!"

I was offering you a great gift, Ishtar said pointedly. *It's not everyone who gets to experience the divine happiness of a goddess firsthand. I could have made you all brainless like Enki did with his forge workers, but purging human sins requires empathy, so I gave you all named souls derived from my own divine power. Those names are the only reason you were able to survive my death. Every demon still in existence is alive because of* me. *Again, you should be grateful, not whining about how you've suffered in my absence while I've been dead.*

Bex clenched her fists. "Wanting to be free of slavery is not *whining.*"

Then take it up with your slaver! Ishtar snarled. *Gilgamesh is the one who did this to you, not me!*

"I am going to take it up with him," Bex promised, sticking out her hand to show her mother the fire that was still blazing like the sun. "This is the power of your people. It might have started with you, but they're the ones who kept it alive, passing the flame of hope from generation to generation. They never stopped believing that you'd return to save them one day, so if you want their worship, be worthy of it. Take this fire and prove that you're still the Ishtar from the stories, Goddess of War and Merciful Mother of the Riverlands. If you don't want them turning to me, then strike down Gilgamesh yourself and end this! Do that, and your people will praise you again with their whole hearts. *I* will kneel and praise you, because I don't care about prayers or being worshiped. I just want this to end. I want their suffering, my suffering, *all of our suffering* to stop. Do that for us, and I'll make sure everyone knows you are the greatest goddess who was ever worthy of her people's praise."

Bex fell back to her knees as she finished, holding the blazing fire up to her mother like an offering, but the ghost of her goddess stepped back.

No.

"Why not?" Bex demanded. "I thought you wanted—"

I want the worship that's mine by right, Ishtar snapped, backing away even farther. *But I'm not falling for the same trick twice. You think I can't see what's happening? The Morrigan, that uncivilized barbarian, arranged this situation specially to lure me out. She even sent you to me knowing that I've always had a weakness for your earnestness, but it's not going to work. You think that fire is something special? It's nothing, leftovers, not even a fraction of the power I once possessed. If I take that flame and march back into the open like the idiot you're asking me to be, what do you think is going to happen?*

Bex frowned at the wrath burning in her hands. "I don't—"

I'll die, the goddess said flatly, crossing her arms over her transparent chest. *If I couldn't beat Gilgamesh* at the height of my power, there's no way I can possibly beat him with that. It's just common sense.

"Then what was it all for?" Bex cried, shooting back to her feet as the fire spread down her arms. "All my lives and deaths, five thousand years of fighting—what was the point of any of it if you're not even going to try?"

Oh, darling, Ishtar said, giving her a pitying smile. *The fighting* was *the point. I always knew you were never going to win. I only let you go back so you could continue being a thorn in Gilgamesh's side. That haughty brat was using my demons like they were his property. Just because I knew I couldn't beat him didn't mean I was going to stand aside and let him get away with that, so I threw you under his feet. You've been spoiling his plans and costing him stress for eons. It might be petty, but knowing Gilgamesh was suffering has given me much solace during what would otherwise be an extremely depressing afterlife, and it made you happy too.*

She reached out to pet Bex's hair again. *You always were such a hopeful little creature, and you worked so hard. That's why you were my favorite. My other queens grew cynical and resentful, but you always believed the best. Even after Paradise fell, you sincerely thought you could get it back, and I just didn't have the heart to tell you how foolish that was.*

"So you lied to me?"

I let you dream, the goddess replied, brushing Bex's ashy hair behind her ear. *There was no harm to it, especially since I got to dream with you. The Paradise you kept for me inside your heart was beautiful. I almost didn't want to let the witches burn it down, but you were practically dust by that point, so I thought, why not? You were going to snuff out soon no matter what, so why not let you go out with a bang? I thought it would make you happy and put one last little thorn in Gilgamesh's boot. I never dreamed you'd take it this far.*

"I didn't 'take it' this far," Bex snarled, yanking out of her mother's reach. "We *made* it. Adrian, Lys, Iggs, Nemini, Kirok, Desh, all of us—we fought tooth and nail to get to where we are today, and we're not stopping. I don't care if you say winning is impossible. We still have to try, because if we quit, it really will have all been for nothing. If we don't defeat Gilgamesh, he'll rebuild the Hells and recapture us one by one. Considering he's locked in his palace, working on some giant move, it might be even worse. I'm not standing around waiting for that to happen."

Bex looked down at the flames burning all over her body. Flames that no longer hurt, because she was no longer fighting them. She was mad at Ishtar too now, and she wasn't backing down.

"If this is the fire we've got, then this is the fire we'll use," Bex said, offering her flaming hand to the ghost of her mother one last time. "If you want to keep being worshiped as our goddess, take it and save us. If you're too afraid to even try, then give me a new name and I'll fight Gilgamesh for you. I'll do whatever it takes, but fighting for my people's right to exist without some warlock's boot on their necks isn't a 'thorn in Gilgamesh's boot'. It's the promise I've been living and dying five thousand years to achieve. There's no way I'm giving up now when we're so close to the finish line, so either you take the power your people have offered, or I'll take it for you."

That's enough, Rebexa, Ishtar warned. *I know you're upset, but the plan you're proposing is ridiculous. We already fought Gilgamesh with everything we had and failed. The idea that we can beat him now when he's stronger than ever and we're little more than echoes is insane. The only thing we can do at this point is bide our time and wait for his mortality to run its course. Once he dies as all humans eventually must, everything will go back to the way it was.*

That was the same logic Enki had used, and now as then, it sent Bex into a rage.

"And what about the rest of us?" she roared. "What are *we* supposed to do while you wait for Gilgamesh to die? Suffer for another five thousand years?"

It's not ideal, her mother admitted. *But it's the best we're going to get, and it's not as if you have to endure with the common rabble. Despite how you're acting at the moment, you're still my favorite daughter, and you've brought enough magic in with you to make our afterlives quite comfortable. We could restore this phantom desolation back into a proper Paradise and wait out the remaining years in peace. That way, when Gilgamesh does finally succumb, we'll be in a prime position to rebuild.*

She flashed Bex a winning smile. *You said you wanted to stop suffering, right? In that case, all you have to do is put the fire down. Let your anger go, and I'll grow you a fresh bank of grass to sleep on like I did when you were a little girl. Wouldn't that be lovely?*

Her smile was so sweet by the end that it made Bex's heart ache. For the first time since she'd arrived in this place, Ishtar looked like the mother Bex remembered, but it was all a lie. This wasn't just a ghost of the brave, loving goddess she'd thought she known. Bex was starting to think that Ishtar had never existed in the first place, because the *actual* Merciful Mother of the Riverlands would never invite her daughter to sleep on the grass while their people suffered and died.

I can see you're going to be foolish, Ishtar said with a sigh as Bex clutched the fire tighter against her chest. *This is why I made you to be a sword and not an advisor. You never could see the bigger picture.*

"I don't want to see your bigger picture," Bex spat. "In fact, I don't understand why Gilgamesh is so terrified of all of you rising again. With the exception of the Morrigan, every god I've ever met has been a coward. I don't think any of you would fight him if you did come back."

Don't be stupid, Ishtar scolded. *I already explained to you what folly that would be. Only idiots fight battles they can't win, but our plan was never to fight Gilgamesh when the wheel turned. That would just be repeating the mistakes of the past, which we're all far too wise to do. Our plan is much cleverer. When the Great Wheel turns again—as it must, since no chain lasts forever—we're going to reset the world.*

Bex went still. "What?"

We're going to reset the world, Ishtar repeated with the look of someone who's just played their final card. *Why bother fighting when we can just start the whole thing over again from scratch? We would have done it before we lost the first time, but clever Gilgamesh started his coup by killing Anu, and the way Paradise is built, I couldn't turn the wheel without him. That's a design flaw I'll be correcting in the next version, by the way, but what do you think now? Still want to throw yourself at a losing battle?*

"Yes!" Bex cried, staring at her mother in horror. "I'm doing this to *save* people, remember? If you reset the world, doesn't that mean everyone who's alive right now will die?"

Technically, Ishtar admitted. *But their souls will be reborn again with no memories, so they won't care, and it will take care of so many problems. We can destroy all knowledge of Gilgamesh's heretical sorcery, remove the pagan worship of the Great Cycles, and set humanity back to the Bronze Age, when they were more manageable. It'll be so much better than things are now, and you'll get to return to Paradise with a fresh population of demons who have no memory of the traumas of slavery or the war. This way gets you everything you want, so you really should reconsider my offer.*

"There's nothing to consider," Bex snarled. "If your idea of victory is killing everyone, then I've got nothing left to say to you."

That's too bad, Ishtar said, her ghostly face truly disappointed. *I wanted to avoid this if I could. As I said, you've always been my favorite, but I'm afraid you've gone too far this time.*

Bex gave her a scathing look, but Ishtar just raised her horns. *Rebexa the Bonfire,* she announced in a ringing voice that shook the ash, *I command you by your name: Surrender the magic you've collected and leave this place, never to return.*

She held out her hand as she finished, fingers ready to receive, but Bex just glared at her.

"No."

Her mother's jaw fell open. *You don't get to say no!* she cried. *I commanded you by your name!*

"I don't have a name," Bex said with a smirk. "That's the whole reason I'm here, remember?"

That shouldn't matter, Ishtar insisted, stomping her transparent feet. *I'm the one who gave you that name in the first place! Every spark that lives inside you came from my body. So long as you walk, burn, and breathe, you* are *my creation. Now,* **give me the magic, Rebexa***!*

"No," Bex said again as her eyes widened in recognition. "And my fire doesn't come from you. It was given to me by the Blackwood, and it burns because of all the people who haven't given up. I control the Bonfire now. Not you, not Queen Rebexa, not Gilgamesh, *me*. *I* decide who and what I burn for, and I'm nowhere near finished."

Then you are dead, Ishtar said, baring her teeth. *Get out!*

The moment she spoke the order, the same hand that had dragged Bex into this place smashed hard against her back. It felt like being slammed into a wall, but Bex held her ground. She didn't actually want to stay in this burned-out tomb another second, but she refused to let Ishtar shove her around. She locked her feet in place for a solid minute, staring her mother in the eye to make sure Ishtar knew she was no longer the one in charge. Only when the dead goddess was looking truly terrified did Bex finally let go and leave, jumping out of the ashes the same way she'd jumped out of Adrian's bonfire.

The flames were the same as well. The conversation with her mother felt like it had taken ages, but Bex must've actually only been gone a few seconds, because the fire she came back to was the same raging inferno that had nearly killed her earlier. It was still hot enough to burn her to a crisp, but Bex welcomed the pain this time, because she knew what that heat meant now.

It was just like the Morrigan had said. This fire didn't belong to the ghost of Ishtar or any of the gods. It was theirs—hers and her demons'. It was *their* wrath, *their* righteous fury to see Gilgamesh's wrongs made right, but even more than that, it was their hope for the future. The Morrigan had stirred them up with old anger, but the reason the demons were so mad in the first place was because they wanted a better world. One where they weren't slaves or tools or anything that belonged to someone else. A world where they were their own masters and could live how *they* wanted.

That had always been Bex's wish, and the moment she embraced it—not as the Sword of Ishtar, but as a demon in her own right—the fire stopped burning her skin. It was still overwhelming but not in a way that was scary or painful. The flames were more like hands lifting her up, pushing Bex higher than she ever could have managed on her own with a single, united wish.

Fix this, they begged. *Stop this. Let us go home.*

"I will," Bex promised the fire. "I swear it on my—"

She stopped in a panic. She still didn't have a name. Ishtar had tried to use her old one and failed, but she couldn't be a queen without a name. She was still trying to figure out what to do about that when she heard voices beyond the flames. Not the whispered plea from the heart she'd answered earlier. These were actual throats yelling audible words. One word, specifically, being chanted over and over by hundreds of thousands of voices.

"*Bex!*" they cried. "*Bex, Bex, Bex, Bex!*"

And just like that, Bex realized she was overcomplicating things. She didn't need a new name from some outside authority figure. She already had a name given to her by people she respected. The ones she was *actually* fighting for, because Iggs's voice was in there, as was Lys's and Desh's and even Nemini's. Just as the Morrigan had promised, their pleas were the ones that mattered, the ones she'd been born to answer, and the moment Bex accepted that, the crown landed on her head like an anvil.

It hurt more than anything ever had. The new horns seared their way out of her skull like red-hot pokers, and not just her normal two. She was crowned with six horns now just like Ishtar, and as soon as they finished growing, a gleaming black sword appeared in her hand, followed by a familiar voice in her head.

My queen, said Drox, sounding very confused. *What has... What did... Why do you have a different name now?*

"It's a long story," Bex said, hugging her sword to her chest. "I'll have to tell you later, but I am *so* glad to see you!"

I am overjoyed to see you as well, Drox said warmly. Then his voice dropped. *But you don't have to tell me. I can see what happened in your memories, though I'm not sure I want to believe it. Is it true that Ishtar abandoned us?*

"It is," Bex admitted, clenching his hilt. "But I won't. I'm seeing this through to the end, but you don't have to go down with me. You've always been loyal to the gods. If you don't want to be dragged into treason with me, you can—"

Don't insult me by finishing that sentence, Drox interrupted with a growl. *I am the Blade of Wrath, forged for your hand alone. The only thing I have to say is that I apologize for leaving your service. It will not happen again. I am yours until I shatter. Now, what do you wish me to cut?*

Bex broke into a grateful smile. Straight and to the point, that was her Drox. He was already raring to go, but the voices were still chanting outside, which meant Bex still work to do.

With that, she lifted her head and waved her hand. The roaring pillar of fire pulled back like a curtain at the motion, revealing the square far below, which was a shock. Bex had felt the flames pushing her up, but she hadn't realized she'd been literally lifted into the air. That said, being high up actually made things much easier. If she'd been low enough to actually see people's reactions for this next part, she might have been too self-conscious to say it. They were the ones who'd put her on this path, though. It was only right that they hear the result from her own lips, so Bex took a deep breath and lifted her gleaming blade high over her head.

"*Demons of the Riverlands,*" she cried in a queen's booming voice that filled the city. "Your anger has been answered. I am Bex of the Bonfire, sword of my people! By my new name, I swear I will fight for all the children of the Riverlands until Gilgamesh is dead and we are all set *free!*"

The words flowed out like a torrent, but it was the answering roar that Bex felt most. As soon as she spoke her new name for the first time, the crowd of demons shouted back so loud that the ground trembled. The sound crashed into her like a wave, surrounding Bex in a pillar of raging fire as they hung their hopes and prayers upon her.

I never realized worship was so potent, Drox said as the power flooded over them. *This is a force far greater than mere wrath. No wonder Ishtar was so mad at you for taking her place.*

"Then let's not waste what we've been given," Bex replied, gathering the storm of flames tight around her as she raised her blade. "Ready?"

Always, her sword said as his hilt settled firmly into her palm. *Forever.*

Bex grinned at her partner and swung with everything she had. She swung with her own wrath plus the wrath of her people. She swung with their sorrow, swung with their pride. Swung with the fear left behind by five thousand years of oppression and the desperate desire that it was almost over. Everything that had brought them to this point, Bex channeled into her sword, lashing out in a sky-splitting strike that roared like a river of fire through the empty air above the part of the White City that was not yet covered in trees and straight into the fortress of the enemy.

Chapter 6

A few minutes earlier.

ADRIAN WOKE TO THE EXTREMELY UNPLEASANT SENSATION OF BEING BOILED ALIVE.

He surged to his feet with a curse then leaped out of the piping-hot cauldron someone had placed him inside, burning his hands in the process. He was still stripping out of his scalding-hot clothes when a familiar weight leaped onto his shoulder.

"*Adrian!*" Boston cried, shoving his head against the underside of his witch's chin. "You're up early."

"I'm surprised I'm up at all," Adrian said, wringing the water out of his rapidly-cooling shirt as he looked around in shock at the last place he expected to see again.

He was in his cabin. *His* cabin, from *his* Blackwood. That was his cauldron in his fireplace that he'd just been boiling inside, but while he definitely hadn't left the fire going, everything else looked exactly the same. The pottery mugs from where he'd served tea to his father while explaining his plan to grow roots into Heaven were even still sitting on the table. If he climbed into his loft, he was sure he'd find the cell phone he'd left charging on the window solar panel a week ago.

It was all exactly as he remembered, but this definitely wasn't Seattle. The forest he could feel through his freshly reburied heart felt far larger than the eleven-acre grove he'd grown on Bainbridge Island, and much, *much* older. No amount of witchcraft could grow taproots longer than fifty feet in less than a century, but Adrian swore the roots of his new heart tree went all the way down to Earth. He was still prodding them in confusion when he heard the familiar creak of his front door.

"Look at you!" cried a voice he knew as well as his own. "I should've known you'd be out early. You never could stand to wait until the treatment was completed."

Adrian looked over his shoulder in surprise to see his mother standing in the doorway. Like everything else since he'd woken up, Agatha looked exactly as he remembered, but the scene behind her was a total shock. It was hard to make out details in the dark, but it looked like his cabin was *inside* the branches of a giant conifer. Also still in Gilgamesh's Heaven, if the reports he was receiving through his new and shockingly extensive root system were to be believed, which meant his plan had *worked*. He'd grown a connection back down to Earth! But the size of it was... was... It was overwhelming. He'd never been directly connected to a forest this enormous. It felt like he'd been wired straight into the Great Cycles themselves, and suddenly, Adrian needed to sit down.

"And *that's* why you stay in the cauldron until the treatment is complete," his mother said as Adrian sank to the floor. "Boston, why did you let him get out? He's barely got enough blood to function."

"You know I can't control him, Lady Agatha," replied that cat, who was still on Adrian's shoulder. "He's always done exactly as he pleases."

"That would be why Muriel picked him," Agatha admitted, giving her son an indulgent smile as she picked up the wet coat he'd stripped off and hung it by the fire to dry. Adrian's broom was already there, propped in its usual spot against the hot rocks to bake off the lingering damp from the Hells. The carved raven head gave Adrian a self-satisfied wink when he glanced at it, and the witch dragged a hand through his dripping hair with a sigh.

"Will someone please fill me in on what I missed?"

"I suppose an explanation is in order," his mother said as she walked to the linen chest to grab him a towel. "The short answer is that you lived up to expectations. A few centuries ago, when the witch hunts forced us to move our heart trees from the Old World to the New, your aunts and I concocted a plan. We would use our relocation as cover to start a project we'd long been considering, a way to break Gilgamesh's stranglehold on our coven. You remember the grove your cousin Olivia was working on?"

"Of course," Adrian said, catching the towel she tossed him and scrubbing it over his face. "They were the biggest trees in the Blackwood other than the heart grove itself, the work of generations."

"And now that work is finished," Agatha told him proudly, waving her hand at the gigantic branches pushing against the cabin's windows. "Muriel knew that one day, I would bear a child capable of overthrowing Gilgamesh, so we grew these trees in preparation. We didn't know when exactly it would happen, but the moment I saw your four-year-old eyes light up as you watched me working at my cauldron, I knew you were the one. Since that day, everything we've done has been in support of the miracle you just achieved. A prince of Heaven strong enough to earn Gilgamesh's respect but principled enough to defy him. A witch tied to the Blackwood tightly enough to grow his own grove, yet rebellious enough to earn the loyalty of the last demon queen."

She huffed as she walked into his bedroom to grab him some dry clothes. "It was hair-raising work. There were *so* many details to get right, but our Muriel is nothing if not meticulous. Even I wasn't sure you'd pan out at times, but she always insisted you were our best shot, and as usual, she was right."

Agatha returned to the main room with a smile, but Adrian took the folded black shirt she handed him with a grim expression.

"So it was all a setup from the beginning?"

"From before the beginning," his mother corrected, holding out his witch hat, which she must've used magic to dry, clean, and reshape while he was unconscious, because it looked brand-new.

"You've been our weapon since before you were born, Adrian of the Blackwood," she murmured as she placed the pointed hat on his head like a crown. "I waited so long to have a son who loved the forest as much as I did. All the princes I bore to Gilgamesh were clever. Some of them even learned a bit of my magic, but you were the only one who could truly be called a witch."

She was still adjusting the hat on his head when Adrian's arm shot up to grab her wrist.

"What about the rest?" he demanded, glaring at her with eyes that, now that he'd been bled dry of all his quintessence, were once again the same gray-blue as his father's. "My brothers, the other princes, did you give them all up to Gilgamesh?"

"Without a moment's hesitation," his mother replied. "I'm a witch, Adrian. Sacrifice is in my blood, and yours. You would have sacrificed yourself just now had we not been waiting to catch you."

"That's different," he insisted, squeezing her wrist tighter. "They were *children*."

"So were we," Agatha said in a cold voice as she yanked her hand away. "My sisters and I were barely out of our first decade when the new god known as Gilgamesh showed up to burn our forest. He kept us as slaves in those early days while he was perfecting his sorcery. I was sixteen the first time I seduced him and seventeen the first time I fed a lock of my hair to the Morrigan to ensure I'd bear him a son. I've been repeating that cycle ever since to ensure our coven's survival, and to ensure we'd get our revenge someday."

She leaned down and tapped Adrian on the chest. "*You* are that revenge. Ours and the Blackwood's. The fire the Great Forest poured through you into the Queen of Wrath is the same fire Gilgamesh used to burn our ancestors. He tied them to their own heart trees and torched them to ash, but the forest has deep roots, and witches do not forget. He thought he stole you from me like he steals everything, but you were, are, and always will be *ours*. The moment you gave your heart to the forest, Gilgamesh's fate was sealed."

Her voice was ringing with ancient anger by the time she finished, but all Adrian could do was lower his eyes. Nothing she'd said had surprised him. His family always put the forest first. It was the first thing witches swore when they took the coven oaths, but

Adrian's heart was only partially roots. The rest was still angrily, bitterly human, which meant it hurt to hear his mother talk so proudly about molding him into a weapon to stab into his father's heart.

"I know this isn't what you wanted to hear," Agatha said as she reached up to touch her son's face. "But none of it means that I don't love you. I've loved all the sons I surrendered to Heaven."

"You just loved the Blackwood more," Adrian finished as he leaned away.

"The heart of a witch is the forest," Agatha reminded him with a sad smile. "I'm sure you would've behaved differently, which is fine. A child should strive to be better than his parents, but I'm not ashamed of what I did. Because of my actions, our coven has a chance to finally be free of Gilgamesh. *You* have the chance to be free, as do your beloved Rebexa and her people. Remember that before you judge me and your aunts too harshly, hmm?"

"There's no point in judgement," Adrian said, turning away from her to finish putting on his dry clothes. "The past cannot be changed. The present can, though, so let's focus on that before we lose the opportunity you did all this to achieve."

"Spoken like a true Witch of the Flesh," his mother said proudly, marching back toward his front door. "This way."

Adrian got dressed as fast as he could before snatching his broom off its hook. His boots and coat were still drenched, so he left them drying by the fire and followed his mother onto the front porch in his shirtsleeves and sock feet. As he'd already seen through the windows, his cabin now sat like a birdhouse in the branches of his enormous new heart tree. Adrian hadn't realized just how much quintessence Gilgamesh had poured into him until he saw the scale of the tree it had grown, but what truly shocked him was what he could feel below it.

"Is this whole tree a rootway?"

"It is," Agatha said proudly as she grabbed her own broom from where she'd left it propped beside his front door. "Like I told you, we've been planning this for a long time. The entrance on our side has been ready for centuries. Muriel has been sitting beside it ever since the Queen of Wrath left for the Hells just to make sure we didn't miss our cue, and it's a good thing she did. You cut it very close. Your body was already technically dead by the time we caught it. If you hadn't had such a strong connection to the Blackwood, even the cauldron couldn't have saved you."

Hearing how near he'd come to death made Adrian wince, but his mother didn't notice.

"Someone had to stay and make sure you didn't boil over, so I volunteered to watch the pot while Muriel and Lydia went back for the others," she continued. "That left no one to keep an eye on the demons, but we'd already summoned the Morrigan, so she took care of that part."

"Wait, the Morrigan?" Adrian repeated in alarm. "The Morrigan is *here*?"

"In the flesh, bones, and soul," Agatha assured him. "Her role in this is as critical as yours. Having her around also freed Lydia and Muriel to focus on widening the rootway enough to bring our coven through while still leaving room for the former Hells slaves to get out, so it was a two-birds-with-one-stone sort of situation."

For the first time since he'd come back to life, Adrian smiled. "You're going to let Bex's demons evacuate down the rootway? That's uncommonly kind of you."

"Kindness has nothing to do with it," his mother said. "It doesn't take Muriel's foresight to see that the fastest way to secure the Queen of Wrath's cooperation is to help her demons. That's why we showed up at the collapsed Anchor in Seattle, and it's why we're making room for them now. We need the Bonfire Queen focused on destroying Gilgamesh, not fussing over a bunch of half-starved demons. Assuming she survives the transformation, of course."

"What transformation?" Adrian asked in alarm. "What did you do to Bex?"

"Nothing she wouldn't have eventually done for herself," his mother replied in the cryptic voice he'd always hated. "Your part in this was planned to the second, but the Bonfire of Wrath has always been a wild card, so we asked the Morrigan to give her a little push, just to make sure the timing lined up."

"What timing?" Adrian demanded, grabbing his mother's shoulders. "What did you do?"

The Witch of the Present flashed him a knowing smile, which made Adrian angrier than anything she could have said. He could forgive his mother for manipulating his life. They were both witches, after all. Living and dying in the service of the Blackwood was part of the deal, but Bex was different. She was already fighting with everything she had. Pushing her any harder was just cruel at this point, but before

Adrian could force an answer out of his mother, something flashed bright enough to white out his vision even through the thick branches of his tree.

The shock wave landed a split second later, shaking the entire tree with an explosive *boom*. Adrian had just grabbed the doorframe to keep from being thrown off the porch when the light shifted from blinding white to familiar fiery red-orange. Sure enough, when he swung his head toward it, he saw flames flashing through the branches. Enormous ones from a raging bonfire as tall as his tree that was currently lighting up the skies of Heaven.

"Well, well," Agatha said brightly. "Looks like your firecracker came out on top. Muriel thought she would. Now things can *really* begin."

She rubbed her hands together in anticipation, but Adrian was already on the move, scooping Boston—who was still getting back to his feet from where the shock wave had knocked him over—off the floor before leaping onto his broom. He caught a final glimpse of his mother waving farewell before she and his misplaced cabin were lost behind a wall of thick fir needles, leaving Adrian flying Bran at top speed toward the flames that shone like spotlights through the branches ahead of him.

"Are you sure that's Bex?" Boston yelled over the howling wind as he clung to Adrian's shirt. "I've never seen her bonfire go that big before."

The fire was absolutely enormous. Even when she'd turned into a tornado of flame in the Hells, her light hadn't been this bright. It looked like they were flying into an erupting volcano. Adrian didn't know what the Morrigan could've done to push her that far, but he was bracing for the absolute worst. When they finally burst through the fir tree's thick outer limbs, though, what he saw was the exact opposite.

There was no raging fire or out-of-control storm, just the outline of a woman glowing brighter than his eyes could look at. She shone like the sun that was missing from Heaven's sky, like a spear of light that went from the tree-covered ground straight up to the firmament. She was *so* bright, Adrian couldn't actually make out what she was doing, but it looked like she was talking to someone. He was flying closer for a better look when a black sword appeared in her hand.

The weapon was the only part of her that wasn't shining, making its path easy to follow as Bex—or at least the brilliant creature he presumed was Bex—swept the sword through the air in front of her. It looked like she'd swung at nothing, but the moment the blade moved, an arc of light shot off its point to slam into Gilgamesh's shielded tower.

Adrian had lived through a lot of scary magic in his life, but he'd never felt anything like this. The burning razor wasn't even aimed in his direction, but he swore he could feel its sharpness in every cell of his body. The strike cut through air, cut through sound, cut through the unknown magic of the gods that was the foundation of Paradise itself. It sliced through the golden bubble around Gilgamesh's fortress like a red-hot wire through spun sugar before slamming into the palace itself.

The attack hit the white stone like a comet, burning a line of glowing destruction from the thick base where all the spires connected to the top of the frontmost tower where Adrian had been kept prisoner.

He swore he saw the windows of his old workshop shatter back into sand before a cloud of dust and debris exploded upward, and the whole tower began to tilt.

It was only one out of a dozen, but Adrian still held his breath as the front tower of Heaven's Holy Palace—the one with the golden balcony where his father had brought him to watch Bex's defeat—toppled like a chopped tree. It fell sideways into the city to the palace's west, crushing the ornate white buildings and throwing a plume of sparkling dust into the air that rose higher than all but one of the palace's remaining gold-roofed spires. The crash was still echoing through the empty White City when the shining creature Bex had become suddenly wobbled.

Her blinding light vanished at the same time, leaving the Bex Adrian remembered from this morning plummeting out of the sky like a shot bird. Fortunately for them both, Bran was quicker on the uptake than his witch. The broom started moving before Adrian could even think the command, darting into the perfect position to catch the falling queen as she flew by.

"Gotcha!" Adrian cried, trusting his broom to keep them balanced as he snatched Bex out of the air. Boston managed to stay on as well, digging his claws into his witch's back as Adrian dragged Bex onto the broom in front of him. He was feeling her limbs to make sure she wasn't hurt when he saw something that made him freeze.

The pale woman gasping on the broom in front of him looked like Bex. She had Bex's lovely face and glowing eyes, her dark hair and small frame, but her head was crowned with not two, not four, but *six* towering black horns. They were the same shape and size as her old ones, but instead of just poking out of her forehead, these new horns encircled her entire skull like the points of a crown. They were so tall and spearlike that Adrian had to watch where he put his face so he didn't lose an eye. But although the new horns were like nothing he'd ever seen, the dazzling smile on her face was one hundred percent pure Bex.

"*Adrian!*" she cried, throwing her arms around him. "You're okay!"

"I'm fine," he said, dodging her spikes. "But are *you* okay?"

"I'm amazing," Bex replied in a dazed voice as her now very dangerous head whipped back toward the plume of white dust that was still rising from the broken tower. "Did you see that shot?!"

"I did," he assured her. "I also saw you fall out of the sky."

"Yeah, I might have gone a bit too hard," she admitted, though her smile didn't budge. "But I did it! I actually got damage on the Palace of the Highest Heaven!"

She grabbed him as she finished, almost knocking them both off the broom as she pulled Adrian into a rib-creaking hug.

"We did it!" she cried as golden fires flared back up all over her body. "Ishtar said it was impossible, but we did it! We did it! We did it! *We did it!*"

Her voice was borderline hysterical by the end, but Adrian didn't want her to calm down. He just hugged her back, leaving the flying to Bran and the panicking to Boston as the four of them dropped out of the sky toward the grass-covered square.

They were still ten feet above the ground when Bex suddenly hopped off the broom. She lit back up as she did so, exploding in a column of fire that missed Bran by inches. She raised her sword at the same time, greeting the enormous crowd of demons, who were all screaming so loudly that their voices shook the ground. There was so much chaos that Adrian didn't realize the packed square was crammed with more than just demons until he set his broom down beside her.

"I don't believe it," Boston said, pushing the brim of Adrian's hat down with his paws as he climbed onto his witch's head for a better view. "Did your mother bring the *entire* coven?"

It certainly looked that way. It was hard to see through all the celebrating demons, but there was a torrent of Blackwoods coming into the square. Black-dressed women were pouring out of the rootway and zipping through the branches of his tree on their brooms. From what he could feel through his new roots, they'd brought their support staff as well, all the partners and adult children and other family members who weren't witches but still lived under the Blackwood's protection.

It looked like a full-on invasion. Bex's demons were still too excited about what their queen had done to pay the witches much attention yet, but the crow-shaped Morrigan was watching the incoming army with pride from her perch on top of the Hells' Gate, completely ignoring the very angry-looking Lys, Iggs, and Nemini who were standing in front of her.

"Oh, ho, ho," the Morrigan laughed, finally turning her beak to the demons, who looked like they were about to jump her. "You see? It turned out exactly as I said. Now get out of my sight before I change my mind about eating you."

If she'd said that to Adrian, he would've scrambled away as fast as he could, but Lys had always been fearless. All they did was flip the giant crow off before leaping off the black cube and flying down to their queen on their dusky, still-bandaged wings.

"*Bex!*" they cried as they landed practically on top of her raised sword. "You did it!"

Bex responded with a whoop that made Adrian's ears ring, grabbing Lys out of the sky and spinning them around. It was absolutely *not* something she should've been doing given the state of Lys's shoulder, which was already bleeding through the bandages again, but Adrian couldn't bring himself to tell Bex to stop. Lys was already falling to their knees on their own, staring up at Bex with an expression of holy wonder.

"I still don't believe it," they said, raising a trembling hand. "Your horns, your sword—Ishtar has given us a miracle!"

It might've been Adrian's imagination, but he would've sworn Bex flinched at Ishtar's name. Whatever the look meant, though, she hid it immediately. Or maybe the expression was shocked off her face when Nemini ran over to grab Bex's head.

"You have a new name," she announced, peering deep into her sister's glowing eyes.

She said that like an accusation, and Bex flinched again. Before she could reply, though, Iggs elbowed his way in.

"Who cares about that?" he cried, giving his queen a crushing hug before whirling to point at the cloud of dust rising from Gilgamesh's broken palace. "Did you see what she did to that tower?" He slammed his fists together with a fang-toothed grin. "Oh, it is *on* now!"

"Gilgamesh won't know what hit him," Lys agreed, looking more fired up than Adrian had ever seen them as they surged back to their feet. "So what's the plan from here? Fly back up and chop off some more architecture?"

Both of those questions were aimed at Bex, but she turned to look at Adrian instead, grabbing him by his shirt sleeve and pulling him down so she could whisper in his ear.

"What *is* the plan?" she hissed. "The witches are here because of you, right? What are they planning to do?"

"I have no idea," he whispered back. "I was being boiled up until just a few minutes ago. My mother told me they're readying the rootway to evacuate everyone who can't fight back to Earth, but I don't know the plan aside from that. Since the Old Wives brought everyone in the entire forest, I presume they're here to fight, but I don't..."

Adrian's voice trailed off. He'd been talking very fast, trying to relay all the important information as quickly as possible, but the moment he mentioned the evacuation, Bex's entire face lit up like a sunrise.

"The witches are going to help my people escape?" she asked, her fiery eyes shining. "They're going to get them to safety?"

Adrian had barely started his nod when Bex covered her face with her hands. She stayed that way for several seconds, but though her shoulders didn't so much as quiver, he could smell the salty tang of her tears. So could the rest of her crew from the looks on their faces, but Bex had always hated crying in front of others, so they all dutifully pretended it wasn't happening. Adrian did the same, though he didn't see what she had to be ashamed about. Bex had spent almost two hundred lifetimes working to save her people. Of course the relief would feel crushing when it finally happened. The demons weren't evacuated yet, though, which meant they still had work to do.

"I need to coordinate with my coven about what the plan is from here," he said, drawing attention away from Bex to give her an excuse to keep her head down. "There's no way Gilgamesh can ignore a direct attack on his fortress, so we should probably expect some sort of retaliation soon. I'll take Bex with me so she can speak to the Old Wives directly. Lys, can you start organizing the demons to make sure those who need the most help get out first when the rootway opens for evacuation?"

Lys shot him a look so scathing, Adrian swore he could feel their eyes carving *I don't take orders from you* into his skin. To his enormous surprise, though, the demon didn't actually say the words out loud. They just nodded and turned to address the others.

"Nemini, you stay with the queen until she orders otherwise. I'll take point on organizing the evacuation. The quicker we get everybody who can't fight out of here, the sooner those of us who *can* fight will be free to do so. And speaking of fighting, Iggs, do you have any guns left in that goblin bag of yours?"

"I've got everything we need," Iggs promised, patting the knapsack of Solomon's Armory, which never seemed to leave his shoulder. "I've been waiting for this day my whole life."

"We all have," Lys said, shooting him a sharp-toothed smile. "I'm putting you in charge of the defense team. Go round up everyone who can still hold a weapon and get them armed. I want a wall of demons ready and waiting when Gilgamesh finally decides to get off his throne and hit back."

Iggs saluted and rushed off to do as Lys commanded. Lys followed right on his heels, hopping behind him in short flaps from their injured wing. This left Adrian standing alone in front of the Hells' Gate with Bex still hiding her face and Nemini giving him the flattest of all flat looks. Even the Morrigan seemed to have flown away while he wasn't looking. He was wondering if he should say something to break the awkward silence when Bex finally lowered her hands.

"Let's get away from the square," she said, her face hard and determined like the last five minutes hadn't happened. "If a counterattack is coming, I don't want it anywhere near the tree we're going to be using as an evacuation ladder. Where's the Blackwood leadership?"

Adrian had no idea. He was about to suggest returning to his cabin, since that was the last place he'd seen his mother, when Boston poked his cheek with a paw. When he looked down to see why, his familiar nodded at a stone circle that was suddenly blocking the wide, elegant boulevard that led out of the square toward the palace.

The standing stones must've popped out of the ground like a mushroom ring, because Adrian was positive the circle hadn't been there a few minutes ago. He could already see the points of dozens of black witch hats moving over the tops of the rocks, though, and his face split into a grin.

"They're over there," he said confidently, dropping his broom to the ground so Bran could change into his wider, much-more-comfortable-for-three-people raven form. "Shall we?"

Bex nodded and climbed onto Bran's wing without another word. Nemini got on right behind her, sitting in her usual position at the raven's tail. Adrian got on last, stepping onto the ridge of Bran's back before tapping his foot to launch them all back into the air.

Chapter 7

BEX COULD HAVE DIED FROM EMBERASSMENT. She never used to be a crier, but here she was, breaking down in front of Adrian, *again*. He would never judge her for that, of course, but Bex was judging the crap out of herself. She'd finally landed a real hit on Gilgamesh and secured freedom for her people. Now was the most important time of all her lives to *keep it together* and be a queen, but she just couldn't get her stupid body to stop.

I don't see why you hold yourself to these absurd standards, Drox said inside her head. *As we saw during your battle with the Prince of Sorrow, suppressed emotions are weaknesses easily exploited by a knowledgeable foe. Expunging them in the company of trusted allies is therefore a sound tactical move that a wise leader should employ.*

That was one way to look at it, Bex supposed, but Drox's military assessment of the value of tears didn't stop her from grinding her palms into her eyes as Adrian flew them over the now intensely chaotic plaza toward the incongruous new standing stone circle that had suddenly appeared on the main road to Gilgamesh's palace.

It certainly looked like a witch's invasion camp. The trees in this part of the forest were miniatures compared to Adrian's skyscraper-sized Douglas fir, but they were still as big or bigger than the tallest trees in his forest back on Bainbridge. They were thick, too, transforming the once blindingly white Heavenly boulevard into a secluded grove. Moss grew on every paving stone, and water dripped constantly down the fern-covered walls of the massive apartment blocks, which now looked more like crumbling marble cliffs.

It was the complete opposite of the normally bone-dry and colorless Holy City, which meant she should've loved it. Now that she'd defied her mother, however, Bex had a different opinion. As much as she'd hated Gilgamesh's monochrome architecture, there had been a point to it. All that dry white stone had maintained Paradise as a land of death, not the fertile Riverlands that the Anchors still mimicked. Bex had denied her mother the demons' fire, but that didn't mean the old rules didn't still apply. If Ishtar—a goddess of life and fertility as well as war and death—got her claws into all this vegetation, she'd be able to pull herself back up no matter what happened with Gilgamesh.

That thought was scary enough to make Bex forget all about a few embarrassing tears. She had the upper hand right now because Ishtar was weak, but if her mother found the strength to rise again, everything could flip. They had to beat Gilgamesh before that happened, but Bex wasn't even sure what the victory conditions were anymore.

How can you think such a thing? Drox demanded as Adrian's broom set them down in the moss at the circle's edge. *The goal is what it has always been: destroy Gilgamesh and retake Paradise.* His voice grew smug. *We already leveled one tower. Just keep swinging me and we'll bring the whole castle down in no time.*

"I don't think it's going to be that easy," Bex whispered, looking down the straight road ahead of them at the fortress that still rose over the city like a white-and-gold mountain.

The dust from her earlier attack had finally settled, revealing movement on the palace's battlements. The defensive ramps were so delicate and golden that Bex had assumed they were purely decorative. Now, though, there were figures lined up on the walkways that spiraled around the bottom of each tower.

Bex cursed under her breath. Even at this distance, she could make out rows of the same golden archer constructs that had shot at her the first time she'd come to the Holy City. Now that the big shield was out of the way, she could also see dozens of lion cannons positioned on the roof of the main floor all the towers branched out of.

That was the most frightening sight of all. Bex didn't know if the cannons were out of range or if Gilgamesh simply hadn't given the order to fire yet, but there were as many lions facing them now as there'd been when Heaven opened fire on the Seattle Anchor. Even with the extra firepower from her new horns, Bex wasn't sure if she could block that many shots. Her best move would be to charge in and melt the cannons like she'd done before. There was no way Gilgamesh didn't know that, though, which meant he'd probably already set up a counter for—

Bex.

Bex froze, causing Adrian, who'd been helping her off the broom, to look up in alarm.

She was alarmed, too. All her life, Drox had always called her Rebexa, but that wasn't her name anymore. It couldn't be, because the ground of Heaven didn't crack under her feet when she hopped off Bran's broomgrass wing. She was the one who'd picked it, but it still hadn't quite sunk in yet that her name was really and truly just Bex now, and she wasn't sure how she felt about that.

You can decide how to feel later, her sword said sternly. *But so long as the weapons of the enemy are facing us, we are on the battlefield. Accurate information is the most important factor here, and the truth is that you are no longer Rebexa. You are Bex now, and Bex has allies. Whatever Gilgamesh has in store for us, you do not have to face it alone. The witches of the Blackwood stand with you, as do all the demons of the Nine Hells. Even the wild Morrigan, who never participated in anything back when Paradise belonged to the gods, has come to lend her aid. This will not be like all the times you died alone. This last life has already been your greatest. Let us keep moving forward and see how we can make it greater still.*

"Sounds like a plan," Bex said with a nervous smile. "You've gotten a lot better at pep talks."

Thank you, my queen, Drox replied proudly. *I've been working to improve.*

"I'm sorry," Adrian said, confused. "Are you talking to me?"

"Her sword is back," Nemini explained before Bex could answer. "I'm sure he has a lot to say."

"Drox has always been a blade of many opinions," Bex agreed, striding into the stone circle to get away from this topic since talking about Drox in front of Nemini felt cruel. The former Queen of Pride might have her horns and name back, but her sword was still broken into a thousand pieces.

Bex had thought about asking Adrian to examine it since he was so good at fixing things, but there'd been no time. She was already running late again. By the time they walked in, the huge circle of gray stones was full of witches. They were all wearing the same black clothes and pointed hats, so it was hard to tell who was in charge, but Bex recognized several of the women who'd run the festival back in the Blackwood as well as the three Old Wives. She'd only seen the white-haired old crone once before, but she recognized Adrian's mother and Muriel, the young-faced Witch of the Future.

All three of them were standing in front of the circle's biggest stone. The Morrigan was there as well, watching everything from the top of the rock in her crow form. The gathering wasn't only witches, though. Captain Roga, the war demon in charge of the tower where Bex had defeated the Queen of War, was there, along with three salty-looking war demons in modern clothes that Bex vaguely remembered pulling out of the Lowest Hells. Desh was nowhere to be seen, which meant Lys probably had him busy helping with the evacuations. But while the Hells demons were an expected sight, the wrath demon standing next to the witches with her horns respectfully lowered was a total surprise.

"Zargrexa?" Bex said, running to meet her. "I can't believe you're here!"

"I could be nowhere else, my queen," the village leader replied, bowing her horns even deeper. "You stormed the Hells and freed Ishtar's children from bondage. Had you not specifically wanted a small team, we all would have gone to fight beside you. I thought we would have to wait for your return to rejoin the war, but when the witches announced they were coming to Heaven, we knew the moment was upon us."

The old demon raised her graying head with a proud smile. "I've brought ten thousand demons from those you saved at the Seattle Anchor. They're coming up the roots as I speak, along with this."

She handed Bex a small bottle full of something that looked like freshly-squeezed pomegranate juice.

"What is it?" Bex asked, holding the bottle up to the dappled light. "A potion?"

Zargrexa's smile widened. "The best sort of potion. That is a bottle of liquid wrath."

"Did you say 'liquid wrath'?" Adrian asked, suddenly darting over to join them. "You mean someone finally figured out how to bottle emotions?"

Zargrexa shot her queen a nervous look. This confused Bex for a second before she remembered the village leader had never actually met Adrian before. She was about to start frantically assuring her that he wasn't a prince despite how he looked when she noticed Adrian's eyes were back to their usual blue-gray.

The realization went through her like a jolt. There'd been so much going on she hadn't even noticed, but Adrian's creepy mirror prince eyes were gone. It must have happened when he'd used up all his white blood to grow the tree, because Adrian finally looked like himself again, which in turn made Bex so happy she couldn't keep the goofy smile off her face.

That must have been proof enough for Zargrexa. The old demon changed her tone at once, clasping her hands in front of her and bowing her horns before Adrian in a show of great respect.

"I'm not sure who discovered it, Honored Witch," she said, answering his question. "The Old Wives of the Blackwood, may Ishtar's blessings be forever upon them, knew of our hunger problems and were working on a solution. Shortly after the queen left, the witch in charge of our camp came by with a cauldron full of this liquid as well as barrels of other bottled sins for all the different types of demons. It's not as energizing as true sin from the rivers, but it held off starvation, especially for the demons of Hate and War, who have trouble finding proper sustenance during happy events like festivals."

Adrian stared at the little bottle in wonder, but Bex's eyes were still locked on Zargrexa. "How much wrath did you bring?" she demanded. "I found the rest of our people, but they're on the edge of starvation."

"We figured they would be," Zargrexa said. "I told the witches that my queen was certain to find the rest of our tribe and that the exit from Limbo would leave them starving. We would be in need of much sustenance, and the daughters of the forest provided. When I left, every wrath demon who could not join the fight themselves was tending a cauldron full of liquid wrath. We should have enough to feed our entire population."

She looked past the standing stones at the crowd that still swamped the entrance to the Hells. "Where are they, my queen? I see many of our horns in the crowd, but not nearly as many as I expected. Have you ordered them to hold the perimeter?"

Her red eyes were full of hope when she turned back to her queen, but Bex's throat was so tight she couldn't answer. She didn't want to tell this woman who'd been through so much already that Gilgamesh had worked half their people to death before she'd even arrived. This was supposed to be their glorious victory, but Bex's mouth tasted like ash when she forced herself to tell Zargrexa the truth.

"They didn't make it," she said. "We saved as many as we could, but Gilgamesh had already…"

Her voice broke apart despite her best efforts, and Zargrexa lowered her head.

"I'd feared as much," the wrath demon whispered, clutching her wrinkled hands tight. "I can't explain it, but I knew in my bones that something horrible had happened. I worried it was your death since we could no longer feel you, but this…"

She stopped there, wiping the tears from her eyes before looking back at her queen.

"We will fight," she promised. "It's what the others would have wanted, for we are the demons of Wrath, the only tribe who never kneeled! I know they would want us to avenge their deaths and take back our home from that false and murdering king. I will go now to make sure those who survived are fed, but I will not leave this place until Gilgamesh is dead."

"Then we will fight together," Bex said, reaching up to grab the taller woman's shoulder. "Welcome to the final battle of the war, Zargrexa."

The old demon bowed low at that, stooping all the way to the ground to touch her horns against the toes of Bex's boots before she sprang back up and ran into the crowd, yelling in Riverlander for her people.

Bex watched her go with a lump in her stomach. Hearing that her wrath demons wouldn't starve now that the witches had invented bottled emotions should have been great news, but so much had happened in the last twenty-four hours that Bex didn't know how to feel anymore. Telling Zargrexa about the wrath demons they'd lost had left her numb inside, but there was nothing she could do about it except keep pushing forward.

With that in mind, Bex pulled herself straight and turned around to face the delegation of Blackwoods that had been waiting patiently since she arrived. She wasn't sure if they'd actually been waiting for her or for Adrian, but he'd stuck steadfastly by her side, as had Nemini. It was put-up-or-shut-up time now, though, so Bex raised her heavy new horns as high as she could and stepped into the center of the stone circle.

"Witches of the Blackwood," she said in a formal voice. "Thank you for coming to our aid once again."

"It is only fitting that victims of a mutual enemy should band together," replied the sharp-eyed Old Wife of the Past, whom Bex was pretty sure was Adrian's Aunt Lydia.

"As I'm sure Zargrexa already told you," Agatha continued when her oldest sister paused, "we have taken every possible step to assure our victory this day. We bring with us ten thousand demons from the survivors of the Seattle Anchor. We've also secured an escape route for the victims of the Hells as well as food and shelter for them within our Blackwood."

"It is our aim that the new Bonfire Queen should be free to attack Gilgamesh at full force without the burden of worrying that she's left anyone behind," Muriel, the young Witch of the Future, finished.

"Thank you," Bex replied, unsure which witch she should be looking at since they seemed to speak in rounds. "We are deeply in your debt."

"It is we who are beholden to you," said Lydia, Witch of the Bones, as she pointed a knobby finger at Drox's ring on Bex's right hand. "Our forces are unsuited for direct combat. We can provide support from the air, but we'll be relying on your demons to push the main assault."

Which explains why they were so eager to remove the noncombatants, Drox whispered in her head. *A camp full of starving refugees is an obvious target. By evacuating our wounded, they free you to be their attack dog.*

"I am always happy to attack the tools of Heaven," Bex said, both to the witches and her sword. "But I'm even more happy to know my people will be safe. If you promise to evacuate those who are unable or unwilling to fight, I'll gladly lead the charge. Captain Roga?"

She'd expected the war-demon captain to jump at the sudden call-out, but he was a soldier from horns to hooves, and all he did was step forward. "My queen?"

"What's our army looking like?"

"Fierce," he replied proudly. "We have many who are weakened even among the war demons, but this is the fight we've been waiting for all our lives. If these witches can provide us with food, I'm certain I can get you a fighting force worthy of your new name."

Bex was about to tell him good job when Nemini suddenly spoke.

"Do we have time for that?" she asked in a surprisingly sharp voice. "Given how hard Gilgamesh was working you all in the Hells, he's obviously in a hurry. That fits with what Adrian was saying as well, as does the fact that we have yet to see any retribution. It's been over twenty minutes since Adrian first grew his tree and ten since Bex sliced one of his towers in half, but we haven't seen a single prince."

"Maybe he's out of princes," Bex said hopefully. "We have been burning through them pretty fast."

"Gilgamesh never runs out of princes," Nemini replied, pointing a calm finger at the white castle covered in golden lions and constructs. "Even if he's running low on active sons, his fortress is well defended. I've been fighting Gilgamesh since the day he first marched into Paradise. He's an audacious general, not a cautious one. If he's holding back, it's because he feels he has no need to attack us, not because he's afraid."

"Then he's an idiot," Bex growled. "We all know Gilgamesh is up to something. He's *always* up to something, but there's no way the thing he's using all this new sin iron to build is so powerful that he doesn't have to worry about the army standing in front of his..."

Her voice trailed off. Bex hadn't actually thought about the words until they came out of her mouth, but after what her mother had said about resetting the world, Gilgamesh's intense focus suddenly seemed a lot less suicidal. There might be an army on his doorstep, but he was already inside his citadel with the Crown of Anu, the Sword of Ishtar, the Hammer of Enki, and who knew what else at his disposal.

Gilgamesh had always stolen his powers. His sorcery, the warlocks' use of demon names, even Heaven itself all came from the gods, so if they could turn the wheel to reset the world, then Gilgamesh...

"Oh, ho, ho," the Morrigan cackled from her perch on the tallest stone. "The little fire finally sees it, does she?"

"The future is rarely clear to those in the present," Muriel observed, turning to gaze up at the palace towers Bex had yet to destroy. "Gilgamesh's greatest strength is that he's always kept his eyes upon it. But focusing on the future blinds one to what is happening right now."

"And right now is always when we die," Agatha finished, turning to Bex with an expression that was nothing like the kindly mother she liked to play. The woman who faced her now was the Old Wife of the Flesh, Witch of the Present, and she had only one question.

"Do you understand what must be done?"

"I do," Bex replied, looking over her shoulder at the plaza full of rushing demons. "There's no time to wait for the army to organize. I'll march right now with whoever's ready."

"*We* are ready," promised Lydia, looking less like a crone and more like a vengeful wraith as she gripped her raven-carved broomstick. "Our coven has spent the last two hundred years preparing for today. This time will not be like all the ones before."

"Because if we fail this time, there won't be another chance," the Witch of the Future finished.

"We'll never get a chance if we keep wasting time talking," the Witch of the Present scolded her sisters before returning her gaze to Bex. "If we take care of your weak and wounded, can you fight unhindered?"

"I'm going to do that no matter what," Bex promised. "If my guess is right"—she looked up at the Morrigan, who nodded her black beak—"then this is now an all-or-nothing fight. That means no breaks, but it also means no rules." She pointed at the golden peak of the castle's highest tower. "You can fly, right? Can you take me straight to the top?"

She was pretty sure that was where Gilgamesh was hiding. Going straight for the head was usually a good strategy, but the Morrigan was already shaking her head.

"We can, but it won't work," the goddess said, turning her black beak toward Gilgamesh's gleaming towers. "Everything you see in front of you is an illusion built to flatter the gods' vanity and serve their convenience. Gilgamesh divided Paradise in two so that it would be easier to oppress Ishtar's demons, but what he calls 'Heaven' is just another factory for processing human souls, same as the Hells. Even if I flew you to the top of the tallest tower, Gilgamesh would not be there, because overseers do not live with workers."

"Then where is he?" Bex demanded.

"Somewhere else," the Morrigan replied, searching the empty sky with her beady eyes. "This is my first time setting foot in the folly known as Paradise, so I don't know where that is, but I *do* know there will be a gate. The gods have always created divisions and hidden places to suit their needs, but even their most secret spaces must always have a door or a bridge back to the living world. The connection can take many forms, but if they don't have something tying them down, their creations would be washed away by the stream of time that flows through the void."

She snapped her beak back to Bex. "My suggestion is to follow the chains. They also can't be interrupted or the strength that binds the Wheel would snap. Follow them, and you'll find Gilgamesh."

"If we're looking for chains, I know where they are," Adrian volunteered. "But I'm not clear about what's going on. Why are we in such a hurry all of a sudden?"

"Because Gilgamesh is probably about to end the world," Bex explained.

Adrian's already pale face turned ashen. "Why would he do that?"

"So he can restart it anew," the Witch of the Present replied with a sigh. "For all that he claims to hate the gods, he always did love pretending to be one."

"He's about to stop pretending," Muriel warned, gazing into the middle distance like she was staring down a horror only she could see. "I've never been able to foresee exactly what Gilgamesh is plotting, so nothing is certain, but resetting the world would be the most efficient way to solve his problems, and he's always been an efficient man."

"Whatever he's working on, I don't intend to let him finish," Bex said as she turned back to Adrian. "Can you fly me up to somewhere everyone can see?"

"Of course," he said, pulling his broom off his back and dropping it to the ground so it could turn back into a raven. "Hop on."

Bex was already stepping onto the broom's wings before he finished. Nemini got on next, followed by Adrian, who still looked confused but determined not to slow things down despite that. He had them twenty feet off the ground in seconds, giving Bex a high platform to address her people.

"Children of the Riverlands!"

The chaos in the plaza surrounding the entrance to the Hells paused as all the demons stopped what they were doing and looked up at their queen. When Bex was certain she had everyone's attention, she drew her sword and pointed him at Gilgamesh's fortress.

"Our enemy is on the move," she announced. "We'll have to go even faster if we want to stop him, so I need everyone who's willing and able to fight to meet me on the road to the palace. Those who cannot join the battle, your job is to get down the roots to safety as quickly as possible and deny Heaven the opportunity to attack our flank. Our allies, the witches, have food ready to help those who are too weak to make the journey. Do whatever you must to get back on your feet, but do *not stop moving* until you're out of Heaven!"

You should command them by your name, Drox suggested as the plaza exploded into chaos. *What's the point of taking Ishtar's power if you don't use it?*

"Because I don't want to use it like that," Bex grumbled, pulling him back into his ring. "My people gave me a name so I could set them free. I don't want them to spend what could be their final hours scrambling to obey an order they can't ignore. If I do things this way, at least they'll die free inside their own heads if we fail."

She'd been talking to Drox, but Adrian was the one who whirled around. "Okay, *what* is going on?" he demanded. "What might we fail? How is Gilgamesh going to reset the world? And while we're at it, why do you have six horns now?"

Presumptuous human, Drox muttered. *You don't owe him an explanation, my queen.*

"Yes, I do," Bex said with a scowl. "Adrian told me what he was doing before he did it. I'd be a terrible partner if I didn't give him the same courtesy. Also, no matter how hard we rush, it's going to take at least thirty minutes to get the first attack force in position so we're not running into battle one at a time like a bad kung fu movie."

"I'm curious as well," Nemini said from the back of the broom. "Not that knowing the future changes it, but it's still comforting to know what to expect." Her yellow eyes flicked up to Bex's horns. "I'd also like to know your new name since it feels like you're officially my queen as well now."

"Wait, I am?" Bex said, shocked. She hadn't had time to think too deeply about what accepting power from all nine varieties of demon actually meant on a metaphysical level. Now that Nemini mentioned it, though, Bex realized she could feel the pride demons the same way she normally felt her wrath demons. She could feel *every* sort of demon, actually, which was pretty overwhelming now that she was paying attention to it.

I don't see why you're so surprised, Drox said as Bex grappled with the new sensations. *What do you think all those extra horns signify? You took Ishtar's place. Her demons pray to you now. Not that that changes much since you've been acting like a queen to every demon you've met since the fall of Paradise, but it's nice to have some new powers to go along with all the extra responsibility.*

Bex hadn't even considered that angle yet. She knew her firepower had gotten a boost, but the way Drox and Nemini were talking made her think that her new name had much more to it than four extra horns and bigger flames. There was no time to sit down and figure it all out, though. The demons in the square below were already scrambling to obey her orders, and Nemini and Adrian were still waiting for their explanation.

She really did owe them one. They'd been nothing but patient, and it wasn't like her new crown came with an instruction manual. She'd figure herself out eventually. Right now, though, the people she depended on most had to come first, so Bex put her arms around her allies and pulled them close to explain all the world-upending things that had happened to her in the last twenty minutes.

"Well," Adrian said shakily when Bex finally finished, "I'm very glad we never managed to cut more than one chain now."

"It was a good plan given the information we had at the time," Bex said, reaching out to pat his arm. "How were we supposed to know that Ishtar was planning to destroy everything the moment the gods came back? She was *supposed* to be on our side."

"The gods have never been on anyone's side but their own," Nemini stated in a matter-of-fact voice.

"So much for the 'Merciful Mother of the Riverlands'," Bex agreed bitterly. "But at least we know what we've gotta do now."

"And we've got the power to do it," Adrian added optimistically, shooting another look at Bex's magnificent new horns. "You took the prayers of all demons and used them to give yourself a new name! Does that mean you're the new Ishtar now?"

Bex shrugged. "Maybe? Sort of? I don't know. All I wanted was for Ishtar to help us, but she wouldn't do that, so I said *I'd* do it, and then I ended up with this forest on my head."

She reached up to smack her horns and nearly hit Boston, who'd put his paws on her back to get a better look at her new headgear.

"What I want to know is why do you have *six* horns," the cat said in a fascinated voice. "If your new authority stems from the combined wishes of all demonkind, shouldn't you have nine horns? One for each type?"

"She has six horns because Ishtar has six horns," Nemini explained before Bex could open her mouth. "It's a mark of her divinity, not a direct representation."

Adrian's face lit up. "So you *are* like Ishtar!"

"If I am, it's only because she wouldn't do her damn job," Bex said angrily. "I don't care about gods or crowns. All I want is for demons to be able to live in peace without having to be anyone's slaves. *Why is that so hard?*"

Her black ring was buzzing like a hornet by the time she finished, causing Bex to lapse into another of her whispered finger arguments that Adrian didn't even bother trying to eavesdrop on anymore. Bex and Drox had always had their own dynamic. He was far more concerned about everything else she'd said.

Ever since his first conversation with the Morrigan, Adrian had been focused on cutting the chains as the magic bullet to bringing down Gilgamesh. If the gods were serious about a reset, though, that made them as much of a threat as the Eternal King. He supposed that didn't actually change much since, aside from the Morrigan, the gods had *never* helped them, but it was still depressing to know their one-cut solution was off the table. Even if Bex was some kind of mini-Ishtar now, beating Gilgamesh was always going to be an uphill battle, and now they had to do it *without* accidentally bringing back the gods. That sounded like fighting a war on a tightrope, but the factor that still worried Adrian the most was his father.

He shot another nervous glance at Gilgamesh's palace, but nothing had changed since the last time he'd looked thirty seconds ago. The constructs were still standing ready on the battlements, and the lions were still gleaming on the roof, but nothing had opened fire. The glittering shield hadn't gone back up, either, which struck Adrian as crazy, considering that Gilgamesh had lost a tower and a good chunk of the fancy mansions near the castle. There should have been some kind of retaliation by now, but the White City was as empty and silent now as it'd been the first time he and Bex stuck their heads out of the Hells. It almost felt like Gilgamesh wanted them to think they had victory in the bag and didn't need to rush.

If that was the image the Eternal King had chosen to project, then Adrian's first instinct was to charge the doors as fast as possible. He wasn't a general by any stretch, but Adrian had a pretty good feel for how his father thought now, and in his opinion, Nemini's earlier assessment—that Gilgamesh was holding back because it served him, not because he was afraid—had been right on the money. If Gilgamesh was keeping the pressure off and giving them room to breathe, then that room had to be his goal. He *wanted* them to feel like they had time to prepare, which meant that time itself had to be his victory condition.

In that case, they were already falling behind. Adrian had known his father was working on something huge since before he'd been kidnapped up to Heaven. Since they were all still alive, the king must not have finished it yet. That explained why he was giving his enemies so much room to dally, but it also meant they could still stop him if they moved fast enough. Bex had already figured that much out herself, but despite her big call to war earlier, only a handful of the most eager demons had actually made it to the rally point.

More were on the way, but it took time to move that many people. The same went for the Blackwoods. The Old Wives' preparation was amazing in hindsight, but even the giant tree he'd grown with all of his quintessence blood could only funnel so many witches into Heaven at a time.

Add in the hundreds of thousands of weakened demons frantically trying to go back down the other direction and the whole situation was starting to feel impossible. The only reason Adrian wasn't already falling into a panic was his firm belief that his Aunt Muriel wouldn't have brought the coven here if they really didn't have a chance. The same went for the Morrigan. The goddess of prophecy definitely wasn't the sort to waste her time on lost causes, which meant that victory had to still be possible. They just had to find and stop Gilgamesh before he finished... whatever it was he was doing.

Once again, Adrian found his lack of knowledge supremely frustrating. His only consolation was that he didn't need to understand something to break it. He just had to get close enough to throw the wrench into his father's works. Fortunately, when it came to being destructive, Adrian knew exactly whom to talk to.

"If speed is the name of the game, then we'd better get moving," he told Bex when she finally stopped whispering at Drox. "Is it okay if I set you down at the rally point?"

"Of course, but where will you be?" Bex asked with a concern that warmed Adrian's heart.

"Not far," he promised as he landed his broom on the road where the first batch of battle-eager demons was already waiting. "I just need to take care of some long-overdue family business."

That statement earned him a funny look, but one of the qualities Adrian loved best about Bex was how she always seemed to know when to step back. She didn't even ask what kind of business he was talking about. She just said, "Don't take too long."

"I won't," Adrian promised, giving her a quick kiss on the cheek before kicking his broom back into the sky to go find his brother.

Finding a Prince of Gilgamesh was normally pretty easy, but locating Leander in the swirling sea of demons rushing either to war or away from it turned out to be a tall order. Every time Adrian convinced a demon to slow down long enough to answer his questions, none of them seemed to know who he was talking about. He was starting to think Leander had vanished into thin air when he felt his brother step into the rootway.

The moment the banished prince's bare foot came down inside his heart tree, Adrian ordered the roots to snatch it. The forest here was so big now that he could feel every muscle in the prince's body go stiff as he realized he was trapped. He started struggling immediately, but it was too late. Adrian had already flown over, pulling Bran to a stop just shy of the warehouse-sized opening in the fir tree's base where two entire populations—the Blackwood witches and the demons of the Hells—were switching places.

Fittingly, Leander was on the side that was going down. The far, *far* side, as if he wanted to put as much distance between himself and the arriving Blackwoods as possible. He was carrying a wrapped body Adrian assumed was Bex's sister Mara, but none of the other unconscious queens Leander was supposed to be keeping an eye on were anywhere to be seen.

The prince didn't even have the decency to look guilty when Adrian hopped off his broom in front of him. He just lifted the hand he'd been using to tear the roots off his bare feet and gave his youngest brother the scowl to end all scowls.

"What do you want?"

"I want to know what the hell you think you're doing," Adrian said, scowling back. "You promised Bex you'd help her if she rescued Mara. You don't get to turn your back on that and run away through *my* tree just because you got what you wanted."

"Better than dying here," Leander snapped, clutching Mara tighter. "I saw how many horns were on the Queen of Wrath's head when she came out of that fire. Add in the Morrigan's presence and even an idiot can see what's coming. This is no longer a simple rebellion. Those fools are about to kick off a second war of the gods. Even if they win, the devastation will be catastrophic, so I'm taking my princess and getting us out of here while the concept of 'out' still exists."

"You can't run away from something this big," Adrian argued. "Where were you even planning to go? The Blackwood?"

"Never," Leander spat. "I'd *never* cower in the forest my mother sold me to Gilgamesh to protect. Even if I was willing, the Blackwood is the first place our father will crush for his revenge. I have a much better plan in mind. I'm going to go back down to Earth, where the teleportation ban isn't in effect, and then I'm taking us to Father's private island. No matter what happens up here, Gilgamesh would never allow his precious collection to be destroyed, so I'm going to take Mara down to his wine cellar and hide there until somebody wins. Once the fires die down, we'll see about making something out of the ashes, but my part in this is finished."

"No, it isn't," Adrian said, grabbing his brother by the neck of his filthy white silk tunic. "Bex pulled you out of the Lowest Hells. She left her people and braved the toxic flood to help you save your precious princess. She could have taken Mara and left you to rot down there, but she *didn't*."

"And I've paid her back for that," Leander snarled. "I helped her escape the inescapable Hells. I fought my own brother to the death alongside her wrath demon. I did *everything* she asked of me, but this goes too far."

He looked at the woman bundled in his arms. "You're welcome to die with your love if you want to, but I'm keeping mine alive. And before you try guilting me again, know that it won't work. You have to have honor to feel guilt, but I'd happily trade the lives of every demon and human on this planet to see my Mara smile again."

Leander finished with a defiant look, and Adrian let go of his collar with a sigh.

"If that's really how you feel, then you're making the wrong choice," he warned. "Running away might save her for a little while, but there's no future for your Mara if Gilgamesh wins. You're right that this is no longer just a rebellion. The reason the Morrigan and Bex are pushing so hard is because we're already in Gilgamesh's endgame, and the future he's planning doesn't include witches or demons."

He stabbed a finger at the unconscious woman Leander was clutching like a lifeline. "The only thing that can save your beloved now is if Bex wins, so if you actually care about Mara like you say you do, you won't leave our victory to chance. You'll fight with us to make it happen, or you might as well have killed her yourself."

That last part was cruel, but Adrian didn't take it back. If Mara was all his brother cared about, then Mara was the lever he would use, because they needed Leander. He was their inside man. If anyone knew where Gilgamesh was hiding, it would be him. But while Adrian's threat had clearly struck a nerve, Leander still wasn't moving.

"You don't understand," he whispered, his black-bloodstained hands shaking where they clutched Mara's wrapped body. "I *can't* fight Father, and not just because he's a better sorcerer than I am. No prince can fight Gilgamesh because he controls the quintessence in our blood."

Leander looked pointedly at Adrian's once-again-human eyes. "You got free because you're the damn golden child the entire universe bends over to save, but I've never been so blessed. If I give up *my* quintessence, I won't just lose my sorcery. My true age will catch up with me, and my body will turn to dust. If I go in as I am now, though, Gilgamesh will be able to put me on my knees with a flick of his finger. I'll be no better than a demon defying their queen, so it's pointless to ask me to help."

"I don't know," Adrian said with a smile. "I've seen a lot of demons defy their queens recently. But just because you can't face the king directly doesn't mean you can't fight. If nothing else, we need your help navigating the palace, because we don't actually know where Gilgamesh is right now."

The desperate look fell off Leander's face. "Oh," he said, straightening up. "Is that all you need?"

"That's it," Adrian promised. "Just take us to Gilgamesh, and we'll do the rest. I'll even have my forest hide Mara's body to keep her safe while you're away."

Leander scowled. "You mean take her as a hostage."

That was *not* what Adrian had meant, but he didn't bother to correct his brother, because Leander had already sighed.

"Very well," he said, cradling Mara to his chest. "It's pointless to stay in denial when presented with facts. You're right. I knew running was a temporary solution, but do you think you can actually win against Gilgamesh?"

"I think we've got a good chance," Adrian said. "As you're constantly complaining, our mother always puts the Blackwood first, but she's brought the entire coven to Heaven for this. She'd never take such a huge risk if she didn't believe it would pay off, but even sure bets can fail without support, which is why we all have to do our part. If we *do* win, though, you can be absolutely certain that Bex will make sure her sisters survive. That makes this a fight for Mara's future, and isn't that what you said you'd do anything to protect?"

"Don't turn my own words against me," Leander muttered. "But very well. I'll help, but you have to swear on your forest that you'll protect Mara with everything at your disposal. No matter what happens to the rest of us, Mara *must* survive. Swear that, and I swear I'll guide you to Father."

"Done," Adrian said, sticking out his hand.

Leander shook it grudgingly before returning his grip to his princess. "Where can I put her so she'll be safe?"

Adrian looked around the crowded tunnel for a moment before pulling his brother over to the rootway's far wall and giving the wood a knock. The new forest responded at once, opening the swirling roots to reveal a hidden grotto that looked like a wooden bunker complete with a mossy bed hidden inside a nook in the wall. Adrian was certain none of that had existed a second ago, but just like Heaven itself, the forest up here seemed to have looser rules than the groves he was used to working with back on Earth. Adrian wasn't sure if that was a good change or a bad one yet, but the extra wiggle room did make it easier to accommodate his brother as Leander carried Mara inside.

"Where are the rest of the queens?" he asked as Leander set Mara carefully on top of the moss.

"I left them with the evacuation team," Leander replied as he arranged the Queen of Sorrow's dark hair behind her head so it wouldn't get tangled. "The queen's favored lust demon came into the building we were using as a shelter and started yelling at everyone to get to the tunnel. They were already prioritizing the unconscious, so I left the queens in their care."

That was pretty irresponsible behavior for someone who'd volunteered to look after Bex's sisters, but if Lys was on it, Adrian wasn't worried. They'd absolutely make sure the other queens made it down the rootway safely. Right now, his job was to get Leander to the front, but no matter how strongly Adrian stressed their need to hurry, the prince refused to leave until he'd tucked the feather comforter he'd clearly stolen off some warlock's bed around Mara's shoulders.

"I'm going to win us a future," he whispered, leaning down to kiss her fingers. "Wait for me."

"She doesn't even remember him," Boston muttered before Adrian shushed him, holding his cat impatiently in the doorway of the new bunker until his brother finally finished fussing and walked out to join him.

Chapter 8

DESPITE BEX'S BEST EFFORTS, they didn't get underway for another thirty minutes. She'd dealt with big crowds before, so she knew that was actually lightning fast, but it still felt like victory was slipping through her fingers with every minute that ticked by.

It didn't help that the army that did show up looked so shabby compared to the grandeur of Gilgamesh's palace. Zargrexa and the demons from the Seattle Anchor had come prepared with the weapons and combat armor they'd gotten from the witches, but the demons from the Hells had nothing but the guns from Iggs's bag and the clothes on their backs. Most of them weren't even wearing shoes. She knew she shouldn't underestimate them for that, but it was hard to feel like a mighty queen when half her army was starved and barefoot, not to mention grossly outnumbered.

That was the real problem Bex didn't know how to overcome. Thanks to the hard deadline, lack of any communication except yelling and word-of-mouth, and the congestion caused by the evacuation, only fifteen hundred demons actually made it to the rally point. She could've doubled that number if she'd been willing to wait another hour, but even if they'd had a full day to rally everyone into position, nothing could change the fact that the majority of the demons they'd freed from the Hells were in no condition to fight. Plenty had volunteered anyway, but Iggs and Captain Roga—who was leading the war demons, their largest contingent of actual soldiers—had ended up sending most of them away again for being too weak or too wounded to join the battle. Including, to everyone's consternation, Lys.

That had been a whole thing, but Bex had put her foot down. Thanks to their fight with the Prince of Hate in the Hells, Lys still had a giant bleeding wound through their shoulder. They'd also stayed up to manage the camp while Bex slept, which meant they'd been awake for two days straight.

Putting Lys on the bench for the final assault was a sorry way to repay such devotion, but between the constant blood loss, the lack of lust to feed on, and the sleep deprivation, Lys was looking even worse than the demons they'd rescued from the Hells. Taking them into a battle in that condition was just asking for them to get killed, so Bex had ordered Lys to stay behind and coordinate the evacuation instead. A critically important job that Lys absolutely did not want.

"I can't believe you're doing this to me," they groaned over the black plastic comm in Bex's ear. "This is the final assault on Gilgamesh. You can't leave me out!"

"A battle is fought on many fronts," Bex replied sagely as she followed Iggs's scout team into the silent streets beyond the mossy edge of Adrian's forest. "The only reason we're able to have this conversation right now is because you remembered to charge the comms. You've always been our ace when it comes to logistics, and getting our people out of the line of fire is arguably the most important job of this entire operation. If I don't save my demons, what am I even fighting for?"

"Don't feed me that 'wise leader' crap," Lys snarled. "I'm the one who taught you all that stuff! I know *why* you're not bringing me along. I just hate it. I've been fighting at your side for centuries, but when our big moment finally arrives, I get left behind with the witches!"

"What are the Blackwoods doing, by the way?" Bex asked.

"Don't change the subject."

"I'm serious," Bex insisted. "I thought they came to fight, but we're the only ones out here."

Lys sighed at the obvious distraction, but they'd been a soldier for too long to ignore something as important as troop position.

"So far as I can tell, the witches are all still up in the big tree," they reported. "They've been arriving in a steady stream since the rootway opened, but other than the support teams distributing bottled sin, I haven't seen so much as a stray cat in the last twenty minutes. Even the Morrigan's vanished."

That didn't sound good. Now that they were out of the tree cover, Bex could see there were even more war constructs and lion cannons on the palace battlements than she'd initially estimated. Both were bad news for her army of mostly unarmored infantry. She'd been counting on the Morrigan's big fat target to draw some of that fire, but Heaven's blue sky was empty.

"Do you think they're going to be coming out of their tree anytime soon?" she asked nervously.

"Not sure," Lys replied, followed by a glugging sound that Bex *really* hoped meant Lys was finally drinking one of the witches' bottles of liquid sin.

"They're up to something, though. I can feel the magic rising like the wind before a thunderstorm."

That was a relief to hear, though Bex was all too aware that feeling magic didn't mean it would arrive in a timely fashion. Witchcraft was an infamously slow art, and Bex's army was coming up on the palace fast. Adrian had a comm of his own, so she supposed she could've just radioed him and asked, but she didn't want to interrupt anything important and risk pushing the schedule back even further.

"The Blackwoods always come through," she said, as much for herself as for Lys. "Let's just focus on our own job. The palace is probably going to start firing soon. I'll do my best to stop the lion cannons, but I want you to keep our people as deep in the big tree's shadow as possible in case any shots get through."

"You're using Adrian's heart tree as a bomb shelter?" Lys whistled. "That's harsh."

"That's war," Bex said grimly. "We don't have enough advantages to waste any. We'll make use of what we've got and focus on getting our wounded out of harm's way. The fewer targets we give the enemy, the less we'll have to worry about."

"I'll get on it, then," Lys said grudgingly. "Ishtar guide your sword, my queen."

It was the same blessing Lys always gave her before battle, but the familiar words made Bex wince. Not counting Drox, who shared her head, Adrian and Nemini were the only ones she'd told about what had happened with Ishtar. She'd thought about telling the others, but revealing the ugly truth of the goddess who'd been worshiped as the mother of their race for eons right before the biggest battle of their lives felt like a terrible tactical decision.

Honestly, Bex didn't even know if she'd *ever* spread the truth wider than she already had. What good would it do for someone like Lys, who'd been a devoted follower of Ishtar all their life, to know that their goddess didn't even consider them worth saving? That useless knowledge would bring only pain, so Bex kept her mouth shut and focused on the fight in front of her.

It was going to be a tough one. Just like when she and Adrian had first poked their heads out of the Hells, Gilgamesh's capital was silent as a tomb. Now that they'd left the neon-green grass and bubbling water of Adrian's forest, the armed column of demons was the only thing moving in the entire city. The architecture got fancier as they got closer to the palace, but otherwise everything was the same monotonous white, marred only by the occasional hunk of blackened debris from the destroyed tower.

Bex smiled every time she caught sight of one. The rubble was a good reminder that Gilgamesh's fortress wasn't as perfect and unassailable as it appeared. As they marched into the final ring of buildings surrounding the palace, she spotted the top half of the tower she'd chopped lying to the left of the road they were walking down. There were no crushed buildings directly in their path, but the blocks west of their position had all been flattened.

The sight was enough to make Bex grin. She kept her eyes on the gap she'd made in the skyline as they marched closer, moving from the middle portion of the city into the even fancier neighborhood that seemed to be reserved for Gilgamesh's most favored sycophants. Finally, when the white mansions had grown so tall and ornate that it felt like they were walking through a marble canyon, Bex spotted the entrance to the palace itself.

It was separated from the residential buildings by a white wall that was much smaller than the one surrounding the city, but still annoyingly tall at twenty feet. The ornate golden gate was already open, so they didn't have to worry about bashing their way in. But the wall combined with the tall buildings on either side meant that Bex's entire army had been channeled into a long line, the front of which was now in perfect shot from the palace's battlements.

The whole setup was clearly designed to be a killing jar, but no arrows were raining down on their heads yet. Nothing had fired, actually, which made no sense. They were so close now that Bex could see the bowstrings in the golden constructs' articulated hands, but not a single metal soldier was moving. The lion cannons' mouths were closed as well. If Bex hadn't caught glimpses of movement through the tower windows, she could almost have believed the palace was as empty as the city.

The whole thing reeked of a trap, and Bex held up her fist. The stop spread through the marching army like a slow wave. Once everyone had come to a halt, she turned and waved for Leander to come and join her at the front.

The prince tromped up the line. Bex had barely seen him since they'd left the Hells, but Adrian must've said something, because the normally bossy son of Gilgamesh had been oddly obedient since

Adrian had dropped him off before flying up to join his coven. He hadn't argued with any of her orders, but from the way he kept constantly looking over his shoulder, Bex could tell Leander's heart was no longer in the fight.

"Hey," she said, snapping her fingers in his face when the prince glanced back at the giant tree for what had to be the millionth time. "I need you to focus. What's going on in there?"

She pointed at the silent castle, and Leander turned around with a sigh, using his hands to shield his mirrored eyes from the glare as he scanned the white battlements.

"Looks like the standard palace defenses," he reported a few moments later. "Though it is strange that we were able to get this close."

"You think they're luring us in?"

Leander gave her an *Are you kidding me?* look, and Bex fought the urge to roll her eyes.

"Let me rephrase that," she said, rubbing her temples. "What *kind* of trap are we walking into?"

The prince pursed his lips as he gave her second question some apparently serious thought.

"Something that needs us to be very close," he said at last. "The palace can fire on anything within the Holy City's walls, but Gilgamesh is too cheap to destroy his own capital if he doesn't have to. When the lions didn't start roaring the second we came up from the Hells, I suspected he was waiting until we were in bowshot because arrows don't destroy buildings, but we've been within the constructs' optimal range for a good five minutes now and still nothing." He squinted up at the battlements again. "They must be waiting for us to walk into the palace itself."

"That would be suicide," Bex argued, pointing at the empty white courtyard she could see through the fortress's gate. "There's two hundred feet of open pavement between the palace wall and the front steps. We'll be sitting ducks if we step into that."

"We're already sitting ducks," Leander pointed out. "As I said, the only reason we're not already full of arrows is because whoever's running the defenses has chosen to let us live. Probably so we'd stand around talking about it like we're doing right now. You did say Gilgamesh's objective was to waste our time, and what wastes more time than a nervous army?" His thin lips curved into a mirthless smile. "This way he doesn't even have to spend ammunition to stop us, which makes it the most Gilgamesh move I've seen yet."

"Then let's not let him keep making it," Bex snapped, calling her sword into her hands. "I'm going to spring the trap. The rest of you stay here and wait for my signal."

Leander waved for her to be his guest. Iggs, however, looked shocked and furious. Nemini didn't look too happy, either, but Bex shook her head.

"If they're going to shoot at something, I'd rather it'd be me," she said before her demons could object. "I'll report what I see over the comm, so listen for orders. Leander, did Lys give you a radio?"

When the prince shook his head, Bex pointed at Iggs. "Get him on the channel," she ordered. "I'm going in."

With a firm look back at her army to make sure no one got any heroic ideas, Bex lifted her six new horns high and marched down the last half block into the grand plaza that surrounded Gilgamesh's palace.

It took all of her willpower to do it. She was the one who'd pointed out they'd be walking onto open pavement, but actually stepping out onto all that exposed stone when thousands of mechanical archers had their bows pointed at her head sent Bex's fight-or-flight instincts into overdrive.

The palace itself wasn't helping either. It looked *so* much taller now that she was standing directly below it. Just trying to see the tops of the towers from way down here was enough to give her vertigo, and the courtyard in front of her was equally discomfiting. The stones were cracked in places where pieces of the tower she'd destroyed had fallen, but someone must've cleaned up the rubble, because there wasn't a pebble out of place. Just an empty, two-hundred-foot-wide expanse of blinding-white pavement leading up to the curved steps of the palace's main door, which looked almost like the entrance to an enormous, super-ornate train station from this angle.

That felt like a silly way to describe the fortress of her ancient enemy, but that was seriously what it looked like. The bottom level of Gilgamesh's palace was lavishly decorated with arches, reliefs of heroic-looking sorcerers, and ornate cuneiform inscriptions. Since the lowest floor also served as the base for all those towers, though, it had been built in a long, sturdy rectangle reinforced with columns and lined with wide white steps leading to multiple golden doors that looked like they'd been built to admit hundreds of people at a time.

The only buildings Bex knew of that were designed like that were train stations. The courtyard even had white stone benches along the walls so people could sit down. The seats were all empty now, of course, but the grooves worn into the stone spoke of centuries of use. Same for the wheel ruts in the plaza's otherwise-pristine paving stones and the foot-traffic hollows that dimpled the palace's white steps.

Put it all together and Bex felt like she was staring at the universe's fanciest transport hub. Considering what Adrian had told her about the entrance to the chains being inside the palace's main floor, though, that actually made sense. As the only reliable connector between Earth and Heaven, Gilgamesh's palace basically *was* a train station. A realization that only made the vast emptiness feel even eerier when Bex walked out into it alone.

It felt like trying to sneak across a stage. Even the normally soft steps of her rubber-soled combat boots sounded like banging hammers as Bex made her way across the open pavement to the stairs that led up to what was clearly the main entrance. She was readying Drox to slice through the heavy golden doors when they suddenly began to swing open.

Bex froze in place, holding her sword ready in front of her as the huge palace doors creaked open to reveal—not an army of warlocks or a firing squad of sorcerers, but a single man. Not even an armored man. This individual was dressed in a spotless version of the same white silk shirt and trousers Prince Leander had been wearing when Bex found him in the Lowest Hell, though this man's outfit also included matching white slippers. But while his clothes made him look like a lost guest from a five-star hotel, the white sword at his side and the mirrored eyes in his handsome face felt right at home.

"Welcome, Bex of the Bonfire, newly crowned Queen of All Demons," Gilgamesh's son announced in a ringing voice that filled the empty plaza. "I am Petros, Prince of Fear and defender of the Palace of the Highest Heaven. It is with great respect that my illustrious father, Gilgamesh, the Eternal King, welcomes you to his home. In his glorious name, he has bidden me invite you in so that we may discuss our differences like civilized individuals."

The prince stepped to the side as he finished, revealing a golden table set with an artistically arranged feast of fruits, wines, cheeses, ice water, and fresh bread. There were two chairs with white fur cushions and a floating clay tablet with a golden stylus that seemed to be acting as a magical recording device. It looked exactly like what she'd expect from a peace talk with Gilgamesh, if Bex had ever bothered to imagine such a thing. But though the prince had yet to touch his sword, Bex backed several steps away.

"He's lying," Leander's voice said calmly over the comm in her ear.

"No shit," Bex whispered back, glancing up at the thousands of constructs still standing like statues on the palace's battlements. "But why tell a lie so obvious? He has to know it won't work."

"He's probably just wasting our time again," Iggs said on the same channel. "I bet the food isn't even real."

"It's a bad-faith negotiation for the purpose of stalling your advance," Leander agreed. "You should kill him."

"No argument there," Bex said, eyeing the prince, who was still smiling at her like a morning TV host. "What does his sword do?"

"I don't know," Leander confessed. "The Prince of Fear has always been in charge of the castle's defenses, so his abilities were kept secret from the rest of us in case of rebellion. He's been doing that job for longer than I've been alive, though, so it's safe to assume he's good at it."

The prince certainly didn't look afraid. He was also still standing inside the palace's giant doors, which wasn't a place Bex wanted to step into alone, even with her new horns. That said, she also didn't want to charge her army into a prince. Getting inside the palace would protect them from the shooting gallery, but even if they outnumbered him a thousand to one, trapping her demons in a room with a prince sounded like a quick way to get them all killed. She was still trying to figure out the right move when a new voice spoke over her comm.

"Keep him talking," Adrian said. "And see if you can get him to step out of the building."

"Why?" Bex whispered, flicking her eyes to the empty sky. "What are you planning?"

"I don't want to spoil it," Adrian whispered back, sounding enormously pleased with himself. "Just stall for a few more minutes, and try to get him over the vine if you can."

Bex was about to ask "What vine?" when she saw it. There, growing along the bottom of the white step the prince was standing on, was a tiny green tendril. It was no bigger than an electrical wire, but it'd somehow managed to grow all the way over the palace wall, across the empty plaza, and up the stairs without Bex—or seemingly anyone else—noticing. The vine got even longer as she watched, working its way along the inside corner of the step like water flowing down a crack, and suddenly, Bex was having a hard time keeping the smile off her face.

"The Eternal King must be pretty scared if he wants to have a civil discussion with the likes of me," she said, striking a confident pose as she plunged Drox's point into the stone at her feet. "I don't mind listening to what you have to say, but I'm not doing it in there. If you want to talk, you'll have to come down to me."

"But the banquet table is all set," the prince argued, waving at the lavish spread behind him. "And the light is strong in the plaza. This could take quite a while. Surely you'd rather sit in the shade?"

"I don't need shade," Bex said, crossing her arms stubbornly over her chest. "And I don't want your fancy food either. I won't draw arms if you don't, but I'm not discussing a damn thing unless you're man enough to come stand out here under the arrows with me."

For the first time since the doors had opened, the prince's dazzling smile slipped. He snatched it back into place a second later, reaching down to fill two golden cups with wine from the cut glass carafe before taking both in his hands.

"As you wish, honored queen," he said as he carried the cups of wine down the steps where the vine was hidden. "Let it never be said that Gilgamesh's household was inhospitable. Even the enemies of Heaven deserve respect and dignity, so if you will not come to me, I am glad to go to you if it lets us speak."

"You're speaking right now," Bex pointed out, uncrossing her arms again in case she needed to grab her sword quickly. "But I suppose you can't help it. Being a font of endless words seems to run in your family."

Once again, the prince's smile sagged a fraction, but he kept his composure as he strode down the final step into the main courtyard to offer Bex her wine cup.

She took it from him like she'd take a hissing viper. But while Bex had zero intention of actually drinking, the wine didn't smell poisoned, which meant it wasn't the threat. *That* would be the prince, who was radiating malice like a furnace despite his sunny smile. Bex really hoped Adrian finished his plan soon, because whatever Gilgamesh was playing at with this fake peace offer, his son's hatred for her was real and bone-deep.

Bex felt exactly the same way about him, except she didn't bother with the fake smile. She held up her golden cup with an honest scowl and tossed it on the ground at the prince's feet, splattering red wine all the way up his white silk trousers.

"That was uncalled-for," the Prince of Fear said in a low, dangerous voice. "I know better than to expect grace from a demon, but I thought you'd at least respect the dignity of a gift offered in hospitality."

"That's just it," Bex growled. "It's not hospitality, because this isn't Gilgamesh's house. It's ours. *Our* Paradise that *your* father stole. If you actually want peace, acknowledge that and leave, or we will throw you out."

"I'd like to see you try," the prince replied coldly, finally dropping the fake smile as he reached for his sword.

The moment his fingers touched it, terror like nothing Bex had ever felt seized her body. She'd seen no attack, but suddenly none of her muscles would obey her, and she wasn't the only one. Bex couldn't turn her head to look, but she knew from the instant deafening silence behind her that her army had also been struck. She could practically hear her demons holding their breath as the now-scowling prince stepped back.

"Open fire," he ordered, giving Bex one last hateful look before a wave of scales—the same snakelike overlapping scales that fear demons used to cover their bodies, only in white instead of black—appeared to cover his face. They covered the rest of his body as well, protecting the Prince of Fear from head to toe as the ranks of golden constructs that had been standing motionless on the battlements this entire time finally loosed their bows.

The wave of arrows was so thick it blotted out even the ever-present light of Heaven. Bex could hear the lions roaring on the roof above, but she couldn't see the white balls of fire through the wall of black-pointed sin-iron projectiles falling toward her head. The sight was even more terrifying than the prince. Him she could fight, but pinned by fear like she was right now, there was nothing Bex could do to block the avalanche of arrows before it landed on the demons behind her. Most of her army didn't have armor, and the prince's fear had frozen them so they couldn't dodge. They were just standing in the middle of the street like target dummies. But before Bex could think of something—*anything*—she could do to stop what was about to happen, a peal of thunder crashed through the empty sky.

The scale-covered prince looked up in surprise. Bex didn't know if that weakened the fear he'd used to grab her or if the noise had simply shocked her out of its grip, but she was suddenly able to look up as well, watching with wide, terrified eyes as a sheet of blindingly bright blue-white lightning engulfed the entire wave of arrows flying at her head.

The torrent of electricity vaporized the wooden shafts in an instant. It couldn't touch the sin-iron arrowheads, but without the shafts and fletching to make them fly true, they'd become little more than dangerous hail. Now that the prince's paralyzing fear had broken, the demons were able to dodge the falling metal easily, freeing them to stare up in new horror at the giant shape that had appeared behind the lightning in the sky.

It was a skeletal hand. Not a human hand, but a huge reptilian claw the size of a minivan. It slashed through the air above Bex like a scythe, cutting the golden battlements off the towers and sending the war constructs that had been standing on them crashing to the ground. The clockwork archers were still falling when the lightning flashed again, lighting up the now midnight-dark sky to reveal the giant skeleton of a dragon.

It was almost as tall as the towers, a fleshless creation of bleached bones held together with ropes of flashing lightning. And standing on its back with her white hair flying behind her like a banshee's was Adrian's aunt Lydia, the Old Wife of the Bones.

"The ancient oaths have been invoked!" the old witch cried, her raspy voice ringing with so much magic, it made Bex's ears bleed. "In return for eons of safe rest within the shelter of the Blackwood, I call upon the bones that slumber within the roots! Rise up, rage of the past! Rise and hunt again until all who threaten our coven are destroyed!"

The undead dragon roared beneath her feet and opened its skeletal jaw to shoot out a wave of crackling blue lightning that eclipsed and consumed the lion cannons' barrage. It wasn't until the deafening thunder shook the ground again, though, that Bex realized the bone dragon wasn't the only thing in the sky. Through its empty wings, she could see hundreds, maybe *thousands* of smaller skeletal dragons diving at the castle like kamikaze fighters.

Each one was only about a tenth the size of the giant dragon Lydia was riding, but the blue lightning that held their bones together exploded when they hit, turning the falling dragons into bombs. They crashed into Gilgamesh's towers like a barrage, shattering the elegant windows and blasting the war constructs into the air. The explosions weren't strong enough to crack the towers themselves, but the golden battlements bolted to the outer walls were blown away in a cascade of deafening thunder and shattering bones.

The silence that followed was so deep, Bex worried her eardrums had shattered. Fortunately, that turned out not to be the case. Her hearing was perfectly fine. The suicide rain of falling dragons had simply stopped, giving way to the soft patter of raindrops as the black clouds—the only clouds she'd ever seen in Heaven's sky—opened above the enormous circle of witches that was now floating above the palace courtyard on their brooms with Agatha in the center, standing on her broomstick like a conductor as she added her voice to her sister's.

"The ancient oaths have been invoked," she said, her calm, rich voice sweeping over the battlefield like a weather front. "In return for the life-pledge of every witch who serves the Cycles, I call upon our pact with the Great Blackwood. Rise up, sorrow of the present. Rise and wash away the enemy who hunts your children and burns your land."

The rain pounded harder with every word, filling Gilgamesh's formerly desert-dry Heaven with a flash flood of churning water that scoured the towers clean. It tore the battlements that had managed to survive the dragons' attack straight out of the stone and washed the war constructs clean off their feet, sweeping them off into the empty city like golden trash caught in a flooding river.

Bex was still watching them float away in wonder when the scaled Prince of Fear suddenly lunged at her. A wave of paralyzing terror came with him, grabbing her body just like before, except this time it didn't stick. This time was different, because this time, a witch was waiting right above her.

"The ancient oaths have been invoked," Muriel said from where she was floating above Bex's head on her broom like a petal in the pounding rain. "In return for heroism yet to be rendered, I call upon the best of all fates yet to be. Rise up, defenders of a brighter future. Rise and know that no malice of the enemy can touch you so long as the forest's rain falls."

The Old Wife of the Future's words were softer than her sisters', but Bex felt them to her bones, because they'd been spoken straight to her. As soon as the witch's voice touched her ears, the prince's paralyzing fear vanished. It must've been washed off her demons as well, because Bex's army was suddenly roaring behind her, charging through the rain to tear apart the war constructs that were still trying to stand in the raging river the plaza had become.

"Don't let anyone enter the palace!" the Prince of Fear bellowed as the demons stampeded past him. "Sorcerers, to your posts! Don't let them—"

His orders were cut short as Bex slammed Drox into his side. The prince's scales were as hard as Havok's armor had been, so she didn't manage to cut him in half, but the blow still sent him flying. He landed on his back on the opposite side of the enormous plaza, coughing white blood out of his lungs as the three witches spoke again.

"The ancient oaths have been invoked," the Old Wives of the Blackwood said in unison. "By our bones, flesh, and souls, we keep the oldest promise. By the past, present, and future, we deliver that which is due. By the tongues of all our coven, we cast down the Witch's Spite, curse of all curses, upon the lands of Gilgamesh, murderer-king of Uruk. So say we all and so shall it be, now, before, and forever more."

A fresh flash of lightning lit up the sky as the final rhyming words of the curse finished, illuminating the damage the dragons had already done, the pounding rain that was presently washing their enemies away, and the shimmering protection that would guard the demons from harm in the future. Watching it all come together was enough to make Bex's knees go weak. She'd seen Adrian do big magic before, but she didn't have to be a witch to know that this curse was magnitudes stronger than the ones he'd used when he'd turned his forest black to kill the Spider's warlocks. Just speaking the words had been enough to send a torrent of red blood pouring from Muriel's lips, but the young-faced witch still looked triumphant as she rose into her sister's rain on a broom carved to resemble a swan.

The scaled Prince of Fear jumped after her, trying to knock the witch back down, but Bex got there first. She kicked the prince back to the wet ground with a boot to his temple. It was a move that would've taken the head off a normal human, but the Prince of Fear must've been as tough as an actual fear demon. He shrugged the kick off like it was nothing, rolling back to his feet with a glare so hateful, Bex could feel it through the mask of scales that covered his face.

"You have no idea what you've just done," he snarled, gripping his white sword, which could no longer paralyze her thanks to the witches, but still had a wickedly curved cutting edge. "You idiot demon. You should have stayed in the Hells where you belong!"

He charged as he finished, running at Bex with a speed she hadn't seen since she'd fought Havok. Fortunately, Drox was quicker on the uptake than his queen. By the time Bex realized she was in trouble, her loyal sword was already swinging. He bashed the white Blade of Fear away like it weighed nothing, but the prince had already pivoted to swing again, attacking with the raw fury of someone with nothing left to lose.

Bex knew that feeling well, but she couldn't afford to do the same. She was fighting for everything now, so she met his attack with skill instead of fury, putting her one hundred and ninety-eight lifetimes' worth of experience to use as she ducked the prince's wild swing to attack his legs.

It was a solid hit, but once again, the prince's thick scales kept her from landing actual damage. Drox's blade slid right off, but the blow still made the prince stumble, driving him back across the rain-soaked courtyard and away from the sorcerers who'd run up to defend the palace entrance that Iggs and the rest of Bex's demons were just starting to assault.

Chapter 9

C‍URRENT LIFE-AND-DEATH SITUATIONS NOTWITHSTANDING, Adrian had never been more excited to watch a curse go off. The Witch's Spite was the stuff of legends, the greatest destructive magic his coven had ever constructed. They'd been building it since the first Blackwood grove was initiated, collecting the bones of every dragon that died in their care, tallying favors done for the Great Forest, and binding pine cones with protective magic so they'd grow into trees that could take hits in someone else's stead at some point in the future.

The Witch's Spite was the greatest expression of Blackwood witchcraft, a monument to the incredible power of patience, preparation, and cooperation with the forest. It famously took a thousand witches working together to spread out the damage when the payment for such an enormous curse came due, which explained why his mother and aunts had arrived with *everyone*. It also could only be cast within the borders of a Blackwood grove, which was where Adrian came in.

"We need more coverage to the west," Boston reported from his perch at the tip of Bran's broomstick. "Bex just kicked the prince over there."

Adrian nodded and moved the vine—a super-long-growing woody variety that his cousin had brought with her from South America for exactly this purpose—as directed.

The vines were the key to all of this. Even with the astounding power of his new heart tree and the full force of his coven behind him, tree roots were slow to spread. Vines, on the other hand, grew like wildfire anywhere there was sunlight. The tropical liana vine in particular could stretch itself practically forever as long as its base was well rooted. A power Adrian had been abusing to the hilt.

It was still hard to push through Heaven's antigrowth protections, but he'd never had so much support, or so much need. Coverage was critical, since wherever Adrian's plants were, so was his forest. That connection was what had allowed the Old Wives to cast the Witch's Spite on Gilgamesh's doorstep. It was also the only way Adrian—and by extension, Boston—was able to see what was happening on the ground.

Looking through his physical eyes while he was communing with his forest had always been difficult. Now that his mother and her apprentices had filled the sky with a thunderstorm, though, it was physically impossible. Bran would throw Adrian off if he tried to fly into that pounding rain, so he and Boston were floating above the black clouds, using the forest's senses to track the battle below. Since plants didn't have eyes like humans, the information was limited, but liana vines were extremely sensitive to both light and pressure, which made them excellent spies. Adrian was making a mental note to ask his cousin for more cuttings when a knife stabbed into his side.

That was what it felt like, at least. When Adrian looked down, though, his coat—which he'd put back on when he'd gone to his cabin to resupply before the fight—was undamaged. There was no spreading bloodstain or gaping wound when he unbuttoned his shirt to check, but he swore he could feel a knife carving into his flesh.

It reminded him of the time the Spider had filled him with phantom daggers, but rougher and more chronic. The Spider's sorcery hadn't hurt until he activated it. This felt like someone was carving their initials into his ribs with a rusty pocketknife.

That last thought was where Adrian found his answer. He *was* getting stabbed, just not in his physical body. This pain came from his heart tree. When he glanced over his shoulder to check, though, the towering dark-green spire of the skyscraper-sized Douglas fir looked normal. He was trying to shift his consciousness over to investigate when Boston galloped down the broomstick to dig his claws into Adrian's knee.

"Get the vines inside the doors!" the cat cried. "Iggs's team is pushing into the palace, but the Witch of the Future's protections can't defend them if they leave the forest's borders!"

"I'm not sure I *can* go inside the doors," Adrian told him through gritted teeth. "The palace is Gilgamesh's private territory. It's a really hard line to cross, especially when I've got something stabbing me in the ribs."

"What are you talking about?" Boston asked in alarm.

"Something's attacking my heart tree," Adrian reported, keeping his words tight and short as he breathed through the pain. "I need to go back and defend it, but the vines here are already overextended. I can't leave them alone."

"Then tell somebody else to go," his familiar suggested. "Our entire coven is here to help! You don't have to do everything by yourself anymore."

Adrian shook his head. All the other witches were busy supporting the Old Wives' three-pronged curse. It didn't feel right to ask them to help him on top of that, but Adrian did know someone who was already at his heart tree and who'd probably love a chance to get into the fight.

Solution in mind, he grabbed his broom tight with his one hand to compensate for the dizziness the pain was sending through his body and reached up with the other to tap the comm inserted into his ear.

"Lys?"

"I'm here," they answered immediately. "Does Bex need backup?"

"No, she's doing fine," Adrian said, reaching through the vines to check the pressure of Bex's feet as she slammed her sword into the scale-covered Prince of Fear. "I'm the one who needs help. Someone's cutting into my tree. I need you to make them stop."

"Can do," replied the lust demon, making this the first and only time they'd ever taken an order from him willingly. "Do you know where the enemy is, and do I need to worry about the tree coming down?"

Adrian looked over his shoulder at the city-block-sized trunk. "I don't think we need to worry about anything falling. Not before we breach the castle, anyway. But the stabbing is making it hard to concentrate on keeping my forest extended to protect Bex."

As always, those were the magic words.

"I'll take care of it," Lys promised. "You just keep that moss under our queen."

Bex wasn't Adrian's queen, and he wasn't working with moss, but he nodded just the same. "Thank you very much."

"Make sure she stays alive," Lys ordered in a worried voice. "I'll let you know when I'm done."

They hung up before Adrian could open his mouth to promise he would, leaving him floating nervously over the lightning-filled thunderhead of his family's ire as the battle for Heaven raged below.

"All right," Lys said, handing the megaphone they'd been using to Annika, the sorrow demon who'd been their best safehouse leader back in Seattle. "I've got to go handle something for the queen's witch. You keep things moving."

"Would you like someone to go with you?" Annika offered, shooting a nervous look at Lys's bandaged wing. "We have several—"

"I'm not pulling anyone else off their job," Lys snapped as they checked their weapons, both the sin-iron dagger under their left wing and the trusty steel combat knife under their right. The steel blade wouldn't even scratch a war construct, but Lys never went anywhere without it. That knife was the one their first Bex had given them after killing their warlock. Lys would die with it in their hand.

"The evacuation is the queen's top priority," they reminded Annika when the sorrow demon didn't stop biting her lip. "It's probably just some idiot war demon acting out. I'll take care of it and come right back. You keep getting our people down that rootway, and make sure you send any new soldiers who come up straight to the front to help the battle at the palace."

"They're doing a good job of that on their own," Annika said, nodding at the river of armed demons pouring out of the four-lane-highway-sized hollow at the base of Adrian's tree. "But are you sure you should be the one to deal with this? No one here would ever question your battle prowess, but you were injured by a Blade of Gilgamesh. Surely you need—"

"What I *need* is for all of us to do our jobs," Lys said firmly, knocking back another bottle of distilled lust from the six-pack the witches had given them. The manufactured sin tasted nothing like the real thing, but it filled Lys with so much energy that they barely felt the hole in their shoulder. The immunity wouldn't last for long, though, so Lys went ahead and flapped into the air.

"Just keep everybody moving," they ordered. "I'll call for backup if I get into trouble."

"As you command, Right Hand of the Queen," Annika said, bowing her horns.

Lys ducked their back and took off, ignoring the pain that was already building in their shoulder again as they flew over the panicked mass of demons Annika and the rest of the evacuation team were desperately attempting to send down the rootway in an orderly fashion.

The crowd noise dropped off quickly as Lys flew, but that was typical of witchwoods. Back in Adrian's forest on Bainbridge, they'd barely been able to eavesdrop on Bex from ten feet away. Not that Lys needed to keep an ear on the queen inside Adrian's forest, but having an actual safe space was a new thing for them, and old habits died hard.

Speaking of old habits, Lys was leaning on one of their favorites right now. Bex liked to attribute their success as a spy to being a good shapeshifter, but the real trick, in Lys's opinion, was attention to detail. Case in point, as soon as they reached the towering trunk of Adrian's new heart tree, Lys stopped flying fast and started flying low. They weren't sure what they were looking for yet, but they went over every nook and fold of the fir tree's gigantic base like they were being paid by the root. Lys had almost made it all the way back around when they finally spotted the culprit.

It was another lust demon, a big one with shimmering wings that were closer to purple than Lys's dusty rose. Just as Adrian had predicted, they were carving something into the tree's trunk. Lys couldn't read what they were writing from the air, but the demon had peeled off a big chunk of the Douglas fir's thick, corky bark to reach the paler wood beneath, which was a crime all by itself in Lys's eyes.

"*Hey!*" they shouted, making the other demon jump as Lys swooped down to land on the gnarled root the carver had been hiding behind. "That tree belongs to the witches who came to our rescue! What in the Nine destroyed Hells do you think you're doing taking a knife to…"

Their tirade trailed off as Lys's eyes finally landed on the knife in question. Given Adrian's complaints about the pain, Lys had assumed the culprit would be using sin iron scavenged from the drowned Hells, but the ornate dagger in the lust demon's hand was white, not black. Lys was close enough now to read what the other demon had been carving, too, and it *wasn't* their name or profanity or even a deranged rant against the queen, which had been Lys's first guess. This was far worse, because the demon was writing in cuneiform.

Thanks to their constant spying, Lys's ancient Sumerian was better than most warlocks', but this text was much denser than the writing they usually saw on Earth. The carving was also enormous, with enough cuneiform to cover a solid three-square-foot block of tree trunk. Despite all of that, however, the actual words were pretty simple.

Like most of the cuneiform Lys encountered, it was a poem. The first verses were nothing but fawning fluff praising Gilgamesh's glory, but the main body contained a florid and highly detailed description of an explosion that would "return everything built by the Eternal King's enemies to dust."

The lust demon had been carving the final stanza when Lys caught them, so it was less of a surprise than it should've been when the demon turned around and looked up at Lys with eyes that flashed mirror-silver.

"Well, well," they said in a masculine voice, letting the winged-demon disguise fall away to reveal a human male in familiar golden armor. "Looks like the Coward Queen forgot to take all her lackeys with her."

Lys didn't bother replying. They just reached under their arm and pulled out their sin-iron dagger.

The prince laughed when he saw it. "Please," he mocked, twirling his own foot-long white knife in his armored fingers. "Don't you recognize me? I'm the Prince of Lust. *Your* prince, so show a little respe—"

The haughty speech became a yelp when Lys dove at him. The prince got his dagger-sized Blade of Gilgamesh into a defensive position with the same annoying speed all of Heaven's sons seemed to be blessed with by default, but Lys wasn't stabbing at him. They were going for the spell behind him. Sin iron would have poisoned the tree, so Lys used their steel blade, gouging a series of furious slashes across the cuneiform the prince had so carefully carved into the Douglas fir's soft wood.

"*You dare!*" the prince roared, whirling around to stab his white blade into Lys's open back. "Die with your queen, you *filth!*"

He brought his knife down as he finished, its gleaming white edge perfectly positioned to sever Lys's spine. But Lys was a seasoned soldier and an even more practiced shape changer. The second the knife's course was set, they shifted their torso to the side, moving their flesh like water to leave the prince stabbing at nothing. But while the change was fast enough to save Lys's back, nothing could save the rest of their body when the prince swung the fist he wasn't using to hold his knife straight into their ribs. The blow sent Lys rocketing sideways into one of the fir tree's gigantic knotted roots, which wasn't nearly as soft or fluffy as the layer of thick green moss made it look.

If they hadn't just consumed an entire bottle of artificial lust, that would've been the end. Lys had never been as good at regenerating as Bex or Iggs. Add in the blood loss from their wounded shoulder and the damage might've been fatal. Fortunately for Lys, the moment the witches had shown up with their bottled sins, they'd taken a page from their queen's old book and started chugging. The results weren't as transformative as Ishtar's glowing water, but they gave Lys enough strength to get out of the splintered roots in time to avoid the prince's next attack, which had been aimed to take off their head.

"Fancy dodging won't save you," the son of Gilgamesh warned, flipping the white knife over in his golden-gloved hand. "Nothing can at this point, because I know who you are. You're the Coward Queen's nursemaid, the one who always runs to find her after she dies."

His handsome face split into a cruel smile. "My brother Leander reported the queen abandoned the fight against him after you were injured. I don't normally take advice from traitors, but my orders were to stall the queen's advance, and I like the idea of killing you far more than carving a bunch of poetry into a tree that keeps growing back over the words as soon as they're cut."

"Only an idiot would expect a Blackwood tree to stay still and let you mutilate it," Lys taunted from where they clung to the side of the giant trunk. "But if you think I'm the easier target, that's your mistake to make. I've faced a lot of puffed-up princes in my time, but you're the sorriest one I've seen yet. Just look at your tiny little sword." They flashed him a smirk. "No wonder your brothers sent you off to do the gardening. I bet you can't even cut me with that thumbtack."

That taunt was the cellophane version of a transparent ploy, but Lys had never met a prince who could take an insult. Sure enough, this one took the bait with a roar, shape-changing the stolen demon wings back onto his shoulders so he could fly up high enough to stab at Lys's heart.

He didn't even get close. The prince was fast, yes, but so was Lys, and more importantly at the moment, they knew how to use their wings. The prince's flying wasn't bad, but his wingbeats were merely efficient. He had none of the grace or natural instinct of someone who'd been born to fly. Lys, on the other hand, had been flying since the first Bex set them free. They dodged the prince's attack by miles, launching up the craggy trunk of Adrian's tree to hide in the night-dark shadows of its interior branches.

It was a stalling tactic at best, but after their last two near-death encounters, Lys wasn't about to try fighting a third prince alone. Unfortunately, they didn't have a lot of other options at the moment. From the thundering blast of Gilgamesh's cannons along with what sounded like *actual* thunder, Bex clearly had her hands full already. Nemini would've been a big help, but Lys wanted her watching Bex's back. Same went for Iggs and Adrian. Lys also wasn't about to call a bunch of normal demons out of the rootway to come get slaughtered. That was the opposite of what Bex wanted, but Gilgamesh wasn't the only one who could push a time limit.

If the Prince of Lust's job was to create disasters that stopped Bex from entering Gilgamesh's palace, then Lys would keep him too busy to cause trouble. They'd stay ahead of his short knife, attacking just enough that he never felt safe resuming his carving but not so much that they put themselves in actual danger.

It was still going to be a throw, but as the superior flier *and* the superior shapeshifter, Lys had the advantage in the dense interior of Adrian's tree. The Prince of Lust could disguise himself as a demon, but could he add owl feathers to his leathery wings to make them soundless? Could he turn his fingers into hooked claws that were perfect for moving through thick branches?

Lys didn't think so. Most lust demons never even bothered learning those tricks, since serving warlocks and scooping sludge in the Hells didn't require such advanced techniques, but Lys was a soldier of the Bonfire Queen. They'd been transforming their body into whatever weapon got the job done for centuries, and they put all of that experience to work now, changing the color of their skin to match the fir tree's dark bark and stretching their fingers into hooks that let them hang off the underside of the thick branches like a squirrel. They'd just gotten themselves nice and tucked away when the prince burst into the canopy.

"Come out and fight!" he bellowed, flapping his wings hard to support his armored weight as he looked around the dark forest of the heart tree's interior. "Or are you as cowardly as your queen?"

Lys's answer to that was to toss a fir cone over his head. The prince didn't even notice it flying by, but he heard when it bounced off the branch behind him. His head snapped toward the sound at once, which meant he was looking the wrong direction when Lys swung up from the branch beneath him to drag their new claws across the prince's unguarded wings.

They didn't manage to slice them to ribbons, alas, but the prince still bellowed in pain. By the time he whirled around, however, Lys was already gone, swooping off on silent wings to a completely different branch several feet above him. They were about to drop down for another swipe they hoped would do some real damage when the prince suddenly pressed his white dagger to his lips.

"Reveal your desires, enemy of the Divine King."

The whispered words were barely louder than the noise of the tree itself, but the moment they left the prince's lips, Lys's entire body started glowing red. This sent them into a panic for a second, because the prince's words hadn't sounded like sorcery. The recitation wasn't long enough, and the prince had been speaking English, not ancient Sumerian. Lys was starting to worry they were facing another Leander-style genius caster when the prince lowered his twitching dagger to his side, and they finally realized what had happened.

This man was the Prince of Lust. That meant his sword had once belonged to the *Queen* of Lust, Lys's native ruler. Not that Lys had ever met their monarch or knew what her sword did, but they *did* know how lust-demon magic worked. Changing shape was only the trappings. What actually made a lust demon a lust demon was the ability to know instinctively what others desired.

Lys did it all the time when they picked their targets, but they'd never had that same power directed back at them. Now, though, their intense desire to destroy this prince and everything he stood for was shining through their camouflaged skin like a beacon, lighting them up for the entire world to see as the prince spun around.

"Got you," he said, flashing Lys a grin as he hurled his white dagger at their head.

Dodging wasn't nearly as easy this time. It was only because Lys's new hook-claws were already dug deep into the tree bark that they managed to fling their body out of the way in time. They'd just finished catching their balance when the Blade of Gilgamesh flipped in midair and flew at Lys again. No matter what direction they dodged, the white blade flew after them like a hornet, so Lys leaped off the tree entirely to go for the only cover they knew would stop it.

They jumped onto the prince's back.

The bastard had been gleefully watching the chase from a safe distance. He was so engrossed in Lys's imminent death that he didn't even notice they were headed straight at him until Lys grabbed him by the wings. Since the prince was still flying, this meant both he and Lys went tumbling toward the ground. Lys was ready to ride him all the way to the *crunch* at the bottom, but the prince grabbed a branch at the last second, almost ripping it off the tree with his weight before the supple greenwood finally stopped his fall.

"You'll pay for that," he snarled, calling the flying dagger back to his hand so he could stab it over his shoulder at the demon who was still clinging to his back.

"That's what they all say," Lys taunted, shifting their body around the prince's strikes as they readied their own sin-iron dagger.

Not to stab him in the back. They'd already learned the hard way with Leander that the sin-iron blade was too short and the prince's armor too thick for that attack to work. Lys needed an easier target, so they stole a move from the war demons and went for the wings instead, slamming the edge of their black knife into the tough cord of bones and sinew that connected the prince's left wing to his back.

Even with sin iron, it was hell to cut through. Given how many times Lys's own wings had been injured, they'd assumed it'd be easy, but cutting through the prince's wing was like trying to saw through a steel cable. Maybe that toughness was why his wingbeats had seemed so stiff, but Lys was committed to the attack. Now that their skin looked like it'd been irradiated, hiding was off the table. It was offense or death, so Lys went after the prince's wing like a mad badger, stabbing and tearing with their short knife until, all of a sudden, the prince's entire wing joint came off in their hand with an extremely satisfying *pop*.

His scream was even sweeter. The Prince of Lust bellowed in pain and fury as he let go of the branch he'd caught to drop them both to the ground. He was already angling to land on top, but Lys changed their body again as they fell, sliding around the prince's torso like a snake before leaping off him entirely to fly back up into the air.

They almost didn't make it. The reason Lys didn't change their body this drastically all the time was because it was exhausting. The entire fight couldn't have lasted more than three minutes, but they were already so tired they could barely get their wings open in time to check their fall. The energy from the witch's tonic was long gone, leaving them coasting on pure adrenaline as they flapped back over to grab the tree trunk. But while it sounded like the prince had hit the ground nice and hard, Lys didn't even have to look down to know he was still alive.

He was already kicking back to his feet in the bloody moss when they finally turned around. The prince regrew the wing Lys had ripped off a few seconds later, pushing it out of his back with the carelessness of a shapeshifter who didn't have to pay for his changes. The price had already been covered for him by the white quintessence dripping down his golden armor. He could clearly do this all day, but Lys was already running close to empty, which meant it was time to make a choice.

Keeping their claws locked into the tree, Lys returned to their original shape and reached up to tap the comm in their ear. No one had said anything over the radio since Adrian had asked for help, but the thunder was still booming from the palace, so the fight there couldn't be finished yet. If Lys called for backup now, they'd undermine Bex's assault. If they kept fighting the prince like this, though, they'd lose the war of attrition. Escaping was also a no-go with their body still glowing bright red from the Blade of Lust's power. Even if they'd been invisible, though, Lys wasn't about to leave this bastard alone to finish carving his spell into Adrian's tree. Those roots were the key to saving the people Bex spent all her lives fighting for. The people *Lys* had fought for for the last two hundred years.

That decided it. If this battle was their last, Lys was determined to go down swinging. It was the same thing they'd sworn to the first Bex after she slaughtered their warlock in front of them. Everything Lys had done since—their devotion to their queen, the countless minions of Gilgamesh they'd slaughtered, the slaves they'd freed—it had all been for this moment. This was the eve of the victory demonkind had been fighting fifty centuries to reach, and there was no way in all the sunken Hells that Lys was going to let a puny little backlines saboteur of a prince take it away from them.

  The resolve had barely crystallized in their head when Lys launched off the tree like a spear. They folded their wings as they fell, ignoring the pain in their shoulder as they dove past the prince to land hard in the moss behind him. They kicked up the moment they hit, throwing wet moss and mud into the prince's eyes to hide their arm as it swept around to stab the full four inches of the sin-iron dagger straight into the joint of the prince's armored knee.

  It was the same hit Lys had taught Bex to use on war demons. It didn't work quite as well on a son of Gilgamesh, but they still got the prince to stumble. The moment he did, Lys shot back to their feet and used their now superior height to reach over the prince's shoulder and slice through the leather strap that held his helmet in place. They snatched the golden protection off his head next, flinging the helmet off to the side as they dropped low to dodge the counter.

  The blow came in like a freight train. The prince's dagger flew over Lys's head close enough to cut the tips off their rounded horns. The flash of pain that followed darkened Lys's vision, reminding them that going toe-to-toe against a prince was exactly the sort of stupid, suicidal behavior they'd always warned

Bex to avoid. There was no getting out now, though, so instead, Lys went all-in, twisting their body into shapes even lust demons weren't meant to take to make sure they always stayed one step ahead.

When the prince came in for a grab, Lys changed the structure of their shoulder to allow their arm to swing past its natural rotation and twist him off. When he swung at their head, Lys collapsed all the space in their spine, shrinking their height by a foot so that his dagger flew harmlessly over their head. They reinforced their rib cage with bone plating, doubled the size of their lungs to process more air, even turned their normally prehensile tail into a bony needle so they could stab it between the scales of the prince's armor.

Every wild shift cost them dearly, but dying with cards still on the table was a soldier's shame, so Lys used every dirty trick they'd ever devised. No matter how cleverly they moved, though, they could never seem to land their sin-iron dagger in a consequential spot. Worse, all the rapid changing was draining their stamina dry. Another thirty seconds of this and the exhaustion would melt their body into a literal puddle. If they didn't score some actual damage before then, they'd have risked it all for nothing, so Lys decided to try something *really* dangerous.

It was easy enough to start. Since they were both fighting with knives, the prince was already very close. All Lys had to do was swing for his throat to get him to dodge to the left. Normally, this was where Lys would've switched to his legs and gone for a trip. This time, though, Lys spun with him, changing the shape of their spine so they could turn the top half of their body in a full circle to catch the prince on the backswing. It looked like they were going to land the hit—it *always* looked like they were going to land it—but once again, the prince changed momentum at the last second, swinging his white dagger up instead to slice across the back of Lys's exposed hand.

The razor-sharp Blade of Gilgamesh went through their skin like a hot wire. Lys had already moved their tendons out of the way, but the pain still caused their hand to open, dropping the knife they'd been gripping onto the torn-up moss at their feet. They were diving to retrieve it when the prince saw his opening and lunged, driving his white dagger up to the hilt in Lys's chest.

The whole fight stopped. Lys clung to the prince's armor, black blood pouring from their mouth. He gripped them just as hard, holding Lys still while he twisted the white blade in their body and shoved it upward, cutting through Lys's ribs and into their heart.

The move was the one Lys had used a thousand times on a thousand warlocks, which was why they were prepared. The prince's strike was in the right place, but Lys had already shifted their heart and lungs down to the relative safety of their stomach. The prince's knife was still buried in their flesh, so it still hurt, but not so much that Lys couldn't reach over their back with the *third* arm the prince had never even thought to expect and stab the black blade of the sin-iron dagger into his exposed windpipe.

The prince's mirrored eyes were right next to Lys's when the knife landed, so they got to watch the shock as it went through him, followed by pain and fear as the prince tried to shove Lys off him only to discover he couldn't. They'd changed their body again, turning their arms into a bony prison that held the prince in place as he choked on his own white blood.

"How?" he wheezed through the quintessence pouring down his throat. "Your knife's on the ground."

"I have two knives," Lys whispered back, giving the sin-iron dagger an extra twist to ensure the internal carotid artery that carried blood to the brain was severed beyond repair. "I switched them when I turned around. The one you made me drop was the steel knife my queen gave to me the night she set me free. This one, though"—they wiggled the sin-iron blade in his throat—"this one's just for you."

The strength in their transformed arms was already failing, so Lys jerked their unnatural third arm as hard as they could, slicing the sin-iron knife through the prince's spinal column to finish the job. With nothing left to hold it, the prince's head tumbled to the mossy ground with a satisfying *thump*, his mirrored eyes wide like he still couldn't believe what had just happened.

Lys couldn't believe it either. After so many years of trying, they'd finally killed a prince, though whether they'd live to brag about it was another story. They'd saved all their vital organs by moving them out of the way, but they still had a fresh gash down their arm and a giant new window in their chest. Add in their still-punctured shoulder from the fight with the Prince of Hate, and Lys's body was losing blood faster than it could regenerate.

They were already on their knees despite having no memory of falling. It was the scariest sensation Lys had ever felt, and though they'd told Bex a thousand times that demons could live through any injury that didn't kill them outright, it was hard to believe when everything felt so cold. Their wounds didn't even hurt anymore. All Lys could feel was numbness and cold, like they'd been turned back into the river clay from which Ishtar had so famously shaped her demons.

That was a beautifully circular thought to end on. But just as Lys was coming to terms with the fact that they'd finally gone and died for their queen, the torn ground beneath their body began to shift. Lys was so weak by this point that it took them several seconds to wake up enough to see the roots that had wrapped around their body.

Lys's blood-deprived brain was still processing that information when Adrian's relieved voice yelled, "*I've got you!*"

Lys blinked in surprise. The words hadn't come through the comm. Adrian was speaking through the roots themselves, his words buzzing against Lys's cold—and no longer glowing—skin like angry bees.

"What were you thinking?" the witch demanded as the roots squeezed tighter. "I asked you to *investigate*, not fight! Why didn't you call for help?"

Because they didn't want to distract him from Bex. Because they didn't want to get anyone else killed. Because there'd been no time. Lys had all kinds of good answers to that question but no breath to speak any of them, so they made do with "Tell Bex I'm sorry."

"You can tell her yourself," Adrian said angrily as his roots curled up to cover Lys's head. "Whose tree do you think you're in? I'm going to try to stop your bleeding now, so hold tight and don't move. This is going to feel pretty weird."

That wasn't much of a threat since Lys couldn't feel anything at the moment. The second the witch stopped speaking, though, Lys felt the tree roots enter the hole in their chest. It felt like worms were invading their body, but while the wiggling was every bit as strange as promised, it wasn't painful. The movement actually felt kind of nice, like Lys's whole being was broken down and returned to the forest. They were relaxing into the sensation when Adrian spoke again.

"I should have checked on you sooner," he muttered, sounding angrier with himself than with Lys. "The damage is much more extensive than I realized. I promise I'll come back and treat you properly soon, but I have to focus on Bex's fight right now. Just stay still and let the roots do their work. They'll keep you together until I return."

Lys could no longer move enough to nod, so they made do with tilting their chin. They were just about to drift away into the beautiful feeling of not being dead when they remembered to say, "Thank you."

"You're very welcome," Adrian replied. "We're a team, aren't we?"

Indeed they were. That was why Lys had been so pissed at him for ignoring Bex back in Seattle. Adrian had certainly redeemed himself now, though, so Lys gave him the greatest gift they could give anyone. They entrusted Bex to his care, closing their eyes as the roots pulled them deeper into the heart tree's protected core.

And above them, on the torn-up moss where they'd just fought, a man's scarred, gold-ringed hand reached quietly through the empty air and retrieved the sword the dead prince had dropped, leaving his son's headless body to rot where he'd been so ignominiously defeated.

Chapter 10

BEX WAS HAVING TROUBLE KEEPING HER FOOTING IN THE RAIN.

The storm seemed to be pouring only on the palace's front plaza, but that actually made the situation worse. Nothing in Heaven was set up to handle weather of any sort, much less torrential rain. There were no drains, no anti-slip texturing, not even an incline to channel runoff. Every floor in the White City was perfectly smooth and flat, so the water just piled up, creating massive puddles over slick white stones. Add in the raindrops slamming into her like bullets, and Bex felt like she was fighting on a Slip 'N Slide at the base of a waterfall.

If it hadn't been working so well, she would've hated it. Demons were sliding and falling every time she looked up, but it didn't matter. The war golems guarding the towers were completely gone, either washed away by the flooding or blasted to pieces by the lightning, and the bone-dragon barrage had obliterated the rows of golden lion cannons on the roof.

With the outer defenses taken care of, that left only the sorcerers inside. Iggs's assault team had already made good headway into the palace, thanks to the Witch of the Future's protections. Spells were flashing like fireworks through the door, but Bex could hear the roar of Iggs's transformed wrath demon followed by the even louder sound of heavy weapons fire. The spells stopped flashing shortly after that as the bulk of the demon army began pouring into the

Tower of the Highest Heaven. Bex would've loved to join them, but she still had an obstacle to overcome.

Despite taking more than twenty hits from the Blade of Wrath, the Prince of Fear was still on his feet. Bex had already driven him to the far end of the palace's walled plaza, but no matter where she struck, the blows never got through. Every time she hit him, the white scales covering his body bent instead of cracking, forming a slick divot that Drox's huge blade slid right out of.

But while that was *very frustrating*, no armor was perfect. She hadn't managed to cut him yet, but Drox's blows were still knocking him around the courtyard. All that trauma had to be doing something. Bex *knew* she'd heard a bone crack at least twice, but every time she was sure she'd knocked him down for good, the prince always got right back up like he hadn't been hit at all.

He must be healing the injuries as soon as we deal them, Drox said in a voice that sounded just as frustrated as she felt. *Go for the neck next. Let's see if he can block a lost head.*

"I *have* been going for the neck," Bex growled, planting her boots on the slick, wet stones as she got ready to take another swing. "But he's too damn slippery to—"

Her complaint cut off with a gasp as the prince lashed out with his white sword, forcing Bex to scramble to the right to avoid contact. That was the other reason she'd yet to land a meaningful blow. Bex could hit the prince all day, but she couldn't afford to *get* hit, because the prince's white sword was a Blade of Gilgamesh. She was stronger and faster than she'd ever been thanks to the six new horns on her head, but none of that mattered if she started piling up unhealable wounds. They were at the foot of Gilgamesh's palace. She didn't have time to take a six-hour soak in Adrian's tub if she broke something. The way things were right now, her only option was to win this fight flawlessly and *quickly*, so Bex stopped worrying about the rain and the magic and the demons fighting in the palace and focused all of her attention on the prince who needed to die.

He must've seen the change, because the moment Bex's hands tightened on her sword hilt, he jumped back to put distance between them and faded into the rain. It was a classic fear-demon move, but Bex wasn't about to be his prey. She lit herself up like a signal flare, digging deep into her frustration to blast her fire so hot that the pouring rain turned to steam before it hit her. This actually made it even harder to see, but the roaring flames expanded her other senses, specifically her sense of touch. Since the fire was part of her, Bex was able to feel the prince's sword enter her flames a full foot away from her actual back, buying herself the split second she needed to whirl around and drive Drox into him instead.

She didn't manage to land the stab, but Drox still hit the Prince of Fear's curved blade, driving its tip into the water-covered ground. Bex stomped her boot on the sword to hold it there and yanked Drox up for a swing at the enemy's center. She'd intended to go for his neck as suggested, but the prince was already yanking his weapon out from under her foot, so Bex went for what she could get and stabbed her sword into his chest instead.

That was the strike she'd been waiting for. Since he'd been restored, Drox was a chopping blade again, not a thrusting one, but that didn't mean he couldn't still run someone through. Bex had driven him straight into the middle of the prince's white-scaled stomach and out the other side, drenching Drox in white blood. She was still savoring the satisfaction of actually doing damage for once when the prince yanked himself off her blade and danced away like being stabbed through the guts was merely a minor inconvenience. He was about to vanish again when Bex lost her temper.

"What in the Hells is wrong with you?" she bellowed, swinging Drox like a bat as she charged after him. "How do you keep *healing*?"

"I'm the Prince of Fear," his disembodied voice reminded her as he faded into the rain once again. "Nightmares wouldn't be scary if they could be killed with brute strength."

"Don't talk like you understand," Bex snarled, pulling Drox into a defensive stance and fanning out her flames to catch the next attack. "That's not your power. You're just a thief like your father."

"It *is* my power," the prince said from behind her, though his voice moved again as soon as Bex spun around. "I am not the oldest or most powerful, but I am the only prince to ever master Fear. My princess killed all her other princes in their sleep because they were unable to understand her."

"Like you'd understand what a *queen* wants," Bex snarled, following the disembodied voice through the rain with the tip of her sword. "She should've killed you too."

"She'll never kill me," the prince replied from her left before flicking to her right. "I'm the only one who can give her what she wants."

"Obnoxious bragging?" Bex guessed as she whirled to slash through the empty air behind her.

"Peace," the prince whispered practically in her ear. "The defeat of the gods at the hands of mere mortals left her traumatized. She was so terrified of us that when the other princes forced her to walk beside them as a princess, she killed them rather than live with the fear. I understood that, so I made her a bargain. If she surrendered her powers, *all* of her powers, to me, I'd never make her wake up again. I'd let her live as a senseless sword, and in return, *I* would be Fear."

"Sounds like a lousy bargain," Bex said as she swung her sword again. "Who'd be afraid of you?"

"Everyone," the Prince of Fear promised. "If the Blackwood traitors hadn't helped you, you'd be crying on your knees in terror before me, because I'm not just a prince of Gilgamesh. I'm the vessel holding the authority Ishtar herself granted to her daughter. I'm *everything* the Queen of Fear used to be before she became too scared of death to use her own powers. Now those powers are mine, and I'm going to use them to add six more horns to my father's trophy wall."

His sword lashed out of the rain as he finished. If Bex hadn't been surrounded by a two-foot-thick wall of flames, he would've sliced the horns off her head before she could duck. Thanks to her fire's warning, she dodged in time, but his sword still got frighteningly close. Close enough for Bex to feel that her sister wasn't really inside the blade.

She was inside of *him*. The indestructible armor that stopped Drox's blows didn't come from the prince's scales. It was the Queen of Fear *inside* the prince's body. That's why he'd been able to heal Bex's damage so quickly. He was using Ishtar's gift of regeneration just like her daughters did.

That thief! Drox roared. *He has no right!*

"He doesn't," Bex agreed, staying low as she moved both hands to Drox's hilt. "But we're not going to get anywhere if we keep attacking like normal. If we want to win this, we've got to hit him so hard that there's nothing left to heal." She braced her feet in the inch-deep water. "Get ready. We're doing the strike that took down the tower again."

That was probably overkill, but the castle-destroying blow she'd used earlier felt like the safest bet. It certainly wasn't as dangerous as grabbing the prince in a bear hug and boiling him to death like she'd done to the first Prince of Greed or turning herself back into the sky-spanning storm of fire that she'd used to char the second. Bex was much more confident in her control these days, but she was also stronger than she'd ever been. A mistake now might burn her entire army to ash along with the enemy, but Drox always knew what he was doing. He wouldn't lose control no matter how hard she swung him, but when Bex dug into herself for the godly power they'd used before, her hands came up empty.

"What the—" she said, spinning to the side to avoid the Prince of Fear's slice at her shoulder. "Where's my fire?"

It's still there, Drox said calmly. *You just can't use it at the moment.*

"Why the Hells not?" Bex cried as she spun again. "I thought I was like Ishtar now!"

You're like her in that all demonkind looks to you for salvation, her sword explained. *But you're not actually a god. The overwhelming fire you used earlier came from the prayers of all the demons in Paradise. They put their faith in you to save them, and so you did. That's how you earned your new crown, but since you're not actually a goddess like Ishtar, that power isn't around all the time. You only get it when people are praying to you, and unfortunately everyone's a little busy right now.*

His blade tilted toward the battle her army was still fighting against Gilgamesh's terrified sorcerers inside the palace, and Bex gritted her teeth.

"Shouldn't you have told me all of that earlier?"

I would have if I'd known, Drox said apologetically. *This is as new to me as it is to you.*

"Well, if I can't shoot a wall of fire, what *can* I do?" Bex asked, turning to parry the white sword as it shot out of the rain again. "You're the only one who can actually see this stuff, so what have I got to work with?"

That's a complicated question, her sword replied. *Give me a moment.*

Bex nodded and assumed a defensive position, but Drox didn't seem to be just distracted while he looked something up. His presence vanished entirely from Bex's mind, leaving her suddenly alone in her skull. She was still trying to get her bearings when something shot out of the pounding rain and crashed into her back.

Fortunately for Bex, it was the prince's scaled foot, not his sword. It would've been game over if he'd planted a Blade of Gilgamesh in her spine. *Un*fortunately, while a kick was much better than a stab, it still sent Bex flying, launching her out of the pounding rain, over the castle wall, and into the clear sky of the empty city beyond.

The moment she left the witch's rainstorm, the prince's fear slammed back down on her like a snapping bear trap. For several horrible seconds, every muscle in Bex's body was locked in terror. She couldn't even curl over to protect her head when she landed, which meant she crashed into the line of mansions outside the palace in the worst way possible, slamming headfirst through a gold-tiled roof.

The impact shattered her skull for a second before her regeneration snapped everything back into place. It still hurt like all the Hells, but the intense pain turned out to be a blessing in disguise, because it shocked Bex out of her overwhelming terror, allowing her to roll back to her feet before the prince landed on top of her.

He came through the hole she'd made like a missile. By dint of pure experience, Bex had rolled to her feet with her sword already in position, but the paralyzing panic from earlier had snuffed her bonfire, leaving her weak and disoriented as the Prince of Fear slammed his white blade into hers.

She barely managed to keep her grip on Drox. Now that she was back under Heaven's clear sky, terror was radiating off the prince's body like cold from an iceberg. It wasn't enough to freeze her completely again—Bex was still a queen herself, after all—but it drained her strength and made her movements sluggish. Every block was a near disaster, and she couldn't hold her ground at all. Each hit drove her backward across the ruined bedroom they'd crashed into. The scaled prince was just about to drive her off the balcony when the intense fear suddenly receded.

Bex had no idea why. Thanks to all the backing up, she was even farther away from the palace now than she'd been when she'd landed. She couldn't even see the witches' rainstorm from this side of the building, so how—

She got her answer when she spotted a line of leaves unfurling along the balcony railing beside her. Bex didn't know when they'd appeared, but the building she'd crashed into was suddenly covered in curling vines. They were all small and new, but the green of their leaves was healthy and shockingly green against the white stone. Their smell was strong as well, an intense mix of resinous sap and grass combined with the familiar loamy scent Bex would never forget even if she reincarnated a thousand more times.

It was the smell of Adrian's forest. She didn't know when it'd happened, but his Blackwood was suddenly all around her, and the stronger its presence grew, the more the prince's fear receded. The rain still hadn't made it over, but so long as the scent of leaves and loam was in Bex's nose, she seemed to be in the clear. Now that she was no longer panicking, it was actually easier to fight under a clear sky than in the pounding rain, so Bex decided to make her stand here, using the prince's momentary surprise at her sudden resurgence to slam Drox into his leg.

She'd hit him with the flat of her blade instead of the edge for maximum concussive damage. Bex knew from experience that shattered bones took a lot more energy to repair than stabs or cuts. If the prince's regeneration worked the same way hers did, then all she had to do was keep breaking him until he no longer had enough energy or quintessence or whatever he was using to heal.

Considering Adrian had had enough magic in his white blood to grow that giant tree plus an entire forest, Bex wasn't sure how realistic that plan was, but it was the best idea she had. She was about to leap on the prince and hit him again when Drox suddenly popped back into her head.

I'm finished.

"Finished with what?" Bex asked as she slammed her blade down like a hammer. Unfortunately, the prince moved at the last second, so she ended up driving Drox into the floor instead. The resulting impact shattered the building they'd been fighting in, forcing Bex to jump out the broken window before she got buried in rubble. She landed on the empty street outside, boots splashing in the river of rainwater that was flowing out of the flooded palace. The green vines were here as well, so at least Bex didn't have to worry about the fear, but she wasn't sure where her opponent was. She was scanning the collapsing building for any sign of where the prince would attack from next when Drox answered her question.

I'm finished with my assessment, he explained calmly. *As the Blade of Wrath, it is my sacred duty to provide you with the best strategy for every encounter. I can't do that without a full understanding of your capabilities, so I also have the ability to assess your divine powers.*

"Great," Bex said, falling into a defensive crouch as she tried to watch every shadow at once. "What's the verdict?"

Complicated, Drox replied. *Your powers as the Queen of Wrath remain unchanged, but there are a lot of new things surrounding them that I've never seen before. It's honestly more information than I was created to handle, so I am not yet able to give a complete analysis of your—*

"The basics will be fine," Bex interrupted, turning in a tight circle. "Just give me an idea what I'm working with now."

It would be easier to say what you aren't *working with,* Drox replied. *You occupy a unique position I've never seen before: greater than any queen but not yet a god. Your abilities seem to fluctuate depending on the amount of faith you're receiving at any given moment. With enough prayers behind you, you should technically be able to do anything that Ishtar could. While your subjects are busy evacuating and fighting, however, it looks like you're limited to the abilities Ishtar granted to demonkind.*

Bex looked at her sword in shock and nearly lost a leg when the Prince of Fear shot out of the alley behind her to take advantage of the lapse.

"Demonkind?" she repeated as she whirled out of the way. "You mean I can armor my skin like a war demon or change my shape like Lys?"

Something like that, Drox muttered in a frustrated voice. *Like I said, your new abilities are very hard to read. I was only made to be Wrath's sword, not all these other demons'. I don't know what to do with their—*

"I do," Bex said, stepping back into an attack position. "Let's give it a try."

Give what a try?

Bex couldn't explain. It was more of a realization than a technique, like suddenly remembering you had toes. They were easy not to think about if she wasn't actively using them, but as soon as Drox had pointed them out, Bex was suddenly aware of a whole new landscape very similar to her fire. Things she simply *was* now, not things she used.

It'd felt so natural she hadn't even noticed, but when Bex reached out for them, the new powers reached back like they'd always been a part of her, flooding her perception with sensations she'd never felt before but that still felt like extensions of her own body. *Literally* her own body, because the very first one Bex tried covered her skin in fear-demon scales that looked just like the prince's. The only difference was that Bex's scales were black instead of Gilgamesh's unholy white. As black as the blood that boiled in her veins when she stopped defending and covered her sword in flames to slice through the buildings where she'd last seen her enemy.

The strike was nowhere near as powerful as the one she'd used to knock down Gilgamesh's tower, but Heaven's over-embellished white mansions were much less sturdy than the palace of its king. One swing was all it took to reduce them to rubble, flushing out the scaled prince, who suddenly looked much less sure of himself.

"You really are a monster, aren't you?" he said, flipping his curved blade over in his hands.

"You should take a look in the mirror," Bex suggested, gripping her own sword.

It was impossible to tell behind his white scales, but Bex swore the prince smiled at that.

"Gilgamesh originally earned his fame as a hero by slaying monsters, you know," he said as he braced his clawed feet. "They were also creations of the gods, tools designed to spread fear so mortals would panic and pray for salvation. My father is the one who freed humanity from such abuses. He's spent his entire life protecting mortals from things like you. Now I shall follow in his footsteps by ending the Queen of the Hells for good."

Bex rolled her eyes behind her new protective scales. She was still trying to process just how far Gilgamesh had misled his son when the Prince of Fear leaped into the air. He kicked off the rubble of the broken building behind him and launched at her from an unexpected angle that forced Bex to roll out of the way before she got skewered.

"Gotta give you credit," she said when she made it back up to her feet. "You're one of the fastest princes I've ever fought. Pretty impressive when you consider how much armor you're wearing, but your speed and scales won't save you from *this*."

She lashed out with her flames, covering the wrecked street in a raging inferno fueled by her wrath at this idiot who was attacking her when Gilgamesh was the monster who needed to be stopped. As always, her flames didn't touch Adrian's plants, but they turned all the luxury goods packed inside the Heavenly mansions into kindling. It was the sort of satisfying power move she'd wanted to pull from the start, but even Bex had a hard time getting a bonfire going in a rainstorm. Out here in the clear, though, nothing was holding her back, so Bex let her fire roar, covering the entire block in a sea of red-hot flames.

"Not so easy to hide in a burning city, is it?" she yelled as she watched the prince jump from house to house ahead of the destruction. "Why are you running, monster hunter? I thought you were going to slay—"

Her taunt turned into a gasp when she felt the prince's white sword cut through her flames like a spear. She'd thought she was looking straight at him, but the Prince of Fear was suddenly behind her. If Bex hadn't been covered in scales of her own now, his blade would've torn straight through her back, but she was more than just her people's wrath now. She was also their fear, a wall against anything that would hurt them, and that wall held firm. Firmer than the prince expected, because he stumbled when his sword slid off her just like Drox had been sliding off his scales all morning, giving Bex the opening she'd been waiting for.

"You want to be like your father?" she yelled, letting go of Drox so she could whip around and grab the prince by his neck. "Then look upon what he has wrought! Let me show you what your king defends, and then we'll see if you want to keep being his loyal servant."

The prince was taller than she was, so Bex couldn't lift him off his feet like she wanted, but that didn't matter. Her new scaled fingers still dug into his neck like daggers, but she didn't rip his head off like her anger was urging her to. She ripped into herself instead, reaching out with Sorrow's power this time as she opened the floodgates and poured five thousand years' worth of suffering straight into the prince's brain.

He screamed as it swallowed him. Bex screamed as well, but she didn't let go. She didn't want to kill a prince who thought he was dying a hero. She wanted him to understand, wanted him to *feel* what her people had suffered at his father's "heroic" hands. The only cure for lies was the truth, so Bex poured it straight down his throat, holding him with one hand while she reached out to her people with the other.

She had to drop her guard to do it, but that didn't matter anymore. The prince was no longer capable of fighting back as Bex reached through the connection she'd forged with every demon who'd given her her name. They were no longer actively praying to her for salvation, but they were all still there, and they answered when Bex called, offering her their sorrow just as readily as they'd offered their wrath.

The result was a wave of tragedy strong enough to wash all of Heaven under. If Bex had been the one being hit, she would've sunk even deeper than she'd fallen when the actual Blade of Sorrow hit her on the chain. Fortunately, she was just the conduit this time, but that was still enough to bring tears to her eyes as she poured her people's sorrow—their suffering, their grief, their loneliness and pain, their lost loved ones, everything Gilgamesh had stolen—into the prince.

They were both on the ground by the time she finished, but Bex was the only one who stood back up. When she finally unclenched her scaled hand from his throat, the Prince of Fear was sobbing in the fetal position. He showed no reaction when she poked him and did not respond when she called his name. Bex was wondering if it was possible for someone to die of grief when a man suddenly stepped up beside her.

"Now you see my princess's suffering."

Bex jumped. She'd assumed the newcomer was Adrian, but Prince Leander was the one standing next to her when she turned her head.

"War wasn't the only one who hated the duty Ishtar sentenced her to," he told her quietly. "Mara despised it as well. Who wouldn't loathe being forced to consume the entire world's sorrow? She only did it because her demons would've had to consume the poison by themselves if she'd abstained, and as you can see from my brother, no one should have to suffer that alone."

"If you want me to apologize, it's not happening," Bex said, pulling back her new scales so Leander could see her face. "He knew what Gilgamesh was doing in the Hells and still supported him. He should feel the pain that he ignored."

"I wasn't asking for mercy," Leander promised as he glared at his sobbing brother. "Fear was my father's loyal dog. Unlike me, he served most eagerly. That's why he was entrusted with the job of guarding the final gate, but..."

He trailed off with a sigh, and Bex looked over just in time to see his gaunt face grow stricken.

"I hate all my fellow princes," he explained at last. "But Mara hated her powers even more. He's sinking in the sea of her sorrow, of all your sorrows." Leander's thin hands squeezed into fists. "Mara never wanted anyone else to feel that way. So please, for her sake, would you put him out of his misery?"

Bex sighed. When Leander put it that way, it did sound monstrous. She hated Gilgamesh with everything she was, but she'd never enjoyed been cruel.

Compassion is a queen's prerogative, Drox agreed. *And you can't get your sister's hand back while her prince is trapped in a sorrow-induced coma.*

"Fair enough," Bex said, trying not to let her relief show on her face as she reached down to press her hand against the prince's scaled forehead.

She felt her people's sorrow the moment she made contact. It was like dipping her fingers into an ocean of suffering, but even though Gilgamesh's loyal prince was the one drowning in it, Bex still hated that all of that pain had come from her demons. The whole reason she was doing this was to free them from such suffering, so Bex did the only queenly duty she'd always been good at.

She burned it.

It took more effort than she was used to. Unlike rage, the tears of sorrow were wet and cold. They didn't burn easily, but Bex had always been a bonfire. Her new name didn't change that, and eventually, everything was consumed. The prince, the sorrow, the suffering, the pain—she ignited them all, transforming the Prince of Fear into a pyre that rose to the sky. She burned until even the ashes were consumed, and when she pulled her flames back at last, the only thing left on the ground was a woman's severed hand curled into a terrified fist.

"It's okay," Bex whispered as she reached down. "I've got you. You don't have to be afraid any—"

A blast of noise knocked her off her feet. It was so loud that Bex didn't even recognize the sound as a bell until she saw Gilgamesh's fingers reaching through the air to grab her sister's hand just like he'd done in Adrian's clearing. Bex surged back to her feet with a roar, but even with all her new powers, she was still too slow. Gilgamesh grabbed the Queen of Fear's hand and vanished before she could reach him, leaving her diving at nothing.

"You *thief*!" she screamed, bellowing up at the golden palace that still towered above them. "I'll burn your whole kingdom to ash!"

"I wonder why he did that," Leander said in a much calmer voice. "Does he still need the queens' hands for something, or did he just not want you to have it?"

"Either way, he's *dead*," Bex snarled, brushing the ash off her tattered clothes.

As always since she'd learned to control it, her fire hadn't touched anything she wasn't furious at, but the fight had still taken a toll on her outfit. Everything was technically still in one piece, but her leggings were sporting some unfashionable new holes, and her beloved black bomber jacket definitely looked worse for wear. That was her fault for wearing it into battle, but the damage on top of Gilgamesh's thievery still had Bex seething as she reached up and mashed the button on her comm.

"Iggs," she barked, "is the fight at the plaza finished yet?"

"Yeah," came the tired reply. "It was rough. The front hall was packed to the rafters with sorcerers, but we pushed them all back with minimal casualties on our side. I'm guessing you took out the prince?"

"Like trash," Bex said, zipping up what was left of her tattered coat. "Leander and I are headed your direction. Don't go any deeper in until we get there."

"We won't," Iggs promised. "We need a breather after that fight anyway. I thought we'd have bigger numbers for the main assault, but half our army still hasn't made it up the damn road. If the witches hadn't rolled in with their death storm, we'd all be goners."

"Good thing we've got reliable allies, then," Bex said, smiling at the swarms of witches she could see flying around on their brooms now that the thunderstorm was breaking apart. "It's like I said back in Adrian's clearing. Gilgamesh made enemies of the entire world, and he's paying the price."

"You reap what you sow," Iggs agreed, his voice oddly tight. "I'm afraid I have to pass out now. See you when I wake up?"

"I'll be there," Bex promised, calling Drox back to her finger as she ran into the still-flooded plaza, leaving Leander trailing far less urgently in her wake.

Chapter 11

THE FRONT OF GILGAMESH'S PALACE was swarming with witches by the time Bex arrived. They were everywhere: using their brooms to sweep the rainwater dumped by the storm into buckets, picking up bones dropped by the undead dragons, helping the vines that grew everywhere get better traction on the palace's smooth white stone. Several were tending to demons who'd been wounded during the assault while others were up on the battlements, sorting through the scrap left by the lightning-struck constructs. A whole team was up on the roof between the towers, taking apart the giant lion cannons with blowtorches, while their cat familiars watched from a safe distance like a line of furry vultures.

It seriously looked like the witches were scrapping Gilgamesh's army for the gold, which Bex found both hilarious and practical. As she'd seen from the Pumpkin Festival, there wasn't much money to be made off a forest, and pillage was the victor's right. Gilgamesh had certainly helped himself when he'd invaded Paradise. Bex found it delightfully appropriate that he should suffer the same, especially since her demons were also helping themselves.

They should be focusing on what comes next, Drox muttered, turning nervously on her hand. *We haven't won yet.*

"Oh, let them have it," Bex scolded, smiling at the demons who were gleefully prying the gold decorations off the palace doors. "They deserve a little joy."

The sight certainly made her smile. They'd been fighting a losing battle for so long that even something as small as stealing Gilgamesh's porch décor felt like a life-changing victory. The forces from the Seattle Anchor were still arriving, which meant most of the demons who'd participated in this fight had come from the Hells. They'd lived and died in toxic darkness, scraping sins out of filthy water, while the warlocks who commanded them lived in luxury. If anyone deserved a little looting, it was them.

"Great Queen."

Bex tore her eyes away from the pillaging just in time to see the war-demon leader Roga kneel at her feet.

"We've taken control of the plaza and the entry halls," he reported as he lowered his helmet of broad, flat horns. "The Queen of Pride and General Iggs await you inside."

Bex arched an eyebrow. She wasn't sure when Iggs had become a general, but she wasn't about to undermine him in front of the war demon. He'd certainly been doing the job, which was good enough for her.

"Thank you, Captain Roga," she said, looking over her shoulder at the river of demons that was still marching toward the palace from the giant tree. "I want you to hold this position and organize the new arrivals. We'll use this opportunity to rebuild our forces while I go find our next target."

"Yes, Great Queen," the war demon said, then he flicked his dark eyes up. "Um, about the looting. Should we—"

"It's fine," she assured him as her face split into a grin. "This city was built on our people's backs. Way I see it, they're just taking back what's owed."

The war demon looked extremely relieved to hear that, probably because it meant he wouldn't have to tell a bunch of delighted demons they had to stop.

"Just keep order and don't let any fights break out," she said. "I'm going to talk to our allies."

The captain ducked his horns again and turned around, yelling to his troop of war demons that the queen had given her permission. This caused a huge cheer as the war demons ran off to join the others in stripping Gilgamesh's palace. Bex watched them go with a grin as she crossed the still-wet plaza to the white steps of the palace's main door, where the three Old Wives of the Blackwood were waiting with their brooms.

The moment Bex's boot touched the first stair, all three witches turned to look at her like their heads were attached to the same string. That would've been spooky if Bex hadn't already heard them finishing each other's sentences during the big curse earlier and pretty much every other time they did something important. She'd already secretly started thinking of them as three faces of the same lady anyway, so this was par for the course. Bex was much more concerned to see that Adrian wasn't waiting with them.

"Where is—"

"Inside," the Witch of the Future said before Bex could finish.

"He's the only one of us who can go in," the Witch of the Present explained. "It seems Gilgamesh has banned all daughters of the Blackwood from entering his palace."

"Wisest move he's made in years," the Witch of the Past agreed, pushing her stringy white hair away from her face as she stared up at the towers. "Pity. There's a lot of good bones in there."

She finished with a hungry smile, and Bex caught her flinch just in time.

"Thank you for your help earlier," she said, bowing her horns as much as she dared with so many demons watching. "We couldn't have taken the plaza without you."

"I'm glad we were able to put our ancient spite to good use," Agatha said, glancing through the open doorway. "Especially since it doesn't look like we'll be able to be of further assistance."

"If we could storm the palace ourselves, we wouldn't have needed Adrian or the queen," Muriel reminded her sisters. "There've been some variations, but all the main parts are still going according to plan." She turned back around to Bex before lowering her head just as slightly as Bex had dipped her horns. "This means the future of our coven is now in your hands. We wish you good luck, Queen of All Demons."

The other witches bowed as well, and Bex stepped back in alarm. "Just my hands? Does that mean you're done?"

"Hardly," Lydia said, glaring at Bex with blue eyes that gleamed like cold gems in her wrinkled face. "Who do you think is going to hold the line out here? Or keep ferrying your refugees back to the land of the living? Just because we can't storm the fortress with you doesn't mean we're not fighting."

"I didn't mean that," Bex said swiftly. "It's just..."

She'd hoped for more help. The witches' magic had been incredible. If it'd just been her and her demons, Bex doubted they could've taken the palace steps without heavy casualties, much less pushed inside. They'd made progress faster than she'd ever dreamed, but even with more demons coming up the tree roots to join them every minute, there was still a lot of palace left to cover.

"Don't make that face," Muriel said. "It's not as if we're abandoning you. In addition to holding the city, as my sister said, we're lending you our best weapon. Adrian was chosen for this. He will not fail us, or you."

"I never thought he would," Bex said, pulling her tattered coat tighter around her shoulders. "Guess I'm going in, then. Thanks for all the help."

The three witches nodded in unison, but when Bex started up the stairs toward the palace's towering doors, a bitter voice spoke behind her.

"Is that all you have to say?"

The words were sharp as steel knives, and Bex looked over her shoulder to see Leander standing at the bottom of the steps, staring up at the three witches with centuries of anger etched into his gaunt face.

"I'm standing right here," he told them. "A son of your own Blackwood, a child you gave away, yet you have more words for the demon than you do for me." He clenched his fists tight. "Have you nothing else to say for yourself, *Mother*?"

The witches of the Past and Future looked away, but the Witch of the Present, the target of his words, stared him down with cold blue eyes.

"No."

Leander flinched like the word was a physical blow, but Agatha's expression didn't soften.

"I would never insult my children by asking their forgiveness," she said. "I cannot ask it, because I am not sorry. I am a mother, yes, and a sister and a woman in my own right. But before all of that, I am a witch. The love I bear for you and all my sons is buried with my heart beneath the Blackwood. A sacrifice to the Great Forest, just like the rest of my flesh."

"Is that supposed to comfort me?" the prince spat.

"Acts of war comfort no one," the witch replied. Then, to Bex's shock, she lowered her eyes. "But I am sorry you turned out so kind, Leander. Most of the sons I bore Gilgamesh were happy to enter his service. I even let him name all of you so I would be less inclined to grow attached. It mostly worked, with two exceptions. Adrian was the second, but you were the first."

Her hands tightened on her owl-carved broomstick. "You were a thoughtful, clever child, and your witchcraft was so beautiful. I would have kept you with me if I could, but the time was not yet right, so I obeyed my sisters and let you go."

"Gilgamesh had already seen your potential," Lydia said. "He would have killed us for keeping such a sorcerer from him."

"Agatha has always been weak when it comes to her children," Muriel agreed. "That's why we are Three. Two can be strong when one is not."

"Forgive me if I don't find that inspiring," Leander growled, stomping up the stairs so that his back was to all three witches. "You're no family of mine," he declared when he reached the top, placing a hand on Bex's shoulder. "Mara's little sister is dearer to me than any of you, and kinder to those in her care. I have disagreed with Gilgamesh on every principle of my life, but in one judgement he was entirely correct." He cast a final glare over his shoulder. "The Blackwoods are all heartless witches."

The Old Wives said nothing in reply. They simply stood on the steps, watching Leander's back as he vanished through the palace doors. A few seconds later, Bex ran after him, chasing nervously after Adrian's brother as he turned the corner and came to a sudden stop.

"Hey," she whispered, her head turning frantically between the plaza outside and the prince in front of her, who stood with his fists clenched and his shoulders shaking like he wanted to scream. "Are you—"

"I have nothing more to say," he informed her crisply. "Go ahead and find the others. I'd like a minute alone."

Bex held up her hands at once, backing away from the former Prince of Sorrow like he was an unexploded bomb before she turned and hurried deeper down the gold-decorated hall that her grinning demons were gleefully tearing apart.

It didn't take long to find Iggs and Adrian. Bex only had to turn one corner and there they were, together in the middle of a huge hall that looked like a ballroom that had been set on fire. Iggs was still in his big red form, lying on his back with Adrian right beside him and Boston floating above his head on Bran, keeping watch from above.

"Hey!" Bex shouted as she jogged over. "Man, am I glad to see..."

Her voice trailed off in horror as she got close enough to see what had been hidden by Adrian's back.

"*Iggs!*" she screamed, sprinting the rest of the way to his side. "What happened to you?"

"I'm fine," her demon croaked, opening one swollen eye to give Bex a gap-toothed grin. "It was only a few sorcerers."

"A *few*?" Bex repeated, staring at his body, every inch of which was covered in third-degree burns, stab wounds, and foot-wide bruises. "You look like you got hit by an entire Anchor all at once!"

"The hallway was pretty packed," Iggs admitted with a wince. "But I was already in a full rage by that point, so I just went for it."

"He took them all on," Nemini said, appearing out of the shadows behind the shattered door to Bex's left. "The war demons were quite impressed."

"Hells yeah, they were impressed," Iggs said proudly, raising his battered arm. "The demons of Wrath are second to none when it comes to—"

"Stop moving," Adrian snapped in his terse doctor voice, reaching up to snatch Iggs's arm back down before returning to the green salve he'd been smearing frantically all over Iggs's torso.

"Will he be okay?" Bex asked nervously.

"He'll be fine if he *stops moving*," the witch growled as he started rubbing the salve in with both hands like Iggs was a lump of bread dough. "Believe it or not, this is already much better than he looked when I arrived. Demonic regeneration is truly a miracle. He should be back on his feet in two hours if he can just hold still and not interrupt the process."

"And I keep telling you, we don't *have* two hours," Iggs growled back. "Look over there."

He jerked his head toward the other end of the room, pointing with his horns, since he couldn't move his hands. When Bex tore her eyes off his mesmerizingly horrific injuries long enough to see why, she spotted a huge stone staircase leading down.

"What's that?"

"The entrance to the chains," Iggs explained. "The sorcerers I fought were just the rear guard. By the time we made it into the palace, most of Heaven had already gone down the chains back to Earth."

"So?" Bex said, failing to see the problem. "I don't care if they run. Fewer enemies is better for us, and the residents of Heaven have always been cowards." She frowned. "Honestly, I'm most shocked that Gilgamesh had allowed it. I thought he'd order his followers to fight to the death, not buy them time to escape."

"They're not escaping," Adrian said, keeping his eyes on his work. "They're the counterattack."

He lifted one green-smeared finger to point at the enormous pile of empty golden chests lying along the burned room's wall.

"Those boxes were filled with quintessence the last time I came through here. Normally, the residents of Heaven are too dependent on the magic of Paradise to leave it. With that much quintessence, though, they can do anything. Go anywhere." He curled his salve-covered hand into a fist. "I can already feel them through my tree. They're attacking the main Blackwood."

"What?" Bex said.

"Gilgamesh is attacking the Blackwood," Adrian repeated, looking up at her with wild eyes. "He didn't just seal his palace to keep us out. He was guarding his advance. Other than the sorcerers who stayed behind to support the Prince of Fear, this whole fortress is empty! He used the time we spent getting ready to move his own people—the original army that conquered Heaven—into position to attack our forest!"

"No," Bex said, stumbling backward. "That can't be right. Why would the witches be here if that was happening? Doesn't your aunt see the future?"

"They're here because they made a choice," Nemini answered before Adrian could. "Gilgamesh's primary goal is to stop us from interrupting him. That's why he's attacking the Blackwood after five thousand years of ignoring it. He's trying to get us to turn around."

"He's doing a damn good job!" Bex yelled in a panic. "If what Adrian's saying is true, I just sent all our wounded into a war zone!"

"They're not in danger yet," Adrian said, determinedly staring at his work as his hands moved faster and faster. "My roots connect to the center of the Blackwood, and I just felt the attack begin. Gilgamesh's sorcerers will have to cut through twenty miles of old-growth forest before they reach the demons in the heart grove."

"And there are still witches in the Blackwood," Boston added from his perch on Bran's broomstick. "The Old Wives would never leave the forest completely unprotected. The Three probably brought just enough people here with them to safely cast the Witch's Spite."

"That's still too many," Adrian said as his hands started to shake. "We're the biggest coven in the world, but we're not an army. There can't be more than a hundred witches left in the main grove."

"There's other things as well," Boston argued. "I was wondering why the Old Wives didn't bring the living dragons as well as the dead ones, but now I understand. They left them behind to counter the counter."

"If the dragons were capable of defeating Gilgamesh, they wouldn't be hiding in our forest," Adrian countered grimly as he smeared the last of the salve under Iggs's neck. "Honestly, at this point, distance is our best defense. The main Blackwood spans hundreds of miles. Even stacked with quintessence, it'll take Gilgamesh's soldiers a while to cut through that much forest. I already talked to my mother, but she says they're not going back. Nemini is right. The Old Wives have already made their bet." He looked up at Bex. "We have to defeat Gilgamesh before his army reaches the forest's heart."

"Okay," Bex said as she processed all of that. "How long does that give us?"

"Depends on whether they have a prince with them or not," Adrian said as he cleaned the last of the salve off his hands with a handkerchief from his coat of infinite pockets.

"Gilgamesh has gotta be running short on sons by now," Iggs insisted. "I saw the Prince of Hate eat it with my own eyes, and Leander's with us, so that's two down."

"I don't think Greed is back, either," Adrian said, thinking. "At least, I didn't see him during the week I was here. Bex beat the Princess of War earlier, but she's paired with Alexander. He's Gilgamesh's Crown Prince, so he's probably still active, but Lys killed the Prince of Lust, so that's another one—"

"Wait, Lys killed a prince?" Bex interrupted. "When did that happen?!"

"Just a few minutes ago," Adrian said. "I felt someone messing with my tree, so I asked them to check it out."

Bex went still. "You sent Lys to fight a prince alone?"

"Not on purpose!" he cried, waving his hands. "I didn't know it was a prince yet! And by the time I found out, Lys had already won."

Her whole body was shaking by the time he finished. "So they didn't... Lys is still..."

"Lys is still alive," Adrian assured her with a smile. "They've got multiple Blade of Gilgamesh wounds now, but I've wrapped them in my roots to keep them stable. After we win here, I'll go back and heal them fully, but they won't die so long as my tree stands."

Bex's shoulders slumped in relief. "I was wondering why they hadn't said anything over the comm in a while," she muttered, rubbing her hands over her face. "I should have checked in on them sooner, should've been more careful. Lys could've died, and I wouldn't even—"

"They didn't want to distract you," Adrian said, wrapping his arm around her shoulders. "They didn't tell me what they were doing either. By the time I realized the fight was happening, it was already over. But everything turned out okay! Lys is going to be fine, and they *won*. I'm still not sure what the Prince of Lust was trying to do, but I'm pretty sure Lys's quick thinking saved my tree, and all of us."

"Of course they did," Bex said, scrubbing her eyes. "Lys has always been a hero."

"And it's about time they added a prince to their trophy list," Iggs added with a smile of his own. "You realize they're going to be insufferable after this, right?"

"I can't wait," Bex said, grinning at her demon as she pushed back to her feet. "I got the Prince of Fear, by the way."

Adrian blinked at her. "What?"

"For our prince count," she clarified. "I killed Fear, and there never was a Prince of Pride, so if War's prince is still in the palace, that only leaves Envy unaccounted for."

"I don't think he'd go to the Blackwood," Adrian said, tapping his wooden pinky thoughtfully against the polished floor. "Envy's the prince who almost killed me when I stuck my head through the door at the bottom of the Seattle Anchor. I'm pretty sure he's in charge of the black desert where all the chains come together, and from the state of his armor, I don't think he ever leaves it."

"That's great," Iggs said as he pushed himself into a sitting position. "If there's no prince in the attack force and Heaven's not coming out of the sky to blast them, I bet the Blackwood can hold off Gilgamesh's army no problem."

"Not when they've only got a skeleton crew," Adrian said, glaring sharply at Iggs until the demon got the message and lay back down again. "Not having a prince will slow Heaven's forces down, but unless we all go back right now, the Blackwood is as good as lost, which is the whole reason Gilgamesh is attacking it. He wants us to turn around and give up the assault."

"Which means that's the last thing we should do," Bex said, looking up at the scorched ceiling. "It feels weird to say, but I'm glad Gilgamesh is being so ruthless. It proves we're on the right track. The Blackwood's where he gets his princes. He'd never burn that bridge unless he was desperate."

"Or he felt its loss was inevitable anyway," Nemini pointed out in her usual monotone.

"The Blackwood did attack him first," Adrian agreed. "But he was already moving his forces into position well before I grew my tree, so..." His voice trailed off as he shook his head. "You know what? It doesn't matter. No matter what Gilgamesh is, was, or will be doing, we still have to stop him, so let's just focus on that."

"Works for me," Bex said, rising back to her feet. "First step is to find him. The Morrigan said to follow the chains, so let's start there. They're down those stairs, right?"

Adrian nodded and rose to his feet as well. Iggs, however, looked panicked. "You can't go down there alone!" he cried, flopping on his back like a bandaged fish. "That's where all the sorcerers ran!"

"I wouldn't be much of a queen if I was afraid of a few sorcerers," Bex reminded him. "And I wasn't planning to go alone. Adrian and Nemini are coming with me. Leander's here, too, but he's working through some stuff, so we'll leave him as a backup for now."

"Stuff?" Adrian repeated with a worried look.

"He ran into your mom," Bex explained. "It wasn't a pleasant reunion."

Adrian winced. "I can see how he'd need a moment after that. Is he going to be okay?"

"I have no idea," Bex said honestly. "But he's still going to fight, so that's good enough for now. We'll swing back and pick him up once we know where we're going. Iggs, you lie there and make sure no one follows us. Call me on the comm if anything happens."

"Yes, my queen," Iggs replied, bowing his horns as far as he was able on his back.

"Boston, you and Bran stay with him," Adrian ordered. "Make sure he doesn't move."

Iggs scowled at that. Boston, however, looked incredibly relieved. "I'll take utmost care of the patient," he promised, hopping off the broom to sit on Iggs's bandaged chest, which made Bex's cat-loving demon suddenly look much less mad about being left behind. "Good luck."

Adrian nodded and turned toward the stairs, offering his hand to Bex as he went.

She took it without hesitation. "Thank you for saving Lys," she whispered as they walked across the room. "And Iggs. And me, while I'm at it. Your vines pushed back the prince's fear."

"That was Aunt Muriel's magic," he insisted, squeezing her fingers. "I merely provided the foundation, but I'm happy it worked. We'd never actually cast the Witch's Spite before."

"Hell of a first run," Bex said as they started down the giant staircase, which was even more blackened and battle-scarred than the rest of the room. "Is this big walkway how Heavenly citizens got down to the Anchor Markets?"

"Yes," Adrian said. "Or at least, that's what I assume it's for. These stairs were closed off the last time your princess dragged me through this part of the palace."

"Don't mention her," Bex said with a shudder. "Just thinking about Gilgamesh making a princess version of me still gives me the creeps."

"She was never you," Adrian assured her. "But she was *definitely* creepy."

Despite just asking him not to talk about it, Bex wanted to hear more. She wanted to talk to Adrian about all sorts of things, but there was no time. The chamber at the bottom of the scorched staircase was already coming into view.

Like everything she'd seen in Gilgamesh's palace so far, it was enormous. Between the soaring ceiling and the long list of destinations carved into the floor, Bex felt like she was walking into a station from the grand age of railroads. The room's circular walls were pierced with multiple doorways leading to hallways that were lined with even more doors, which Bex presumed were the entrances to all the various Anchors. But while she spotted plenty of good places for an ambush, she didn't see any chains, or any people. Either the sorcerers Iggs mentioned earlier had already fled down to Earth or there was another level to this place. She was looking around for a second staircase when she finally spotted someone.

Bex had no idea how she hadn't noticed him sooner. The man was directly ahead of them at the dead center of the giant circular room. He was kneeling on the ground with his head bowed all the way over so that his forehead was pressed flat against the marble. Between the humble position and his filthy clothes, Bex's first thought was that he was a demon slave who'd been left behind when all the masters ran. Then she saw the white sword lying on the ground beside him.

Her boots squeaked to a stop on the slick-polished floor. Adrian froze a second later, his blue-gray eyes flying wide. Nemini was the only one who didn't seem surprised. She simply moved a little closer to Bex, her snakes hissing protectively on her head as the bowing prince lifted his empty, dirty hands and said,

"I surrender."

Chapter 12

"WHAT DID YOU JUST SAY?" Bex demanded.

"I surrender," the prince repeated, finally sitting up to show them his mirrored eyes, which weren't even looking at Adrian yet but still managed to make his whole body tremble.

It was a natural reaction. Adrian had only spoken to this prince for less than a minute of real time, but he'd stared at his dirty face for what felt like hours during the Walking Memory. His armor was even dirtier than the last time Adrian had seen it, so coated in black dust that the ornate gold was no longer visible. He looked more like a coal miner than a son of Gilgamesh, but it was impossible for Adrian to forget the prince who'd almost killed him with a single flick to the forehead. That was *definitely* the man from the chain desert, the Prince of Envy.

"You're surrendering?" Bex said, her voice deeply skeptical. "Why?"

"Because you are here," the prince replied. "The Prince of Fear would die before he allowed the Coward Queen to enter the Palace of Heaven, so if you are standing before me, that must be what has happened." He glanced at the white sword on the floor beside him, and then he bowed his head again. "My brother is a much better fighter than I am. If he couldn't beat you, I have no hope. All I can do is put myself at your mercy and beg you not to cut the chains."

Adrian let out a relieved breath. *That* was why the prince was acting this way. He still thought Bex was here to destroy the chains and bring back the gods. That idea was totally off the table now that Bex had told him what Ishtar had said about resetting the world, but the Prince of Envy didn't know that. If the chains were still his primary concern, maybe he could be reasoned with. He certainly didn't seem as fanatical as other sons of Gilgamesh Adrian had met. But before he could tell the Prince of Envy they weren't here for the chains, so there was no reason to do anything extreme, Bex beat him to the punch.

"The chains are worth that much to you?"

"They are worth more than life itself," the still-bowing prince replied. "Gilgamesh's chains are the only protection this world has against the return of the divine tyrants. I know you think the gods will restore your kind to Paradise, but their rule was anything but paradise for humanity. The fact that Gilgamesh was able to free us from their hold once is the miracle of our race. I'm not so cocky as to think we'll be so lucky twice."

He pressed his head even harder against the floor. "Please, Queen of Wrath. I'll do anything you say. Just please don't cut the chains. Don't bring the cruel gods back to trample everything humanity has built."

"Anything, huh?" Bex said, pulling Drox into her hand and tapping his black blade against her shoulder as she made a show of thinking the prince's words over. "All right. I'll spare the chains, but in return, you have to call off the attack on the Blackwood."

The bowing prince shook his head. "I cannot. Only the king himself can end an operation that's already underway."

"Then take me to Gilgamesh and I'll tell him myself," Bex offered with a smile. "Do it quick, or I'm chopping this whole place apart."

It took every bit of Adrian's self-control not to gape at her in wonder. That was the most bald-faced lie he'd ever heard Bex tell, but it wasn't a half-bad one. If this prince really was the true-blue Gilgamesh believer he appeared to be, then he'd have no doubt that his king could easily defeat the Coward Queen, which meant he might actually do as she said.

Sure enough, the Prince of Envy nodded immediately and pushed up from his bow. "My father is a wise and civilized king," he said with a relieved smile. "He despises war in all its wasteful forms, so I'm certain he'd be willing to negotiate if you came to him in good faith. Call off the demons who are ransacking his palace and send the witches back to their tree, and I'll take you to King Gilgamesh."

Bex shook her head. "That wasn't part of the deal. You take me to Gilgamesh now—the *actual* Gilgamesh, not his throne room or his study or his Crown Prince stand-in, but the man himself—or I chop everything you just bowed your head to protect."

The prince heaved a long sigh. "Very well," he said, wiping the black grime from his gloved hands. "I'll take you straight to him. Just put away your—"

"Don't listen to him."

The dirty prince stopped with a jolt, his grimy face—which had just been the picture of defeated resignation—twisting into a hateful scowl as Leander marched down the stairs.

"He's lying to you," Leander said as he stomped into the room. "That is Hector, Prince of Envy, and the chains aren't the only realm he looks after. He's the custodian of all of Gilgamesh's sacred spaces. If you follow where he leads, he'll strand you in an endless labyrinth between worlds until you die of starvation."

"I see you've turned full traitor, Leander," the Prince of Envy spat, snatching his arm down to grab his sword, only to come up empty. The white blade that had been lying on the floor beside him was now clutched in Nemini's hands where she stood behind Bex, who no longer looked like she was bluffing about chopping everything apart.

"Gotta admit, you almost had me for a moment," Bex said, pulling Drox off her shoulder to point his black blade at the scowling prince. "Was all that stuff about protecting the chains a lie as well?"

"Absolutely not," the Prince of Envy insisted, pulling himself up straight and proud even though his hands were still empty. "The chains that hold the Wheel of Reincarnation are the greatest creation of Heaven and the only thing that protects humanity from being the playthings of the gods. Not that my demon-loving brother cares about that. Leander would sacrifice every human on the planet if his precious Mara asked him to, and he'll do the same to you if you get in his way."

"Big words from a liar," Bex said as she stalked closer to the dirty prince. "But I don't care about cutting chains anymore. I'm here to kill Gilgamesh, and while I'm sure he's very hidden, I also know that the chains are how I get to him. You're just the person standing in my way, so either you get out of it or…"

Her voice trailed off as she slammed Drox's point into the floor. It didn't look like she'd hit the marble that hard to Adrian, but either the stone was weak here or those six horns had boosted her strength even more than he'd realized, because the entire circular chamber cracked when her sword came down. She was about to hit it again when the Prince of Envy threw out his hands.

"*Stop!*" he cried. "Please, Queen of Wrath, you don't know the calamity you're courting! The Wheel has already been strengthened by the water and life the witches brought with them into Heaven. The chains are at their limit. If you jostle them now, the bound Cycle of Reincarnation could break free completely and all the gods will return, but *not* as your saviors. They hate what humanity has become and will use their power to reset the world and everyone in it. You, me, the Blackwoods, your demons—everyone will die if you let them rise!"

"I'm already aware," Bex said, moving her sword back to her shoulder. "But what *you* don't understand yet is that Gilgamesh is planning to do the same thing."

For the first time since they'd arrived, the Prince of Envy looked genuinely surprised. "That's ridiculous," he said. "Gilgamesh is the Eternal King, humanity's champion. More importantly, he already has all the power he could ever want. He would never throw away his throne."

"That's where you're wrong," Adrian said, stepping forward to stand beside Bex. "I've spent a lot of time with our father lately, and he's anything but satisfied. You accuse Leander of being a slave to his princess, but Gilgamesh is the one who'd *actually* sacrifice the world to get what he wants, and you're standing here fighting to let him."

"Shut up," the Prince of Envy snarled. "What do you know? You're not even a real prince. You're just the tool Father used to repair the Queen of Pride's horns, which you then *stole* and put back on her head!"

He pointed at Nemini, who shrugged.

"You've always been in the demons' pocket," the prince went on. "You even became their queen's lover! You're no better than our harlot of a mother, but unlike the rest of you degenerates, *I* know what has to be done. You think I'm unaware of our father's true nature? I've known he was a lying, despotic king from the day he first brought me here, but I still follow him because, for all his faults, Gilgamesh is the only one who can protect us from the gods. He's the strongest human that's ever lived, and unlike *her*"—he stabbed his finger at Bex—"he's actually on our side. He dreams of ruling humanity, not destroying it. I'd bet our future on his greed any day, and I'll *never* let you reach him!"

He yanked his arm back as he finished, and the white sword in Nemini's hands exploded into a white-carved woman. She was the dirtiest princess Adrian had ever seen, with lines of black sin-iron dust caked into all the carved folds of her dress. Her body was cracked and battered like she'd been rolled down a mountain, but her golden eyes were calm and deadly as she kicked her way out of Nemini's grasp and ran to her prince. She turned back into a sword the second he touched her, and the Prince of Envy lurched down to plunge his blade—which was long, thin, and tapered like a giant needle—into the stone Bex had already cracked.

The moment the Blade of Envy struck it, the floor beneath their feet vanished. Not broke, not gave out, *vanished*, leaving Adrian frantically waving his arms as he began to fall. The Prince of Envy smirked at his distress from his perch on the one remaining spot of solid ground, which looked like a circle of stone floating in the air. The rest of the giant arrival hall was gone, leaving everybody but the enemy prince falling into what appeared to be an enormous sandstone cavern with an ancient city nestled far, far at the bottom.

The change was so unexpected, it actually shocked Adrian out of his panic. He had no idea what had just happened, but the Prince of Envy was now high above them, left behind as Adrian, Bex, Nemini, and Leander plummeted down the cavern toward the city like coins tossed into a well. Adrian was kicking himself for leaving Bran behind with Boston when Leander grabbed him by his coat sleeve and yelled, *"Fifty Steps of the Pilgrim!"*

Adrian's stomach lurched with the familiar swinging feeling of teleportation. Unlike all the times he'd moved himself, though, there was no ringing bell. This was simply a blip, like he'd been inside the eye of the world when it blinked, and then suddenly he and Leander were falling through the air *above* the Prince of Envy.

The filthy prince had just enough time to look up in surprise before they landed on top of him. The giant sandstone cavern vanished a second later, returning the arrivals room to its previous state as the three sons of Gilgamesh fell sprawling onto the cracked floor.

"*You*," Envy snarled, shoving Leander off him as he raised his long, needle-sharp white sword again. "Sorcery won't save you this—"

"*Binding of Deepest Bedrock*," Leander replied, looking at his brother with a superior smile.

The sneer fell off the Prince of Envy's face. Adrian was feeling pretty shocked as well, but he didn't let that slow him down as he dived behind the brother who wasn't actively trying to murder him.

"What does that spell do?" he whispered frantically.

"It prohibits movement," Leander replied with the smuggest grin Adrian had ever seen. "Until I revoke it, no one who has heard my voice can walk more than ten paces from their original position. Just look at your feet."

Adrian glanced down in alarm. Sure enough, his black boots were ringed with ghostly chains. He couldn't feel them while he was standing still, but when he jumped back in surprise, the transparent chains tightened like a slipknot. He could still move if he pushed, but the binding pulled tighter with every step, and his face broke into a smile.

"Nice work," he told his brother. "But why did you trap us as well? And why didn't you teleport Bex or Nemini?"

"Because that's how the Binding of Deepest Bedrock works," Leander replied with a shrug. "And because you were the only person close enough for me to grab before we fell out of range. Trust me, I'd much rather have gotten one of the queens."

Adrian felt the same. "Where did they go?" he asked nervously, reaching down to touch the now solid-seeming marble under his feet. "What was that place?"

"I'm not sure," Leander said, keeping his mirrored eyes on the Prince of Envy, who was standing at the far edge of the binding, muttering his own sorcery under his breath. "As keeper of Gilgamesh's private spaces, Envy has access to all manner of pockets and subworlds that our father created to house his projects over the years. The Hells, the chain desert, Limbo, even Heaven itself are all created spaces and thus technically part of Envy's domain, but there are hundreds more, most of which are top secret. That cavern, for example, was nowhere I've ever seen before."

"Well, we need to figure out how to get back to it," Adrian said anxiously. "Bex and Nemini are trapped down there!"

"I'd love to," Leander said. "But..."

His mirrored eyes flicked to the white sword in Envy's hands, and Adrian sighed.

"Right then," he muttered, moving closer to his brother. "What's the plan?"

"Be very careful," Leander whispered, never taking his eyes off his brother's sword. "The Princess of Envy is a contrary creature. She always longs to be somewhere else, which is what allows her to move between so many different places. She can cut a path to any location her wielder is aware of, but her true power is jealousy."

Adrian scowled. "How is being jealous a power?"

Before Leander could answer, the Prince of Envy whirled around. Whatever sorcery he'd been muttering must not have been able to beat Leander's, because the prince lashed out at Adrian with his sword instead. Adrian instinctively tried to defend with his own sorcery before remembering he couldn't do that anymore. He'd used up every drop of his white quintessence blood growing his new tree, which meant he was back to being just a witch.

Under any other circumstance, Adrian would've counted that as a major win. In the current situation, however, it was a serious problem. He'd grown his vines all the way around the palace by this point, but this room was made of solid stone with no windows or skylights. He'd loaded his coat with fresh spell reagents when he'd stopped by his cabin before the assault, but it was all raw materials. He hadn't had time to prepare any throwable curses, and he didn't think his brother would be polite enough to wait while he set one up. But just as Adrian was realizing that his lack of preparation was about to get him killed just like Boston had always said it would, Leander shouted at the top of his lungs.

"*Ishtar's Charging Bull!*"

Sorcery leaped from his words, and a giant spectral bull appeared in front of Adrian, its curved horns already in position to knock the Blade of Envy away. The spell's shape hadn't even finished solidifying, though, when the needle-sharp Blade of Envy shimmered like a mirror, and a *second* sorcerous bull appeared, colliding with Leander's in a blast of sorcerous power that knocked all three princes flat on their backs.

Adrian was the first to get back up. He scrambled to help Leander next, hauling the prince, who'd been lying at the edge of the glowing binding's range like he'd just been run over by a truck, back to his feet.

"I see what you meant now about jealousy being Envy's power," he said as he steadied his brother's weight. "She's a mirror sword."

"She's much worse than that," Leander warned, clinging hard to Adrian's arm. "The Blade of Envy doesn't just duplicate attacks. She adds her prince's sorcery on top as well. As you just saw, any sorcery I throw will bounce back with the same strength I used *plus* the Prince of Envy's." He shook his head with a grimace. "We should call for help."

"Help from whom?" Adrian demanded. "I'm the only Blackwood who can enter the palace, Iggs is injured, and the rest of the demons can't stand up to a prince. Even if they could overwhelm him with numbers, he'd just teleport them all to Limbo or somewhere even worse."

"Then what do you suggest we do?" Leander snapped. "Because unless you want to get blasted to the floor again, my sorcery is useless."

Adrian fell silent. He still had the comm Bex had given him in his ear. One tap was all it would take to call Iggs and tell him to send Boston or the war-demon captain or anyone else to help. That felt like the strategic move, but Adrian hated the idea of calling Bex's people into a battle they couldn't win.

He didn't like any of his options, but Adrian was going to have to come up with something soon, because the Prince of Envy was already back on his feet. He lurched at them with a snarl, straining against Leander's invisible chains as he struggled to get within striking distance. And it was there, watching Envy's jaw clench as he tried his hardest to murder his brothers, that Adrian got his idea.

"I know attack sorcery is out," he whispered to Leander as he pulled them both to the farthest end of the binding spell's ten allowed steps, "but you can still cast defensive spells, right?"

"Sure, if you want to hide in a cage while that filthy fanatic beats his way to us," Leander grumbled.

"A cage would be perfect, actually," Adrian said with a smile. "Do it."

Leander looked at him like he was crazy. He must have truly been at his wit's end, though, because he did as Adrian asked, speaking a line of sorcery that went much too fast for Adrian's sorry understanding of ancient Sumerian to follow. The moment the final word left his lips, a ring of stone sprang from the floor and flew toward the ceiling like a spear, closing the two brothers inside a cylinder of what appeared to be solid granite.

"There," Leander gasped as he fell back to his knees. "That's the biggest Seven Walled City I can manage. Envy isn't an idiot like Hate, though, so it won't take him long to—"

"I don't need long," Adrian promised as he closed his eyes. "Just watch my back."

He heard Leander squawk in protest, but Adrian was already gone, leaving his body behind as he plunged himself into the embrace of his new forest.

Bex was falling toward a city she'd never seen before. She had no idea where she was or how the Prince of Envy had dropped them here, but she was picking up speed at a terrifying pace. Whatever was happening, it would definitely end in a splat if she didn't do something fast, so Bex kicked her confusion out of the way and called as much fire as she could.

The blast of flame lit up the entire cavern like a miniature sun, but at least it stopped her fall. She was still adjusting the burn to a level that would keep her hovering without cooking everything else in the vicinity when two arms suddenly came out of nowhere to wrap around her neck. The rest of Nemini followed immediately after, falling out of Bex's shadow until the other queen was clinging to her back like a monkey.

"Where are we?"

"I was hoping you could tell me," Bex said, turning up her fire again to compensate for the added weight. "Where's Adrian?"

She was certain he'd been right beside her when the floor vanished, but Bex didn't see Adrian or Leander anywhere up here or down in the strange city below. But while it was a huge relief not to see his body lying broken on the ground, Bex was now more confused than ever.

"What in the Hells is going on?"

"This isn't the Hells," Nemini replied unhelpfully. "It's somewhere else."

"I already figured out that much," Bex grumbled, craning her neck as she tried to look in every direction at once. "What I want to know is where we are and how do we get back to Gilgamesh's palace."

Going up didn't seem to be the answer. Thanks to her raging bonfire, Bex had a great view of the top of the cavern they'd been dropped into, which seemed to be one solid arch of sandstone. There were no gaps or cracks that might lead to an exit, and definitely no spiral staircase back to Heaven. The walls below appeared solid as well, which was annoying. So far as she could tell, the Prince of Envy had dropped them into a completely sealed stone room that had an ancient city at the bottom for some reason. Bex was no archaeologist, but if any of those buildings were less than a thousand years old, she'd eat her new horns. They also looked oddly familiar, almost like she'd been to this city before, but Bex didn't remember any—

I do, Drox said calmly in her head. *That is the ancient capital of Uruk.*

"Uruk?" Bex repeated, causing Nemini to glance up in surprise. "As in Gilgamesh's Uruk?"

The very same, her sword replied. *It's even still got the fire damage you caused when you came down here to punish the king at Ishtar's behest.*

The stone and mud-brick buildings did look pretty torched now that Drox mentioned it, but Bex was getting a bad feeling.

"Why would Gilgamesh seal his ancient home city inside a cave?"

I don't know, but there's something moving down there.

So there was. Thanks to the light of her fire, Bex could see a dark shape moving along the city's stone-paved streets. It looked like a wandering building, but when it turned around, Bex saw that it was a bull. A gigantic black bull with horns as wide as the road it was standing on. Bex was still staring at it in confusion when Nemini's arms tightened around her neck.

"That's the Bull of Ishtar," she whispered.

"No way," Bex whispered back. "Ishtar's bull is dead. Enkidu killed it, so I killed Enkidu. That's why Gilgamesh went to war with us in the first place."

"True," her sister said. "But creations of Ishtar don't tend to stay dead, do they?"

That was a good point.

"Gilgamesh must've made this place to contain it," Bex muttered, squinting at the rummaging monster through the glare of her fire. "I can't think of any other reason he'd bury his former—"

Her voice cut off like a switch as the bull's giant head snapped up to look at them. For three long breaths, it stared straight at her, its eyes gleaming like black glass in the light of Bex's bonfire. Then a wave of malice and judgement stronger than anything Bex had ever felt fell over her like a smothering blanket, and her fire went out.

She dropped like a stone, limbs wheeling uselessly in the suddenly pitch-black air. There'd been no warning, no sense of being attacked, but no matter how hard she tried, Bex couldn't get her fire to ignite again.

They would've crashed to the ground right in front of the bull's nose if Nemini hadn't been so quick. Just a few seconds after they started falling, her sister threw out her arm. A wave of shadow snakes followed, flowing off of Nemini's body like water to grab the top of an ancient dovecote. They swung the queens through the window next, moving like a rope to toss them onto the wooden floor at the dovecote's base.

"Nice catch," Bex gasped as she pushed herself up. "But why didn't you move us through the shadows? That probably would've been safer. And cleaner." She glanced down at the centuries' worth of calcified dove droppings under their feet, but Nemini shook her head.

"I can't carry you that way anymore now that you've got a name again," she explained as the snakes returned to her horned head. "You'd be torn off of me and vanish into the void."

"Oh," Bex said with a wince. "Snakes are fine in that case, but why are your powers working when my fire isn't?"

She'd been talking to Nemini, but it was Drox who answered. *Because only you were judged,* her sword said, his deep voice tight with worry. *I don't know how Gilgamesh got it in here, but that is absolutely the Bull of Ishtar, a monster crafted by the goddess's own hands just like she made you. Unlike her queens, though, who were built to rule, the bull was created only to destroy.*

"If it's Ishtar's creation, why is it targeting me?" Bex demanded. "Haven't I got a big enough crown?"

She pointed up at her new horns, but Drox's ring trembled on her finger.

I think your horns are the problem, he said. *You're wielding powers no queen should have, and Ishtar's Bull was built with a simple mind. It probably thinks you're a traitor.*

That made sense, but the real kicker came from Nemini.

"Your fire is still tainted with the death of Enki," the other queen reminded her. "That's as good a reason as any for a weapon of the gods to turn on you."

"Fair enough," Bex said with a sigh. "Do you think the Bull of Ishtar would listen to my side of the story if I talked to it?"

No, Drox replied immediately.

"Then we do this the hard way," she muttered, peering through the dovecote's window at the dim outline of the city beyond.

If her night vision hadn't been so good, she wouldn't have been able to see even that much. Now that her fire was out, the sealed cavern was pitch-black. Fortunately, Bex's eyes had always been excellent in the dark. Even with nothing but her own ember glow to work with, she could still make out the bull's giant shoulders poking over the flat tops of the single-story buildings one street over. It was weaving from side to side, methodically shoving its giant horns through each building as it searched for her.

"Looks like the bull has no problem seeing in the dark, either," Bex whispered as she called the Blade of Wrath to her hand. "It doesn't seem to know where we are, though, so now's our chance to catch it by surprise. Nemini, you stay here and grab me if I get into trouble. I'll run along the rooftops and hit it from the..."

Her voice trailed off as she looked down at her empty hand. The one she *knew* she'd just called her sword into, but Drox was still in his ring on her finger.

I'm so sorry, my queen, he said before she could ask. *I'm trying to obey, but something's—*

His voice cut off as the ring started shaking harder against her skin. *It's no use,* Drox said in a furious voice. *I can't get out! There's an edict blocking me that I never realized was there, a sacred command that forbids me from being drawn against Ishtar's personal weapon.*

"Well, that's just great," Bex muttered as she curled her empty hand into a fist. "No fire, no sword. What am I supposed to do? Punch it to death?"

"Maybe it will pass us by," Nemini said calmly from her crouch on the dovecote's dropping-covered crossbeam. "If it can't find us when your fire's out, maybe we can just sit here and wait for—"

The rest of Nemini's reasonable advice was drowned out by a deep animal bellow. The noise roared through the cavern, shaking the buildings like an earthquake. The sound had no variation, nothing that could possibly be labeled as words, but the message it caried was clear nonetheless.

Reveal yourself, Godslayer!

Bex flinched as the command vibrated through her bones. She'd done her best not to make a sound, but one slipped out anyway. The moment the squeak of surprise left her lips, she felt the bull's gaze land on her despite the wall that should've been in the way.

There you are.

"Run!" Bex shouted, grabbing Nemini and leaping out of the dovecote seconds before the bull's giant horns smashed through it. The two queens landed on the road below in a shatter of smashed mud bricks, but while Bex could no longer see Nemini's snakes in the dark, they must've been already busy. She barely had time to crash into the ground before something giant yanked Bex back to her feet and shoved her after her sister, who was already running down the narrow alley.

Bex sprinted after her as fast as she could, not even taking time to glance back at the sounds of destruction filling the cavern behind them. If the buildings were slowing the bull down at all, Bex couldn't tell, because the explosion of shattering stone didn't let up, and neither did the roars.

Traitor! the bull bellowed as it smashed through the city after them. *Godkiller! Unclean!*

"You're one to talk!" Bex yelled as she pumped her legs faster. "You're rampaging for Gilgamesh, you idiot!"

The bull didn't listen. Bex didn't even know if it understood human speech, but it didn't slow down at her words, or even to turn. When Nemini whipped them around a corner, the bull simply smashed into the buildings on the other side, using the bricks to slow its momentum and bounce it back the right direction with no concern for its own safety.

After three of these collisions, Bex realized the bull didn't need to be concerned. No matter how big or pointy the buildings it crashed into were, nothing seemed able to pierce its black hide. Bex didn't know what that damn thing was covered in, but the bull went through the city like an icebreaker through a frozen sea. She and Nemini, however, were rapidly running out of cover.

"How does Gilgamesh even have a capital anymore with that monster smashing through it?" Bex shouted over the destruction as she chased Nemini down yet another twisting alley.

"I think we're the first ones to come here in eons," her sister observed in a voice that sounded far too calm for someone running for her life. "There's no dust or signs of age on anything. It's like this whole place was baked in clay and cut off from time."

"*We're* about to be cut off from time if we can't find a way out of this," Bex reminded her, glancing over her shoulder at the pile of broken buildings the bull's horns were driving in front of it like a bulldozer.

"Okay," she said, forcing herself to calm down and *think*. "My fire won't burn and Drox is stuck in his ring, but your powers still work. Is there anything you can do to help? Knock the bull over with your void touch or something?"

She glanced at her sister hopefully, but Nemini was already shaking her head. "I already tried touching it earlier," she confessed. "But the bull has no ego to break. It exists purely to serve Ishtar, so…"

Nemini trailed off with a shrug, and Bex sighed. "What about your snakes?" she asked instead. "Can they slow it down, at least?"

"No," Nemini said, her voice still as calm as ever, even when she had to duck under a flying piece of roofing. "What you perceive as snakes are actually the fragments of my broken sword. They can puff themselves up when they sense I'm afraid, but they're not actually any stronger than I am myself. They're also still Enki's creations, which means they definitely can't stop the Bull of Ishtar."

"Of course," Bex muttered, putting on an angry burst of speed as they turned onto one of the large straightaways that led to the ancient fortress on the city's lone surviving hill. "How is it the gods are always useless when we need them but somehow become unbeatable forces of nature when they're used against us?"

It wasn't actually a question, but Nemini answered just the same. "Because Gilgamesh arranges things that way. His entire rule has been one long play to transfer the gods' power bit by bit into his own hands. It only makes sense that he'd be very good at it by now."

"Nemini," Bex growled through gritted teeth. "I love you, but I seriously don't want to hear praise for Gilgamesh right now."

"Sorry," her sister said. "I was just trying to help."

"I know you were," Bex said, keeping her eyes on the cobbled street as her boots flew over the uneven stones. "And I'm not mad. I'm just scared because I have no idea how we're getting out of this."

Those were hard words to admit, but there was no point in saving face in front of Nemini. Her sister had stuck with her through Bex's worst and best. She deserved the truth, not queenly bravado, but Bex seriously at her wits' end.

You could try one of your new powers, Drox suggested.

"I don't think fear-demon scales are going to do much against those giant hooves," Bex huffed. "Another demon's power might work, but I'm not exactly practiced at using my new modes yet, and the bull isn't leaving a lot of room for error."

As if to prove her point, a giant crash sounded behind them as the bull slammed through a two-story building, sending Bex's sense of impending doom ratcheting up yet another notch. As scary as being chased was, though, the destruction was actually their biggest problem. She and Nemini could run for a long time, but at the rate the bull was going through buildings, they were going to be out of cover very soon. Once that happened, it'd be just them and Ishtar's rampaging weapon on an open field.

She and Nemini were fast, but if they had to start vaulting over rubble while the bull ran unhindered, they were going to get trampled. Bex was scrambling to think of something, *anything* she could do to prevent that when Nemini's head snapped up.

"My power could do it."

"You have a power?" Bex blurted out before she realized how stupid that was. Of *course* the Queen of Pride had a power. All Ishtar's daughters had powers like Bex's fire and War's control over weapons. They were what Gilgamesh stole to make his swords. Since Pride had never been a princess, Bex had no idea what Nemini's ability was, but she was super excited to find out.

"What is it?" she asked eagerly, running up beside her sister. "And can it stop a charging bull?"

"It could stop an army," Nemini said, but her voice was still flat. "Unfortunately, I can't use it."

"Why not?" Bex demanded. "Adrian gave you back your horns and name. Why can't you use your own power?"

"Because, like my sword, I am no longer what I used to be," Nemini confessed, keeping her eyes on the shaking road as they ran up the hill toward the ancient keep that must have been Gilgamesh's original palace. "The power of Pride requires absolute confidence. You have to know without doubt that you are better, superior, more capable than anyone who's ever come before. I used to feel that way about everything I did, but when I came face-to-face with the void, it changed my perspective. I know now that, no matter how powerful an individual might seem, we're all insignificant compared to the infinite arc of the boundless universe. It was a truly enlightening vision, but while I am forever grateful to have seen the truth, that same understanding unfortunately makes it impossible for me to feel superior to anyone anymore."

That was a very Nemini answer, but Bex had to clench her jaw to keep from screaming in frustration. She didn't blame her sister—it wasn't Nemini's fault that she'd been enlightened—but it was *so frustrating* to have a solution teased in front of her only to have it snatched away again a second later. She was wondering why Nemini had bothered bringing the subject up in the first place when Bex realized her sister wasn't finished.

"You don't have that problem, though," Nemini said, glancing over her shoulder at her sister. "Unlike me, you are still what Ishtar made you to be. Whereas I had no interest in leaving the void, you couldn't wait to get out of it and get back to your duty. I told you once that you're the queen I should have been. Now that every demon has bowed their horns to you, that's literally true. You're the Queen of *all* demons now, including Pride, which means you should be able to use the power I no longer can."

Bex was panting too hard to gasp properly at that, but she still managed to gape at her sister. It was true she'd covered herself in scales and attacked with weaponized tragedy to end her fight with the Prince of Fear, but those were both things that normal fear and sorrow demons did. Drox had told her earlier that without active prayers, Bex was limited only to the powers Ishtar had granted to demonkind, but it hadn't occurred to her that definition included other *queens'* abilities as well.

It still didn't feel possible. Surely a change that important would've come with a sense or a trigger or *something* to let Bex know it was there, but she didn't feel any different than she usually did. Nemini wasn't the sort to suggest something unless she was sure of it, though, so Bex swallowed her misgivings and asked, "How do I do it?"

"I already told you," her sister said patiently. "You have to be proud. Remember that you are the greatest queen, a divine force nothing can defeat. You must pin your horns to the sky and plant your feet so firmly on the ground that they can never be moved. Do that, and the mountains themselves will bow before you."

Bex was cringing by the time Nemini finished. "I see why you can't do it anymore," she muttered. "That sounds like a lethal amount of ego."

"It was the Pride of Ishtar," Nemini agreed. "Gods aren't known for being humble. It should still work, though, assuming you can pull it off."

That was a big assumption. Bex had stood up to Ishtar for her people's sake, but the idea of planting her feet and trying to stop a charging bull with nothing but her own hubris sounded like a good way to turn herself into a speed bump. She also still didn't know if the bull would let her use it. He'd already sealed her fire and her sword. What if he'd cut her off from everything else as well?

I think it will work, Drox said. *For all its power, the bull is merely Ishtar's tool. He judged you as a misbehaving queen, but you are Ishtar's daughter, born of her own divine flesh. That means you outrank a lowly beast.* Her sword's voice grew deadly. *It's time that fool remembers just whom he presumes to judge.*

Easy for Drox to say. He'd always been the first to remind Bex of her position. Still, the idea of taking all his puffed-up queen talk and saying it herself like she really felt she was superior made Bex want to bury herself in the dirt. She didn't know what else to do, though. This was literally their only idea, so Bex did the same thing she'd been doing all her life. She shoved her fears aside and went for it, slamming her feet into the ground as she whirled around to face the bull head-on.

Since they'd been running up the steep hill toward Uruk's old stone castle, this put Bex on higher ground. Good thing, too. She'd gotten used to bluffing during the seven years she'd spent as a burned-out husk, but it still took every nerve Bex had to hold her ground as the gigantic bull thundered toward her. If she'd been lower than those horns, she would've crumpled on instinct. For at least the next few seconds, though, Bex stood above them, and she used the extra height to maximum advantage, lifting her own six horns to the cavern's dark sky as she commanded, "*Stop.*"

The word tore out of her the same way her fire did. Her actual flames were still smothered by the bull's censure, but nothing could change that Bex was the one all of Ishtar's people had bowed to. She was the queen who'd destroyed the Hells, stood up to a goddess, and cut Gilgamesh's fortress in half. With a lot of help, admittedly, but the whole point of being a leader was that people followed you. Bex wasn't strong because of her horns or her fire or her name. She was strong because she had strong people who supported her without reservation. They were the ones who'd lifted her up to where she was now, and pride in them was the mountain she stood on as she stared the charging bull down.

"Stop," she said again.

The bull roared and tossed his horns, turning the stone road to gravel as he stomped his sharp hooves. For all the destruction and noise, though, he was no longer moving forward, and for the first time since the Prince of Envy had tossed them down here, Bex's face split into a smile.

"Kneel," she ordered.

The bull bellowed again, but his knees still hit the ground, going down one leg at a time until his giant belly was pressed against the road.

"That's better," Bex said, breathing deep to hide her crushing relief. "Can you speak?"

The bull snorted through its giant nostrils. Just like before, though, the meaning still came through clearly.

Of course. I am a divine creation, not some dumb animal.

"Then why are you charging around like one?" Bex snapped, getting angry again now that the terror of impending death was subsiding. "We're all children of Ishtar here, so what are you—"

Liar! the bull trumpeted. *I know you! You are the Blade of Ishtar, and yet your flames are tainted with the blood of Holy Enki! You are a godslayer! A traitor! You—*

"And you are dead," Bex reminded him, waving her hand at the stone roof high above their heads.

"The mortal hero Enkidu slew you five thousand years ago, after which you were sealed down here by Gilgamesh the Traitor, conqueror of Paradise and murderer of the gods." She crossed her arms over her chest. "If you're going to point your horns at me, know that all of mine are pointing back. This war's a lot more complicated than it used to be, but we are both creations of the gods. The important thing now is to decide whose side you stand on: Gilgamesh's, or your fellow children of Paradise?"

I stand with Ishtar, the bull snorted. *But what do you mean I am dead? I'm a creation of the eternal gods. I cannot die!*

"I don't know how you ended up here," Bex told him honestly. "But if you'll stop raging for a moment and look around, you'll see that we're not on Earth or in the Riverlands anymore. We're stuck in one of Gilgamesh's prisons. My sister and I were trying to escape when you attacked. I can take you with us when we go back to Paradise, but only if you promise to stop trying to kill me."

Never! the bull roared, tossing his head. *You are a godslayer!*

He ended with his black nose stuck obstinately in the air, and Drox made a disgusted sound inside Bex's head.

Don't waste your time on this oaf, my queen. His rage-drunk mind can't possibly understand the nuances of all that has changed in the past five thousand years.

"Perhaps," Bex said. "But I was a loyal weapon of Ishtar myself not that long ago, so I understand where he's coming from." She frowned for a moment, and then she glanced back up at the bull, who was already pushing at the limits of her new pride.

"How about we make a deal?"

The bull looked disgusted. *I don't bargain with murderers.*

"This bargain doesn't involve me," Bex promised. "I won't even be there. I'm just offering you a chance to trample some actual traitors."

The bull stopped fighting at once. *Continue.*

"There's a great forest down in the living world where the armies of Gilgamesh are gathered," Bex explained in her best tempting voice. "Why waste your time in this dark, boring place, chasing one godslayer, when you can trample thousands of them? They're mortals, too. Easy to crush."

An army of mortals, you say? The bull perked up. *I haven't crushed one of those in ages.*

"You can crush these to your heart's content," Bex promised. "They're servants of the enemy, slavers who've befouled Paradise. They're down there right now, seeking to destroy the last power capable of dethroning Ishtar's murderer. If you trample them, you'll be avenging her death."

Yes! Yes! the bull bellowed. *I would do anything to avenge her! Even in this strange land, I knew that she was gone.* His black eyes flashed as he started fighting Bex's command to kneel even harder. *I will destroy them all!*

"Then you'd better not trample me, because I'm the only one who can get you down there," Bex said. "You also have to swear on Ishtar's name that you won't hurt the trees or the witches who guard them. Only Gilgamesh's servants shall die. Promise me that, and I'll let you get up."

I promise! I promise! the bull cried. *Take me to them! Let me crush them!*

"We'll head right over," Bex promised, easing back her hold to let the bull rise to his feet again. "Just let me talk to my sister first."

The bull nodded and started kicking his hind legs excitedly. If he hadn't been a murderous monster the size of a barn, it would've been cute. As it was, the shaking from his pounding hooves was collapsing the last parts of the ancient city that hadn't already been trampled. That was a shame considering the age of the place, but since the city was Gilgamesh's, Bex was having a hard time feeling guilty.

"That was well done," Nemini said, patting her sister on the shoulder. "You're a better Pride than I was."

"I know that's not true, but thank you," Bex said, wrapping her arms around her tattered jacket as the storm of nerves she'd been desperately holding back finally shook through her. "Have you been able to reach anyone on the comms yet?"

"No," Nemini said. "But I saw Leander teleport out with Adrian while we were falling, so I'm sure they're working on it."

Bex heaved a relieved sigh. Leander was still a question mark, but if there was anyone she trusted to rescue them, it was Adrian. Her clever witch always found a way. She just had to be patient and wait, so that was exactly what Bex did, sitting down next to her sister on the doorstep of Uruk's ancient palace while the Bull of Ishtar continued his happy, ground-shaking dance on the dark road in front of them.

Chapter 13

ADRIAN HAD NEVER WORKED SO HARD to sink into his forest.

Merging with his Blackwood was normally like sinking into water, but he wasn't on a prepared bed beneath his heart tree. He was on Gilgamesh's palace floor. A hard stone floor built to reject every aspect of life. Adrian's vines had already wrapped all the way around the building, but like every other part of the Blackwood except for himself and Boston, they couldn't cross the threshold into the actual palace. He was still technically inside his forest because he had plants surrounding him, but Gilgamesh's fortress was like a burn zone where nothing could grow.

That severely limited what Adrian was able to do, but ingenuity was the soul of witchcraft, and it wasn't as if he didn't have a good foundation to work from. His heart was pumping at the base of the biggest tree he'd ever grown. His body might be just a tendril pushing into the wasteland of Gilgamesh's control, but his roots ran all the way back to the land of the living. He just needed to—

His progress was interrupted by a loud *bash* right next to his head. The hit cracked the stone cocoon of the Seven Walled City like an eggshell before Leander, who'd been standing over Adrian like a guard this whole time, muttered something under his breath. The walls pulled themselves back together a second later, and his sorcerer brother let out a sigh of relief.

"Sorry," he muttered. "I've reinforced the outer rings, though if you could work faster, that would be good."

Adrian nodded and lay back on the ground again, closing his mind against the increasingly violent banging coming from the Prince of Envy to focus on his pulse. He could feel it strong and steady despite his heart not being inside his body, and Adrian threw himself into its waves like a harbor seal, diving down, down, down as fast as he could away from this dead land to the place where life still thrived.

There was a lot of it to choose from. Adrian had been growing trees since he was seven, but he'd never been plugged straight into the Great Cycles like he was now. No wonder his mother had been able to move their entire coven through his roots. Between the ocean of quintessence he'd poured in from his end and the centuries-long witchcraft the Blackwood Coven had prepared to meet it, the taproot of his new heart tree went all the way to the roots of the Great Blackwood itself.

He'd always felt the Great Forest at the edge of his consciousness. Now that he'd dived in headfirst, though, Adrian was suddenly swimming through primordial magic. He swore he could feel the Great Cycles turning around him, which was terrifying because they had no care for him. The engine of life was bigger than any individual soul, and it rolled over him like a boulder down a hill. It would crush his soul to pulp if he wasn't careful, but Adrian had always been quick on his feet, and he knew exactly where he was going.

Faster than he'd ever moved in his life, Adrian darted through the enormousness of the living world's magic for the little patch of green that belonged to him. This was why it was always best to grow good roots from the start. Despite being poisoned with quintessence and having its heart tree ripped out and moved to the land of the dead, Adrian's forest on Bainbridge Island was still right where he'd left it.

He could feel the roots of his witchwood as they slumbered in their seasonal hibernation, feel the cold water of the famous winter rains that had finally arrived in Seattle. He couldn't feel his cottage since his mother had picked it up and stuck it in his new branches like a birdhouse, but his garden was still there. The beds were dead and neglected, but the soil was rich and would be ready for planting again in the spring. And hidden in that soil, buried under the large stone that used to serve as the step for his back door, was the treasure he was searching for.

Adrian snatched it up like a hunting hawk. The wrapped object was small and compact, but while he had no problem carrying it with him through the roots, getting it back to his physical body proved much more challenging. His heart might be woven into the tapestry of the Great Forest, but the vines he'd wrapped around Gilgamesh's palace were simply too small and young to transport an object of that size. No matter which direction Adrian turned it, the wrapped package kept getting stuck. He was starting to feel really frantic when a voice he'd completely forgotten about suddenly spoke in his ear.

"You guys still okay in there?" Iggs whispered over the comm. "I'm hearing some pretty scary noises."

"Iggs!" Adrian cried, snapping out of his delve into the forest to grab the plastic speaker in his ear. "Fantastic timing! Put Boston on."

Anyone else would've been insulted by the idea of being passed over for a cat, but Iggs had always understood witches the best of any of Bex's demons. He handed the comm over immediately, and Adrian heaved a sigh of relief as Boston's voice came over the speaker.

"So I just push down on this button when I want to talk?"

"*Boston!*" Adrian cried, yelling over Iggs's hasty explanation. "I need you to go to the front door of the palace and grab something from the vines. You don't have to bring it all the way to me, and don't unwrap it. Just run it to the top of the staircase we went down and toss it in."

"Don't unwrap—" Boston repeated in confusion, then his voice grew furious. "Wait a minute. I know what you're doing! Adrian, that's very dangerous. Are you sure you want to—"

"Dead sure," Adrian said, glancing up at the cracks that were forming in the stone walls faster than Leander's now-constant stream of sorcery could repair. "Do it quickly, we're almost dead."

Those must've been the magic words, because the next thing Adrian heard was the *thunk* of the comm hitting the floor as Boston darted away.

"Were you just talking to your cat?" Leander asked tersely.

"Yes," Adrian said as he stood back up as much as he could inside their shelter, which was now very small. "Don't worry. Help is on the way."

Leander stopped straining long enough to give him a scathing look. "Help from your cat?"

"Boston is a fully initiated member of the Blackwood coven," Adrian informed him proudly. "He's also got my broom, so he should be—"

The rest of his assurances were knocked out of his head when something hit Leander's sorcery hard enough to shatter all seven walls. His brother was sent flying, but Adrian managed to hold his ground, staring defiantly into the cracked, dirty face of the sneering Princess of Envy.

"Well done," her prince said as the princess lowered the fist she'd just used to crack open Leander's Seven Walled City. "Now that the insects are out from under their rock, this should be quick."

"Are you sure you want to take that risk?" Adrian stalled frantically. "I'm still the only prince who can use witchcraft and sorcery together. That makes me very valuable to Gilgamesh. Surely you don't want to anger—"

"That line won't work on me," the prince interrupted as his princess moved around Adrian to wrestle his arms behind his back. "Perhaps all that cowering made you forget, but I'm the Prince of *Envy*. I hate every son Father raises above me. It's not my fault. I've always striven to be the rational one, but no prince is immune to the influence of his sword. That's why my princess and I are normally kept far away from the others, but Father doesn't care what happens to us anymore. After Alexander's disastrous loss of the

Hells, Gilgamesh has washed his hands of this place, which means I'm finally free to eliminate the competition."

"Doesn't that mean you *shouldn't* care about killing me?" Adrian asked frantically, struggling against the princess, who seemed to be trying to wrench his arms out of their sockets. "If Gilgamesh has abandoned us, why do you still care about being his top prince?"

"Because he *will* care," the Prince of Envy explained. "Father's busy changing the very nature of this world. He doesn't have time to burden himself with stupid family drama, but he will take note of who was effective and who wasn't."

He pointed a finger at the arched ceiling overhead. "Alexander made his first big mistake in centuries when he failed to halt the Coward Queen's incursion. That means there's a rare opening at the top. If I can prevent you two traitors from interrupting Gilgamesh's work, he might just make *me* Crown Prince instead."

The princess who was currently mauling Adrian's arms trembled with joy at the possibility, but Adrian had to fight the urge to roll his eyes. What was it with these people and sucking up to a king who so clearly didn't care about anything but himself? The princesses he could understand—they were programmed to worship Gilgamesh—but his brothers were human. They had no excuse for this brain rot, but it was clearly pointless to say as much to Envy. The prince was already bouncing on his heels like a kid who couldn't wait to run and tell his father what he'd done, which meant it was time to try a different tactic.

"Okay," Adrian said as he slumped against the princess in defeat. "You win. I'm tired of fighting losing battles, and I hate Alexander too. If I have to die, I'd rather do it helping you steal his position than waste my life for nothing, but I want a favor in return."

"I'm not sparing anyone's life," Envy warned him. "Leander's head is worth as much as yours, and the queens are never coming back."

"It's nothing like that," Adrian assured the prince, doing his best to look pathetic. "It's just... I left my cat upstairs. If this is truly the end, I'd like to hug him one last time before I die."

The prince's mirrored eyes narrowed. "That's a very suspicious request."

"It's an earnest one," Adrian promised. "I might be a son of Gilgamesh, but I was raised as a witch. We Blackwoods are a sentimental bunch, especially when it comes to our animals. I just want to say goodbye, and surely the future Crown Prince of Heaven isn't afraid of a cat?"

The Prince of Envy frowned even harder, but just when it looked like he was about to say no, Leander spoke from the floor.

"Just let him do it, Hector," he said in a pained voice as he pushed himself off the cracked marble. "He's our baby brother, and Father always says that mercy is the privilege of the strong." He flashed the Prince of Envy a sneer. "You'll look weak if you deny him."

"As if you weren't always the weakest among us," the other prince snapped, but his face was set in a scowl.

"Oh, very well," he said as the Princess of Envy released her death grip on Adrian's arms. "You can say goodbye to your pet, but only if you call it here. I'm not letting you out of my sight."

"Perfectly acceptable," Adrian said as he rubbed his aching shoulders. "Thank you very much."

The Prince of Envy rolled his eyes and gestured for Adrian to get on with it. The witch did so with great humility, crouching down and turning to face the staircase, where he could already feel his familiar waiting.

"Here, Boston," he called. "Here, kitty, kitty."

It wasn't possible to share emotions through the familiar bond, but Adrian still swore he felt his cat's disgust land on him like a wet blanket. In this as with every task his witch assigned him, however, Boston was a consummate professional. He galloped down the stairs exactly like a scared pet running to its owner. He even meowed, jumping into Adrian's arms in a moving display of animal devotion.

"It's under my left foreleg," he whispered when Adrian caught him. "I had Iggs stick it there with tape from his first aid kit and covered it in a Nevermind."

"You are absolutely brilliant," Adrian whispered back, giving his cat a completely genuine hug of relief.

"Just be careful," Boston murmured as Adrian began to gently pry the wrapped object out of the nest of tape his familiar had heroically allowed to be stuck to his fur. "It's not fully cured yet, so the potency will be high."

"I'm counting on it," Adrian said, giving his faithful familiar a final squeeze before setting him back on the ground to run to Leander, who was crouched several feet behind Adrian like he was bracing for impact.

"Are you finished?" the Prince of Envy asked impatiently.

"I'm finished," Adrian said, raising his hands to his face as if he were saying a final prayer. "Do your worst."

The prince smiled at this clear display of surrender, but Adrian hadn't been talking to him. He'd breathed those words over the object Boston had smuggled into his hands. The curse that was now crawling out of its wrapping to reveal the five-inch-long black body of a preserved wasp. Its wings weren't dried all the way through yet, and its body was still soft in places where the magic hadn't finished. The wasp was actually a lot less ready than he'd expected, but it still shot out of Adrian's palm like a bullet, streaking across the white room to drive its half-inch-long stinger into the exposed skin of the dirty prince's face.

The Prince of Envy screamed when it happened. Adrian screamed, too, falling to his knees as the burning venom raced through his system. Deploying the karma wasp always resulted in at least one sting for the caster, but this time was so much worse than when he'd used it on the Spider. Adrian was normally pretty invincible when it came to poison, but Boston must've been dead-on about the increase in potency. The toxin flowing through Adrian's system was strong enough to dim his vision. Using the wasp was still worth it, though, because as hard as the poison was hitting him, it was hitting the Prince of Envy even harder.

"You underhanded *witch*!" the prince roared, frantically loosening the hard collar of his golden armor as his head began swelling up like a balloon. His princess ran to help at once, but the prince shoved her away.

"Don't bother with me," he snarled. "*Kill him!*"

That wouldn't be hard. Thanks to the karma wasp's poison, Adrian couldn't even open his eyes all the way right now. Killing him should've been the work of a second, but when the Princess of Envy turned around to rip his head off, Leander's arm shot out first.

"Band of a Thousand Irons."

The sorcery had barely left his lips before the princess toppled over with a band of metal the size of a telephone pole wrapped around her body. Because she was still the Princess of Envy, the same iron band clapped around Leander as well, slamming him to the floor. He took the fall gladly, grinning the whole way down, because it no longer made a difference. No matter how helpless he'd just made himself, the Prince of Envy was choking too hard to follow through.

Adrian was choking too. He wasn't sure if the karma wasp was even more potent than he'd initially realized or if the Prince of Envy's power was reflecting the full poison back at him, but he'd never been stung this badly in his life. If he hadn't spent thirteen years training to resist poisons, he'd have died in the first thirty seconds. He *was* trained, though, so he was able to hang on, but every blood vessel still felt like it was filled with acid. It burned worse than anything he could remember, but at least all that gasping in pain meant he could still breathe, which was more than Adrian could say for his enemy.

The Prince of Envy's entire face was black with poison now. His eyes had been reduced to two puffy slits, and his neck was so swollen that his own armor was choking him even with the unlatched collar. The karma wasp was still darting around stinging any bit of exposed flesh it could find, but the prince was no longer trying to swat it away. All of his attention was focused on sucking air through his swollen throat, but every breath he managed was shorter than the last until, finally, he couldn't get one in at all.

That was when it truly ended. The prince had already fallen to his knees, but the moment his breathing stopped, he toppled like a felled tree. His princess screamed when she saw it. She still couldn't walk thanks to the metal bar Leander's sorcery had used to bind her, so she wiggled on her belly like a worm, dragging her iron-wrapped body across the floor until she lay beside her dying prince. She was begging him not to die when the Prince of Envy's bloated body finally went still.

"*No!*" she screamed when she saw it. "You can't leave me! I can't be the only one without a prince! I—"

"Silence."

The command was so sharp and cold that even Adrian stopped gasping long enough to watch Leander sit up, despite the weight of the iron manacle that was still wrapped around his body, and fix the sobbing princess with a look of pure disdain.

"Your beloved is dead," he told her. "That makes you a masterless sword, the lowest of the low. As a son of Gilgamesh, I now rank above you. By that authority,

I command you by your sacred name: Kesra, Princess of Envy, release all mirrored sorcery and return to your sword."

The princess had kept screaming the entire time Leander was speaking, but as soon as he said her name, her cries stopped like a flipped switch. The metal bindings holding Leander vanished a second later, setting him free as the white Blade of Envy, a needle-sharp sword once more, toppled to the ground.

"That was a lot of fuss," Leander said, wiping the sweat from his brow as he turned to Adrian. "Are you going to live?"

"He'll make it," Boston answered when it was clear Adrian was still too busy going into toxic shock to do so on his own. "My witch is second to none when it comes to poison, but why did you order her back into her sword? Iggs told me you smashed the Princess of Hate."

"Because the Princess of Hate is an unstable menace in any form," Leander explained while he slowly pushed back to his feet. "Honestly, the same could be said for the Princess of Envy, but unlike Hate, we still need her."

"For what?" Boston asked as he wiggled his body under Adrian's legs and elevated them to improve blood flow.

"She's the key," Leander said. "I assume you want your queens back, yes?"

"Yes," Adrian wheezed, reaching out to his forest for help, since his body wasn't clearing the poison quickly enough.

He should've done it that way from the start. The moment he opened himself to the Blackwood, the venom drained out of him like water down a cliff. He'd been worried about dumping such a large dose of poison into the ecosystem, but this forest was much bigger than his grove back on Bainbridge, and it was eager to help. He could almost feel the tree roots pushing him back to his feet as he groggily climbed off the floor.

"Okay," he said when the room had slowed to an acceptable level of spinning. "How do we get Bex back?"

"The same way Hector sent her off," Leander replied, pointing at the sword lying on the ground. "Without her prince, the Blade of Envy can no longer use sophisticated abilities like attack reflection, but wanting to be somewhere else is part of Envy's base nature. That means she should still be connected to all the secret places Gilgamesh allows his sons to access. Also, thanks to the loyalty verses carved into her core, she's currently unable to refuse the command of any son of Gilgamesh, including traitors like us. All you have to do is tell her what you're looking for, and the sword should do the rest."

"If that's all there is to it, can you do it instead?" Adrian asked tiredly. "I want to rescue Bex as fast as possible, but I'm still pretty dizzy from the poison. You seem to know a lot about this, so why don't you go ahead and—"

"Absolutely not," Leander said, crossing his arms over his chest. "I already told you: Mara is the only sword I'll ever use. If you can't pick up a weapon yet, we'll wait until you can, but I'm not being unfaithful to my one true beloved just so you can save a little time."

That was simultaneously the dumbest and sweetest thing Adrian had ever heard. He didn't even bother trying to argue with his brother. He just took a deep breath and stumbled forward, trusting his forest to flush the last traces of the poison out of his system as he leaned down to shakily pick up the Blade of Envy.

The sword bit him the second he touched it. In hindsight, Adrian supposed he should have seen that coming. Between Drox and the princess version of Bex, he'd never met a Blade of Ishtar or Gilgamesh that wasn't stabby. If he'd been thinking ahead, he would've put on a glove. He hadn't been, though, so he was forced to endure the bloody fingers as he gripped Envy's hilt hard.

"Bring back the Queens of Wrath and Pride," he commanded. "And *don't* drop anyone else in this time."

That probably wasn't the right wording, but Adrian didn't know where the prince had sent them, so it would have to do. Thankfully, the sword still seemed to get the message. She fought and gnawed and dragged her point along the stone, but eventually she did as Adrian ordered, opening a much smaller section of the floor to reveal the same sandstone cavern and empty city he'd glimpsed before Leander had teleported them out.

The *destroyed* city. Adrian hadn't gotten a good look at the buildings the first time, but he was certain they hadn't been leveled when he'd left. He took the destruction as a good sign since wrecking Gilgamesh's property was Bex's signature, but he didn't see the burning light of her bonfire anywhere. He was still searching for it when something jumped at him from the ground below.

Adrian leaped away from the hole with a yelp, and not a second too soon. The moment he got out of the way, a giant bull exploded through the opening Envy's sword had made in the floor. It was the size of a house with horns as long as railroad ties and eyes that gleamed like black glass, and riding on its broad back were Bex and Nemini.

"*Adrian!*" Bex cried, leaping off the bull, who couldn't seem to get her off its back fast enough. "I knew you'd find us!"

"I'm sorry I didn't do it sooner," he said, catching her in a hug. "Are you okay?"

He should've started checking for wounds the moment she came into reach, but Bex looked so bright and happy, and she felt so *good* in his arms. He'd already locked himself around her, dropping his face to her shoulder so he could breathe her in, when Leander cleared his throat.

"If you're finished," the prince said tersely, "I'd appreciate it if someone could explain what *that* is."

He pointed at the giant animal Nemini was still sliding off of.

"It's the Bull of Ishtar," the Queen of Pride replied as she landed on the ground. "He agreed not to kill Bex in return for getting to destroy the servants of Gilgamesh who are raiding the Blackwood."

The bull tossed its head with a snort, and Bex turned around in Adrian's grip to give it a scowl.

"Would you shut up?" she growled at the animal, who hadn't said a word that Adrian had been able to hear. "I've already told you a million times that we're on the same side. And speaking of, a 'thank you' wouldn't be amiss. You'd still be stuck in that crypt of a city if it wasn't for Adrian, so how about you chill on the death threats?"

The bull stomped its sharp hoof, clearly insulted. It must not have said anything too egregious, though, because Bex nodded as if that were the end of the matter.

"Thanks again for getting us an exit," she said, wiggling out of Adrian's arms far too quickly for his taste. "Looks like the Prince of Envy is dead."

"He is," Adrian said, keeping his eyes on Bex both because he loved looking at her and so that he wouldn't have to look at the horrifying spectacle of the Prince of Envy's bloated corpse. "But credit for that one goes to Boston. We were losing until he came in with the curse."

"Just doing my part," Boston said humbly, though his chest was still puffed out to maximum fluffiness. "But what's this about a bull for the Blackwood?"

"He wants to crush the enemies of Ishtar," Nemini explained. "Bex told him the best way to do that would be to go to your forest."

"It would indeed," Boston agreed, trotting over to the giant bull. "This way, comrade. I'll direct you to the front."

The bull's black eyes lit up with excitement at those words. He'd been looking dangerously surly, but he followed Boston up the stairs like an eager puppy, squeezing his giant shoulders through the arched doorway at the top.

"How is your cat able to talk to the Bull of Ishtar?" Bex asked in amazement.

"Boston can talk to most things," Adrian replied proudly. "One of the many, many reasons witches have familiars. It's not all cat hair collecting."

"I never doubted that for a second," Bex assured him, reaching up to tap her comm. "Iggs, you there?"

"*Bex!*" the wrath demon cried in relief. "Thank Ishtar! Boston just came by with a giant bull. What in the Hells have you been doing?"

"It's a long story," she said. "I'll tell you later. Right now, I need a status report. Are you still down?"

"Nope," Iggs reported. "I got the feeling back in my legs a few minutes ago, so I hobbled out to the front hall with the others. My left arm's still not in great shape, but I'm mostly functional. Why do you ask? Is it time to push the assault?"

"Sort of," Bex said, looking at Adrian. "I want you to round up everyone who's still in fighting shape and lead them back to protect the Blackwood."

"What?" Iggs said.

"*What?*" Adrian cried at the same time. "Bex, no! I appreciate the gesture, but Gilgamesh is attacking the Blackwood specifically to draw troops away from his palace. If you send your demons to help us, you'll be playing right into his hands."

"That's why I'm doing it," Bex said, craning her neck back to look at the arched ceiling above them. "We needed an army to get through the front door, but we're not actually here to occupy the palace. Our *only* target is Gilgamesh. Normal demons can't survive in a fight like that, which means a big force will just get in the way and give me more to worry about. Leaving them at the bottom of the tower is a waste, though, so I'm taking a page from the Eternal King's playbook and doing my own feint. Iggs?"

"Yeah?"

"I want you to put on a big show," she ordered. "Round everybody up and march that bull to the rootway like you're putting on a rodeo parade. Make sure everyone in Heaven knows that we're pulling back to defend the Blackwood." She turned back to Adrian. "Is Lys awake yet?"

He poked through his roots for a moment before shaking his head. "Not yet, but they can be."

"Great," Bex said. "Wake them up and tell them to change into me. Don't let them actually *do* anything. Just pretend like I'm injured and falling back. We want Gilgamesh to think he's winning."

"But that will make all of *our* people think we're losing," Iggs argued.

"Only for a few minutes," Bex promised. "As soon as you're back on Earth, you can tell everyone the truth. The important thing is to make *Gilgamesh* believe his plan worked. If he thinks he's a genius who successfully manipulated his enemies into falling back, he'll lower his guard, which will make the actual assault easier when Adrian, Nemini, Leander, and I hit him from behind."

"I see," Iggs said thoughtfully. "That'll be a nice fake-out if he falls for it, but can the four of you actually beat him?"

"If we can't, then keeping the army here won't change that," Bex argued, reaching up to touch her new horns. "The whole point of putting on these antennas was so that I'd be strong enough to toe-to-toe it with the Traitor King, but I can't focus on winning if I'm constantly worried about the rest of you. That's why I'm sending you to a place Gilgamesh doesn't control. I also really want to save the Blackwood. It's the least we can do after all their help, so think of this as two birds with one stone."

Iggs's growl was rumbling over the speaker by the time she finished. He obviously didn't like that plan one bit, but he'd always been the most obedient of Bex's soldiers, so all he actually said was "Yes, my queen."

Bex smiled in relief. "Thanks, Iggs."

"Just make sure you beat him, okay?" the demon grumbled. "I'd hate to have come all this way for nothing."

"It definitely wasn't for nothing," Bex said. "We destroyed the Hells and freed our people. No matter what happens from here, nothing can ever take that victory from us. That's why I need you to make sure everyone we saved makes it over the finish line." She bowed her horns. "I'm trusting you to take care of our people, Iggerux."

"I will," he promised with a bow Adrian swore he could hear over the comm's speaker. "I'll protect them all until you return to us. May Ishtar guide your sword and grant you victory, my queen."

Bex's whole body stiffened at Ishtar's name, but her voice was as steady as ever when she replied. "I pray for your success as well. We're going silent now. Good luck."

"Good luck," he replied as the comm cut off, leaving them standing in silence around the dead prince and his dropped sword.

"Well," Leander said when the quiet had stretched to an uncomfortable length. "I only heard half of that, but I assume we're continuing the assault on our own."

"That's the plan," Bex said, unzipping her poor tattered bomber jacket and dropping it on the ground so she was left in her short-sleeved—but still intact—T-shirt. "I realize neither of you take orders from me, so I'm asking this next part as a personal favor. Will you come with me to kill Gilgamesh and put an end to this forever?"

"Of course," Adrian said at once. "But *how* are we doing it? Even if you succeed in convincing Gilgamesh that you're retreating, we still don't know where he's hiding."

"The Morrigan said to follow the chains," Bex reminded him. "And this is the place where all the chains connect. It's also the only room inside the palace that was being guarded by a prince, so I'm guessing the entrance to Gilgamesh's bunker is somewhere around here."

That struck Adrian as sound logic, but Leander was shaking his head.

"My father would never hide anywhere so accessible," he informed them in a haughty voice. "Also, this is just where the general public enters the bridges to Earth. The chains themselves are hidden in yet another of Gilgamesh's private areas so that he doesn't have to compromise the aesthetics of his palace with giant ugly chains that are constantly flaking sin iron. Fortunately for us, we've already secured the key."

He pointed at the Prince of Envy's sword, and Adrian's eyes lit up.

"We might have done better than that," he said excitedly, using his coat to protect his hand this time as he grabbed the white blade off the ground where he'd dropped it when Bex appeared. "Envy's sword is connected to all of Gilgamesh's secret places, right? Doesn't that mean we can use it to cut straight to him?"

Leander scowled. "I can't imagine that actually working, but I suppose it's worth a try."

It absolutely was. Adrian was already swinging the sword, actually, keeping his focus on the gnawing blade as he ordered, "Open the way to Gilgamesh."

The command was simpler than the one he'd used to bring back Bex, except this time, nothing happened. The white sword just sliced through the air like any normal piece of metal. Adrian tried the order two more times with different wordings before dropping the blade with a disgusted huff.

"Useless hunk of junk."

"Let's not be so hasty," Leander said. "Just because Gilgamesh took the extremely simple precaution of not leaving his door unlocked doesn't mean he's unreachable. I've never dealt with the Morrigan personally, but even I know she's famous for not giving clues unless they're important. If she said 'follow the chains,' that is likely the way, so why don't you try asking the Blade of Envy for those instead?"

Adrian didn't want to touch the bitey sword again if he could help it. His hands were already covered in enough cuts, but Leander looked dead serious about never using any sword other than Mara, so he sucked it up and bent down to grab the white hilt one more time, gritting his teeth against the pain as he ordered, "Take us to the chains."

The moment the words left his mouth, the needle-shaped sword slashed the air open in front of him. The space beyond the cut looked as black as the void between worlds, but when Adrian leaned closer for a better look, he saw that was just an optical illusion. The other side of the cut was actually quite brightly lit. He was just staring directly into a rope made of twisted chains.

"Whoa," Bex said, her already pale face turning the color of paper as she peered through the hole. "That's high."

She was right. The place Envy's blade had cut into looked like what would happen if all of Heaven was invisible. If he looked down on this side, Adrian saw the cracked marble floor beneath his feet like always. When he looked through the hole, though, he could see all the way down to the bright-blue water of the living world far, far, *faaaar* below.

They were so high up that the islands of the Anchors looked like tiny specks. The Rivers of Death that rose from them were little more than blue flashes, while the chains were even smaller. They didn't even look golden from this angle. They were more like black threads that followed the blue lines of the rivers to a point where the water suddenly vanished.

Even compared to Gilgamesh's other artificial spaces like Limbo and the black desert, it was super weird. The raging Rivers of Death literally disappeared into thin air about a mile below. Adrian supposed that must be where they flowed into the Hells, but seeing all that rushing water simply cease to exist hurt his brain. The inner workings of the gods were famously beyond mortal comprehension, though, so he supposed that was what he got for poking his head behind the curtain.

He was far more concerned with the fact that he didn't see anything above them but chains vanishing into blackness. That didn't seem right, but the rest was exactly what he'd asked for. The Morrigan had said "follow the chains," and those were definitely chains. They were even twisted together in a way that made the giant links of smooth black metal actually climbable. Bex was already leaning through the hole to grab the closest one, sliding her fingers over the sin iron until she found a good handhold.

"This is it," she said, turning around to grin at the others. "Come on! The sin iron's corroded in places, so there are plenty of pits to dig your fingers into. Just be careful not to jostle the chains too much. We don't want Gilgamesh to feel us coming."

Adrian worried that was inevitable. He liked Bex's idea of pretending to retreat, but he secretly suspected it was more about keeping her demons out of harm's way than tricking Gilgamesh. From what he'd seen of Heaven so far, his father seemed aware of everything that happened here. Adrian was certain that Gilgamesh already knew they were coming, but he was also certain that Iggs would never have obeyed an order to retreat if Bex hadn't phrased it as part of a military strategy.

Whether she'd been telling the whole truth or not, they were in the thick of it now. Nemini had already started scaling the chain after Bex, and even Leander was bracing his bare feet against the sin iron to haul himself up. That left Adrian as the last one through. He wasn't leaving without his partner, though, so Adrian waited at the threshold until he heard the familiar patter of cat feet racing across the stone floor.

"I'm back!" Boston cried as he galloped down the stairs. "The bull is delivered. What did I miss?"

"Nothing much," Adrian joked, pointing the Blade of Envy at the hole he'd cut in the air.

"That doesn't look safe," Boston observed as he clambered up Adrian's coat to his shoulder. "Are we really going in there?"

"I am," Adrian said. "But you don't have to. I'm sure you already heard Iggs yelling about it, but Bex is sending all her demons back to Earth to defend the Blackwood. You're free to go with them if you—"

His voice cut off as he felt the thump of Boston's lashing tail hit this back.

"Adrian Blackwood," his cat said stiffly, "I am your familiar. It is my sworn duty to assist you in your work no matter what. Also, as was just established five minutes ago, you'd be dead without me."

"That I would," Adrian agreed wholeheartedly. "But I still wanted to give you the option."

"Your consideration is appreciated but unnecessary," Boston assured him. "I already made my choice eighteen years ago when I became your cat. Now let's get moving before the others leave us behind!"

He leaped off Adrian's shoulder as he finished, landing on the chain with the flawless grace of a curious cat.

His witch wasn't nearly so brave. Adrian took one look at that enormous drop and whistled for Bran. His broom appeared at once, shooting down the stairs from the room where he'd set it down to tend to Iggs.

He grabbed hold of the raven-carved broomstick the second it got close, but while Adrian was overwhelmingly relieved to have Bran back, he wasn't sure he'd get to use him. The hole he'd cut made it look like the twisting chains were going up through empty space, but when Adrian poked his broomstick through to check the flight conditions, he discovered he'd cut into yet another illusion. There only *appeared* to be tons of room. In reality, though, Gilgamesh's chains were tightly surrounded by an invisible wall, almost like they were running up the inside of a pipe.

That made a lot of sense, considering the entire purpose of this space was to run chains through the palace without being seen. They were basically crawling up the wiring on the inside of Gilgamesh's walls. The unexpectedly tight quarters didn't seem to bother the others, but it left Adrian with little room to fly. He'd been hoping he could take everyone up on Bran's raven, but it looked like there wasn't even enough space to fit his broom form without risking damage to his bristles.

That was bad news. Adrian was no slouch climber, but the chains were very tall, and the drop was *definitely* fatal. Climbing seemed to be the only way, though, so Adrian grabbed Bran's leather strap out of his pocket and slid his broom onto his back with a sigh. He was about to hop through the hole and grab onto the chain like Bex had when he realized he was still holding the Blade of Envy.

That was an easy choice, at least. Adrian didn't even hesitate before he dropped the white sword on the ground. Leaving the Blade of Envy behind was a risk, but whatever Leander said about rank, he was fed up with her constantly chewing on his hand. Bringing a princess who hated their guts on a secret mission sounded like a terrible idea in any case, so Adrian happily chucked her, taking a moment to wrap his bleeding palm with a handkerchief before he reached through the hole to grab the chain and start climbing after Bex and the others.

And behind him on the cracked floor of the arrivals room, unseen through the already closing cut in the world, a man's scarred, olive-skinned hand reached out of nowhere to pick up the crying sword Adrian had left behind.

Chapter 14

"So, you've got the powers of all nine queens now?" Adrian asked, looking up at Bex from his precarious hold on the chain several links below.

"That seems to be the case," Bex replied, doing her best not to sound overconfident as she hauled herself up the gigantic ladder of twisted sin iron. "I can also use powers from normal demons. I'm pretty sure I could even grow wings like Lys's if I tried."

"Then why don't you?" said Boston, hopping casually from link to link like they weren't all dangling over a miles-high drop into a sea of souls. "I'm no expert on demon magic, but now seems like a good time to spontaneously develop flight."

"I agree," Bex said as she reached for the next handhold. "The problem is I don't know how to use it. Lys makes flying look easy, but I'm pretty sure if I sprouted wings and tried to take off, I'd just end up plummeting to my death. Same goes for shapeshifting. Again, Lys makes it seem so simple, but spontaneously rearranging your organs doesn't sound like the sort of thing that should be attempted without a *lot* of practice."

"You probably should leave that one alone for now," Adrian agreed, but his eyes still shone with excitement. "What about the others, though? Have you tried any of them?"

"Just Fear's scales, Sorrow's sorrow, and the Queen of Pride's ability to make people kneel so far," Bex reported. "I'm sure I can do more, but it's hard to figure out what's available, since I don't feel any different than I did before War tore my horns off."

"What do you mean 'hard to figure out'?" Leander demanded from his safe perch on the inside of a giant link twenty feet above them. "You already know what powers each type of demon possesses. Can't you just do that?"

"Can you do a card trick after only seeing it once?" Bex grumbled, focusing on her hands as she hauled herself up to the next ledge. "Just because I know something's possible doesn't mean I know how to do it. It's not like these new horns came with a manual."

The prince shook his head and made himself more comfortable on the link twenty feet above the one Bex was currently hauling herself over, which was just obnoxious. Bastard had been using his *Fifty Steps of the Pilgrim* spell to avoid climbing the slippery, poisonous sin iron. Bex respected the ingenuity, but it was *super* annoying that he could just sit up there acting all superior while the rest of them struggled.

She'd thought about asking Adrian if they could use his broom, but she figured the witch wouldn't be climbing if flying was an option. Space was *super* tight in here. It might look like the chains were hanging in empty air, but every time Bex stuck her limbs out too far, she bumped an elbow or a knee against an invisible barrier that felt as hard as a steel pipe. It was like they were following the chains up a drain spout, and the higher they got, the more the walls closed in, leaving less and less room for Bex to squeeze her body through as she pulled herself into the seemingly-infinite dark.

"I hope it's not too much farther," Adrian panted below her. "All this sin iron is making Bran sick. I can feel him shaking through my back."

"I'm not feeling so great myself," Boston confessed, lifting his paw to examine his toe beans, which definitely looked darker than usual.

"I don't understand," the cat grumbled, glaring at his feet. "I'm a Blackwood just like Adrian, *and* I've endured all the same poison training. Why is he tolerant to sin iron and I'm not?"

"Because you're not Agatha's son," Leander replied from above. "The Witch of the Present's resistance to both sin iron and quintessence are the two main reasons Gilgamesh accepted such an obvious enemy into his bed." He made a disgusted sound. "They bred us for our traits like dogs."

"Well, I'm *extraordinarily* happy that princes are immune to sin iron right now," Adrian said as he held out his arms for Boston, who for once didn't gripe as he jumped down and wiggled into the protected, sin-iron-free safety of his witch's coat. "This whole thing would be impossible if we weren't."

"I wish I was immune," Bex muttered, shaking her stinging hands. "My regeneration is keeping up with the damage, but it still feels horrible." She looked over at her sister. "How're you keeping up, Nemini?"

"I'm still in existence," came the exhausted-sounding reply. "I know time is an illusion, but I'd still like to know when this particular experience will be over."

"Me too," Bex said, craning her neck back to glare at Leander again. "Hey, show-off! Why don't you teleport up a few more rungs and see how much more of this we've got to climb?"

Leander rolled his mirrored eyes but did as she requested, vanishing with a mutter of sorcery only to reappear a few seconds later.

"That was fast," Bex said. "Were you even able to see anything?"

"No, because I didn't make it," Leander explained tersely. "There's something blocking the way above us."

"What is it?" Adrian asked.

"If I knew that, I would have said," Leander snapped, gazing at the darkness over his head, which looked exactly the same as all the other darkness they'd been climbing through for the last twenty minutes. "Unfortunately, just like all the other walls in here, I can't see what's in the way. The chain keeps going, but I can no longer push my body into the empty space between the links. It's like the chains are passing into a place where I can't go,"

"You mean like a barrier?" Adrian asked, pulling Bran off his back. "Let me see."

Adrian's broom must have definitely not been feeling well. Due to the small space, the witch had to hold him straight up and down like a pole. The odd arrangement shouldn't have been an issue—Bex had seen Bran pull off way more complicated moves—but the broom seemed barely able to lift Adrian off his feet. It was more like a helium balloon making his body lighter, but Adrian still had to kick off the chains to actually reach the place where Leander was. He pulled it off eventually, but he only managed to get a few feet higher than his brother before Adrian suddenly stopped.

"Leander's right!" he called back down a second later. "There's something stopping me up here!"

"Can you break it?" Bex yelled back.

Adrian switched his arms, holding Bran in his left hand so he could give the blackness a good *thwack* with his right. When that didn't seem to work, he climbed around to the other side of the chains and tried again. That must not have done anything either, though, because he floated back down again a few moments later.

"That's as much as Bran can take," he said as he landed on the chain right next to Bex. "I couldn't figure out how to get past the blockage, but I did manage to get a good feel for its shape."

"What shape?" Bex asked, sticking her leg out behind him so Adrian, who was only holding onto the chain with one arm, wouldn't fall.

"It's kind of like a rubber stopper," he said, pointing at the seemingly infinite darkness over their heads. "The chains can pass through it, but everything else gets blocked, including us." He frowned. "I probably should've expected something like this in hindsight. Gilgamesh has been obsessing about these chains for the last five thousand years. Of course he'd have something to keep people from just climbing straight up into his secrets, but I'm not sure how we're going to get through."

"We'll just have to go around," Leander said, leaning off the chain to run his fingers over the invisible walls beside them. "Gilgamesh has always been an orderly man. Even if this is a separate hidden space, it's still probably close to where the actual chains come up."

"That makes sense," Adrian agreed, looking at the blue water glittering miles below. "I can't imagine a place like this is cheap to maintain, and the most efficient path between two points is always a straight line. The barrier must also be expensive, or else he would've filled the whole pipe with it." His face broke into a smile. "I bet that plug is the bottom of wherever we're ultimately trying to go."

"So all we have to do is bash through the ceiling and we're there?" Bex asked, smiling back as she pulled out her sword. "That's easy, then. Drox can cut through anything."

"Let's not be rash," Leander said swiftly, putting up his hands. "I agree we're likely close to our goal, but if you start slashing in a tight space with a sword that can 'cut anything,' you might slice through something critical and doom us all."

"Then how do *you* want to do it?" Bex snapped as she pulled Drox back into his ring.

"By going out the same way we came in," Leander replied with a superior look. "Unlike the Blade of Wrath, the Blade of Envy was built for this task. She's also dulled by the loss of her prince, which means she shouldn't be able to damage anything we don't want her to. She's basically a safety sword at this point, *and* she happens to conveniently be already in our possession."

"Not really," Adrian said sheepishly. "I kind of left her behind."

Leander whirled on him in a fury. "Why in the Hells would you do *that*?"

"Because the whole point of doing this was not to get caught," Adrian reminded him, giving the prince an exasperated look. "The princesses are all Gilgamesh's spies. You can't execute a sneak attack while carrying the enemy's camera."

Leander still looked livid, but Bex thought Adrian had been very forethoughtful.

"We don't need the Blade of Envy," she insisted. "We were just talking about how I've become the Swiss Army knife of demon powers. That means I should be able to do anything Envy could."

"We were also discussing how you don't know how to use your powers yet," Leander reminded her tersely. "You also don't know where you're going. Envy's power relies on knowledge to work because even she can't be envious of a place she's never heard of. You're proposing to use a power you've never tried to go to a place you can't even picture. How do you think that's going to end up?"

"Better than hanging off a poison chain at a dead end," Bex snapped as she started hauling herself up the links again. "You're making this way too complicated. There's a wall between us and where we want to be, so I'll break it down. Easy-peasy."

"Of all the blockheaded notions," Leander muttered. "You can't just bash your way through everything!"

"Why not?" Bex asked, climbing faster. "That's how we've won everything so far."

"I suppose one should never underestimate the power of brute force and ignorance," Leander muttered as he teleported beside her. "Just *please* don't hit it too hard. I don't think the Prince of Envy was lying when he said the chains are exceptionally fragile at the moment. If you crack them by accident and end up resurrecting the gods, this will all be for nothing."

"I'll be careful," Bex said, flashing him a fanged smile. "Though if you want to make yourself useful, you could go up there and find me a good spot to hit."

Leander gave her a scalding look, but he did as she asked, teleporting up to the place where the chains all came together in a final black twist. Bex still couldn't see the barrier he and Adrian had been talking about, but she hadn't been able to see any of the walls in this place. Sure enough, when she finally made it up to the spot where Leander was waiting, her towering new horns bumped against an invisible barrier that felt even harder than the walls around it.

"Okay," she muttered, pressing her hands against the invisible surface. "Let's give this a try."

It's thick, her sword warned. *I could still cut through it, but the rude prince has a point about the chains. If we hit as hard as we need to get through, there's a good chance we'll damage something we don't mean to.*

"What about the walls?" Bex asked, moving her hand off the vertical invisible barrier to the horizontal one beside it. "Are they an easier target?"

Significantly, Drox said. *But you'll still want to use Envy's power.*

"Sure. Can you tell me how to do that?"

No, because it's not mine, her sword replied bitterly. *I didn't get a manual either. You're just going to have to use it and see.*

Bex swore under her breath. Blind was her least favorite way to fly. She was tempted to use Drox anyway despite the risk, but she *really* didn't want to cut a chain and bring Ishtar back by accident just because she was uncomfortable. The wall felt thinner than the ceiling, and Leander had already said they should be very close, so Bex decided to give Envy's power a go.

Decision made, she closed her eyes and pressed her fingers firmly against the invisible barrier. It felt just as hard as every other time she'd bumped it, but Bex forced herself to stop thinking about how difficult it was going to be and approach the problem like a queen. A *different* queen, which was the really tricky part. As Queen of Wrath, Bex normally just burned anything that got in her way, but stopping the bull with Pride's power had forced her to be prideful. By that logic, accessing Envy's abilities probably required her to be jealous of something.

That was going to be a problem. Bex was legitimately proud of many of the things she'd accomplished, but she didn't envy Gilgamesh in the slightest. She loathed him, which felt like the opposite. If Bex had learned anything from her own powers, though, it was that a queen's abilities largely depended on mindset. The reason Nemini couldn't use her power despite getting her horns back was because she was no longer capable of feeling superior to others, not because she wasn't a queen. Likewise, the reason Bex didn't feel a damn thing stirring inside her now wasn't because she lacked Envy's power but because she couldn't even imagine being envious of Gilgamesh. *That* was the factor that needed to change, so Bex squeezed her eyes even tighter and focused on the things she didn't normally like to think about.

She thought about how hard she'd had it through all her lives, how much she'd struggled. She thought about all the times she'd died in vain or worse, gotten others killed. She thought about how bitter she'd felt back when she'd thought she'd already wasted this life and that the only thing her current incarnation was good for was building up a stockpile of deathly water so the next Bex could have a better start.

She thought about all the bitter, horrible, depressing things Drox usually scolded her for dwelling on, and then Bex thought about Gilgamesh. She thought about how he got to do whatever he wanted while his sons and minions did all the work. She thought about how he had a private island all to himself while she'd spent the last seven years scrounging to be able to provide her demons with a Winnebago. How he and his people lived in luxury while her demons slaved for their scraps.

Even Adrian had liked Malik so much that he'd lied to her. Gilgamesh was charming, rich, and brilliant—the man the gods had adored before he'd beaten them and continued to respect even after they were dead. Ishtar herself had been head over heels in love with him while Bex, her own daughter, was treated as merely a useful tool. Gilgamesh wasn't even part of the mortal world anymore, but all of creation still seemed to revolve around the precious Eternal King, and Bex was *sick* of it. Why couldn't she be the one with the power to give her people whatever they wanted? Why didn't she have a private island hidden from the world's troubles where she could relax with Adrian? She'd certainly worked hard enough to deserve it, but her efforts always fell flat while Gilgamesh seemed to succeed without even trying. It just wasn't fair.

As soon as that awful feeling festered inside her chest, the invisible wall Bex was pressing her hands against began to crack. She leaned into the pressure at once, taking all the toxic jealousy she'd just cooked up and feeding it into... not a fire, exactly. Envy didn't burn like Wrath. It was more like a vise that was forever squeezing tighter, a pit that only sucked you deeper the more you thought about it.

It definitely wasn't the sin she'd been born to burn, but that didn't mean it didn't need to be destroyed, because the deeper she sank into Envy's power, the more Bex hated it. She didn't want to be jealous of Gilgamesh's sad, self-serving life. She wanted to be happy with her own, to make a *better* world than his selfish dreams could envision. Gilgamesh's power to change the world was what she was actually envious of, and the moment Bex embraced that, the invisible barrier shattered under her fingers.

It felt like breaking through a metal plate. The wall right next to the ceiling had fractured like glass. To get through it, though, Bex had to peel each shard back like a piece of metal sheeting. This feeling turned out to be even more accurate than she'd initially realized when Bex poked her head through the hole to discover she'd just broken through the solid-gold floor of the most glittery, most ostentatious room she'd ever laid eyes on.

It reminded Bex of the famous circular theater Shakespeare had built for his plays. Like that building, this room was several stories tall, perfectly cylindrical, and big enough to hold several hundred people. Unlike the medieval Globe Theatre, however, this room was entirely covered in gold.

Not gold leaf either. The floor she'd just broken through was a four-inch-thick plate, and the curving walls were just as bad. The gold on them was so thick it looked wrinkled, though after a few blinks, Bex realized that wasn't because the soft, pure gold was collapsing under its own weight. It was because the entire room was covered in a carving.

The details were hard to see, since everything was the same shiny, metallic color, but after several seconds of staring, Bex was able to make out the image of a city. It was done in the same realistic style as the stone carvings of demons being tortured that she'd cringed at in the Hells, except this art was shimmering and beautiful. The carving spanned the entire room, covering the multistory walls in a glittering panoramic image of an ancient walled city seen from a single high point. Not until she'd gawked at it for several seconds, though, did Bex realize she'd seen this view before.

The color was obviously different, and the gold was much, much brighter than the dark cavern, but that was definitely the ancient city of Uruk. She'd seen a destroyed version of this exact view from the steps of the palace on the central hill. She was still gaping at it in wonder when Adrian wiggled his way in beside her.

"What is this place?" he asked, opening his coat so Boston could get a look as well. "An art gallery?"

"Going by the glare, it's probably the throne room," Leander called from behind them.

Bex *did* see a throne, now that he mentioned it. Everything was so glittery she hadn't noticed it at first, but the section of the circular room farthest from where she'd come up had a giant golden dais leading up to an ornate throne made of—what else?—solid gold.

"Couldn't he think of anything else to use?" Bex grumbled as she hauled herself onto the shiny, slippery gold floor. "I thought Gilgamesh was supposed to have *good* taste."

"Throne rooms are always displays of a king's wealth and power," Adrian said as he scrambled after her. "This is a bit much, though."

"It's blinding," Bex complained, putting her hand over her glowing eyes to shield them. "There's so many reflections in there that I can't even see where the light's coming from."

"Never mind the décor," Leander said as he teleported in beside them. "What's important is why did we come out *here*? I thought you were going through the ceiling?"

"It was too tough," Bex said with a shrug. "This was right next to it, though, so we should still be very close."

"Close doesn't cut it in Heaven," Leander scolded. "This is the throne room at the top of the main tower, but other than the fact that Gilgamesh carved all the wall art himself, it's not actually special. I thought we'd come out in the king's private chambers or, better still, his treasure vault, but this is useless."

"I wouldn't call it useless," Adrian said quickly, coming to Bex's defense before she lost her temper and told the former Prince of Sorrow exactly where he could shove his opinions. "Is there more to this place? A room above us, perhaps?"

"No," Leander said. "This is Gilgamesh's personal tower where he keeps his private quarters and treasury along with the Sanitorium where the princes are reconstructed, but those are all below us. The throne room is at the tippy-top because Gilgamesh considered it thematically appropriate for the Eternal King to sit at the literal pinnacle of Heaven, but he never actually uses this room anymore now that there's no one left that he needs to impress." Leander frowned in thought. "Why would the chains go up here?"

"Well, we're not going to find out by standing around," Bex said, reaching back to help Nemini, who was looking positively ill.

"Whoa," she said, gripping the other queen hard. "Are you okay? Did the sin iron get to you?"

"It's not the sin iron," her normally stoic sister whispered as her fingers clamped down on Bex's. "There's something terrible here. Can't you feel it?"

Bex didn't. Other than the eye-searing brightness, the throne room actually felt much better than the chains had. But while Bex was delighted to be somewhere open, bright, and non-toxic again, Drox was also trembling on her finger.

The Queen of Pride is right, he whispered. *Be on your guard, my queen.*

"I'm going to need a better hint than that," Bex told her sword irritably. "What am I supposed to be on guard against?"

When Drox failed to reply, she glanced back at Nemini, but her sister wasn't even looking at her anymore. She was staring across the circular room at the golden throne on the opposite side. A throne that, Bex realized with a start, someone was sitting on.

She didn't feel bad that she hadn't spotted him earlier. The man's golden armor was the same color as everything else in this gaudy place, causing his body to blend into the throne like a chameleon's. Considering where he was sitting, her first guess should've been Gilgamesh himself, but although Bex had never seen the king in anything other than his propaganda art—hardly a reliable source—she already knew it wasn't him. The man on the throne looked too haggard and impatient to be the Eternal King, and there was no crown on his dark, curling hair. He also had only one eye, which Bex could never imagine Gilgamesh enduring. Her best guess was that this was yet another prince, but while there was a sword at his hip, it wasn't white. She was still trying to figure it out when Leander suddenly stepped forward.

"Brother."

Ah, Bex thought, moving her feet into an attack stance. So this *was* another prince, and not one Leander liked, given the way he'd spat that word like a curse. Bex was starting to get the feeling that none of Gilgamesh's sons liked each other, but while Leander looked ready to throw down right then and there, the prince sitting on the throne just looked sad.

"Leander," he replied, "I'm relieved you made it out of the Hells."

"No thanks to you," Leander snarled back, pulling himself to his full, lanky height. "What are you doing, sitting in that chair? Has Father finally given up?"

"I'm sitting because I'm tired," the new prince said, turning his single silver eye toward Bex. "Thanks to *someone's* refusal to die, I haven't gotten more than four hours of sleep together in two months."

"You could've died instead," Bex offered, stepping up to stand beside Leander. "Which prince are you? I never was able to keep all you golden bastards straight."

"*That* is Crown Prince Alexander," Leander informed her before the prince on the dais could even open his mouth, "Gilgamesh's most reliable paper pusher and the Prince of War."

"That explains why he doesn't have a princess," Bex said as she lifted her own sword.

"The loss of my partner was unfortunate," Crown Prince Alexander agreed, settling deeper into his golden seat. "But also inevitable. Father has always despised war in all its forms. Even if my princess had survived, there was never going to be a place for her in Gilgamesh's new kingdom."

"Then you already know what he's doing," Adrian said, clutching Boston in his arms as he stepped forward to join Bex and Leander. "Alexander, *brother*, please listen. I know how good Gilgamesh is at making bad ideas sound noble, but you have to believe me when I say this isn't a good path for any of us. We believe that Gilgamesh is going to use the power of the gods to reset the world and establish himself as the new divinity. You have to help us stop him!"

"Why would I do that?" Alexander asked, turning his head slightly to the side so that he could stare directly at them with his good eye. "Even if your ignorant accusations had merit, what part of our current world deserves saving? The death? The suffering? The destruction and exploitation of every natural wonder? The witches who dabble in black magic and sell their children for power?"

"And you think Gilgamesh's world would be better?" Bex demanded. "He's a murderer, a tyrant, and a slaver! Any future he makes will be just as twisted and self-centered as he is. Just look at the disaster he calls Heaven."

"You have no idea what you're talking about, Coward Queen," Alexander snarled. "Your creators were the ones who pushed us to this point! Yes, my father is cruel, but he is also brilliant. He alone was able to defeat the gods and return this world to humanity. But even after the gods were slain, they were too selfish to die. The Heaven you criticize is indeed a flawed compromise that none of us wanted, but my father was only doing what needed to be done. For five thousand years, he has been our bulwark against *your* gods. You say he enslaved your people, but from our perspective, he has kept millions of enemy soldiers from overrunning the world."

He stabbed his finger at her. "*You* are the demon here, daughter of Ishtar! You lead an army of parasites who feed off the very people Gilgamesh fought to save. You're not even organic lifeforms. Ishtar's demons are tools crafted for the convenience of a delusional regime that sought to remake humanity in the gods' own image. What Gilgamesh did to your kind was not slavery but containment. If you have a problem with that, take it up with the one who built you to be used in the first place."

"I *have* taken it up with her," Bex growled, clutching her sword. "I'm not here to fight for Ishtar or any of the gods. I'm here to win freedom for *my* people, who never asked for any of this! The gods may have built them, but you're the bastards making them suffer *right now*."

"If that's what you're here for, you're too late," Alexander informed her with a sneer. "The war is over. Father already has everything he needs. I'm only keeping watch to make sure his victory is not disturbed."

"And then what?" Leander asked, putting out a hand to stop Bex, who was already readying her sword to take off the Crown Prince's head. "You're still being the good son, Alexander, but Father doesn't value goodness. The moment he gets what he wants, he'll toss you aside just like he did the rest of us. I know you understand that, brother, so why are you still helping him?"

"Because he's the only way any of us get free," Alexander replied with resigned acceptance. "You're too young to know this, Leander, but while I am Gilgamesh's oldest living son, I am far from his first. I was born only two thousand years ago. Over those twenty centuries, I've seen more of my brothers die than I can count, mostly because of her."

He nodded at Bex, who winced despite her best efforts.

"I've seen so much death," the Crown Prince continued. "I've *caused* so much death. So much suffering and destruction and loss, and for what? To keep a bunch of stubborn gods in their graves."

Alexander shook his head with a sigh and sank lower in his golden chair. "I'm tired," he said. "Tired of war, tired of bickering warlocks and vain, scheming princes. I've wanted to enter the Sleep for ages now, but after so many years, I was the only one capable of running Father's empire. If I quit, all the balance and order I'd spent my entire life constructing would fall apart. I couldn't stand the thought of returning to chaos, so I stayed and worked. I hated every single second, but I did it all perfectly. That's why Gilgamesh trusts me most of all his sons. I'm the only one who understands the world of peace and order he's trying to create for all of us."

"If you're so important to Father's vision, why didn't he take you with him?" Leander asked, crossing his arms over his chest. "Why are you sitting alone in this empty room, waiting for the likes of us?"

"That was my choice," Alexander replied with a sad chuckle. "For the record, Father did invite me to join him. I was the one who refused. The new world King Gilgamesh is making will be splendid, I'm sure, but as I already told you, I'm tired. I've done my duty. I worked for two thousand years to help Father achieve his great dream, and now I intend to rest. When the current world ends, I'll end with it, and so will all of you." He smiled. "It is the *Epic of Gilgamesh*, after all. Minor characters like us don't belong in the final stanzas of his victory."

"Don't lump us in with you," Bex growled, raising her sword again. "You're free to die all you want, but we're not the Eternal King's lapdogs, and we're *not* giving up just because Gilgamesh says it's over."

"That we are not," Leander agreed, taking Bex by surprise when he stepped into a battle stance beside her. "Unlike you with your one blind eye, we can see this for the farce it is, and without your sword, you can't stop us."

It might have been Bex's imagination, but Alexander looked disappointed.

"I knew you wouldn't see reason," he said bitterly, rising from the throne at last. "For such a clever man, you never could make the right decision, Leander. That's why I brought this."

He clapped his armored hands together, and a figure stepped out from behind the towering throne. The golden room was so glittery that it was hard to make her out at first, but Bex already knew it was a princess. There was no one else whose carved feet made that musical clacking sound when they walked, but it wasn't until Leander went stone-still beside her that Bex finally realized *which* princess she was looking at.

Like all of Gilgamesh's dolls, she was incredibly beautiful with a willowy body and long, straight hair that cascaded over her shoulders like a waterfall, but her face was the saddest thing Bex had ever seen.

"Leander?" she whispered, her carved hand trembling where it clutched a square of blue silk around her narrow shoulders. "My love, my prince, is that really you?"

Leander stared back at her like he'd seen a ghost. "Mara," he choked at last, stumbling forward. "But it can't be. How is this—"

"I had her reconstructed," Alexander explained, placing his hand on the princess's shaking shoulder. "She's your Mara again."

"But... you said she'd already been wiped," Leander insisted. "You told me she was gone!"

The Crown Prince shook his head with a *tut*. "You should know by now that Gilgamesh never actually throws anything away. We kept all her old memories just in case we needed them. It was a tactical precaution, though in the end, I'm afraid my reasons for bringing her back were entirely sentimental."

Leander looked confused, and Alexander sighed again.

"I told you," he said irritably, "I'm tired of my brothers dying, so after Father ordered the destruction of the Hells with you still in it, I had her wipe reversed. I wanted somebody else who remembered you, somebody I could mourn with. I figured there'd be no one better for that than the Princess of Sorrow, but what started out as a tragedy might have just turned into a happy ending."

He extended his arm, pushing the princess forward with the hand that was still clamped around her shoulder.

"Here," he said, looking Leander dead in his mirrored eyes. "She's yours. Your princess, just like before. Father's even agreed to let the two of you assist him while he finishes his work. You can finally be together with your beloved in a place with no war or gods just like you've always dreamed, and all you have to do to is bring me the heads of the Coward Queen and Prince Adrian."

Bex went perfectly still. Everyone on her side of the room did as all eyes turned toward Leander. The Prince of Sorrow was staring at his princess like she was everything he'd ever wanted, but just as Bex was getting ready to put her sword between him and Adrian, Leander said, "No."

Alexander's confident face went blank in shock. "What?"

"No," Leander repeated, gripping the golden floor with his bare, dirty feet. "You've told me so many times that I could earn Mara's freedom if I just did this or killed that, but you never once kept that promise."

"Because you were never successful," Alexander snapped.

"That shouldn't have mattered!" Leander roared. "You've always claimed I'm your favorite brother, but you hold my beloved to my throat like a knife every time Father snaps his fingers. You go on and on about how the gods mistreated humanity, but you've helped Gilgamesh treat us even worse, and I'm *sick* of it! You think you're the only one who's tired of this nonsense? I've been exhausted for four hundred years! Mara was the only bright spot in my entire miserable existence, but I'm not so stupid that I'm going to betray the allies who *have* been honorable toward me and turn myself into a dog for Gilgamesh *again* in the hope of a happy ending that's been forever promised and *never come true!*"

"Don't do this, Leander," the Crown Prince warned, gripping Mara's shoulder. "I've offered you a great gift. Don't throw it away like a fool."

"You're the one being a fool," Leander snarled. "You know better than anyone that Father's not the glorious king he pretends to be, and yet you let him do whatever he wants! You say it's because it keeps back the gods, but I know the real reason. You're a coward! You say you're tired of seeing your brothers die, but who was it who stood by and let Father send them to their deaths? Who drags us to him so that we can be punished? No wonder you're so tired. You've been complicit in everything Gilgamesh has done! Now you want me to join you in licking the boots that kick us, but I will not."

He pulled himself straighter. "I refuse to be anything less than the noble prince my beautiful princess deserves. *She* is my paradise, so I don't need Gilgamesh's condescending invitation. With her by my side, I already have everything I could ever want. I know she feels the same, so come, Mara!" He threw out his hand. "*Run to me!*"

As soon as Leander called out to her, the horrible sadness fell off Mara's carved face, replaced by a look of pure fury as she reeled back and slammed her carved elbow into Alexander's stomach. That shouldn't have been enough to hurt a prince by itself, but Mara was also the Princess of Sorrow. The moment she touched him, Alexander's armored body seized up with a sob, leaving him crippled as she tore herself free and ran for her prince. Alexander recovered the instant she stopped touching him, but by that point, Mara was halfway across the room, reaching out her hands for Leander, who was already there to catch her.

He must've teleported. By the time Bex realized he was no longer standing next to her, Leander was sweeping his princess into his arms. She crashed into him with a sob, pressing her carved white lips against every bit of Leander she could touch. That normally would've creeped Bex out, but this wasn't the normal obsessive princess attachment. Every clutch and kiss was filled with what looked like true affection, so much that even Bex couldn't help but smile.

She'd already signaled Nemini to move forward and help her protect the lovers, though she wasn't terribly worried. Now that his scheme to bribe Leander into betraying them had failed, the Crown Prince was outnumbered five to one. Bex was hoping he'd just give up since he seemed like such a sad sack, but Alexander didn't look like he was planning to step aside. He'd already drawn the black sword Bex had noticed him wearing at the beginning, the one she just now realized strongly resembled her own Drox.

"*Stop*," he commanded in the language of the Riverlands.

The order fell on the throne room like a hammer. The only time Bex had felt anything like it was when the eight stolen voices of the queens had commanded every demon in the Hells to kneel. She'd been hornless at the time, so it had hit her hard, but even that pressure was nothing compared to this, because those voices had been mere echoes. This was the real thing, because the sword in Alexander's hand wasn't a Blade of Gilgamesh. It was the blade Enki had made for Bex's mother, the weapon Gilgamesh was always holding in his statues while the carvings of the defeated queens sobbed at his feet.

Ishtar's sword.

"Maranea," he said in a voice so full of stolen power that even Bex shuddered. "By your sacred name, I command you: Kill everyone in this room except for me."

Bex sucked in a breath. She had to get that sword out of his hands, but before she could even take a step in the Crown Prince's direction, Leander cried out in pain as Mara ripped her white-carved arm off his shoulders and stabbed it through his chest.

Chapter 15

THE STAB WAS SO FAST IT SEEMED INSTANTANEOUS, but everything that followed looked like it was moving in slow motion. Leander didn't even seem to understand what had just happened. He kept clinging to his princess with a confused look on his gaunt face while gallons of white blood—far more than any human body should've been able to hold—poured out of his sundered chest and landed on the throne room's golden floor.

For what felt like an eternity, nobody moved. Even Bex's feet were rooted in shock. When she finally managed to overcome it, she raced forward and yanked Leander off his princess, whose arm was *still* sticking through his chest. This caused even more blood to dump out of him, but while Bex was trying to get Leander to safety, the prince was fighting back.

"No," he wheezed, grabbing at Bex with weakened, blood-slicked hands. "Don't take me from her. I can't leave her like this."

"Don't be stupid," Bex hissed, pulling him harder. "She's a Blade of Gilgamesh, the Traitor King! Of *course* they used her against you the moment your loyalty went in the wrong direction."

Leander made another gurgling sound of protest, but Bex had had enough. She hauled him out of danger and shoved him at Adrian, who was already digging his medical supplies frantically out of his coat, before turning to put herself between the wounded Leander and the enemy. She'd just gotten into position when Bex caught another glimpse of the Princess of Sorrow's face.

It was enough to make her pause. The princess might have the same carved body and tooled-gold eyes as all of Gilgamesh's dolls, but the look of abject horror on her face belonged solely to Mara. If ivory and gold had been capable of producing tears, she would've been weeping rivers, but her smooth-carved cheeks were dry. She didn't even have enough control over her body anymore to open her lips and let out the scream Bex could see building inside her as Gilgamesh's weapon lifted her perfectly carved bloody hand and swung again.

Bex was fast enough this time. She sidestepped the blow and struck back, swinging Drox like a bat to bash the terrified but still deadly-looking princess with the flat of her blade.

Mara didn't even try to dodge. She took the hit full across her front, letting Bex throw her across the circular throne room into the wall on the opposite side. She landed with enough force to flatten the golden carving of ancient Uruk, but the real damage came when she slid to the floor, revealing the cracks Bex's hit had opened all over her carved body.

"No!" Leander screamed, fighting Adrian's grip as the witch tried desperately to keep him still. *"Don't hurt her!"*

"Yes," Mara said at the same time, giving her sister a desperate look even as her cracked body pushed itself back up with the janky motion of a marionette. "Do it again, Bexa. Shatter me before—"

Her plea cut off as her body shot forward, her carved white feet slipping on the slick gold floor as she charged recklessly at the enemy. Her movements were so obvious that Bex could've hit her with her eyes closed, but she didn't even raise her sword. She spun out of the way instead, letting the Princess of Sorrow run right past. When she was in the clear, Bex turned to Nemini, who was standing directly behind her as usual.

"Can you keep Mara off me without hurting her?"

"Probably," Nemini said, glancing at the princess, who was already wheeling back around for another charge. "But what will you be doing?"

"Stopping this tragedy at the source," Bex growled, turning to glare at the Crown Prince, who was still watching from the golden dais with Ishtar's stolen sword at in his hand.

Nemini's lips curved into a slight frown. "Be careful. He was War's prince for a reason."

Bex didn't care. She'd already defeated War once, and she'd rather fight Gilgamesh himself right now than keep hitting the sobbing Mara.

"Just keep everyone alive," she ordered, getting into position. "This shouldn't take long."

The Queen of Pride nodded and stepped up to take Bex's place, facing off against their tragic sister while Bex launched herself across the throne room to drive Drox's blade into the Prince of War's heart.

That was the plan, at least. Unfortunately, Drox's point didn't get within a foot of the prince's golden armor before he stepped out of the way. The move was so fast Bex's eyes could hardly track it, but by the time she slammed her boots into the slick floor to course correct, the prince was already behind her.

"Rebexa," he said in the same commanding voice he'd used to order her sister, "kill yoursel—"

"That's not my name, asshole!" Bex roared, spinning around to unleash a blast of fire straight to his face. The flames were roaring around her body by this point, stoked by the wrath of what had been done to her sweetest sister. Their heat was already turning the golden floor under her feet to mush. The conflagration should've scorched the flesh off the prince's quintessence-caked bones, but Alexander paid the fire no attention. He simply flicked his wrist.

What happened next was too fast for Bex's brain to follow. One moment, her fire was about to cook his face. The next, it was gone, cut out of existence by a sword so sharp, the fabric of reality snapped and frayed wherever its edge rested. Bex was still trying to wrap her mind around the concept when that impossibly sharp sword swung at her.

She barely got her own sword up in time. She blocked with Drox out of five thousand years of habit, but the moment the Blade of Ishtar touched her own, Bex knew she'd made a fatal mistake. Her Drox was normally an unbreakable wall. Even when he'd been whittled down to a sliver, he'd never failed to stop an attack. But when the enemy's sword met Bex's this time, that unthinkably sharp edge sliced through him like a razor, cutting the unbreakable metal of the gods, the blessing of Enki himself, like it was paper.

If Bex hadn't been burning with the combined fire of all of Ishtar's demons, the prince would've cut her sword in half before she'd realized what was happening. Bex *was* burning, though, and she moved as fast as her flames, snatching Drox back into his ring before the prince's terrible weapon could do more than nick him.

That quick thinking saved her sword. Unfortunately, it also left Bex without a defense when the prince swung again, his stolen sword moving so fast she didn't have a prayer of dodging. Frantically, Bex pulled up the fear-demon scales she'd used against today's first prince, but she already knew it was useless. If a Divine Blade of Enki couldn't stop it, flesh and bone had no shot. The prince's sword didn't even slow down as it sliced the black scales off her with effortless grace to cut into Bex's side.

It was the same place she'd gotten hit the first time she'd faced a prince at seventeen. Bex had gotten faster over the years, so the wound wasn't as deep this time, but the damage was still done. She could actually feel her regeneration recoiling from undoing the work of Ishtar's weapon. The result was a gush of hot black blood running down her side as she rolled to a stop and whirled back around to face the smugly smiling prince.

"Now you understand," he said, turning Ishtar's black sword to show Bex the cutting edge, which was so sharp that blood didn't even cling to it. "I might not be able to name you, but no creation of Ishtar can defeat their goddess's sword."

"And you're telling me this why?" Bex demanded, pressing a hand against her wound. "Surely you don't think I'm going to surrender now?"

That was what the princes who talked to her in the middle of combat were usually after, but Alexander shook his head.

"It wouldn't matter anymore if you did," he said as he stepped back into his stance. "Didn't you hear me earlier? This world is as good as gone. You could throw yourself at Gilgamesh's feet, and he would no longer care. It's already over. We're just killing time until the countdown's finished."

"If that's how you feel, why don't you get out of my way?" Bex offered. "It'll save you a lot of pain."

The Crown Prince didn't bother with a response. He just attacked, moving faster than any opponent Bex had ever fought as he swung his sword at her neck. She moved just in time to save her head, lighting up in an explosion of fire the second the prince got close. If she couldn't block his sword, Bex reasoned, she'd burn off his hands instead. Even the Blade of Ishtar still needed to be swung, but no sooner had her flames shot out than the prince's sword flicked back, and all the fire she'd just thrown at him vanished without so much as a puff of smoke.

He cut them out of existence, Drox explained when he felt her shock. *The Blade of Ishtar is the sharpest tool Enki ever made. It can cut things I can't even conceive of.*

"Then we'll just have to get it out of his hands," Bex snarled, drawing her sword again.

She pulled on her own power at the same time. Not the Bonfire of Wrath again. This was an ability Bex hadn't tried yet but had already seen in action. She even had a pretty good idea of how it worked. All she had to do was focus on her refusal to let this son of her hated enemy take anything else away from her. Gilgamesh already had enough, as evidenced by the golden room they were standing in. To demand her defeat as well was pure greed, and the moment Bex threw that sin onto her fire, the notch Ishtar's Blade had put in Drox repaired itself.

The hole in her side closed up as well. Not because it had healed—her regeneration still refused to touch any damage done by Ishtar's sacred weapon—but because that was Greed's power. Her sister permitted nothing of hers to be stolen, and now that Greed's demons had bowed their horns to her, neither did Bex.

She could already feel the protection wrapping around her like a fist. While the Queen of Greed's power was squeezing, nothing that belonged to her could be taken or broken. Bex wasn't sure if that protection extended all the way to death, but after watching Greed's sword put the haughty prince she'd diced back together in Adrian's forest *and* repair the madman she'd burned to a crisp in Limbo, she was feeling pretty confident. Keeping the power up took a lot of energy, but Bex's flames were getting her nowhere, so she threw it all in, pouring herself down Greed's maw as she dug her boots into the softened gold floor and charged, turning the tables on the Crown Prince as she swung for *his* head instead.

He dodged the attack with room to spare, moving with beyond superhuman speed to strike Bex's open flank. She spun around to meet him, slamming Drox's blade into the Sword of Ishtar. Just like before, the black blade cut straight through hers. This time, though, Bex was able to push back, using Greed's power to replace Drox's sword as fast as Ishtar's blade cut it. The victorious smile was still spreading across her face when Alexander hooked the toe of his golden boot around the back of her ankle and yanked Bex's legs out from under her.

She fell on her back with a slam. The prince's sword followed, almost slicing her in half before Bex rolled away. She'd thought she'd made it until she felt a cold breeze on her left shoulder and realized Ishtar's unthinkably sharp blade had cut her arm off.

Bex was still staring at the bleeding stump in shock when Greed's power reversed it. Just like when the princess pulled her prince's white blood back into him, Bex's severed arm picked itself up off the floor and stuck itself back onto her shoulder like the damage had never been done. It was an unnatural, almost comically macabre sight, but the moment Bex saw it, she saw her path to victory.

Be wary, Drox cautioned as she rolled back to her feet. *Greed's power is not natural to your body. You were made to burn, not to replace. If you keep using it so recklessly—*

"It's the only thing that works against him," Bex argued, fixing the circling prince with her eyes as she raised Drox's once-again-pristine black blade. "We'll just have to end this quick."

A tremor of fear ran through her sword at those words, but Bex didn't have time to heed it. The prince was already swinging for her knee, his sword moving like a bolt of black lightning. Bex couldn't possibly dodge something so fast, so she didn't even try. She opened her defenses instead, practically offering the prince her leg, because if his sword was in her thigh, then it couldn't block her counter. She could already feel her balance tilting as the black blade cut in, so Bex swung with all her might, throwing what was left of her weight into the strike that should have taken off the prince's head.

"Should have" turned out to be the operative phrase. The blow had looked certain when she'd started, but by the time Drox's blade was actually within range of his neck, the prince had already ducked. His attack changed with him, transforming what had been a chopping strike into a thrusting one as the prince's body went down and forward, driving Ishtar's thin black sword like a nail through Bex's kneecap.

She howled in pain. Even with Greed's power reversing it, that hit hurt so bad she saw spots, especially since the prince still hadn't pulled his sword *out*. He used it as leverage to push her over instead, toppling Bex back onto the floor she'd just gotten off of. She responded with a kick from the leg he wasn't pinning, slamming her boot into the prince's armored elbow, but not nearly hard enough. The moment she made contact, the prince shifted his weight, fading under her foot and spoiling the kick's momentum. He twisted his sword at the same time, almost taking off the bottom half of her right leg before Bex got herself together and ripped free, dumping a ton of black blood on the floor in the process.

Greed's power pulled it right back into her, but the few seconds it took for her mangled leg to revert back to its pre-injured state felt like running a marathon. It was the biggest wound she'd undone yet, but while Bex did eventually get her knee—and even her leggings—back together, her heart was pounding like a jackhammer.

I warned you, Drox said as she gasped. *You can't keep this up.*

"What else am I supposed to do?" Bex demanded, rolling to the side just in time to avoid the prince's next deadly swing. "This is the final prince before Gilgamesh. If I can't kill him, we did all of this for nothing."

It's going to be the last thing you ever do at this rate, Drox snapped, his voice more terrified than Bex had ever heard it. *Please, my queen, you can't—*

"I can," Bex said, tightening her grip on his hilt as her eyes flicked to where Adrian was still saving Leander's life. "I have to, or it's all over."

There was nothing Drox could say to that. Even if he'd had something, Bex didn't have time to listen. She'd already launched into her next attack, ignoring the sword flying at her stomach as she leaped into the air to bring Drox's enormous blade down on the Crown Prince like a guillotine.

Adrian had never been so scared in his life, which was saying something, considering the past six months. He thought he'd become hardened to fear by this point, but there was something uniquely terrifying about seeing Bex—the fastest, strongest, most unbeatable person he'd ever met—being forced back by a prince who moved faster than lightning and cut through anything he touched without breaking a sweat.

Even thinking about it felt like a betrayal, but Adrian was pretty sure the Crown Prince was better than Bex. Add in his unbeatable sword that could cut through Drox's blade *and* slice her fire out of the air, and it was no wonder that there was now a pit where Adrian's stomach used to be. The only good thing he could say about the situation was that at least the horrific damage she was taking seemed to be instantly repairing itself.

He wasn't sure how she was doing that, actually. Adrian was used to Bex's amazing regeneration by this point, but he'd never seen Drox heal before. He would've called it a miracle if it hadn't been so clearly taking a huge toll. He'd seen Bex go entire fights without getting winded, but this battle had lasted less than a minute, and she was already gasping like a landed fish.

He *had* to go help her before she ran out of whatever she was using to power her miraculous recovery, but Alexander was moving too fast for Adrian's once-again-mortal eyes to follow. He'd get cut to ribbons if he tried to stick his nose into their fight. Also, as much as Adrian wanted to focus on Bex, he had his own problems to worry about.

"Would you *stop moving*?" Boston snarled, sinking his teeth in Leander, who hadn't stopped thrashing in Adrian's arms despite the enormous amount of white blood he'd already dumped on the floor.

"I can't!" Leander cried, lurching against the bandage Adrian was attempting to tie around the hole in his chest. "I have to help her!"

"You can't help anyone if you bleed to death," Boston pointed out, smacking the frantic prince on the head with his paw before turning to Adrian. "You should knock him out."

"I'd love to," Adrian replied through gritted teeth as he wrestled with his bloody brother. "But princes are immune to most common poisons, and I didn't think to grab any uncommon ones from my cabin before we ran off."

"Who said anything about poison?" Boston huffed. "Just hit him over the head. I know blunt trauma is risky, but you can't possibly do more damage than he's already doing to himself."

Adrian didn't know about that. Even for a Witch of the Flesh, the brain wasn't something that should be damaged on purpose. Leander really was going to bleed out if he didn't stop thrashing, though, so Adrian decided to try a different tactic.

"Calm down and listen," he said, pressing the ball of his palm into Leander's wound until the prince collapsed on the ground with a gasp. "Your princess is not in danger. Look and see for yourself."

He grabbed his brother's chin with the hand he wasn't using to grind into his wound and yanked his head around to face the battle happening on the opposite end of the throne room from Bex's. Adrian hadn't had time to glance in that direction yet, so he wasn't actually sure if what he'd said was accurate, but he'd overheard Bex telling Nemini not to hurt Mara, and despite being revealed as a queen herself, Nemini *always* did what Bex said. That fact held true yet again when Adrian turned to see Leander's princess swinging wildly at Nemini, who was not swinging back.

It was a shocking sight to see. Despite working with Bex's team for almost half a year now, Adrian had never gotten the chance to watch Nemini fight for real.

She normally just knocked her opponents out with a touch. That trick must not have worked on princesses, though, because while Mara's wild attacks were leaving openings so big that even Adrian could spot them, Nemini never tried to touch her. She was just keeping Mara busy, exactly as Bex had ordered.

That would've been great if Bex's fight with the Crown Prince had been going better. The way things were looking on the other side of the room, though, Adrian decided he'd better do something before they all died tragically on Gilgamesh's threshold.

"Leander," he whispered, keeping his voice as low as possible, even though none of the combatants were paying attention to them. "Do you have a spell that can restrain a princess?"

"Nothing that will work on her," the prince whispered back, his frighteningly gray face pinched as he stared at his beloved. "Mara's not as physically powerful as War or Wrath, but she knows all my spells' limitations. She can easily break out of any of my nonlethal restraints, and I'd never use a lethal one."

"I know you wouldn't," Adrian said, using his brother's distraction to finally finish wrapping the bandage around Leander's perforated chest. He just hoped he'd stemmed the bleeding in time. A chest wound like that would have killed a normal human in seconds, but the princes' quintessence bodies seemed as sturdy as the queens', so Adrian had hope. He was checking his pockets to see if he had anything that might help with Leander's pain when his brother began pushing to his feet.

"What are you doing?" Adrian hissed, grabbing his arm. "Don't move yet! We just tied you back together!"

"I have to move," Leander wheezed. "I have to stop them. This fight is killing her!"

Adrian didn't see how he'd arrived at *that* conclusion. If anything, Nemini looked like the one who was having a hard time. Adrian had known for a while now that she had some sort of instant-movement power, but he'd never seen her use it like this before. The Queen of Pride was blinking all over the throne room like an afterimage, her normally emotionless face scrunched up in concentration as she fought to stay ahead of Mara's wild jabs.

She must not have been able to dodge them all, because there were splashes of black blood on the golden floor beneath their feet. The Princess of Sorrow, on the other hand, looked completely uninjured. Adrian would even go so far as to say she was winning. Then he caught a glimpse of Mara's face, and he understood what Leander had meant.

Gilgamesh's princesses had never had the biology necessary to produce real tears, but the Princess of Sorrow was certainly trying. Her carved white face was twisted in anguish, and her golden eyes were squeezed shut as she tried in vain to stop herself from attacking her sister. She looked like a puppet fighting against its strings, but no matter how hard she tried to throw the battle in Nemini's favor, her body kept attacking with the ferocity of the weapon Gilgamesh had carved it to be. It was a heartbreaking sight, but then, everything about what Gilgamesh had done to Ishtar's people was a tragedy, and Adrian was sick of seeing it.

With that, he let go of his still-bleeding brother and started digging through his pockets. He'd filled his coat from his cabin before they'd marched on the palace, but most of what he'd grabbed was raw materials. He hadn't had time to craft anything useful out of them yet, but Adrian had an idea for how to cheat on that. He might not have Gilgamesh's quintessence blood in his own veins anymore, but Leander had spilled a ton of his, and while Adrian had sworn never to touch sorcery again, picky witches were dead witches.

Someone was almost certainly going to die in the next few minutes if he didn't do something, so Adrian grabbed a handful of leaves, sticks, and sticky sap out of his supplies pocket and dropped them on the golden floor. He got down on his knees next, using his bare hands to scoop his brother's white blood over the materials. It was a total hack job, but improvisation was a Witch of the Present's greatest strength, and Adrian had gotten pretty good at speeding up witchcraft with sorcery. It helped that he'd done this spell a thousand times before. All he had to do was mash the appropriate ingredients together with the power of the living forest that once again thrived inside his heart, use quintessence to replace the normal twenty-eight-day curing period, and when he pulled his bloody hands aside, what he wanted was sitting right in front of him.

"Is that a sap trap?" Boston asked, leaping onto his shoulder. "How'd you get it so big?"

"It's easy to make a big one when you don't have to bury it for an entire lunar cycle," Adrian replied as he hefted the round, sticky, piney-smelling enchantment—which was roughly the size and weight of a bowling ball—off the ground. "Instant results mean no cracking or moisture loss."

His familiar looked disgusted by that, as well he should. Adrian would be the first to admit that sorcery was *not* good witchcraft. It was, however, what they had.

"Nemini," he said, reaching up to touch the comm that was still in his ear despite everything. "Can you hold her still for a moment?"

The former void demon didn't reply. Adrian wasn't sure if that was because she hadn't heard him over the life-or-death struggle she was locked in with the Princess of Sorrow or if she was just being her usual taciturn self. He was wondering if he should ask again when a reply came over the speaker.

"Five seconds."

Again, Adrian wasn't sure what that meant, but he got the trap ready, lifting the heavy weight over his head with both hands as he watched Nemini and the carved copy of the Queen of Sorrow careen around the room. Mara must have been getting desperate by this point, because her eyes were open again, and she was begging her sister to kill her. It was heartbreaking to listen to, but Nemini bore it with the same stoic blankness as she bore everything, dodging the princess's lethal swings with careful steps as she led her back around to the opposite side of the circular throne room from where Bex was fighting.

The moment they reached the far wall, Nemini changed tactics. Instead of dodging the princess's punches, she got in close and grabbed her arms. Snakes erupted out of the floor as she did so, passing through the gold like ghosts only to become solid again when they wrapped around Mara's thrashing body. No single snake seemed strong enough to stop her on its own, but together with their queen, they held the princess in place, forcing her to be still for a critical second as Nemini said, "Now."

The second her voice spoke over the comm, Adrian threw the trap. It wasn't a particularly good throw. The ball of wood and fir sap was heavy and unwieldy, and while Adrian was in decent shape thanks to all the yardwork his craft required, he'd never been good at sports. Fortunately for all of them, this spell didn't require accuracy. All he had to do was break the ball somewhere close to the princess, and the trap did the rest, exploding on impact to cover the white weapon of Gilgamesh from head to gilded toe in thick, dark, inescapably sticky fir sap.

The blast caught Nemini too, but in the time it took Adrian to realize that, she'd already used her movement power to get free, reappearing behind him before he'd even noticed she'd vanished. She was still covered in sap, though, so much that it immediately stuck her feet to the ground again. Adrian was digging through his pockets for a solvent when Leander rushed toward Mara.

"It's okay," he said, stopping just before he got stuck in the explosion of sap as well. "It's all right, Mara, it's over. You're safe."

He leaned as close as he could get, but Mara's gold eyes were still wild.

"It's not over," she insisted as her doll-like body fought the sap with superhuman strength. "It will *never* be over. Even if you kill the Crown Prince, that order was given with the Blade of Ishtar."

"Then we'll take the sword from him and cancel it," Leander promised. "I'm going to save you!"

The princess's frantic expression grew soft. "If you truly mean that, then kill me."

"What?" he said as his face grew desperate. "*No!* You said we'd run away. That we could be together for—"

"There is no forever for us," she said, her voice quiet and calm even as her hands strained against the sap toward his throat. "I wanted to believe in it, but after having my mind erased and then returned, I know exactly how much this life doesn't belong to me. Even if you revoke the order of Ishtar's Blade, I'll always be a puppet. Gilgamesh's voice will *never* leave my head, and I... I..."

She dropped her golden eyes with a sob. "I'm tired of being someone else's weapon," she whispered. "Even if you're with me, this body will never be my own. I want to be myself again. I want to be *free*, Leander, and we both know there's only one way for that."

The prince took a shuddering breath. "I know," he said, dropping his mirrored gaze to the floor. "I'll always fight for whatever makes you happy, but if the Queen of Sorrow's hand is returned, what happens to you? Will you forget everything that happened? Everything we..."

His voice trailed off, and Mara's golden eyes softened. "I hope I forget," she said. "I hope we can both forget these centuries of suffering and humiliation, but just because this cursed existence will finally stop doesn't mean my love for you will end."

"I don't see how it could do anything else," Leander replied bitterly, placing a hand over his bandaged chest. "I'll always be the son of your most hated enemy, while you'll go back to being Ishtar's weapon. There's no way we can—"

"Of course there's a way," the princess said, giving him a smile so warm and genuine that it made her carved face look almost real. "All princesses love their princes, but I loved you more than I was made to from the very beginning. I loved you so much that Gilgamesh considered it a flaw and tried to fix me, but he could never make it go away, because it wasn't a princess's love. It was mine. I wanted you for myself, Leander, and that's why I'm not afraid. I know that whatever form I end up in, there will never be a version of me who doesn't love you."

Leander didn't make a sound, but tears were rolling down his face by the time she finished.

"Is this—" He stopped to swallow. "Is this really what you want?"

"Yes," she said, her gold eyes moving nervously to the white hand that had almost broken free of the sap. "Keep your promise, Leander. Set me free. Break this prison Gilgamesh built and let me be myself again. *Please.*"

That "please" was the final straw. As soon as his princess begged him, Leander started muttering under his breath. Adrian's ancient Sumerian wasn't good enough to follow what he was saying, but Mara's must have been, because she started sobbing in relief. Her carved body heaved against the sap prison as the spell went on and on, building in power until Adrian could feel it crackling over his skin like electricity.

Even Alexander glanced away from his fight with Bex for a moment, but he either felt no need to stop it or couldn't take the risk, because the Crown Prince didn't interrupt his brother as a crackling ball of power built in Leander's hands. It grew until it looked like he was holding a miniature black hole, spinning above his fingers with a high-pitched whine so sharp it felt like a knife was stabbing into Adrian's ears. Then, just before the noise became unbearable, the prince pointed the crackling ball at Mara.

"Royal Verse Fifteen," he said in a shaking voice. "Heavenly King's Eternal Banishment."

Adrian ducked and covered as Leander finished, but there was no explosion. All he heard was a *pop* as the crackling ball floating in front of the prince's palm vanished, and so did the princess. There was no shattering of enchanted ivory, no scream of pain. The Princess of Sorrow was simply gone, and stuck to the sap where she'd been was a woman's elegant hand with a thick black ring on its graceful finger.

Leander fell to his knees in front of it and dug his bloody hands into the sap to retrieve the only part his beloved had left behind. This, of course, got him stuck immediately, but he didn't seem to care. He just knelt there, clutching the queen's hand until Adrian finished unsticking Nemini and moved over to start rubbing solvent on his brother.

"You did the right thing," he told him softly as he worked.

"It doesn't feel that way," Leander muttered, staying perfectly still even after Adrian got him unstuck. "She was my world, and I destroyed her."

"You put her happiness above your own," Adrian said, patting his brother on the shoulder. "That makes you her prince in a way Gilgamesh's power never could, and I'm sure the real Mara will feel the same way when we bring her back."

Leander's shoulders were still shaking, but he nodded, clutching Mara's hand to his bandaged chest like a talisman. He did not, however, stand up.

"Do your legs not work?" Adrian asked, suddenly nervous.

"Nothing works," Leander confessed in a pained voice. "I was able to push through for Mara's sake, but now that she's gone..."

His voice trailed off as he looked down at his ruined body, and Adrian sighed.

"You can answer my questions from there, then," he said, crouching down beside his brother as he pointed at the fight that was still raging across the throne room. "How do I help Bex beat Alexander?"

"I'm not sure you can," Leander replied sadly. "Alexander's loyalty has always made him Father's favorite, but he's never had a talent for sorcery. To correct this flaw, Gilgamesh adjusted Alexander's body to send his quintessence inward. All princes are stronger and faster than the human limit, but Alexander is in a class by himself. That's why he was given the Sword of War. He might spend all his time behind a desk, but he's the fastest and strongest of all

Gilgamesh's sons and the best swordsman aside from the king himself."

He looked back down at the bloody hand clutched against his chest. "Alexander's the one who taught me how to use a sword when I first arrived in Heaven. Mara belonged to another prince back then, but when I fell in love, Alexander was the one who convinced Father to let me wait for her."

Leander smiled. "All Celestial Princes are brothers, but Alexander was the only one who ever acted like it. That's why Gilgamesh trusted him so much. No matter how bad things got, Alexander always saw us as a family, and a good son never disobeys his father."

"I wish he'd disobey a little," Adrian muttered, tapping his wooden pinky finger nervously as he watched Bex take yet another horrific blow across the shoulder. She'd been getting hit like that since the fight started, and while the new wound repaired itself just like all the others, it took a terrifyingly long time. Long enough to make Adrian shoot back to his feet.

"Nemini," he said, glancing at the queen who was, of course, standing right behind him. "Can you help Bex?"

"If I could, I would've done so already," the former void demon replied in a flat voice that somehow still managed to sound accusatory. "But I'm not fast enough for that fight. If I went in there, I'd just get hurt and distract her."

That was also Adrian's worry, but, "How are *you* not fast enough? You were just teleporting all over."

"It's not teleporting," Nemini insisted, reaching up to touch the giant crown of her horns. "Even with my name restored, part of me will never forget being nothing. Nothing is always present in the places we're not looking, but while Sorrowful Mara was trying not to see me so she wouldn't hurt me, the Crown Prince's one eye is sharper than most people's two. He's always looking everywhere, even behind him, which makes it impossible for me to sneak in without getting stabbed."

"What about if you *did* get stabbed?" Adrian asked desperately. "I can heal you, so you wouldn't die."

"Even you couldn't heal that," Nemini said, pointing at the black blur that was the Crown Prince's sword. "Bex did a lot to break us free, but we're still Ishtar's creations. Even if her sword is in someone else's hands, our flesh will still refuse to heal what our goddess cuts. The only reason Bex isn't dead is because she's using Greed's power, which reverses damage instead of trying to heal it." Her lips quirked in a small smile. "I'm actually very impressed she figured it out, but I don't have a power like that. I don't even have Pride's power anymore or I'd already be making the Crown Prince crawl on the ground."

Adrian cursed under his breath. So much for getting help. It was really starting to look like they'd have to rely on Bex to win this battle by herself. He'd normally count that as a sure bet, but even Adrian, who'd never swung a sword in his life, could tell that this fight was going very badly for her. If she didn't find a way to tilt things back in her favor soon, Bex was eventually going to hit a wall she couldn't climb.

Just thinking about that made Adrian feel helpless, which, ironically, was what gave him his next idea.

"Could you drop him into the void?"

Nemini frowned in thought. "Probably," she said at last. "Princesses are immune because their egos are overridden by Gilgamesh, but princes are human. Very proud humans, which means they fall far. The trouble is making the connection. To expose the Crown Prince's illusion of ego, I'll have to touch him with at least one whole hand. That means getting close, which I've already explained is a death sentence."

"Not if he can't see you," Adrian countered excitedly, digging into his pockets for more raw spell materials. "And before you say it won't work, I'm not talking about your nothing movements. I'm referring to good old-fashioned sneaking."

Nemini's frown curved deeper at that, but Leander was the one who spoke next, which was a surprise because Adrian thought he'd already passed out.

"How is she going to sneak up on two people fighting in the middle of an open room with no cover?"

"We don't need cover," Adrian insisted, motioning for Boston—who'd already realized what he was planning—to start moving the fir branches he'd used for the sap trap into a wider circle. "This is witchcraft."

"Don't witch spells take a long time?" Nemini asked.

"Not this one," Adrian promised, keeping his eyes steadfastly on his work as the fight across the throne room grew more and more dire.

Chapter 16

BEX WAS LOSING.

It wasn't as overwhelmingly obvious as the drubbing the Queen of War had given her over the Holy City, but the tide was definitely against her. Slowly but inexorably, she was losing ground, and since she'd sent all her demons away to Earth, she had no way of regaining it. She still didn't regret her choice—their army would do more good in the Blackwood than they would've up here, not to mention they had a *much* higher chance of surviving that fight than they would've storming Gilgamesh's palace—but it wasn't looking good.

The nonstop usage of the Queen of Greed's power had left her exhausted, but Bex still hadn't managed to put a single scratch on her enemy. The Crown Prince was simply too good, and his sword was too strong. A more tactical fighter would've given up and retreated ages ago, but the demons of Wrath had always been stubborn, and there was nowhere to go even if she had wanted to run. The only way any of them lived was if she got through this, so Bex gritted her teeth and kept pushing, methodically testing the prince's guard for any hint of weakness. She was still searching when she made the mistake that almost ended her for good.

Like everything in this fight, it was a matter of inches. She'd been retreating, leading the prince around the giant golden throne in the hope that having something in the way might compromise his perfect guard, when her boot slipped off the edge of the raised dais. She recovered her balance immediately, but the gap had already opened, allowing Prince Alexander to stab Ishtar's sword past Drox, under Bex's arm, and into her stomach.

It was a clean skewering, but Bex had been run through before. She knew how to handle both the wound and the pain. But when she focused Greed's power on the damaged parts to return them to their original form, all she got was a throbbing shot of pain.

The unexpected agony made her stumble again. She would've fallen off the dais had Drox not stabbed his blade into the gold floor, using himself as a lever to throw Bex sideways a split second before the Crown Prince's sword sliced through the air where she'd been.

"Thanks," Bex muttered as she caught herself against the wall. "Just let me—"

She stopped there, focusing hard on her wound as she reached for Greed's power again. The pain was still there, chewing at her insides like a trapped rat, but Bex had always wanted more than she'd been given. Unlike Envy, Greed was a sin that came naturally to her, and eventually she made it work, pushing the pain back with her own flames until the wound in her stomach finally reversed itself.

You can't do that again, Drox warned as she pushed off the wall.

"I know," Bex muttered, backing away to put distance between herself and the Crown Prince, who was watching her wounded movements like a predator. "But I can't win this if I do nothing but defend."

He hits you even when you do *defend,* her sword scolded. *Your footwork is slipping.*

Because she was exhausted. She was technically still uninjured thanks to Greed's power, but every part of Bex was so tired she could barely stand. That painful push was almost certainly the last one she had in her, but the fight wasn't close to over. Alexander didn't even look winded as he stalked toward her, which *sucked* because he wasn't even the last fight. Bex still had to face Gilgamesh after this, and suddenly, she wasn't sure she could do it.

None of that, Drox snapped, knocking his hilt against her hand. *If your mind gives up, you're finished no matter how much strength is left in your body. You're the one who said you'd do what Ishtar wouldn't. Are you going to let your people die just because some snot-nosed son of Gilgamesh got his hands on your mother's sword?*

Of course not. Bex would fight until she died, but even as she moved back into attack position, part of her was whispering that Ishtar had had that "unbeatable" sword when she faced Gilgamesh, and she'd still been defeated. *Everyone* who'd faced Gilgamesh had been defeated, including Bex herself. He'd smacked the first Rebexa, the infamous Executioning Blade of Ishtar, out of the sky like a buzzing gnat, so what hope did she—

You have every hope, Drox snarled, digging into her palm. *The only way Gilgamesh becomes actually undefeatable is if you believe him to be. The gods lost because they underestimated him, but you will lose if you over*estimate *him. You must see him exactly as he is: a human opponent who is still susceptible to death. That goes for the prince in front of you as well. He is also merely a man holding a sword that has already been defeated, but* *you are different. You are the queen who rose from her own ashes, and you will be their end.*

Bex smiled. Drox had always been good at talking her up, or maybe she was just susceptible to inspiring speeches because she wanted to be inspired. She wanted to believe that she was the one who could stop this, the one who could finally win. That was the dream she'd sold to all her demons, the dream Lys and Iggs and everyone else who followed her had laid down their lives for. Bex could quit on herself, but she would never quit on them, so she planted her boots one last time and made a calculated lunge at the place the prince's guard looked weakest: his left shoulder.

Just one hit, she told herself as her sword flew. One good shot was all she needed, because princes couldn't heal like demons. If Bex could wound him even once, she'd flip the momentum back to her side, so she poured every bit of fire she had into going faster, closing the distance between them like a flaming comet.

He still saw it coming. The damn prince was the fastest opponent she'd ever faced. He must've estimated her trajectory ahead of time, because his sword was already in position to block hers before Bex's feet left the floor. If she'd still been the fighter she was two months ago, that would been all it took, but if there was one thing Bex had learned from all those losses to Havok, it was how to improvise in the air. The prince had set his blade to stop her current trajectory, but she was the Bonfire Queen, which meant she didn't have to stay on course. One quick blast of fire was all she needed to change her direction in mid-flight, flipping her body to transform what had been an overhead chop into a sweeping strike from the ground.

The cocky prince wasn't expecting that. Bex saw the surprise flash over his one-eyed face a split second before his sword moved. As fast as they were both going, though, that single moment of shock was all it took for Bex to slide past his guard and drive Drox's blade straight into his armored armpit.

The resistance of her sword slamming into the prince's golden armor was the sweetest thing Bex had ever felt. The angle wasn't the greatest since she'd flipped herself upside down, but this was the first solid hit she'd landed since the fight began. She carried it through with everything she had, blasting her fire behind her like a rocket as she pushed up and through, cutting armor, flesh, and bone until her black sword came out the other side.

His left arm hit the golden floor a second later. It wasn't as good as cutting off his sword arm, but Bex didn't care. His cry of pain was still music to her ears. Feeling better than she had since the fight started, Bex landed on the golden throne and whirled to keep pressing the attack. By the time she actually made it all the way around, though, the sight that was waiting for her shocked all the joy straight out of her body.

The Crown Prince's arm was back. His golden armor was still missing, but his left arm was once again connected to his shoulder like it had never been cut. That made no sense, though, because Bex could see the arm she'd severed still bleeding on the floor. How had he grown it back so quickly? How had—

"Don't look so confused," the prince chided, flashing her a superior smirk as he held Ishtar's sword up for her to see. "This is the personal weapon of the Goddess of Life and Death, the same goddess who blessed your cursed kind with regeneration in the first place. Of course it has the power to heal something as inconsequential as a severed arm." He shook his head. "What a terrible daughter you are. You should really have more faith in your—"

His bragging cut off with a choke. Bex backed away, watching for the trap this had to be, but the Crown Prince wasn't even looking at her. He was staring at something else, something far in the distance that only he could see. The prince's hands opened a second later, dropping Ishtar's sword as his arms—both his new naked left one and his armored right—shot out like they were trying to catch something.

Whatever it was, he must not have made it. The Crown Prince was still straining when his body toppled, falling straight forward like a cut tree to land face down at the foot of the throne where Bex was crouching. She was still staring at him in dumbfounded confusion when Nemini appeared on top of the fallen prince's back, pulling something black off her head that looked a lot like Adrian's coat.

This just made Bex blink even harder. Nemini popping out of nowhere was business as usual, but she normally did it where Bex couldn't see. This was completely different, because now that Bex was staring straight at her, she was starting to realize that Nemini had been there the entire time. She just hadn't noticed her, which felt impossible until she saw Adrian running over.

"*Bex!*" he cried, jumping up on the giant throne to throw his arms around her. "Are you okay?"

"I'm fine," Bex lied. She felt nothing like fine, but she didn't need medical attention, so it was good enough. "What in the Hells just happened?"

"A Nevermind," the witch replied, looking cockier than she'd seen him in a long time. "Alexander's eye was sharp, so Nemini couldn't sneak up on him the normal way, but even an incredible warrior like him only has enough brainpower to look for threats. He can't actually keep an eye on everything, especially things specifically enchanted to be beneath notice, so I put a Nevermind charm on my coat and put my coat over Nemini, who—"

"Dropped him into the void," Bex finished, smiling at her sister. "Nice work."

"Not that nice," Nemini said, poking the twitching prince with the toe of her shoe. "I still couldn't get close enough with him darting around like that. It was only when he stopped to brag that I finally saw my chance. His new naked arm was also helpful. It gave me something to grab onto."

"That's still nice work," Bex insisted, collapsing onto the throne with an exhausted sigh. "Better than I could do."

"You did very well," Nemini said, giving her a rare smile. "You were the only one who could have held out against him for so long. You gave me the opening. I merely used what was available."

Bex frowned. "What was available?"

The Queen of Pride nodded at the golden body lying still as stone on the floor. "The Crown Prince was very convinced of his own rightness, and no one falls harder than the self-assured. His pride at being Gilgamesh's reliable right hand had become his whole identity, so he had nothing left to grab on to when I ripped the curtain of ego away." Her smile collapsed into a frown again. "He'd dug a deep pit in his heart to bury the suffering he knew he was causing others. I don't know if he'll ever be able to climb back out."

"Good riddance," Bex said darkly as she pulled Drox back into his ring. "Bastard used Mara against us."

"He did worse than that," Adrian said, taking a seat beside her on the throne's massive arm. "If I understood Leander correctly, Alexander's the one who actually pressed the button that flooded the Hells. Even if he was just following orders, there's no excuse for genocide."

"He can make his peace with the void, then," Bex said, turning away from Alexander's still body. "More importantly, where's Mara? And did Leander survive?"

Adrian sighed. "He's alive, but..."

His voice trailed off as he pointed across the shockingly bloody throne room to a miserable-looking figure curled up at the far edge. He was so hunched over, it took Bex several moments to realize she was looking at Leander. Boston was watching over him, but there was no sign of the Princess of Sorrow. Just her prince curled into a fetal position around something Bex couldn't see but already knew was a hand.

"It's probably for the best," she said softly. "Mara deserved to be free."

"They're both free now," Adrian agreed. "Though I'm not sure how long they'll be able to enjoy it."

Bex arched an eyebrow, and the witch leaned closer. "Leander's injuries are severe," he whispered. "I've triaged his wounds, and princes are tough, so I'm reasonably confident he won't die if he stays still and avoids making his condition any worse, but he can't keep going."

"That's fine," Bex whispered back. "He's already fought harder than I expected, and his sorcery would probably be useless against Gilgamesh anyway. He deserves a rest, but do you think you could wake him up for just a minute? He's still our inside man, and I don't know where to go from here."

Adrian blinked in surprise. Then he looked around at the perfectly circular golden throne room with only one obvious door leading to a downward staircase, and he hopped off the throne they'd been whispering on with a sigh.

"Boston?"

The cat looked up.

"I know you just got started, but could you rouse Leander? We need to ask him a question."

"You could have told me that *before* I began the sedation spell," the familiar replied with a lash of his tail. "But fine. He was resisting anyway, so it's not like I've lost much. Ask away, though I'll warn you, he's a bit delirious."

"I can work with delirious," Bex promised as she forced her aching body out of the golden chair—which was oddly comfortable for something made of metal—and hobbled across the room to where Leander was lying in a pool of his own white blood.

"Hey," she said, squatting down beside him. "We still need to get to Gilgamesh. Do you know where we go?"

She gave him a poke as she finished, but the prince didn't respond. He just curled harder around Mara's severed hand. Bex tried the question a few more times with even less success, and eventually she stood back up with a huff.

"This is just great. We finally get to the part where his know-it-all attitude would actually be helpful, and he's out cold."

"Leander's knowledge has been useful many times," said Nemini, who was the last person Bex expected to come to Leander's defense. "And I think we're already in the right place."

"How do you figure that?" Bex asked, waving her bloody hand at the empty room. "This whole place is just one big golden dead end."

"It does look that way," Adrian said as his clever blue-gray eyes darted over the carved walls. "But I'm with Nemini. This was where the chains narrowed and where Alexander was standing guard. He wouldn't waste his time protecting a dead end, which means the path to Gilgamesh has to be in here somewhere."

"You mean like inside the walls?" Bex wrinkled her nose. "Aren't we already at the top, though?"

"Space in Heaven doesn't always work like you assume," Adrian reminded her, pulling his broom off his back. "Let's go see what we can find."

Bex still didn't see how there could possibly be any hidden doors in a room that so clearly took up the entire top of a tower, but if both Adrian and Nemini said this was it, she wasn't stupid enough to argue.

There was something else she still needed to take care of in any case, so while Nemini and Adrian started tapping on the walls, Bex walked back over to the golden throne and crouched beside the still-breathing body of Gilgamesh's unconscious Crown Prince.

Are you sure about this? Drox whispered as she rolled him over.

"No," Bex whispered back. "But I'm already at the top of Ishtar's shit list, so I might as well take everything I can get."

There are different degrees of rebellion, her sword warned. *Stealing the worship of her demons enraged her, but you needed them to win back Paradise, so it could still technically be framed as doing your job. This, on the other hand, is the literal definition of stealing from the gods, and that never ends well.*

"So long as I beat Gilgamesh, I don't care," Bex said, reaching under Alexander's armored body for the sword he'd dropped when Nemini touched him. "Even with all my new powers, I wasn't able to defeat the Crown Prince without Nemini and Adrian's help. I can't take a risk like that against the real deal. I don't care if Ishtar eats me alive. I'm not passing up this opportunity."

I see your logic, Drox acknowledged, but his voice was still worried. *I just hope you don't leave me behind.*

"Don't be crazy," Bex told him with a grin. "I've got two hands, don't I?"

That was supposed to be a joke to reassure her sword, but the moment Bex touched the hilt of Ishtar's black blade, a bolt of magic went through her body hard enough to reset all her thoughts. She'd never felt anything like it, not even when she'd grabbed Enki to stab him. That could've been because the crafter god was already a husk by the time Bex reached him, but the magic contained in this sword was stronger than she'd felt from Ishtar herself.

Just brushing it with her fingers was enough to blast all the tiredness out of her body. That should've been a good thing, but wrapping her hand around the grip made Bex feel so full she worried she was going to pop. How in the world had the Crown Prince managed to hold a blade this potent for an entire fight without his hand falling off?

He probably didn't feel it like you do, Drox said, his voice clearer inside Bex's head than ever despite the chaos filling her mind. *Alexander and Gilgamesh are both human, but you are Ishtar's daughter. Not only do you bear her blood, you command the worship of her demons. You're probably experiencing that sword the same way Ishtar herself did.* His voice grew even more worried. *She's going to kill you for sure now.*

"Pretty sure she was always planning to do that," Bex said, forcing her knotted shoulders to relax as she struggled to get used to the buzzing sword in her hand. "That's why I'm doing this. If I'm damned no matter what, there's no reason not to squeeze out everything I can before I go."

Fair enough, Drox replied. *Just take it slow. I'm connected to your magic and was built to perform at even your highest burn, but that sword's so strong that even I'm having trouble adjusting.*

He did sound much louder than usual. Everything did. When Ishtar's sword was in her hand, the whole world felt brighter and more alive. Her body felt stronger, her senses sharper, which was insane, since she'd already gotten an upgrade when she grew her new horns. Bex had been hoping to score a weapon sharp enough to cut through whatever Gilgamesh was plotting, not to mention the cultural rightness of taking back Ishtar's blade, but it felt like she'd gotten more than she'd bargained for.

Too much more. The new sensations were rapidly overloading her. Even Drox was starting to shake, his ring clamping down on her finger in distress until Bex forced her hand open again, sending Ishtar's black sword clattering to the golden floor.

Maybe we should work up to it in phases.

"Yeah," Bex agreed, undoing the belt sheath from Crown Prince Alexander's waist and wrapping it around her own. When she'd made a safe holding place, she picked up the sword again, using her shirt hem this time. The extra layer of fabric didn't do much, but it took the edge off long enough for Bex to get the sword into its scabbard. She was pulling the belt tight on her waist so it wouldn't slide around when Adrian gave an excited shout.

"Found it!" he cried, tapping the raven-carved head of Bran's broomstick against a piece of gold wall about twenty feet away from the throne.

"Good job," Bex said, hurrying to his side. "How do you know that's the right spot, though? It doesn't look any different from the rest of the wall."

"There's no obvious sign," Adrian admitted, returning his broom to its sling on his back so he could tap his fingers against what looked like just another carved section of the intricate gold depiction of ancient Uruk. "But the important thing to remember about Gilgamesh is that he considers himself an artist.

Why else would a king so famous for being thrifty bother making his creations beautiful? His princesses and palaces and the golden armor he puts on his sons would all still work if they weren't decorated, but they *are*. Dramatically so, because Gilgamesh values both beauty and symbolism. That's why his throne room is covered in a relief of his old kingdom instead of celestial lions or even no carvings at all. Even at the pinnacle of Heaven, he's still presenting himself as a human king, and as a human, this was the place that was most important to him."

Adrian tapped his finger on the market square depicted in the gold relief, but Bex still didn't understand. "What's so special about that spot?"

"Because this is where Gilgamesh began his war with the gods," Adrian explained. "It's the same place he chose to show me when he turned me into a prince, the road where his best friend, Enkidu, was killed by the original Queen of Wrath." He pressed his finger even harder against the carefully worked gold. "This is the place that, in Gilgamesh's mind, justifies everything he does. Of *course* he'd hide his door behind it. It's literally the heart of his entire philosophy."

"It's also the point directly next to where we came out of the chains before," added Nemini, who'd been listening silently the whole time. "I don't know if that matters for a hidden space, but if there is a connection, it lines up."

"Sounds good to me," Bex said, turning her new belt so the sheathed length of Ishtar's sword wouldn't bang against her legs. "How do we get it open?"

"That's the part I'm less sure about," Adrian admitted, taking off his witch hat to push his hair, which had gotten quite shaggy, out of his eyes. "We could try Envy's power again, but I suspect that won't work since you already tried to go straight to Gilgamesh and failed. I also doubt there's a physical hidden door because I've already tapped all over the wall, and I can't hear any difference in density."

"Maybe there never was a door since Gilgamesh teleports everywhere," Bex suggested.

"But the chains don't," Adrian said. "Even if Gilgamesh teleported all the sin iron directly to his workshop, the chains still need an uninterrupted path from Earth to the Wheel. That's what got us up here in the first place, but if the hole was too narrow to climb through, that just means..."

His voice trailed off as he looked over his head, and then his face split into a smile. He ran over to Leander next. Bex thought he was just checking on his downed brother, but when Adrian returned, both of his hands were covered in princely white blood.

"I know, I know," he said at Bex's horrified look. "But it doesn't make sense that Gilgamesh's final chamber wouldn't be sealed with sorcery, and this is the only quintessence I've got at the moment."

"That doesn't mean you have to use it!" Boston hissed, arching his back. "You told me we were done with this!"

"Almost," Adrian said, pressing his bloody palms onto the carving, which was how Bex noticed that the golden edges of the buildings in that spot were slightly rounded, almost as if someone laid their hands in that exact position often.

"Here we go," Adrian whispered, focusing on the point between his thumbs where a large bearded man, the only human Bex had seen in the entire carving, was depicted walking through the square. "*Open.*"

That didn't sound like any sorcery Bex had ever heard. The word wasn't even in ancient Sumerian, but it still worked like a charm. The moment Adrian spoke the command, the wall he'd pressed his hands against vanished, revealing a hallway lined with old brown stone leading farther in.

"There," Adrian said, shaking his hands, which were now perfectly clean. Every bit of blood had been consumed by the spell, leaving his palms soft and scrubbed when he reached for Bex.

"Shall we go have a look?"

She took his offered hand in her shaking one, leaving the gleaming throne room behind as she, Boston, and Nemini followed Adrian into what Bex desperately hoped was the final room of Gilgamesh's palace.

Adrian's heart was thumping beneath his tree as he led Bex down the stone tunnel, which was so old and worn that it looked like it belonged beneath a pyramid. The blocks that formed the walls were huge and covered in cuneiform markings, but not the clean, fancy kind found on Gilgamesh's modern infrastructure. This was cuneiform like you saw in museums, true ancient writing.

"Do you know what it says?" he asked over his shoulder.

Bex shook her head. Fortunately, Nemini was old enough to read anything.

"It's a poem," she reported, her yellow eyes moving in circles as she read the writing carved into the walls, floor, and ceiling. "The first section recounts Gilgamesh's life and heroic deeds. The second is a record of the war, though it's mostly a recounting of the crimes of the gods that led to their defeat."

"Gotta give him points for consistency," Bex muttered. "How far do you think this tunnel goes?"

She moved closer to Adrian as she spoke, walking with her arms pulled in to keep them as far from the walls as possible, though she could also have been avoiding touching the new sword she wore on her hip. Adrian had seen her pick it up because he watched her more than he was comfortable admitting, but while scoring the Sword of Ishtar seemed like it should be the victory of a lifetime, Bex acted like she was carrying a cursed object.

Considering how strained her relationship with her mother was at the moment, Adrian supposed that made sense. He was dying to ask Bex about it, but he didn't want to poke a sore spot, so he answered her question instead.

"There's no way to know how long it is except to walk down it," he said, picking up the pace. "We're in the most Gilgamesh-y of all Gilgamesh's private spaces now. Whatever's in here, it was built for his purposes alone, so I guess we'll arrive when he wants us to."

"Or we'll be trapped forever," Bex muttered.

"He won't do that," Adrian told her confidently. "He'll come down to gloat, if nothing else, and then you can hit him. I'm much more interested in why Gilgamesh chose a tunnel. He's always been more of a grand-decorative-spaces sort of..."

His voice trailed off as the ancient hallway they'd been following suddenly ended in a large stone chamber exactly like the one he'd *just* said was Gilgamesh's style. There was no gold, but the arched walls were covered in beautiful carvings of lions, trees, and fountains. It looked like a naturally occurring cathedral, if such a thing existed, and sitting at the far end was a beautiful waist-high stone basin filled with glowing blue water and lined with eight pairs of horns, plus an empty spot for one more.

"I don't believe it," Adrian breathed. "Is that—?"

He didn't get to finish, because Bex had already run past him. She sprinted down the middle of the beautifully carved cavern and grabbed the closest set of horns, which also happened to be the most familiar.

"That bastard," she snarled, clutching the pair of two-foot-long, spear-sharp, black-ridged horns to her chest. "These are *mine*!"

"They're all here," Nemini said, appearing next to her sister between one blink and the next. "Those are Sorrow's. Those are Greed's. Even War's horns are here."

"This must be where Gilgamesh has been hiding them," Adrian said as he ran over. "But why did he leave them unguarded like this?"

"They weren't unguarded," Bex argued. "Did you not see the fight I was just in?"

"I know, I know," Adrian said, looking around nervously. "But I still expected a trap of some sort. Gilgamesh *is* famous for being suspicious."

"He's also famous for discarding things he no longer needs," Nemini said quietly, looking up at the pale light that shone down through the holes in the elegantly carved ceiling above them.

"I agree," Bex said, handing Adrian her old horns so he could tuck them into his coat, since she had no pockets. "Gilgamesh didn't leave our horns unguarded. He left them behind. He doesn't need the queens' crowns anymore now that he's flushed his demon population."

She looked up at the wall behind the basin where the crowns were displayed, which was covered in the smallest, most elegant-looking cuneiform yet. "What's that? More god cursing?"

"No," said Nemini, squinting at the tiny lines. "It's still poetry, but it's not about the gods or the war. It looks like the stuff sorcerers say when they cast spells."

"What sorcerers say," Adrian repeated, his eyes flying wide as he stared at the cuneiform-covered wall. "Of course!" he cried, running over to touch the carvings Nemini had been struggling to read. "These must be the original verses."

"The original verses of what?" Bex asked.

"Sorcery," Adrian replied excitedly, running his fingers over the ancient markings he still wasn't good enough to read reliably. "Malik—that is to say, Gilgamesh—told me that he created sorcerous poetry so that normal people could use quintessence without getting cooked. All the verses are written down in books so that sorcerers on Earth can learn them, but those books are just copies of the originals, which are famously in Heaven. I thought they'd be carved on golden tablets and kept in a treasury, but now I see. It's all here!"

"Should we destroy it?" Bex asked, walking up to the wall. "If this is the poetry all the sorcerers on Earth are pulling from, then wrecking this wall should mean they're no longer able to use spells, right?"

"I don't know," Adrian said. "I'm not sure if simply knowing the verses is enough or..." His voice trailed off as he thought about it, and then he shook his head. "It doesn't matter. Even if breaking that would destroy all modern sorcery, we don't have time. If Gilgamesh has already abandoned the queens' crowns, he must be very close to his goal. I'd love to wreck this place, but those verses are carved into stone. Breaking them will take too much effort for something we don't even know will work, so let's just leave it for now. Once Gilgamesh is dead, we can come back."

"That's the sort of optimism I count on you for," Bex said, flashing Adrian a beaming smile before turning to Nemini. "I need to ask a favor."

"Anything," Nemini replied with the speed that proved she meant it. Bex must've picked up on that as well, because her smile softened, though her voice did not.

"I want you to grab our sisters' crowns and take them downstairs," she said, pointing at the ring of royal horns that still lined the edge of the water-filled basin. "Pick up Leander and Mara, too, while you're at it. Take it all and carry them down through Adrian's tree to the Blackwood."

"I can't do that," Nemini said, her voice shaking as she stared at her sister. "If I leave, you'll face Gilgamesh alone."

"That's the idea," Bex told her. "You're my backup. If Adrian and I fail, I'm counting on you to restore our sisters and take up the fight. I don't know if there'll still be a world worth saving by that point, but if there is, I'm entrusting it to you. You've fought beside me since the very beginning. Do this for me as well. Be my hope so that I can face this last fight with everything I have."

She reached up to touch Nemini's face as she finished, but her sister smacked her hand away.

"No," Nemini snarled, her whole body shaking in fury. "I know you, Bexa. You're telling me to be your hope so you can die without guilt, but I'm not falling for it. I did all of this for you. Left the void for *you*. If you're gone, how am I supposed to endure?"

"The same way everything endures," Bex replied as she pulled her sister into a hug. "You're the one who told me we all become the same dust in the end. If we're destined to crumble no matter what, then I want to go out fighting the fight I've lived all my lives for. That's my choice, but you never cared about the war or Gilgamesh. My end has always been inevitable, but I promised you'd be free, and free demons don't die fighting battles they have no stake in."

"I'd fight for you," Nemini whispered, clutching her hard. "I'll always fight for you."

"I don't need you to fight," Bex whispered back. "I need to you to live. That's why I'm asking you to do this, because I can't beat Gilgamesh if I'm weighed down by worries and regrets." She hugged her sister tighter. "That's the help I need from you, Nemini. Give me the security of knowing my family got out safe, and I swear I'll tear Heaven down."

Nemini was shaking by the time Bex finished. It was more emotion than Adrian had ever seen her show. He was sure she was going to refuse, but then, to his shock, Nemini nodded.

"I'm only doing this because you asked," she said as she grudgingly started to collect the horns of the seven remaining demon queens from the basin. "For the record, I hate this plan, and I hate your decision, but if it will make you happy, I'll do it."

"Thank you," Bex said, hugging her one last time before turning to Adrian. "Do you want to send Boston with her?"

"Absolutely not!" Boston cried, galloping over from where he'd been busily exploring the hidden chamber. "A witch going into battle without his familiar? He might as well be naked."

"That would be a no," Adrian agreed, reaching down to pet his loyal cat. "We're in this together."

Bex didn't look like she liked that answer, but she didn't push the issue, which proved she understood more about witchcraft than any other non-witch Adrian had ever met. Just thinking about that made his heart feel too big for his chest, which was nice because everything else was feeling pretty scary.

"This is it, then?" he asked nervously as Nemini finished gathering the queens' horns and turned to leave the temple.

"It'd better be," Bex said, washing her face and bloody hands with water from the basin, which shone with the same glittering blue light as the vials of deathly water she used to hoard. "We've beaten every prince and been all over this damn tower. If we haven't made it to Gilgamesh yet, I'm calling foul."

"I'm pretty sure he's here," Boston said as he scaled the back of Adrian's coat with his claws to perch on his witch's shoulder. "I don't know what's above us, but the magic coming down through the ceiling is incredible."

It did feel pretty thick now that his familiar mentioned it. Ironically, the size of Adrian's new forest made it harder for him to sense other magics. If he pushed past the deep pulse of his root-bound heart, though, he could feel hard, hot power beating down on them like the desert sun, even inside the cool dark of the cave.

He was also glad he could still feel his forest so strongly even in this other place. Ironically, that was probably because of the chains. Thanks to their need for an uninterrupted path, this place was the closest to the living world that Heaven got outside of his new tree's roots. That was good news for Adrian since witches drew their power from the Great Cycles of life. Whether it'd be enough to actually beat Gilgamesh was another matter, but at least he wasn't alone this time. Boston was right there on his shoulder, and Bex was by his side, shaking the sparkling blue water out of her hair before she held out her hand.

"Ready to end this?"

"Ready to start something new with you," Adrian replied, leaning down to press a kiss against the back of her fingers as he took her hand. "Shall we go kick out the tyrant and win ourselves a better world?"

He was trying to make her smile, but Bex's expression was something else entirely when he glanced up again. She didn't look happy or sad or even worried. She looked absolutely determined, like she was ready to claw Gilgamesh to atoms with her fingernails.

"We'll do it," she promised, squeezing his fingers tight. "We'll beat him and make a better life for everyone. One where no one has to be a slave and where I'm free to be with you."

Those final words made Adrian's heart skip half a dozen beats. Other than a few wild brunch plans made in the heat of battle, Bex had never said anything about their future before. Now, though, she was smiling at Adrian with that same beautifully shy hopefulness he'd treasured on their one and only date.

It was the look that had made him want to kiss her every second they were sitting next to each other during the stakeout. He had the same reaction now, only this time, there was nothing in his way. Adrian only hesitated long enough for Boston to jump off his shoulder before he picked Bex bodily up off the ground and kissed her, squeezing her against him until every doubt was buried under the glorious mountain that was their future together.

"Right," he said breathlessly when he finally let her go. "Let's go ruin a king's day."

Bex grinned back and grabbed his hand, pulling Adrian across the shady, quiet cavern toward the staircase drenched in harsh white light on the other side.

From her shadow in the corner, Nemini watched her beloved sister run up the stairs with the witch who'd earned her affection. The kiss had been a good one, especially for the current Bexa, who was the shy type. Nemini still wasn't sure what made one reincarnation more bashful than others, but her little sister was clearly very happy. If she hadn't been running off to die, Nemini would've had nothing to complain about, but even for someone who'd built her life around the fact that nothing mattered, that was a hard pill to swallow.

She still wanted to go after them. The only reason she didn't was because she knew it wouldn't help. Even now that her horns were back, Nemini had never been one of the combat queens. Her strength and speed were both mediocre at best, and her regeneration was abysmal. She used to win by bringing her enemies to their knees before they could swing, but that power was gone now, along with her sword, which meant she was more likely to be a liability than an asset.

Nemini knew that was the real reason Bexa had sent her away. Fortunately, she no longer had an ego to be bruised by such an honest assessment. Gilgamesh might have enough pride to sink him like a battleship if she ever got her hands on him, but he might also be so convinced of his power that not even the void could suck him down. Either way, Nemini would have to get within touching range to try, which would most likely end with her getting hurt and distracting Bex, defeating the entire plan. Her heart still dragged at the thought of leaving, but not as much as it did at the thought of getting Bex killed.

That was the one thing she'd never do, so Nemini clutched her sisters' horns against her chest and did as her chosen queen had said, walking down the cuneiform-covered hallway toward the magical door that was still open at the end. She'd just stepped back into the throne room when she noticed something was different.

It was hard to make out through the glare of all that gold, but Nemini's eyes were sharp, and she'd seen this phenomenon before. Neither of the downed princes had moved since the fight ended, but there was a familiar shimmer in the air above Leander. Sure enough, a man's scarred hand reached through the distortion a second later to wrench Mara's severed hand from Leander's unconscious grasp. He'd almost gotten it loose when Nemini dropped her armful of horns and leaped forward.

She'd never make it in time with her slow speed, so she dove for the places where no one was looking only to discover she couldn't. He'd put just a single hand into the room, but when Nemini tried to find a place where Gilgamesh's eyes didn't touch, she found nothing. Nemini swore she could feel his eyes peering inside her when a second hand appeared in the air in front of her and smacked her away.

She flew straight back like a shot, streaking across the bloody throne room to crash into the golden artwork on the other side. She was still sliding down the carved wall when the hand Gilgamesh hadn't just used to swat her finished prying the Queen of Sorrow's severed hand from her prince's grasp. All three hands vanished after that, as did the door Adrian had opened in the wall, leaving Nemini sitting in what was now truly a golden dead end with the scattered horns of Ishtar's queens, two unconscious princes, and no way to go back and warn her sister.

Chapter 17

ADRIAN THOUGHT HE WAS BRACED FOR ANYTHING at this point, but the top of the stairs still took him by surprise. Given the beautifully carved cavern they'd just climbed out of, he'd expected a golden ziggurat or a long-lost temple of the gods. Maybe they'd step out into the ancient fields of Uruk or a palace floating in the sky. All kinds of wild imaginings had flitted through his mind's eye as he climbed the narrow steps behind Bex, but when he finally stepped into the blinding light, what Adrian actually saw was desert.

He recoiled so fast that he almost slipped back down the stairs. The cavern let out into the center of a very black, very *familiar* desert. Black dunes of sin-iron dust rolled away in every direction like waves on the sea, making him instantly afraid for Boston. If touching the sin-iron chains had made him sick, a whole desert full of powderized particles might kill him in minutes.

For once, though, Gilgamesh's dedication to artificiality seemed to be working in their favor. Despite the sea of sin iron that stretched out around them in all directions, the platform where the stairs came up was spotlessly clean. The black dunes came right up to the stone's edge, but with no wind to push them around, the dust seemed to be staying in place. Boston certainly didn't appear to be in distress. He'd already gone up on his hind legs, nearly falling off Adrian's shoulder in his efforts to see more of what was hanging above them in the sky.

That part of the black desert was exactly as Adrian remembered. The sky overhead was as sunless and cloudless as ever, its pale-blue dome interrupted only by the crisscrossing lines of thousands of black chains that bound the gigantic wheel that spanned from horizon to horizon. If Adrian looked hard enough, he could actually see it straining against its shackles. No matter how hard it tried to turn, though, the wheel did not move.

Nothing here did. Bex had come out swords first, but as far as Adrian could see, there was no one to fight. The stone platform where the stairs came up—which was also the top of the cavern they'd just walked through—was quiet and still. There were no chains or golden war constructs or piles of quintessence. In fact, the only thing Adrian saw that wasn't black dust or clean-swept stone was a large golden structure filled with corpses.

He knew that made no sense even as he thought it, but those were the only words that came to Adrian's mind. Directly across the stone platform from where they'd come up was a wall fifty feet tall and at least a hundred feet wide made of gold-and-glass tanks. The tanks were stacked on top of each other in a neat grid, and each one was big enough to hold a fully-grown man. Adrian knew that last part for a fact, because that was what was inside them.

Through the tanks' glass fronts, he could see rows and rows of young men floating in what appeared to be the glowing blue deathly water that Bex drank. They were all dressed in the same white-silk pajama-looking tunic and trousers that Adrian's princess had always badgered him to wear. But while the men's eyes were closed in what appeared to be merely sleep, not death, every one of them was injured. *Seriously* injured, as in missing limbs or sporting fist-sized holes through various important parts of their bodies. A disturbing number were even missing their heads, but what really creeped Adrian out was how much they looked like him.

Not exactly the same. He wasn't looking at an army of clones, but the resemblance was still striking. Every one of the sleeping men had the same dark hair and olive skin that he did. Several also had his nose, shoulders, or feet. The genetics were all right there in front of him, but it still took Adrian an embarrassingly long time to reach the conclusion Bex had apparently figured out the moment she came up the stairs.

"Check out all the princes," she said, carrying her swords over to the wall of tanks for a closer look. "I've never been good at telling them apart, but Drox is pretty sure those are all sons of Gilgamesh that I've killed in my past lives."

"But why are they *here*?" Adrian asked as he ran nervously to join her. "I'd heard that Gilgamesh puts his damaged princes in something called the Sleep, but why's he got them on display in the middle of a sin-iron desert?"

"And why are there so many?" Boston added, hooking his claws into Adrian's shoulder as he leaned back to get a count. "Seven tanks tall by forty tanks wide is two hundred and eighty princes! I had no idea Gilgamesh had so many sons."

"I'm more concerned that he's displaying them in jars," Adrian said with a shudder. "Even by Gilgamesh standards, that's weird."

"Super creepy," Bex agreed, flexing her hand around the hilt of Ishtar's sword. She did this a few more times, wiggling each finger individually like holding the weapon pained them, before finally giving up and sliding the divine blade back into the sheath on her hip.

"Let's keep looking around," she suggested, pulling Drox back into his ring as well as she turned away from the wall of bottled princes. "This is the top of Heaven and the place where all the chains connect, so Gilgamesh has got to be around here some—"

Her voice cut off. When Adrian's head snapped over to see why, Bex was standing perfectly still with her foot raised like she was a video that had been paused midstep. He'd just grabbed her frozen shoulder to see what was wrong when a weight fell over his body.

It felt like he'd been trapped inside an invisible block of iron. He could still breathe, but no other part of him could move. He couldn't even slide his eyes over to see if Boston was in the same predicament, though from the perfect silence on his shoulder, that seemed to be the case. He was wondering if they'd triggered some kind of automatic trap when Adrian heard the soft tap of a man's footsteps walking over clean-swept stone.

"I was wondering when you'd show up."

The voice was the exact one they'd come here to find, but Adrian still felt unaccountably surprised when Gilgamesh stepped around the wall of preserved princes and into his frozen line of sight.

He was dressed like Malik again. No golden armor or Crown of Anu on his brow, just a breezy natural linen shirt with the sleeves rolled to his elbows, perfectly fitted blue jeans, a leather blacksmith's apron, and comfortable-looking calfskin loafers. His scarred hands were decorated with ancient golden rings, but the rest of him looked like a wealthy retiree on vacation, and the more Adrian thought about that, the angrier he got.

"Don't give me that look," his father scolded, even though Adrian's face was frozen and thus couldn't look like anything. "I'm sure this isn't the reunion you were hoping for, but I'm actually glad you're here. Alexander was as loyal and competent a son as any father could ask, but between you and me, he could get a bit dull."

He walked over to clap Adrian on the shoulder that wasn't currently supporting a cat. "No one could ever say that about you, though! You're always a surprise, Adrian Blackwood. A man my age needs those, so why don't you come along and let me show you what I've been working on? I'd appreciate your unique perspective, and I'm sure the fabled Queen of Wrath won't want to miss this."

He reached out to pat Bex on the shoulder as well, and though she was still frozen, Adrian swore he saw her twitch. He half expected her to rip through whatever magic was holding them and bite Gilgamesh's smirking head off. But whatever magic was holding them in place must have been a sort even the new Queen of All Demons couldn't fight, because Bex didn't even move her eyes to follow the king when he stepped away.

"I've prepared refreshments," he announced as he walked back the way he'd come. "It's a joyous day, after all, so come. Let me be your host one last time before the end."

Gilgamesh flicked his scarred hand as he finished. There was no sorcery spoken, no flux of magic. He simply twitched his fingers, and Bex and Adrian with Boston still on his shoulder floated into the air, trailing behind the Eternal King like balloons as he led them around the glowing wall filled with his preserved sons to the other side of the stone platform.

This half was very different. When Adrian and Bex had first come up, the desert, chains, and tanks of sleeping princes were all they could see. Here on the other side of the wall, though, the swept-stone platform was covered in furniture. There was a golden table set with artful trays full of beautifully prepared food, a drink cart with tea, wine, and other refreshments, and what appeared to be a weapon forge made of the same black metal as Bex's Drox.

"Impressive, isn't it?" the king asked as he made his frozen guests sit down at the lavish table. "That forge belonged to Enki himself, you know. I salvaged it from his workshop on the banks of the River Lethe along with several other choice pieces, including that table. It used to be for etching, but as you know, I like to reuse things. I promise it's clean."

He beamed like he thought they actually cared about the hygiene status of the stolen table they were being forced to sit at with magic, and not for the first time, Adrian wondered if Gilgamesh might be mad.

"Go on," the king said, waving his gold-ringed hand. "Eat! That spell only restrains threatening movements. It won't stop you from enjoying hospitality, so please help yourselves. The food will go to waste if you don't."

The moment Gilgamesh said that, the magic freezing Adrian's muscles went slack, allowing him to rest his arms on the table. Boston jumped off his shoulder a second later, shaking his fur like he'd just been dunked in water. Bex was the only one who didn't move, probably because she'd never stopped contemplating violence. Her hands were under the table, but Adrian could see her arm moving one fraction of a millimeter at a time toward the sword on her hip. Actually reaching her blade would take a century at that rate, but Adrian decided to go ahead and stall for time, just in case.

"Thank you," he said, reaching out to take a slice of quiche both to show that he wasn't planning anything threatening and because the food really did look delicious. He hadn't eaten anything since before he'd grown his tree, and he was starving. He was also reasonably certain Gilgamesh wouldn't stoop to poisoning his guests, so Adrian went ahead and made himself a plate.

"May I ask you a question?" he said as he carefully spooned a serving of pâté onto a second golden plate for Boston.

"If you don't mind me working while I answer," Gilgamesh replied, walking back over to the forge, which shone with the brightness of a supernova when he opened the protective door. "I'm running slightly behind schedule."

"I don't mind at all," Adrian said, which was one hundred percent true. If Gilgamesh hadn't finished his plan yet, maybe there was still time to talk him out of it. "Earlier, you said this was a joyous day, but I don't understand how you can call it that. You've lost three princes this afternoon, four if you count Leander's defection. I know you don't care much for the lives of your children, but—"

"Nonsense," Gilgamesh countered. "I care deeply for all my sons. Your murderous queen there is the one who killed them, so if you've got complaints, take them up with her."

"Bex had to defeat them to stop you," Adrian told him angrily. "If you actually love your princes, why are you destroying the world they live in?"

"Destroying?" Gilgamesh repeated, closing the blinding forge before turning around to give him a puzzled look. "Adrian, just what is it exactly that you think I'm doing?"

The way he said that opened a yawning hole in Adrian's stomach. "You're... Aren't you going to reset the world?"

"Reset the world?" his father repeated, his face splitting into a smile like that was the most absurd thing he'd ever heard. "No, no, no! It's nothing like that. Honestly, Adrian, I thought you understood me better. You've seen my art and collections, all the beautiful things I value. I already lived through the Bronze Age once. Do you really think someone like me would roll the world back into that wretched darkness?"

Not when he put it that way.

"So you're *not* going to reset the world?" Adrian confirmed.

"Absolutely not," Gilgamesh said, walking back to the table to take a sip from his wine cup. "The gods are the only ones who benefit from a fearful and ignorant humanity. My views are the complete opposite. I'm a humanist, a proud defender of literacy and culture. Everything I've ever done has been for the preservation of mankind, not its ruination."

"Then what *are* you doing?" Adrian demanded, losing his patience at last. "You dragged me into Heaven to fix the Queen of Pride's horns then ignored me for an entire week. You worked Bex's demons to death producing sin iron and tried to drown the entire Hells. You'd never waste resources like that unless you were working on something apocalyptic, but I don't understand what. Why did you lock yourself up here? Why did you send all your sorcerers to attack the Blackwood? Why did you leave Alexander to fight to the death to keep us from reaching this place? *Why?*"

He was shouting by the end, but his father didn't look offended. He actually looked delighted by all the questions, which made sense in hindsight. Even back when he'd been pretending to be Malik, there was nothing Gilgamesh seemed to enjoy more than talking about himself.

"Why indeed?" he replied gleefully as he walked over to the furnace. "There are five thousand years' worth of answers to that question, but I think the easiest way would be just to show you."

He stuck his hand inside the forge as he finished. Given the blasting heat Adrian could feel all the way back at the table, that looked like a quick way to lose an arm, but Gilgamesh must've had something shielding his bare hand, because his gold rings weren't even warped when he pulled his arm back and held up a sword.

Again, that seemed like a terrible idea. Adrian had never been much of a blacksmith, but even he knew that superheated metal needed to be treated with the utmost care, not waved around. But even though it had just come out of a blazing furnace, the sword—which was long, slender, and white as snow—already looked finished. It had a guard and a hilt made from the same white metal as the blade, and its dual cutting edges were already sharpened to gleaming points.

Even its flat had already been decorated with motifs of rampant lions, which was just ridiculous. Again, Adrian was no swordsmith, but who put a fully finished blade back in the forge? He also didn't understand what the sword was supposed to explain. Its decorated blade and hilt were fancier than the ones the princes used, but otherwise the white sword looked like just another Blade of Gilgamesh. He was trying to puzzle it out when Bex suddenly spoke beside him.

"What in the Hells did you do?"

Adrian glanced at her in surprise, and not just because she'd managed to stop wanting to kill Gilgamesh long enough to move her mouth. He was alarmed because Bex sounded horrified. His first thought was that she must've seen something in the sword that he didn't, but when he looked harder at where her eyes were pointed, he realized she wasn't looking at the blade at all. She was staring into the furnace the sword had come out of. The blazing white inferno, which, now that he was squinting at it as well, Adrian realized was fueled by a pile of severed women's hands burning like charcoal briquettes at the very back.

"You *monster*!" Bex roared, jerking against the binding magic so hard she almost managed to knock herself out of her chair. "*What did you do to my sisters?*"

"Nothing, for once," Gilgamesh replied calmly. "That is Enki's forge, not Ishtar's. Her daughters can't affect it at all. Their swords, however…" He chuckled. "That's another matter."

He slid his white sword back into the glowing oven and tapped its point against a pile of dark objects sitting at the center. They were so small, and the light was so bright, Adrian didn't realize what he was looking at until Gilgamesh actually pulled one out to show them a smoking black ring. The same sort of black ring Bex was currently wearing on her finger, except the one Gilgamesh had removed was cracked and burned like an old piece of scorched wood.

"Enki's forges are powerful but finicky," the king explained as he tossed the burned ring back inside the oven. "The only way to make them run properly is to fuel them with sparks of his own creation, which these days can only be found inside the rings of Ishtar's daughters. Obviously, that makes forging anything using this setup a one-time affair, which is why I waited so long. I knew I'd only get one chance, so I had to make sure that it was perfect."

"Perfect for what?" Adrian demanded. "Whose sword is that?"

"Mine," Gilgamesh replied proudly, pointing the blade at Adrian so he could see its perfect straightness head-on. "What you are looking at is the ultimate pinnacle of sorcery. A divine weapon forged by human hands."

"Okay, but don't you already have plenty of divine weapons?" Adrian asked, taking great care not to look at the Sword of Ishtar on Bex's hip.

"All except the Blade of Wrath," Gilgamesh acknowledged, smiling at Bex, who growled inside the prison of his magic. "But although I did manage to make use of all of them eventually, they were never truly mine. My mortal soul simply could not unlock the full potential of weapons made for the gods' divine creations. But a good engineer never accepts defeat gracefully. I knew how the weapons were made because Enki had described the process to me in detail back when I was his student. Not being a god myself, I was unable to duplicate his exact method, so I began to experiment. I made good progress in the beginning, but none of the materials I had access to were strong enough to withstand the forging process. Even sin iron fell apart when exposed to the raw powers of creation. I was starting to think the whole idea was hopeless, and then I found you."

He waved his sword at Adrian, who winced.

"I told you when we talked in your forest that sin iron has always been an incomplete creation. To balance its formulation and bring out its true potential, I needed sins collected by all nine of Ishtar's demons, and I only had access to eight. Seven, really, because while the sleeping pride demons were still *technically* able to collect sin, the power it should have contained was missing, a void just like their shattered queen.

"For eons, this flaw held back my progress," the king continued bitterly. "Even if I brought the Coward Queen under my control, I had no solution to the Pride problem. It was the wall I could not climb, and then I heard about your miraculous work with the Bonfire Queen."

He stretched out his arms to his son, causing Adrian to tilt back farther in his chair. If Gilgamesh noticed the rejection, though, it didn't bother him.

"You performed even better than I could have hoped," he said warmly. "When you repaired the Queen of Pride's horns, all the sin I'd used the sleeping void demons to collect over the years suddenly became viable again. Even though you defied me and put Pride's crown back on the queen's head rather than in my hands, I still had what I needed. Between the reactivated sins of Pride and all the Wrath I was able to squeeze out of the starving demons of Limbo, I was finally able to forge all nine sins into one perfectly balanced alloy that, when mixed with quintessence and my own command over the magic of Heaven, became one perfect sword."

He showed off the weapon again, but Adrian's patience with his father's drama was at an end.

"But *what* do you need that sword *for*?" he demanded. "What are you going to do with it? Kill the gods again?"

"That would truly be impossible," Gilgamesh said. "If Enki's forge was capable of making weapons that could kill the gods for good, they'd have all murdered each other long ago. Even if I could destroy them permanently, I wouldn't, for without the gods, where would I get my quintessence?"

Adrian went still as he realized what his father was saying. "You mean all that liquid quintessence..." He stopped to swallow. "The white stuff you drowned my forest in..."

"Was the blood of the gods," Gilgamesh finished impatiently. "Where did you think I was getting it from? Even I can't make magic out of nothing."

Adrian had never given it much thought, which was stupid in hindsight. Of course quintessence had to come from somewhere, and as the most powerful beings in existence, the gods were the obvious choice, but... "If all your magic comes from gods' blood, how did you defeat them the first time?"

"By tricking them into giving it to me," Gilgamesh replied with a smug look. "I was their treasured pupil, remember? All of my requests were treated as innocent curiosity, which was one of the traits the gods wanted to encourage. Even when I asked Anu for a cup of his blood to use in an experiment, he never suspected anything was amiss until my first words of sorcery became a spear in his back. This caused more of his divine blood to spill, giving me everything I needed to push the attack all the way to the end."

Adrian wasn't surprised by that story in the slightest. But if his father wasn't about to carry his betrayal to its logical end and plunge his new sword into a bunch of divine hearts, then he was stumped.

"It's all right," Gilgamesh assured him. "True genius often looks like madness from the outside. That's why, even though it cost me my other sons, I'm glad you made it up here, Adrian. It'd be *such* a tragedy if I was forced to perform my life's greatest accomplishment without an audience. I was starting to worry it'd just be me and them."

"'Them'?" Adrian repeated with a frown. "Who's—"

Gilgamesh swept his hand through the air before Adrian could finish. Not the one holding his new sword. *That* stayed at his side, but his empty left hand cut through the empty space in front of him like a saber.

Magic followed the motion in a surge, making Adrian gasp. Even though Gilgamesh had already explained exactly how he did sorcery back in Malik's study, it was still shocking to see someone throw around that much power so casually. Gilgamesh hadn't said a single word. He simply waved his arm, and the black dunes of sin-iron dust that filled the chain desert were blown away, revealing the industrialized horror beneath.

Adrian recoiled in shock. When he'd first stuck his head through the portal into this place, he'd suspected something bigger was buried under the dunes. He'd assumed it was the Anchors at the time, or at least the manifestation of the concept of the Anchors as they existed inside this pocket reality. Now, though, Adrian realized he'd been grossly incorrect. There *were* giant sin-iron structures hidden beneath the black shavings, but they weren't weights attached to the ends of chains. What Adrian saw when Gilgamesh's magic blew the black desert away were coffins.

Miles and miles of matte-black sin-iron coffins stretched as far as he could see to the horizon. They'd been lined up head to foot in an orderly grid, but it still took several seconds for Adrian's brain to accept how *big* the coffins were. They looked like black metal boxes at this distance, but each coffin was actually the size of a three-story building, and the ones closest to the rocky outcropping where Gilgamesh had set up shop were bigger still. The real shocker, however, was the tanks.

Each coffin had a black spigot at its foot that fed into a sin-iron pipe. These pipes ran down into an array of storage vessels that looked like water tanks. The setup reminded Adrian of the buckets used to collect sap from a grove of tapped maple trees. The liquid he could see through the tanks' tiny windows was even thick like syrup, but it shone as white as moonlight.

That pure, soft, glittering radiance was the hallmark of liquid quintessence, but the sheer volume being collected was difficult for Adrian to comprehend. It just didn't seem possible that bodies— even the giant bodies of gods—could produce so much blood, though Adrian would've bet his witch hat that the insides of those coffins were filled with spikes just like the queens' had been down in the Lowest Hells. It was the only way those tanks could be collecting so much white blood, but knowing how it worked didn't make the sight any less horrifying. Even Bex, whose opinion of the gods had done a complete one-eighty during the time Adrian had known her, was visibly shaken by the grim industrial efficiency of it all. Gilgamesh, however, looked delighted.

"Magnificent, isn't it?" he said, his blue-gray eyes gleaming with pride as he swept his scarred hand once more over the abomination his sorcery had revealed. "The divine tyrants who once sought to reshape our species into docile sheep, transformed into fuel for humanity's advancement. Truly, there could be no more fitting end to the saga of the gods' hubris."

"If this is the end, then why are we here?" Adrian asked in a shaking voice. "It looks like you've already got the situation on lockdown."

"The lockdown is precisely the problem," his father explained patiently. "Don't you see it? All of these gods"—he waved his hand again over the coffin-filled landscape—"are trapped in a vicious cycle. They can't die because they're immortal, but they're too afraid to come back to life because they know I'll just strike them down again. My backstabbing was the closest to true death most of them had come, and the experience traumatized them so deeply that they all collectively decided to wait for my life to end rather than risk going through it a second time. Naturally, I was fine with this plan, except for the part where it doesn't work because of *that*."

He pointed his new sword at the giant chained wheel filling the sky above them.

"The Wheel of Reincarnation is not a natural cycle," he said gravely. "The gods created it to catch the souls of their beloved humans as they died so that our entire species could be 'tumbled like rocks in the river' until we met their definition of perfection. To control the souls of an entire planet, the gods had to make a system *so* big that they also ended up trapped inside it. Since the wheel only turned the souls of the dead, however, the immortal gods assumed that would never be a problem for them."

"And then you came along," Adrian said.

"That oversight has been the bane of my existence for five thousand years," Gilgamesh said with a sigh. "I thought I'd scored a clean victory when my army swept through Paradise, but no matter how much the gods and I both want them to stay dead, the wheel they'd built to churn humanity's souls keeps pushing them back up. Even after I chained it to motionlessness, the pressure never ceased."

He shook his head at Adrian. "This is how we ended up in the situation I complained about to you before. I'm the most powerful human in the world, a sorcerer king of unrivaled skill and potential, and yet I've been forced to spend ninety-nine-point-nine percent of my time, resources, and magic coming up with ways to keep the wheel from pushing the gods out of their graves. All the sin iron you see before you is the reason I built the Hells and Limbo in the first place, the reason I allowed Ishtar's demons to survive at all. Do you have any idea how much work and expense it takes to keep nine different kinds of demons enslaved? I would've collapsed the Hells and crushed them all ages ago if I could have, but even when it was imperfect, the sin iron they produced was the only material capable of restraining divine creations like the gods and their wheel."

Gilgamesh smiled at his son. "I thought I'd be trapped in that stalemate forever, but then you bumbled into the picture. Thanks to your efforts, I was finally able to produce a sin-iron alloy capable of withstanding Enki's Forge of Creation. I *finally* have a weapon that can destroy the creations of the gods themselves. Not merely their children or their tools but the great works that required the full effort of their pantheon to bring into existence, the infrastructure they built to change the nature of the world itself! *That* is what I forged this blade to cut, and now that the stage has been properly set..."

He let his voice trail off dramatically, his blue-gray eyes moving purposefully from Adrian to Boston to Bex and then back to Adrian again. When the Eternal King was certain they were all watching, he swung his white sword up in a flamboyant arc.

Or so it appeared, at least. Gilgamesh hadn't set his feet or strained his muscles. There'd been no preparation, no warm-up, nothing that made it look like he wasn't just being theatrical. But just like when he'd blown the black desert away with a sweep of his arm, the moment he swung the white blade over his head, Adrian felt that pulse of power in his chest again right before a great arc of magic flew off of Gilgamesh's blade and into the sky.

It rocketed upward like a glowing scythe, flying higher and higher—higher than Adrian had realized the sky here went—until it crashed into the Wheel of Reincarnation. The sky-spanning creation of the gods was so huge that the hit barely looked like it'd done anything at all. Then the air was filled with the groaning creak of breaking glass as the false cycle all the Anchors in the world had been created to stop suddenly shattered.

Adrian hadn't realized how big the Wheel truly was until it broke. The cycle built by the gods to control all of humanity's deaths and births exploded like a supernova, causing the hundreds of chains that used to bind it to go spinning off in all directions. The destruction whited out the sky, raining bits of crystallized... Adrian didn't even know what it was made of, but it fell all over them like a warm, slightly stinging blizzard. It fell on the coffins of the gods, on the shining tanks Gilgamesh had made to hold his dead sons, on the food-laden table, and on Gilgamesh himself, who threw up his arms to meet the falling debris like a child celebrating the year's first snow.

"It's finally *done*!" he shouted into the newly empty sky. "The shackles of the gods have been broken! Humanity's stagnant souls are once again free to keep flowing toward whatever awaits them in the great beyond!"

"*Does* anything await them in the great beyond?" whispered Boston, leaning closer to Adrian as Gilgamesh waved his sword around.

"Who knows?" Adrian said. "What comes after death has always been a mystery, though what I want to know is what happened before this. If the Wheel of Reincarnation that's supposed to churn our souls has been stopped for five thousand years, where did everyone who died before now end up?"

"Here," Gilgamesh answered, making both him and Boston jump. Adrian hadn't realized his father could hear them, but when he looked away from his cat, Gilgamesh was already striding over like he couldn't wait to explain.

"Human souls were never meant to reincarnate," the king told them authoritatively. "Our reality is just one eddy in the infinite river of time and space. That's why the gods built the Wheel in the first place. They couldn't stand the thought of their favorite pets dying and passing beyond their reach, so they trapped us here like fish in a bucket. It was their greatest crime, and for eons, I was unable to do anything about it. Humans kept being born, but with the Wheel stopped, the souls of the dead could neither move forward nor go back into the system, so they built up here. That's what all this dust is."

Adrian stared at Gilgamesh in horror. "I thought that was all sin iron that'd worn off the chains!"

"Some of it was. Some of it wasn't," his father said with a shrug. "In the end, though, it's all semantics. Sins are just the bits of people the gods deemed unacceptable and shaved off, but it's all the same souls in the end. Their dust is all over Paradise—here, the Goddeath Wastes, the Hells, everywhere. Now, though, thanks to me, all those fragmented souls can move on as they were always meant to." He grinned from ear to ear. "I *told* you I was the savior of humanity!"

Adrian didn't buy that for a second. He could acknowledge that, unlike the rest of Gilgamesh's actions, breaking the Wheel of Reincarnation didn't seem overtly evil. If his father was telling the truth when he said human souls were meant to move on, it could even be viewed as a net good. But while Gilgamesh had always been happy to dress himself up as humanity's champion, Adrian had never seen his father do anything that wasn't of direct and immediate benefit to himself, which made his grandiose language all the more suspicious.

"So what happens now?" Adrian prodded, sitting up straighter in his golden chair. "You finally broke the wheel that's been pushing up the gods. What are you going to do next?"

"How many hours have you got?" Gilgamesh asked with a giddiness that felt oddly dangerous, like a happy drunk getting behind the wheel of a sports car. "Adrian, Adrian, Adrian, you simply cannot imagine how long I've dreamed of this day! How many thousands of plans I've made, revised, and made again. This is the culmination of my life's work, what I killed the gods to achieve. Now that the force that's been pushing them back toward life is gone, they'll cower in those coffins forever, which means the undying gods are now fish in *my* bucket!"

He set his sword down on the table so he could rub his hands together in glee. "They're my eternal source of quintessence now," he said, smiling so widely that it was becoming slightly difficult to understand him. "No more constant monitoring, no more chain replacements, no more regulating every drop of liquid that enters Heaven. I'm free now, *truly* free to be the king I always dreamed of being!"

Adrian nodded. There it was. "You're going to rule the world."

"I've been doing that for eons," his father said dismissively. "The difference now is that I can finally do it *right*. All of humanity's needless wars, the shortsighted destruction of the environment, the enormous suffering caused by hunger and poverty, I'm finally free to fix it all! The only reason I put scales in humanity's eyes to begin with was because my imperfect sin-iron chains couldn't handle the tumult of a truly magical world, but that's all over now. I don't need to worry about chains or Anchors or anything anymore, which means I'm finally free to give it *back*."

He swept his hand over the field of coffins covered in the glowing remnants of the Wheel.

"Just think about it," he said, his voice quivering. "A worldwide magical society with me as its benevolent king. I would dole out magic only to those who would use it best, guide humanity through its follies like a benevolent father. In a single generation, I could eliminate all poverty, injustice, and violence. Not by changing human souls as the gods sought to, but by harnessing the power of mankind's greed. The problem with the current world is that cruelty and selfishness are rewarded, but if I grant magic only to the very best our species has to offer, then humanity will choose to become better on its own! I will usher in an era of peace, culture, and decency greater than any that has come before. I will clean up pollution, cure diseases, uplift the impoverished. I will create a paradise on *Earth*, not in a secret place known only to the gods." He sighed happily and turned to beam at his son. "Can you imagine anything more wonderful?"

It did sound pretty great, but Adrian had already been fooled by his father's silver tongue once. Gilgamesh's ideals always sounded fantastic while he was pitching them, but Adrian had seen the Heaven his father had built. He'd met the selfish sorcerers, the slaving warlocks, all the chosen of Gilgamesh who treated everyone not blessed by Heaven as disposable. The king who'd built that abusive system, enslaved an entire race, and killed so many witches that the Blackwood coven was the last still in operation was the same man sitting here pontificating about creating a perfect world, and Adrian just didn't buy it.

"If your goals are so benevolent," he said, pushing away his untouched slice of quiche, "what about those who don't qualify under your narrow definition of humanity? What about the Blackwood witches and the demons? If you're going to be such a magnanimous ruler, what mercy will you show them?"

Gilgamesh's dark eyebrows shot up, and then he shook his head with a long, disappointed sigh. "That's such a foolish question, I don't even know why you asked it. I've always described myself as humanity's savior, and—as I've already explained to you many times—demons are not human. They're the army of the enemy, Ishtar's *literal* tools. Just look at your pet queen."

He pointed at Bex, who was still straining against his magic so hard that the heat from her contained fire was melting her chair.

"I know she appears beautiful," Gilgamesh said in a hard, angry voice, "but that's the monster who killed your brothers. All the princes you see in the Sleep"—he flicked a finger at the golden wall of corpse-filled tanks—"she's the one who did that to them, just like she murdered my blood brother Enkidu. She's a demon in every sense of the word, and what's even worse is that she seduced you into helping her. That's how dangerous her kind is. If I'm ever going to achieve my dream of a peaceful world, I can't allow such threats to continue. It'd be irresponsible governance, just like it'd be irresponsible to allow my new utopia to be infiltrated by heartless, backstabbing, betraying witches."

"It wasn't a betrayal," Adrian said with a lift of his chin. "We were never on your side to begin with."

"I know." Gilgamesh sighed. "But that's why you and your charming mother and all the other Blackwoods must die. It breaks my heart. It truly does. I despise wasting such talented artisans, but you've proven over and over that you cannot be trusted, and a king has to put his kingdom first. I'm sure you understand."

"I understand you perfectly," Adrian said, putting out his arm so Boston could scuttle back onto his shoulder.

"I am sorry," his father said as he picked up his sword. "If only I'd taken you from your mother sooner, I'm sure we could have seen eye to eye, but I'm still glad you joined me today, Adrian. It pleases this old poet's heart to know that the divine executioner who began my journey and the witch who made it possible were the ones who got to witness my final victory."

He did look happy as he straightened back up, swinging his new white blade a few times to get a feel for its weight before leveling the point at Adrian's neck.

"I'll send your mother to follow you soon," he promised. "She always told me that witches join the Great Blackwood when they die. I don't know if that's true or not now that I've reopened the flow of souls, but wherever the two of you end up, know that I will always remember you with the greatest fondness."

"I'll take it to heart," Adrian promised, opening his arms to accept the blow. "Go ahead."

Gilgamesh smiled gratefully at his son's understanding. But before he could begin his swing—which he was performing with great pomp, just as

Adrian had hoped—Adrian stomped his foot on the ground and pushed his chair backward.

Since this was *not* a threatening action toward Gilgamesh, the sorcery that bound his movements allowed it, dumping Adrian backward onto the stone floor. He rolled the second he hit, ignoring the sound of the white sword whistling through the air where his head had just been to leap at Bex and shove the hand she'd never stopped trying to move the final six inches to Ishtar's sword.

The second her fingers touched it, the Blade of Ishtar sliced through its sheath. It sliced through the magic trapping her in the chair as well, freeing Bex to surge to her feet. She lit up like a rocket as she rose, slashing her mother's sword through the sorcery that was still all over Adrian and into the golden table behind him. The attack sent food, wine, and platters flying everywhere, creating the perfect cover for the flaming Queen of All Demons to leap over Adrian—who'd already flattened himself against the floor with Boston clasped protectively in his arms—and stab her *other* sword, Drox's smoking pitch-black blade, straight at Gilgamesh's aproned chest.

Chapter 18

BEX KNEW THE STAB WASN'T GOING TO LAND the moment she launched it.

Her original plan had been to strike Gilgamesh with Ishtar's Blade using a continuation of the same slash that had cut through the binding sorcery. Drox could've executed that move easily, but while Bex had co-opted a large portion of her mother's power, she wasn't actually a goddess, and Ishtar's sword knew it. It fought her grip like a wild horse, filling Bex's limbs with a power she could barely control.

That was fine for things that didn't move, like sorcery and tables, but it made striking a skilled opponent extremely difficult, which was why she'd gone back to Drox. Her own blade wasn't just steadier and more reliable, he was a true partner who could communicate with Bex instantly through her thoughts, which was how she knew they weren't going to make it. Pulling Drox out of his ring had taken only a fraction of a second, *and* she'd used the flying table as cover to hide her attack until the last possible second, but even so, Gilgamesh didn't look the least bit surprised when she burst through the cover. He mostly just looked smug, taking the time to look Bex directly in the eyes before teleporting away.

Drox stabbed through the space where he'd been half a heartbeat later. Bex was still shifting her weight to stop her momentum when Drox shouted in her head.

Above us!

She leaped sideways the second he called the warning, but she still wasn't fast enough to avoid the rain of glowing swords. Shining white blades that looked like they were made from the same glowing energy as the Heavenly bombardment that had flattened the Seattle Anchor were suddenly falling around Bex like hail. What was left of the golden table was atomized in seconds. Bex was terrified that Adrian had met the same fate until she saw him and Boston diving for cover behind the golden wall of Gilgamesh's sleeping sons.

The sight filled her with both relief and rage. Clearly, Gilgamesh no longer gave a damn about who he hurt, if he ever had. But while she was grateful that Adrian was behind cover, Bex couldn't say the same for herself. Drox had flown up automatically to protect her head, proof yet again that he was the best sword any queen could ask for, but even his restored wider blade couldn't shield her entire body.

We have to move, Drox agreed as the hail of narrow, white-glowing swords rattled off him. *Gilgamesh is fifty feet above us and to the left. I can't tell where the swords are coming from, but they don't seem to have an end.*

"That's fine," Bex said, tightening her left hand around Ishtar's wildly jerking blade. "We'll go to him. Ready?"

Drox responded by going still in her palm. Bex tightened her grip in reply as she leaped into the air, keeping Drox above her head with her right hand while she swung Ishtar's Blade with her left. It was the first time she could remember wielding swords in both hands, but some previous version of Bex must've used a two-weapon fighting style at some point, because her body adjusted without her having to think about it. If Ishtar's Blade hadn't been constantly trying to rip itself out of her grasp, it would've felt almost natural and not like she was swinging a possessed bat.

Bex didn't know if her mother's sword was acting up because she'd disobeyed or if it was simply too powerful for a non-god to handle, but it was the sharpest weapon she'd ever held. Even when it was jerking uncontrollably in her fingers, it still cut the glowing swords out of the air with ease, clearing an attack path as Bex blasted up on her fire toward Gilgamesh, who was standing in the sky with his leather loafers planted on thin air like it was solid ground. She was only a foot away when the smug-faced king teleported again.

Bex was ready for him this time. The moment Gilgamesh vanished, she pulled Drox in close and spun to block the attack she was positive was already coming for her back. That was what she would've done if she could teleport without a word. When Bex actually did make it around, though, the air behind her was empty. She was wondering if Gilgamesh had taken the safer route and teleported much farther to shoot her from a distance when Drox screamed in her head again.

Up!

Her brain didn't even have time to process the one-syllable warning. It was pure luck that her flinch of surprise at Drox's yell caused her to move sideways in time to avoid what should've been a skull-splitting blow. The attack still landed in her shoulder, though.

Gilgamesh's white sword was so sharp she didn't even feel it go in. There was only pressure and a flash of cold against her flaming skin, and then Bex looked over to find that her left shoulder had been cleaved down to the third rib. She could literally see down into her own black organs before her flaming body pulled itself back together.

Ironically, the healing hurt much, *much* more than the initial wound. Bex could feel every burning inch as Ishtar's gift of regeneration fused her together again. But while the intense pain sent tears streaming down her face, Bex had never been happier because the return of her healing meant that she didn't have to keep using Greed's power. Forcing her body to work like someone else's had been exhausting, but her natural regeneration was tied to her fire, and Bex could burn all day.

She did so now with a victorious shout, ramping up her flames to sear the last of the cut away as she slashed Drox through the air directly below her. That was where Gilgamesh should've been given the angle of the attack he'd just finished. As always in this fight, though, Bex was already too late. The moment her sword went down, the Eternal King appeared in front of her with that same smug smile as he ran her through.

Bex saw the sword go in this time, which meant it hurt a lot more. Gilgamesh didn't give her a chance to recover either. Her bonfire had barely started cauterizing the wound when Gilgamesh slid his insanely sharp sword out of her stomach and teleported behind her to stab Bex in the back. *That* pain was still registering when he yanked his sword out and did it again, teleporting around to stab her from the left side, then the right.

Bex lost track after that. All she could feel was pain as Gilgamesh's sword skewered her over and over followed by the scorching heat of her flames repairing the damage. Maybe she shouldn't have been so quick to say she could burn forever. Even with the wrath of all of demonkind behind her, Bex could feel her body growing weaker. Even her raging bonfire wasn't enough to boil away all the blood she was losing, leaving it to fall like black rain onto the shattered banquet below. If she couldn't stop the barrage of constant attacks soon, she was going to bleed out and die in the air before she landed a single hit. It was kill or be killed, so Bex decided to do something crazy.

She couldn't see Gilgamesh anymore through the raging fire and the blinding pain, but she could feel his sword. She hadn't been fast enough to block him before she'd been injured, and she *definitely* didn't have the speed to do so now, but he always attacked with the same straight, stabbing motion. So the next time Bex felt Gilgamesh's blade enter her perforated stomach, she pulled Drox back into his ring and lurched forward, sliding her body down the king's sword to grab the arm he was using to hold it. Since he'd been cocky enough to meet them unarmored, Bex was able to feel his muscles tense through his linen shirt right before she poured her hottest flames straight into him.

The result was a combustion big enough to light up all of Heaven. Bex burned like she was back in the fire she'd become when all the demons of the Hells bowed their horns to her. The difference this time was that, instead of being a pillar of flames that roared into the sky, Bex had focused all her explosive power onto a single, man-sized point. Even the flames on her skin went out, leaving her bleeding like a fountain as she threw every joule of heat she had at the man who'd killed the gods.

The famously *mortal* man. Unlike the Queen of War, who'd taken Bex's flames like the divinely unkillable metal statue she was, Gilgamesh's arm felt fleshy and human in her grip. His boiling blood was red—not princely white—and his charring flesh smelled like any other burning meat.

Impressively, he didn't scream as she scorched him to the bone. He *did* try to push her off with his sorcery, but Bex was still clutching the Blade of Ishtar in her left hand. She couldn't swing it at the moment thanks to the sword's unruly nature and the effort of producing all that fire, but her mother's weapon was so sharp that just holding it still in the right position was enough to slice any sorcery aimed at her to ribbons as she cooked Gilgamesh alive.

And it *worked*. In the space of seconds, Bex's roaring flames reduced Gilgamesh's arm to ash that blew away in the wind whipping off her fire. He almost got away then, but Bex didn't let him. Whenever one part of the king became too charred to hold on to, she lurched forward and grabbed another, impaling herself farther and farther up his sword to grab his shoulder, then his chest. Eventually, with no hand left to hold it, the king's white blade fell out of her stomach on its own, clattering to the bloody stone below as Bex clawed her way up Gilgamesh's body, cremated him piece by piece until there was nothing left but ash.

Even though she was the one doing it, Bex couldn't believe what she was seeing. She'd been saying she was going to burn Gilgamesh for as long as she could remember, but she hadn't thought it would be so...

"Easy" was the wrong word. If her body hadn't been burning with the strength and regenerative power of every demon queen put together, he would've killed her in the first thirty seconds. But while the battle with Gilgamesh had been every bit as brutal as Bex had always imagined, she had thought it would take longer. Not that she was complaining, or taking any chances. She kept burning until Gilgamesh's ashes were ashes. Only when there was literally nothing left to hold on to did Bex finally uncurl her flaming fingers and take a cautious look around.

The first thing she noticed was that, except for smoke and billowing ash, the air was empty. Gilgamesh's sword was also still lying on the ground where it had fallen, its white blade coated in Bex's black blood. That was a good reminder that she needed to finish healing herself, but Bex wasn't sure she had enough fire left. Her body hadn't felt this hollowed out since before Adrian had healed her, but it was all worth it to kill—

Her pain-muddled thoughts stumbled to a stop as a hand wearing a golden gauntlet reached into her field of vision and picked up Gilgamesh's white sword. It seemed to come out of nowhere, but when Bex's eyes snapped up, a man was standing at the head of the destroyed banquet table. He was dressed in a heavier version of the princes' cuneiform-marked golden armor topped with a helmet shaped like a lion's head. Bex had never seen anything like it, but when the soldier finally raised his golden visor, Gilgamesh's face—healthy, whole, and completely unburned—was the one that smiled up at her.

"Now you see why I'm called the Eternal King," he said in the silence of Bex's shock. "Nice job on the fire, by the way. I wasn't expecting that." He smiled wider. "It's always exciting to be surprised. Now how about I show you one in return?"

Bex was still trying to figure out what he meant by that—struggling to understand how he was here at all after being turned to ash—when Gilgamesh swung his white sword up to point at her face.

The world vanished immediately after. There was no pain, no sensation of falling, just blackness everywhere she looked. Her first thought was that he'd teleported her somewhere, but when she tried to flare her fire to get some light, Bex realized the truth was much simpler. She couldn't see anything because she was blind.

Gilgamesh had placed a magical darkness over her eyes. Now that she'd guessed what was happening, Bex could feel his sorcery pressing against her eyeballs like two coins, but her hands found nothing when she tried to pull it off. Ishtar's Sword probably could've cut it, but that would mean getting the jerky, uncontrolled blade right next to her eyes, and then there was the question of what Gilgamesh was doing while she was blind. He'd probably already launched an attack, but Bex couldn't dodge what she couldn't see.

I can, Drox said, leaving his ring to return to her grasping hand. *I might not be able to slice through sorcery like the Blade of Ishtar, but I'm still a weapon of the gods, and I'd have to be blind in every sense not to feel power like Gilgamesh's. It won't be perfect, but if you give me control of your arm, I can defend you while you cut the blinders off.*

That was a good plan, but not in their current configuration. If Bex was going to have any hope of cutting the blinding sorcery off her eyes without cutting off her own head in the process, she needed Ishtar's Blade in her right hand. That would leave Drox with her weaker, non-dominant left arm, but there was no other way this was going to work, so Bex mashed her hands together, blindly switching her swords so that Ishtar's insanely sharp, insanely unhelpful blade was in her right and loyal Drox was in her left.

He took control the second he landed in her palm, jerking Bex's arm up to bash away something she couldn't see.

"What was that?"

No idea, her sword replied, moving her left arm into a defensive position. *Without your eyes, I can only see the names of demons. I feel magic with my other senses. It's normally limited, but Gilgamesh's magic is so strong that I can feel him from several feet away. That should give me enough warning to block anything he throws, but you should still hurry.* Her sword quivered in her hand. *I worry he's surrounding us.*

Bex was worried too. Fighting Gilgamesh was terrifying enough without also having to do it blind. She needed her eyes back as soon as possible, so she yanked Ishtar's sword up to her face, looping the first finger of her right hand over its black guard to gain more fine control. The position should've let her maneuver the blade like a straight razor, but even when she was holding it in her dominant hand, the sword refused to behave. It fought her for every inch, yanking against her grip like it wanted to fly off and fight on its own.

If it could've actually done that, Bex would've been happy to let it, but although the Blade of Ishtar was the most powerful sword she'd ever touched, she'd never seen it move on its own. Maybe Ishtar could've made it fly, but Bex was just a pretender to the goddess's throne. The best she could do was hold the stupid thing still, channeling the Queen of War's unbreakable stance as she slashed up with the black sword's insanely sharp edge.

It still took her three tries. The first hit missed completely, dragged off course by Bex's left arm, which Drox was moving constantly to defend them from whatever Gilgamesh was doing. The second strike almost took off her nose, but the third landed right where Bex wanted, slicing through the thick magic that had attached to her face like an octopus.

The world came back into view a second later. Bex was still where she'd been when Gilgamesh put out her lights, suspended in the air by her blasting flames thirty feet above the stone platform, but she saw no sign of the miraculously resurrected king. Also, everything was still oddly dark. The desert had been blastingly bright when she and Adrian had come up the stairs, but now it looked like a cloud had passed over the nonexistent sun. She was wondering if she'd missed part of the blindness spell when she heard a strange whistling sound.

Bex jerked her head up with a curse. Things hadn't looked dim because there was still a spell in her eyes. It was shady because she was standing in the shadow of a falling mountain.

She had no idea how Gilgamesh had done it, but a rock big enough to crush a city was suddenly plummeting through the empty sky where the Wheel of Reincarnation had been. It wasn't going as fast as an actual meteor, but even at that relatively slower speed, it was so big that getting out of the way was going to be impossible. It was already only a few dozen feet above her head, so Bex did the only thing she could think of. She slammed both her swords together in front of her and blasted all her fire out behind, turning herself into a rocket-stabilized knife as the giant stone crashed down.

If she'd been any less than what she was, that would've been the end. Even the original Rebexa would've been crushed, because no fire was hot enough to burn through all that stone before it hit her. But Bex was no longer that Rebexa nor merely the Queen of Wrath. She was the combined hope of all of Ishtar's creations, and she pulled on every single one, coating her body in both Fear's scales and War's bronze armor to keep her arms from buckling as the falling mountain crashed into her.

She'd never been hit so hard in her life. Even with all her fire blasting, the initial impact almost smashed her into the ground. But Bex was the Bonfire of her people's Wrath, and she had five thousand years' worth of shit to be mad about. When the crashing rock pushed her down, she dug in and pushed back, reaching deep not just into the well of their righteous anger but also their sorrow, hate, and fear. She pulled from the suffering of the war her people had been fighting and dying over for fifty centuries and the pride they'd held onto despite that. She used everything her demons had ever given her, turning herself into a white-hot star as she drove her two swords in like a wedge to split the falling meteor in half.

The giant rock broke with the biggest crash she'd ever heard. Then, as fast as it had appeared, the enormous meteor vanished, revealing a clear blue sky filled with golden lights. They looked like motes of dust floating in the sunlight, except there was no sun in this cursed place, and they were all getting brighter. That was when Bex realized she wasn't looking at motes or lights or anything so benign and beautiful.

They were lions.

A thousand golden lion cannons were standing in the sky above her. Just like the vanished meteor, Bex had no idea where they had come from, if Gilgamesh had pulled them from some ancient stockpile or simply created them out of thin air. All she knew was that they were about to fire. The air in front of them was already shimmering with the first gleams of the destructive white light that had obliterated the Seattle Anchor. But while Bex had smacked the lions' shots away plenty of times, she'd never faced this many at once. She was wondering if she still had time to run when Gilgamesh—whom she'd just spotted standing in the air behind the cannons—waved his golden-gloved hand.

The lions all roared as soon as he gave the signal, unleashing a wave of white fire that, once again, Bex had no choice but to cut through. Just like before, she did it with both blades at once, holding Drox on her left and Ishtar's sword on her right to slice the barrage right down the middle. When her swords made contact with the blinding fire this time, though, the shots didn't bounce off. They exploded, blasting through Bex with enough force to make the world go white.

When she came back to herself, she was lying on the ground in a pool of her own black blood. She must've already healed a lot of the damage, because her body had that tingly, fragile, overused feeling she remembered from the day and a half she'd spent battling Havok nonstop. Drox's voice was buzzing in her ear, but she couldn't focus on his words long enough to comprehend them. The only thing she understood was that she probably shouldn't take another of those.

You absolutely shouldn't take another! Drox yelled through her ringing head. *Your regeneration is nearly instantaneous now that you've got six horns, and you* still *almost died before it could catch you!* She felt his blade shake in her limp hand. *I'm starting to understand how Gilgamesh defeated Ishtar now. You absolutely cannot let him hit you like that again.*

"Not planning on it," Bex muttered as she pushed herself up. "But how are we going to—"

She cut off as the healed injuries she'd been about to inspect were suddenly illuminated by a white light so bright it washed all the color out of the world. Bex didn't even have to look up to know the lions were getting ready to fire again, but if she couldn't block the shots, couldn't take them, and couldn't dodge, what was left to do?

Who says you can't dodge? Drox demanded. *You're faster than you've ever been.*

"Not fast enough when all they have to do is turn their heads," Bex said, glancing around for cover.

There wasn't much. The wall of tanks full of injured princes was still standing, but Bex was pretty sure Adrian was hiding back there, and she didn't want to bring the fire to him, *especially* since she was certain now that Gilgamesh wouldn't pull his punches for his son. She could try diving into the cracks between the giant god coffins, but even with her new improved speed, she didn't think she could make it that far in the few seconds before the lions fired.

That left her pretty cornered, but Bex was used to having her back against the wall. In a way, having no other options was actually freeing, because it gave her the courage to do what she really wanted to.

What's that? Drox asked in a terrified voice.

There was no time to explain. The next barrage of glowing shots was already leaving the lions' mouths, so Bex decided to show him instead as she blasted herself into the air. This put her straight in the path of incoming fire, but now that the shots had left the lions' mouths, their trajectory could no longer be changed, which meant she could dodge them.

Bex did so like a fighter jet, shooting into the sky so fast that the air started to drag like water. She pushed until she was going the same speed as the white shots themselves, which made it even easier to dodge over, under, and between them in midair, but Bex didn't stop there. Once she'd cleared the explosive barrage, she kept going up, using her fire to blast herself faster and faster until she was flying like a rocket at the king hiding behind the cannons like the coward he was.

By this point, Bex was going so fast that the world was a blur, but she still saw Gilgamesh's smug face go blank in shock beneath the visor of his new lion helmet. She saw him tense next, which she realized probably meant he was about to teleport. For once, though, the King of Heaven was too slow.

Bex crashed into him the same way she'd hit the meteor—swords first and blazing like a comet. It was impossible to aim for anything specific at this speed, so Bex settled for just striking her target. And in that, at least, she seemed to be successful. She felt her swords go through Gilgamesh like two guillotines. When she finally stopped blazing and looked back to see how she'd done, though, the result was a mess in every sense of the word.

She definitely hadn't missed. Gilgamesh's golden armor was covered in red blood. It was splattered all over the lions in front of him, almost like he'd exploded. But while the evidence of her victory was painted all around him, the king himself didn't have a scratch. His armor wasn't even dented, and his grinning face showed no sign of pain. It was just like when he'd come back before, but Bex barely had time to gawk before Gilgamesh swung his sword at her.

He was still standing twenty feet away, but that turned out not to matter. Now, at last, Bex understood how he'd broken the Wheel from the ground. His white sword was less than half the size of Drox, but the magic coming off it was like an avalanche. It hit Bex full in the face, sending her body tumbling back down to the ground.

Her flames caught her before she fell too far, but Bex was still a mess. Not in her body—she'd actually escaped with minimal damage this time—but her mind was in chaos. She was sure she'd killed Gilgamesh twice now, but the king floating above her didn't even look wounded. If anything, he was smugger than ever, strolling through the empty air like it was a paved path as he twirled his white sword and looked down on her in pity.

As she watched him gloat, Bex realized this was the same place she always ended up: on the bottom, under Gilgamesh's boots. The view was extra bitter now, because Bex had really thought this time would be different. She'd fought a war, destroyed the Hells, and betrayed her own mother, all to make sure this never happened again. Now, though, Bex was starting to wonder if this ending was inevitable. She'd beaten lots of enemies who were tough to kill, but they'd always had limits, lines she could push them over to win. So far as she could tell, though, Gilgamesh had none of those. His magic was seemingly infinite, his life apparently untouchable. For the first time ever, Bex understood how the gods had fallen before him, but how in the Hells was she supposed to win?

You can't think like that, Drox ordered, digging into her palm. *I already told you, if you start thinking you've lost—*

"I know," Bex said, raising her two swords to face her seemingly unkillable enemy. But just as she was about to plunge back into the fight no amount of positive thinking could convince her wasn't hopeless, she heard the soft sound of glass breaking in the distance right before the smug smile slipped off of Gilgamesh's face.

Three minutes earlier.

Adrian needed to get to better cover.

He'd scrambled behind the wall of princes because it was the only thing up here other than Enki's forge now that the golden banquet table was shattered. But while the tanks Gilgamesh stored his broken sons in had been stacked high, a see-through barrier of glass, gold filigree, and glowing water was not the most confidence-inducing shelter when a battle of almost-gods was going on fifty feet away. The best survival move would've been to run back downstairs into the cavern where they'd found the queen's horns. That was where Boston was tugging him toward, but Adrian couldn't take his eyes off Bex.

She was shining like a supernova. Her body was a white-hot silhouette inside the halo of her flames. Every time she moved, she left a blazing trail, filling the pale sky with an aurora of yellow, orange, gold, and blue fire. It was unspeakably beautiful, unspeakably *powerful* on the primal level that all witches loved. If Adrian hadn't been head over heels already, the sight of her right now would've sealed the deal for sure. As glorious as Bex unquestionably was, though, she didn't seem to be winning.

His eyes weren't fast enough to keep up, but Adrian couldn't miss the stream of black blood that was constantly hitting the ground. Gilgamesh didn't need to speak to cast his sorcery, so it was hard to tell exactly what he was doing, but it looked like he was using a variation of Leander's *Fifty Steps of the Pilgrim* to teleport into all her blind spots. The fact that Bex hadn't already fallen out of the sky meant she was healing the damage, which was good, but Adrian knew better than anyone that Bex had a hard limit. The more blood she lost, the harder she'd fight until she hit the wall, and then she'd die.

Adrian wasn't about to let that happen. He *had* to find a way to help, some edge he could push to shift the fight in Bex's favor. Gilgamesh was still in his casual blacksmithing clothes, so he couldn't be taking this battle seriously. Abusing that overconfidence was probably the winning move, but how? Gilgamesh was using sorcery with no incantations or pauses, and his one sword was moving faster than both of Bex's put together.

As more and more of Bex's blood hit the ground, all Adrian could think was that this whole situation was supremely unfair. Where was Gilgamesh getting all that power from? Was every bit of his body made of quintessence now, or—

A fiery explosion blasted Adrian out of his thoughts. He wasn't sure what had caused it, but Bex suddenly had only one sword, and she was using her free arm to pull her burning body as close to Gilgamesh's as possible. Adrian could see the king struggling to push her off, but Bex was stuck to him like flaming napalm, and the brighter she burned, the more of Gilgamesh vanished.

Literally vanished. The hands she was holding on to Gilgamesh with must've been hot enough to vaporize, because the shadow of his body was disappearing into Bex's light at an astonishing rate. His arm turned to ash as Adrian watched, followed by his shoulder and then his torso. Bex had only been blasting for a few seconds, but at that temperature, a few seconds was all it took to reduce the Eternal King, the slayer of gods, Heaven's immortal tyrant, to dust.

Bex looked as surprised by that as Adrian. She was shining too brightly for him to make out her expressions, but the glowing hand she'd used to grab Gilgamesh was fumbling through the suddenly-empty air. She turned around after that, her flaming head moving in a circle, but other than ashes, the sky was empty. He really did seem to be gone. Dead! *Finished!* Adrian was about to leap out of his hiding place with a whoop of joy when Gilgamesh suddenly reappeared twenty paces in front of him.

It felt like seeing a ghost. He'd watched Gilgamesh's body turn to ash with his own two eyes, but the Eternal King was suddenly right there, standing next to the destroyed table. It wasn't because he'd teleported to safety either. Adrian had been looking right at him when it happened. He'd *seen* the king's body reform itself from the inside out, starting with his bones before moving on to organs, then muscles, then skin.

By the time he'd capped his miraculous resurrection off with a suit of glittering golden armor, fewer than three seconds had passed. It'd happened so quickly that part of Adrian was sure his eyes must've made a mistake, but the rest of him—the witch who'd been trained to be watchful from birth—knew what he'd seen. Gilgamesh had just resurrected himself from the dead, and he *hadn't* used quintessence to do it. Adrian had seen his body rebuild itself from the inside out, and his blood had been unmistakably red. Other than his bones, nothing white had been involved. There'd been no giant bag of quintessence coins or gallons of liquid magic. He'd simply reformed himself out of empty air, but... that was impossible.

Adrian dropped his eyes to the ground. He could hear his father saying something cocky, but he didn't have a spare brain cell left to interpret the words. Every thought in his head was focused on what he'd just witnessed: the miracle everything he knew about sorcery told him shouldn't have happened, yet clearly had. Even his aunt Lydia, the Old Wife of the Bones herself, couldn't pull off a total resurrection on a vaporized corpse, and while sorcery's claim to fame was doing the impossible, the sorcerer still needed fuel to do it. Gilgamesh himself had taught Adrian that, so how had he pulled it off? Where was he getting that insane amount of magic from if it wasn't in his blood?

"Adrian?"

The whisper was soft and close, and Adrian looked over with a jump to see Boston crouching on his shoulder.

"If this is about getting to safety, I already know," Adrian said, heading off the lecture. "But I can't leave Bex alone to—"

"I wasn't going to ask," his familiar assured him. "We both agreed to this fight, which means no running. I only interrupted you because I saw something."

He pointed his paw at the row of glowing glass-and-gold boxes above them. "You see that prince on the corner?"

"Not really," Adrian said, craning his head back. "That tank looks empty to me."

"Precisely," Boston said with a lash of his tail. "It *wasn't* empty when we got here. I didn't see what happened with everything else that was going on, but I remember distinctly that every tank on this wall was full. Now there's one vacant right after Gilgamesh—"

"Brought himself back to life," Adrian finished excitedly, stepping back to get a better look at the giant display case. "*That's* how he's doing it. He must be using the injured princes as replacements!"

"It's too soon to jump to conclusions," Boston warned, but his green eyes sparkled with excitement. "If that were the case, though, it would explain why this wall is here. I thought it was odd that Gilgamesh was storing his injured sons so close to him when he had no problem sending off all the functional ones to die stopping us. If he's using them to give himself extra lives, though, it all makes sense."

"It makes *perfect* sense," Adrian agreed, ignoring the odd darkness in the sky as he pressed his face against the glass wall of the closest tank.

Like all the princes he'd seen up here, the man floating inside it was mortally wounded, with stab holes through his stomach, heart, and head. Now that Adrian knew what he was looking at, he could practically see Drox's old shaved-down shape in the puncture wounds. This prince had definitely been killed by one of Bex's previous incarnations, probably not even that long ago. But while the lack of scar tissue proved that this prince had died from his wounds, there was no white blood clouding the tank's beautifully glowing blue water. If he turned his head sideways and pressed his cheek flat against the freezing cold glass, Adrian could actually see the liquid quintessence shining inside the prince's severed arteries, and that made him more excited than anything.

"I don't think they're just replacements," he whispered. "All of these princes still have their quintessence blood! That's how he's able to—"

"Adrian," Boston interrupted in a terrified voice, his black ears flat against his skull as he stared at the sky. "Do you see what's happening above—"

"No, and I'm not going to look," Adrian interrupted, keeping his eyes firmly on the tank in front of him. "Bex is strong. I know she can handle whatever Gilgamesh throws, but she can't win if he's got a whole wall full of extra lives while she only has one. It's our job to level the playing field, and *this* is how we do that."

He smacked his hand against the glass tank.

"The princes aren't just Gilgamesh's backups," he announced, grabbing Boston's head and forcing him to look. "They're his fuel tanks. This is how he's able to cast so much magic despite having no quintessence in his own body. He's using their bodies and blood instead."

It all made sense now. Adrian had never seen sorcery on the scale Gilgamesh was throwing around. He'd assumed that was due to the experience difference between the master who'd invented the system and his students, but it still felt like too much.

It'd taken all the quintessence in Adrian's body to grow his new tree, but the magic Gilgamesh was doing now—endless teleportation, the complete reconstruction of his body, whatever that giant shadow before had been—was even bigger. Pulling off that many miracles back-to-back required more quintessence than any single person could hold, but Gilgamesh wasn't doing it as a single person. He was fueling his magic using an entire array of princes, and now that Adrian knew that, he knew how to bring him down.

"Cover me," he told Boston.

"Cover you with what?" the cat cried, digging his claws into Adrian's coat as the witch dropped flat on the stone. "There's no forest here!"

"There's about to be," Adrian promised as he pressed his entire body into the ground. "Just keep your eyes on the fight and bite me if something's about to hit us. I'll do the rest."

Boston growled deep in his throat. Adrian hoped it was a growl of approval, because he'd already turned his attention inward, leaving the chaos of Heaven's pinnacle behind to focus everything on his heart, which was still beating far below at the base of his new tree. Through its deep roots, he could feel the battle raging in the main Blackwood grove. Not enough to tell how the fight was going, but it made him feel terrible about asking for resources. He was about to go see if there was an outer grove he could pull from instead when the forest itself forced its way into his mind.

It felt like someone had shoved a handful of roots inside his skull. The Great Blackwood was famous for showing up where it was least expected, but Adrian had never felt it do anything like this before. It was almost like someone was using a spell to thrust the forest's magic directly into his hands. Not that Adrian was complaining, since that was exactly what he needed, but the timing was too perfect not to be suspicious.

That thought survived only a few seconds before Adrian tossed it aside. Nothing was suspicious when your aunt could see the future, and the whole coven knew he'd come up here to finish Gilgamesh. If he actually managed to kill the Eternal King, the army attacking the main Blackwood would collapse on its own. That made Adrian's tree the most important to the forest's survival, and survival at any cost was the first rule of all living things. Look at it that way and it made complete sense why the Great Blackwood was suddenly pouring magic into him like a firehose into a bucket. The only question left was what to do with it all.

As a greedy Witch of the Present, that was Adrian's favorite question to answer. He soaked the magic up as fast as the Blackwood fed it to him and used the power to send his forest surging to the sky. Not Heaven's sky. That place was just another prison, same as the Hells. The *true* path to power followed the chains just like the Morrigan had said, so that was what Adrian did, growing his forest along the same black links they'd used to climb up here in the first place.

Just like during his experiments below the Seattle Anchor, the sin iron killed his plants almost instantaneously, but Adrian was no longer working with potted sprouts from a nursery. He had volume on his side now, and he used it mercilessly, burying the chains in vines, moss, and twisting roots until the layer of dead material was so thick that the chains' poison could no longer reach the new growth that surged over it.

All that coverage took up a lot of room in the narrow, hidden tunnel, but the chains were sagging now that Gilgamesh had destroyed the Wheel they'd been made to hold. Several had already fallen out completely, making room for all the new branches and greenery Adrian was shoving into the hole. The wave of growth hit the ceiling Bex had punched through to reach the golden throne room like a landslide, but the forest didn't have to go around like they had. It bashed its way straight through the plug at the top, breaking the magical base that supported the gods' giant sin-iron tombs like roots cracking a foundation.

That was exactly what Adrian hoped would happen. But as he poured the Blackwood's magic onto his forest like gasoline on a fire, he realized for the first time just how *big* this place was. His forest was spreading like every witch in the world was pushing it right along with him, but it still took a full twenty heartbeats before the first roots started poking over the edge of the rocky shelf Adrian was lying on.

Once the flood of life got going, though, it didn't stop. The moment the roots broke through, the rest of the forest erupted into Gilgamesh's black desert in an explosion of vibrant, violent green. Saplings and vines, flowers and weeds, even the upper branches of his fir tree pushed through the black sand like water welling through a cloth. Within seconds of the first root's appearance, the entire stone outcropping was tilting like a caught kite in a canopy of green, but the real magic didn't happen until Adrian reached up and pressed his fingers against the cool glass of the magical holding tank above him.

    The moment he gave the signal, Adrian's forest hit the wall of preserved princes like a tidal wave. Vines twisted around the golden filigree that held the tanks together until the metal snapped. Roots pushed the stacked coffins into skewed angles while bright-green algae blossomed inside the glass. No one element was enough by itself, but together they created a storm of entropy that even Gilgamesh's precise engineering couldn't stop. Adrian barely had time to scramble out of the way before the wall of tanks broke free of its bolts and crashed to the now moss-covered ground.

    The tank directly next to Adrian shattered when it landed, smashing into a thousand pieces with the unmistakable sound of breaking crystal. All the glowing water poured out when it broke, dropping the prince who'd been floating inside. Adrian had already scrambled back to his feet by the time he landed, flinging his hands up to deal with whatever came next, but the wounded prince didn't attack or even resume dying. Instead, he started to vanish, his flesh evaporating like ether exposed to air.

    That was probably a mercy considering the horrific head wound he'd been sporting, but Adrian hadn't expected his body to disappear like a puddle on a hot day. Gilgamesh had warned him that liquid quintessence was unstable, though, so maybe this was the natural result of keeping all that volatile magic inside a vessel that was no longer alive enough to contain it. Adrian was about to break the next toppled tank open to see if the princes evaporated every time when he heard the muffled *clank* of metal boots hitting the moss-covered stone behind him.

Sorcery slammed into his back a second later. The magic grabbed Adrian like a giant fist, hauling him off his feet and whirling him around to face his furious-looking father.

It was a sign of how angry Gilgamesh was that he didn't bother with gloating or demands. He simply squeezed his golden-armored fist. The magic holding Adrian followed the motion, crushing his body like an apple in a cider press. He was seconds away from being squeezed into sausage when Bex appeared out of nowhere and crashed into Gilgamesh like a flaming meteor.

The crushing pressure vanished that same instant, dropping Adrian face-first into the moss as Bex and Gilgamesh brawled a few feet away. It was a testimony to the Bonfire Queen's restraint that her roaring flames didn't even burn the dew off his new forest's delicate young leaves. Gilgamesh, on the other hand, was being roasted alive, and this time, he didn't seem nonchalant about it. The smug smile was long gone from his face as he attacked the queen with his sword, fists, and legs in a desperate struggle to get out of her grasp and back to killing the forest. A fact that Bex realized much faster than Adrian did.

"*Don't stop!*" she shouted as she sliced Drox's black blade through Gilgamesh's flailing arm. "Whatever you're doing, *keep doing it!*"

Adrian nodded and scrambled away, giving the queen and king plenty of room to brawl while he dug his fingers into the tangle of vines, brambles, and roots that hadn't stopped growing even while he was being squeezed to death.

That was the best part of being a witch. Gilgamesh's sorcery worked only when he told it to, but Adrian's forest would keep spreading whether he was alive or dead. The tree roots had already wound themselves around the unbroken tanks, squeezing the glass like constrictors and working the lids off so the glowing water could spill out.

It took a while. The original tank Adrian had watched the prince evaporate from had shattered when it hit the ground, but they hadn't gotten so lucky with the others. The gold-and-glass constructions looked delicate, but Gilgamesh's craftsmanship was superb, and none of Adrian's plants were supernaturally strong. It took them ages to pry open the well-made seams, but even nonmagical forests could reduce entire civilizations to rubble, given enough time, and with a desperate witch plus the full might of the Great Blackwood behind it, this small woodland was doing a century's worth of work every second. It squeezed and pried and pulled and eroded and grew over until all the once-pristine enclosures looked like old, abandoned fishbowls left out in the sun.

The tanks started snapping like melting icicles after that. The air filled with the sound of breaking glass as the cloudy vessels shattered, exposing the princes inside to the air, where they vanished like mist on a summer morning. Gilgamesh's fighting got more desperate with every son he lost, but while he'd blasted Bex away several times by this point, she always managed to get back on top.

She wasn't even trying to stab him anymore. She'd actually dropped Ishtar's sword on the moss to free both her hands for grappling and covered her flaming body in thick, gleaming scales that looked like a combination of Fear and War demon armor. The new plating still couldn't stop Gilgamesh's insanely sharp sword, but it added a ton to her weight, which helped pin the king down. Considering the magic Gilgamesh had been throwing around earlier, that still didn't seem like it'd be enough. Then Adrian caught a glimpse of his father's desperate face behind his lion helmet, and he understood.

Gilgamesh looked centuries older. The sleeping princes must've done more than just hold his magic and die in his stead, because every time one evaporated, the Eternal King looked closer to his actual age. His formerly robust frame had shriveled to a skeletal husk under the shell of his golden armor, and his skull was clearly visible under the sagging, paper-thin skin that now covered his face. His once-thick salt-and-pepper hair was now white and stringy where it hadn't fallen out completely, and his sharp blue-gray eyes were cloudy with age.

He looked one rattling breath away from death, but he was still fighting like a madman, stabbing Bex's armored back with glowing swords and summoning golden lions to roar their fire in her face. The only reason Adrian didn't get vaporized by the splash damage was because he'd crawled up into the thicket that had formed around the shattered tanks, which

Gilgamesh's destructive magic never got close to no matter how desperate the king became.

Not that it mattered anymore. Only three tanks were left intact at this point, and they were already overgrown. Even if Gilgamesh blasted both Adrian and Bex to dust, the forest's roots were dug in too deep to stop. The Blackwood's will would be done whether a witch was there to help it or not, which made Adrian the smug one as he watched his father's final struggle, holding his breath as he waited for the end.

It couldn't be more than a few seconds away. But then, just before the twining roots crushed the final three tanks, Gilgamesh finally managed to kick Bex off him long enough to teleport.

He reappeared almost a thousand feet away, standing on the lip of one of the giant coffins that contained the gods' bodies. Adrian hadn't realized just how big the sin-iron boxes truly were until Gilgamesh was standing on top of one. It didn't seem possible that any human, especially not one as decrepit as Gilgamesh had become, could affect something that enormous. But while the king's body was so shriveled that his golden armor was falling off him like a discarded shell, his sword was still the divinely sharp blade that had cut the Wheel of Reincarnation from the sky. All he had to do was wave it at the coffin's base, and the pipe that tapped the slain god's quintessence—which looked tiny at this distance but was actually big enough to drive a car through—cut cleanly off the end, creating a waterfall of white magic that Gilgamesh toppled into gleefully.

"*No!*" Bex roared, making Adrian jump. He hadn't noticed her land beside him in all the chaos, but the blast of her fire knocked him off his feet as she rocketed past and dove into the gushing river of gods' blood after her ancient enemy.

Chapter 19

BEX HIT THE WHITE WATERFALL OF QUINTESSENCE like a missile. She wasn't thinking, wasn't listening to the increasingly dire warnings Drox was yelling through her skull, wasn't paying attention to anything except her burning need to finish this. Gilgamesh was almost defeated. She'd seen how shriveled Adrian's attacks had made him, felt his weakening strength with her own hands. Just a little bit more and he'd be dead for good. If he reloaded on magic, though, the fight would start over from the beginning, and unlike the quintessence-fueled king, Bex didn't have a second wind waiting to pick her up again.

If they were ever going to beat him, it had to be *now*, so she dove into the gushing quintessence without a second thought. She could still see Gilgamesh's golden boots in front of her, but the moment her flaming body entered the river, the entire world changed.

It felt like she'd been dropped into Limbo, only instead of a big gray nothing, all she saw was white. Endless, formless, relentless white that poured through her eyeballs and into her skull, filling her mind with a light so bright it burned away her thoughts, leaving her empty. For one blissful second, she floated in nothingness, a nameless ripple floating in an endless sea of light. Then something inside her freshly emptied brain seized up, and a chorus of thoughts exploded where Bex's own should have been.

So many voices were talking at once that it was impossible to tell what they were actually saying. Bex wasn't even sure they were speaking a language she understood, but while the overlapping words sounded like gibberish, the feelings inside them were as plain as day. The voices were envious, fearful, hateful, and sad. They were lustful, warlike, greedy, and proud. Most of all, though, they were angry.

Their furious shouts ripped through Bex like spears, tearing her apart with the intensity of their rage. Their righteous, well-deserved wrath at being imprisoned, tortured, and bled for power at the pinnacle of what was once *their* kingdom. How dare that traitor show his face among them again? But he would pay. One of their best weapons had just fallen back into their possession. Ishtar's Executioning Blade had returned. The only reason she wasn't already swinging at their enemy was because too many divine hands were fighting for control. They squabbled like gulls over the right to wield her, and as the fighting consumed their attention, Bex finally managed to wrest back control.

"*No!*" she roared, driving back the blinding white ocean with a wave of red-hot fire. "I am *not* your sword anymore! I am Bex the Bonfire, sword of *my* people! I'm killing Gilgamesh for their sake, *not* yours! The demons of the Riverlands are slaves no more! We are *through* with you!"

Her defiant words echoed through the emptiness, and then a screech came back so loud it whited out her thoughts again. But when the hands returned to try to take advantage of her lapse, Bex flared her fire even brighter, burning them away with a river of her own wrath, because if there was anything worth being angry about, it was this bullshit. The gods had *lost*. They were nothing but disembodied voices howling in an empty white room, and they thought they could take her over? Make her fight their battles for the prize of being their fawning servant again?

Hells no! Bex was never bowing a damn centimeter to any of them ever again. She was building a new future where demons lowered their horns to no one. *That* was her burning purpose, the meaning behind her new name, and the moment Bex embraced it, all the grasping hands fled, leaving her floating alone in a pool of what felt like glowing white paint.

It was so thick that Bex could barely move her arms through it. She could still hear the voices howling, but the sound was in her ears now instead of her head, which made it easier to ignore. The bad part was that she still couldn't see anything. She knew Gilgamesh had to be in front of her somewhere, but the liquid quintessence was as thick as glue and as bright as a spotlight. It was also still, more like a pool than a waterfall, which meant she must've fallen into the tank at the bottom of the sliced pipe.

That was bad. Her six horns had made her much stronger, but Bex still needed to breathe. She had to get back to the surface, but when she pushed her hands through the thick liquid to start swimming in the direction she was pretty sure was up, her grasping fingers bumped into something that felt an awful lot like a metal boot.

Bex couldn't believe her luck. She forgot all about breathing and lurched forward, wrapping her arms around the two kicking legs that had to be Gilgamesh's. She climbed his body next, working her way up his armored chest like a lemur climbing a golden tree. She didn't have a plan other than to keep him from escaping, but when she reached up to grab his helmet, she felt the too-fast, almost-painless pressure of his impossibly sharp sword slicing through her left arm.

The moment she felt it, Bex knew the limb was gone. She could use her fire to regrow it, but she was too focused on the arm she still had as she frantically called Drox out of his ring. She still couldn't see anything but blinding white sludge, but the overwhelming pain that was finally spreading through her severed shoulder painted a perfect picture of where the sword strike had come from. She only had a second before Gilgamesh moved on, so Bex ignored everything else and swung Drox in that direction, feeding him with her fire so her sword could launch the glowing whip he'd used to slice through Havok.

The result was a line so bright Bex could see it even through the quintessence's glow. She couldn't hear anything over the gods screaming in her ears, but she felt Gilgamesh's kicking legs go still in her grasp, and she knew—*knew*—she'd hit him.

Her body moved on instinct after that. Bex let go of Gilgamesh and blasted herself forward, spending the last of the fire she'd gotten from her anger at the gods to regrow her left arm in an instant. Her hand had just finished reforming when her bare fingers bumped into something hard, metal, and sharp—so sharp that merely touching it sliced a deep gouge into her new palm. The pain was a present, though, because when Bex finally blasted herself out of the quintessence lake she'd fallen into, she was holding Gilgamesh's white sword in her newly-formed hand.

"Give it back!"

The order hit her like a physical force, sending waves of quintessence washing over her head as Gilgamesh rose from the white pool like a figure from legend. They were down in the tank the chopped pipe had connected to, but it could've been the waters of creation from the way Gilgamesh set his golden boot upon the waves and glared down at Bex with silver-mirrored eyes that were no longer clouded by age. He actually looked younger now than he had when they arrived, more like Adrian's brother than his father. Even his battle scars were healed, leaving his skin practically glowing with health under the dripping sheen of quintessence that coated him from head to foot.

The new Gilgamesh was a terrifying, beautiful sight, as close to a god as someone born mortal could possibly become. Bex, meanwhile, looked every inch the demon with her black blood leaking out into the flawless white of the gods. At least, that was what the dead gods themselves were whispering in her ear before she shook their voices away, clutching her stolen sword even tighter as she glared up at her enemy.

"I must congratulate you," Gilgamesh said as he walked over the surface of the choppy pool of quintessence toward her. "You and that brat Adrian forced me to take the plunge I'd been avoiding for five thousand years. I've always felt that a human king should remain human in order to understand his subjects, yet despite my best intentions, here I am."

He spread his dripping arms with a shake of his handsome new head, but Bex wasn't buying a word of it.

"If you wanted to be a good king, you should've tried killing fewer of your subjects," she snarled. "You've been a horrible ruler and an even worse father, and I will drown in this pool with the gods before I let you win."

"So be it," Gilgamesh replied, raising his golden fist. "That sword wasn't made by the gods. They have no claim over its creation, so if it sinks with your corpse, I can easily retrieve it. Quintessence holds no risk for me now that you've forced my hand, so have it your way, Queen of Failure, and *die*."

He swung his fist as he spoke. The pool of quintessence followed the motion, surging toward Bex in a great white wave. She didn't know what would happen when it hit her, and she didn't wait around to find out. As soon as Gilgamesh moved to hit her, she struck back, swinging the white sword in front of her in an arc just like she'd seen him do when he cut the Wheel from the sky.

She'd been hoping for an attack so big it was inescapable, but this new, young Gilgamesh was even squirrellier than the old one. He flickered out of the way before Bex could finish the swing, but the giant sin-iron tomb behind him couldn't dodge. Bex's attack hit it right across the middle, painting an enormous white slash across its pitch-black surface. The mark grew bigger as she watched, burning through the sin iron like a seam of white phosphorus. She was still staring at it in confusion when Gilgamesh reappeared.

"No!" he screamed, throwing out his arms like he was trying to catch something. *"Hold together!"*

Bex had never heard him yell out sorcery like that, but it worked. The moment the command left the king's tongue, the giant slabs of sin iron started pulling themselves back together. The whole pool shook with their effort, but no matter how desperately the tomb tried to obey its king, it couldn't heal the wound, because something inside was pushing out.

It broke through a few moments later, ripping the weakened metal apart like paper. At first, it looked like the coffin had been attacked by four huge spears, but when the white lengths bent to grab the edge of the new hole, Bex realized they were fingers. Four emaciated white fingers the size of telephone poles were ripping the lid off the gigantic sin-iron coffin. When Gilgamesh shouted at the metal to push them back in, the first and longest of the fingers straightened out to point at the tank where Bex was still swimming.

Her first terrified thought was that it was pointing at *her*, but that wasn't the case for once. The finger was pointing at the quintessence, and the moment it did so, all that thick white blood began pouring back up the pipe Bex and Gilgamesh had dived down. It flowed out even faster than it had fallen in, gushing back to the coffin it had been drained from, and as the lake of quintessence vanished, so did Gilgamesh's restored youth.

"No!" he cried, clenching his rapidly skeletonizing fists. *"It shall not be yours!"*

He slammed both fists against his chest in a motion that was clearly meant to call the quintessence back, but for the first time in Bex's memory, the magic didn't obey him. It just kept flowing back to the coffin until the whole tank was empty, leaving Bex standing at the bottom of a deep bowl of sin iron. Gilgamesh dropped to the ground beside her a few seconds later, unable to even hold himself up as all his new white blood—the stolen power of the gods—flowed back to its original source.

It would've been the most satisfying sight of Bex's life if she hadn't been so terrified. The first white hand had a partner now, then two more appeared for a total of four bony arms ripping the coffin apart. Between the emaciated flesh and the waves of returning quintessence, everything inside was blindingly white. It wasn't until the lid broke off entirely that Bex finally saw the figure's shape.

It looked like nothing she'd ever imagined. The gods she'd seen had always been beautiful and only slightly larger than human scale. This monster was as tall as a building. It was so thin that it looked like a skeleton as it pulled itself off the bed of spikes that lined the inside of the coffin, but when it finally rose to its feet, it looked like an angel. A terrifying, biblically accurate one with six wings, six arms, and six black horns that rose from its head like a crown of spikes, the only parts of its entire body that weren't white. Even its eyes were the color of fresh snow, staring down with a look so alien, Bex didn't realize which god she'd accidentally awoken until it pointed one of its many fingers at the once again ancient-looking Gilgamesh and said,

"Perish."

The word was spoken in the ancient language of the Riverlands, but it was the voice that shook Bex's body. She'd never heard it so loud before, but that was absolutely Ishtar's voice, and the moment it spoke, Gilgamesh's body tore itself apart.

It happened too fast to feel real. It couldn't *be* real. If Ishtar could destroy Gilgamesh with a single word, why hadn't she done it during the first war five thousand years ago? It made no sense at all until Bex looked over and saw Gilgamesh's new white blood boiling through his skin.

Ah, she realized numbly. *That was it.* Every other time Gilgamesh had faced the gods, he'd been a red-blooded human. The moment he'd taken their quintessence into his veins, though, he'd become a semi-divine creature just like Bex. He didn't have a sacred name as she did, but the white essence of the gods ran through every cell in his body now. If he could command that stolen power with his sorcery, it only made sense that the original owner would be able to do the same.

It was a suitably ironic ending for a hubristic fallen hero. The same power Gilgamesh had embraced to save himself had become his downfall, leaving the Eternal King of Heaven collapsing like a sand sculpture as the white blood that had powered his entire empire attacked him from the inside out. His flesh dissolved piece by piece, bubbling away like boiling water until the great and glorious Gilgamesh was nothing but a ring of scum stuck to the inside of his golden armor. Bex was still wrapping her brain around the idea that her ancient nemesis was finally and forever dead when Adrian flew in on his broom.

He landed on the opposite side of Gilgamesh's empty armor and reached out immediately to grab Bex's hand as he stared at the towering figure looming over them like the god she was. Bex could feel him trembling as any sensible person would, but he still held his ground beside her. That must have pleased the goddess, because her alien face split into a smile before her white body pulled into itself like a collapsing star.

It took several seconds to squeeze down so much power, but when it was over, the Ishtar Bex remembered was standing inside the empty quintessence tank beside them. She was still a towering presence, but her crown of six horns rose only a foot above Adrian's head, and she was back to only two arms. Her hair was dark again, her dress a shining blend of many colors, and her wings—only two—were once more those of the wise owl. It was the way she'd appeared to Bex in the vision inside the bonfire, the way Bex's instinctive memory was sure Ishtar had always looked. But while this version of Ishtar was unquestionably more approachable, Bex couldn't get the giant truth out of her head. She also didn't bow, a slight the restored goddess did not overlook.

"Now is not the time to be petulant, dearest," Ishtar said, shaking her lovely head. "I created you to be the embodiment of Wrath, not Pride. It seems you've taken over a great deal more than you were made to since last we spoke. Fortunately for you, I am in a wonderful mood."

The goddess's face lit up with a smile that made Bex's heart leap.

"Our conqueror is dead!" she announced, turning her glittering eyes on Gilgamesh's empty armor. "Not that I approve of your methods, but in the end, you did as I commanded. You brought my enemy down. You even delivered him to my grave so that I could deal the killing blow myself!" The goddess clapped her hands in delight. "Those are the actions of a truly loyal servant, and for that service, I am willing to forgive all of your past transgressions. Now bow your horns and return to my side, and I shall reforge you once again into my beautiful, loyal Rebexa."

She finished with a glorious smile, but Bex just moved closer to Adrian.

"No."

The goddess's beaming expression faltered for a second before snapping back into place.

"Maybe you didn't hear me," she said in a decidedly less magnanimous tone. "I am offering to wipe the slate clean. Your sins against Enki, against myself—they will all be forgotten. I'll even spare the life of your handsome paramour."

She winked at Adrian, who shivered.

"This is my reward for your eons of loyal service," Ishtar went on. "But such divine mercy shall only be tendered once. I know many things were said in the heat of our last meeting, but I'm willing to put all that behind us if you bow your head right now and return to where you belong."

She held out her hand as she finished, reaching for Bex not as a daughter but as one would grasp the hilt of a sword. It was a move she must've made often, because part of Bex instinctively responded, stepping closer to her mother before she could drive her foot into the ground.

"No," she said again, digging her boots into the sloping sides of Gilgamesh's empty quintessence collector. "You were our goddess once, but the demons born today don't belong to you." She reached up to grab the six horns that still rose from her head. "They put this crown on me so I could free them from Gilgamesh, but I didn't go through all of that—*they* didn't go through it—so I could turn around and hand them back to you."

"There's nothing to hand," Ishtar snarled, snatching her radiant hand back to her side. "They are demons. Therefore, they belong to *me*. There's no such thing as freedom for them, just like there's no such thing as a crown for you unless I put it there. I am your creator, your *god*. You will bow to me, or you will be destroyed."

Bex lifted her swords in reply, both Gilgamesh's white blade and Drox's black one. The latter was shaking like a leaf against her palm, but he didn't flee back into his ring, which steeled Bex's determination even more. No matter what happened next, she was determined to be worthy of her sword's loyalty. Worthy of everything she'd been given as she moved to stand between Adrian and the furious god that had once been her mother.

Ishtar scowled in reply and held her arm out to the side. Bex wasn't sure what she was doing at first. Then her ears caught the faint ringing of metal right before the goddess's sword flew past her to slap itself back into Ishtar's palm. Drox did the same thing when

Bex called him, so it wasn't surprising that Ishtar could do the same. It was, however, extremely intimidating. Taking a stand against Gilgamesh was one thing, but when the Goddess of War, Life, and Death turned to face her with Enki's greatest masterpiece in her hand, even Bex felt like she was about to faint. She was telling herself to go ahead and get it over with before she lost her nerve entirely when Adrian grabbed her shoulder.

"Not yet," he whispered. "They're almost here."

"Who's almost here?" Bex whispered back frantically.

"Just five more seconds," he promised, giving her a wink. "Trust me."

Bex trusted him with every single life she'd ever had. If Adrian said wait, then her feet were welded to the ground. Unfortunately, the same did not apply to Ishtar. The goddess was already darting forward with her razor-sharp black sword to remove Bex's head. Bex responded by throwing up Gilgamesh's white sword since she'd much rather lose that ugly thing than Drox, but she'd barely gotten the block in position before something huge and dark erupted out of the ground right in front of her.

Bex's first thought was that it was a tree. Adrian's forest hadn't stopped growing since he'd used it to destroy Gilgamesh's prince tanks, and trees were how her witch solved most problems. She was wondering what sort of tree had such dark leaves when the black shape suddenly opened its beak to snatch the charging Ishtar off the ground. It rocketed into the air next, carrying the screaming goddess high into the pale-blue sky. It wasn't until it spread its huge black wings, however, that Bex finally realized what she was looking at.

"That's the Morrigan," she said, staggering back into Adrian. "The Morrigan just ate Ishtar!"

"The Morrigan didn't eat her," countered a familiar voice as Muriel, Witch of the Future and Adrian's youngest aunt, hauled herself out of the hole the Morrigan had just made in the tank's sin-iron floor. "She's disciplining her."

"The gods have always been excessively violent with each other," agreed Lydia, Witch of the Past, who popped through next. "That's one of the reasons the Morrigan left in the first place."

"I'm just glad we got here in time," finished Agatha, gracefully bringing up the rear on her broom. "Not that I didn't think our Bonfire Queen could win, but nothing good ever comes of family trying to kill each other."

The Three Sisters all chuckled like that was an inside joke, but Bex was too alarmed to find anything funny.

"What are you all doing here?" she demanded, finally pushing off of Adrian, who'd been graciously holding her up. "You're supposed to be in the Blackwood, fighting with my demons!"

"The rest of our coven is there," Agatha assured her. "But Muriel foresaw that our work here wasn't finished yet, so we stayed behind with the Morrigan."

"And it's a good thing we did," Muriel muttered, tugging at her shiny black hair. "I don't like giving odds, but your chances against Ishtar after the amount of fire you used to beat Gilgamesh were *not* good, especially since all the demons who could've provided you with more are back in the world of the living."

"All of them?" Bex repeated as a weak smile crossed her face. "Does that mean everybody got to safety?"

"Only if you want to call evacuating into an active war zone 'safe'," Lydia said.

"What matters is they're not here anymore," Agatha added tactfully. "That's about to be very important, Muriel tells me."

The Witch of the Future nodded and turned her blue eyes to the sky. Bex looked up as well, biting her lip as she watched Ishtar stab her sword into the Morrigan's beak. The Morrigan still didn't let go, but she did swoop back down, throwing Ishtar to the ground at the last second so she couldn't use her wings to avoid the impact.

"You *heathen*!" the goddess screamed when she'd clawed her way out of the crater. "What are you doing in this sacred place?"

"Getting a little payback while you're still too weak to fight properly," the Morrigan replied, licking Ishtar's white blood off her beak with a forked black tongue as she set down next to her trio of witches. "Say what you will about Gilgamesh. He always was the best at bleeding you pigs dry. Just look at you! Shriveled up like a raisin."

Ishtar narrowed her glittering eyes. "I will not accept criticism from a barbarian who left the light of her divine kind to live like an animal in the woods. Your opinions have never mattered, and they never will. Now that Gilgamesh is dead, I can restore all the other gods to glory and put the world back in its proper order."

"Really?" the Morrigan said, cocking her giant raven head to the side. "And how do you intend to do that?"

"The same way we did it the first time," Ishtar replied haughtily. "We built the Wheel of Reincarnation once. We can easily build it again. It's simply a matter of time, and we've got plenty of that. After all"—her face lit up with that lovely smile again—"what is time to true immortals? We only cared about it while Gilgamesh was making us suffer, but now that we're back, the years no longer matter. We can take as long as we like to craft a new Paradise that's even better than the first, and then we'll use those tools to roll this planet's timeline back to its verdant beginning. We can erase the damage an unfettered humanity has wrought and start over with a clean slate. Everything is possible again, and it's all thanks to my daughter." She flicked her glittering eyes back to Bex with a sigh. "What a shame she's determined to be a fool."

"What am I being foolish about?" Bex demanded. "You're talking about the destruction of everything that is. All the things we've built, the people we know and love, you're planning to erase them all like it's nothing! Just because the gods live forever doesn't mean the rest of us are junk to be thrown away."

"But you are," Ishtar said in a pitying voice. "Mortality is one of the problems we built Paradise to fix. The only reason I facilitated the Blackwood's decision to fill you with the flames of life is because I had nothing else to work with inside my prison, but that's all behind us now. You could have your immortality back in an instant if you'd just stop being stubborn."

Bex crossed her arms over her chest with a glare, and the goddess sighed again.

"Enough of this," she said, turning back to the Morrigan. "Just because I have infinite time does not mean I have infinite patience. I have a daughter to discipline, gods to wake, and a divine Paradise to put back in order. Just rebuilding the Wheel so we can reset the terrible state Gilgamesh allowed this planet to sink into will likely take a millennium, so I'd like to get started, *if* you don't mind."

She made a shooing gesture with her sword, but the Morrigan just fluffed out her feathers. "Are you sure you've got enough time left to do all that?"

"Of course," Ishtar said, giving the crow a nasty look. "We are *gods*. We have all the time there is."

She said that like it was the only obvious truth, but the Morrigan started to laugh. Just a bit of crow chuffing at first then louder and louder until she was cackling. It was clearly getting on Ishtar's nerves, but before the goddess could raise her sword to strike the giant crow down, the Morrigan stopped.

"All the time there is, huh?" she said, lifting her black-clawed foot. "Not anymore."

She brought her talons down as she finished. It looked like she was just scraping the bottom of the quintessence tank, but the instant the goddess's claws made contact with the metal floor, the world beneath them ripped away like paper.

That was how it felt to Bex, anyway. She grabbed onto Adrian, ready to jump them both out of whatever the Morrigan was dumping everyone into. But while the floor did vanish, it didn't drop them, because it'd never really been there to begin with. This whole place was just another of Gilgamesh's hidden spaces, one of the mini-worlds he'd crafted using the gods' tools to house his secret project. The Morrigan hadn't even destroyed the entire thing. She'd just ripped a hole through the section they were standing on, creating a window into Heaven below.

What used to be Heaven, anyway. Gilgamesh's palace was still there, but the greenery Adrian had brought in with his tree—which used to be confined to just the blocks immediately surrounding the entrance to the Hells—now covered everything in sight. The roads, the white buildings of the Holy City, even the black cube of the Hells' Gate were all covered in verdant jungle. The trees grew right over the giant wall where Bex had melted the lions during her battle with the Queen of War, filling the gray desert of the Goddeath Wastes with blooming, buzzing, overflowing life.

Everywhere Bex looked, plants were spreading their leaves. Flocks of birds flew through the formerly empty sky, and the previously bone-dry air was thick with humidity and the drone of insects. But while all of that that struck Bex as a definite change for the better, Ishtar was staring at the overgrowth like she'd just been stabbed in the chest.

"What is *that*?" she cried, whirling away from the beautiful jungle to shake her sword at the Morrigan. "You black-beaked traitor! *What did you do?*"

"The only thing that could truly defeat you," the Morrigan said, lifting her wing to show the other goddess the trickle of blood running through her feathers from where Ishtar had stabbed her earlier. Ruby-red blood, not white.

"That's right," she said as Ishtar stumbled back. "I wished Gilgamesh luck the first time he fought you, but I already knew he wouldn't win. He couldn't, because there is no such thing as victory against an enemy that cannot die."

"Of course," Ishtar said shakily. "That has always been our strength."

"Has it?" the Morrigan asked, aiming her sharp beak at Ishtar like a spear. "I'm a god, too, as old as you are. I remember when we first found this place, how it shone like a blue-green jewel in the infinite blackness of time. I thought we all understood how lucky we'd gotten, but the moment we set foot in this place, the rest of you started trying to change it. You gave your ambition all sorts of noble names—civilization, improvement, refinement, salvation—but your intentions were always the same. We settled in this place because it was so beautiful, but you couldn't let it be. You kept trying to control it, reshape it, bend it to your will." She stomped forward, shaking the new green world. "You *ruined* the paradise we'd already found in the name of improving what was already perfect!"

Ishtar stumbled away from her rage, but the Morrigan wasn't finished.

"That hubris is why Gilgamesh was able to slay you so easily," she snapped. "He loved my wild son so much, I thought he might finally understand, but his rule was just more of the same. Even in his revenge, he was exactly like you, always trying to control the uncontrollable. It's no wonder he met the same fate, but I am not so foolish. I know that the beauty of this world lies in its wildness, its refusal to be tamed. That unbridled freedom is what tempted us to descend to this realm in the first place, and it's what I've given myself over to now."

"Given?" Ishtar repeated suspiciously. "What do you mean by that? You didn't—"

"I did," the Morrigan said with a proud lift of her beak. "With the help of my beloved witches, I have given my heart, soul, and bones to the Great Forest of the Blackwood. The result is the forest you see beneath us, a verdant new life born from a god's conviction. Born here specifically, in the false Paradise the rest of you built with your magic. Thus has my conviction become tangled up in all of yours, binding us together forever to the endless turning of the Great Cycles."

She delivered those final words like a death blow, but Bex didn't understand. From the way Adrian always talked about the Great Cycles, being tied directly to them sounded like having a mainline into the power of the universe, but Ishtar looked horrified. Terrified, really, covering her face with her hands as her black sword clattered to the ground at the edge of the hole the Morrigan had torn in the world.

"You selfish creature," she whispered through her clenched fingers. "Our entire race worked together to build this place, but you co-opted our efforts and entangled our essences to tie us to your damn forest." She ripped her hands down to stare at the Morrigan in absolute betrayal. "You've killed us all!"

"I prefer to think of it as a gift," the Morrigan said, looking her fellow goddess dead in the eye. "Now that I've bound the magic of the gods to the Great Cycles, we no longer have to live as outsiders. We're officially part of this world now, which means we will age and die along with every other creature caught in the Cycle's turning. Your power and authority have not been diminished, but you can no longer escape the march of time, which means you have two choices, Ishtar, Queen of Paradise. You can stay here and grow old along with the humans you claim to love, or you can rip out the roots I just gave you, reclaim your immortality, and leave."

"Or I could rip out *every* root and burn your forest to the ground!" Ishtar snarled.

"And kill yourself in the process," the Morrigan informed her cheerfully. "That's a possibility now that I've made us all mortal. I'm not afraid of death, so what do you say, sister? Feel like taking a few thousand years to rebuild that wheel now?"

The other goddess stared at her for a long time, blinking her glittering eyes like she couldn't believe what she was hearing. Then, with an urgency Bex had never seen from her before, Ishtar shed her human guise and turned back into the white giant from before. Her sword changed with her, becoming enormous as well as the towering goddess scooped it off the ground and banged its black blade into the sundered coffin beside her.

"*Wake up!*" she bellowed in a voice that shook what was left of Heaven. "Rise, you fools! The Morrigan has betrayed us! We're getting older every second! *Wake up!*"

She swung her sword like a whirlwind as she yelled, moving between the other giant coffins like a storm as she sliced them all open. Bex couldn't see the gods she was yelling at from down in the tank, but she wasn't sure she wanted to. The gods' true faces were terrifying, as was their anger, for they were *very* angry. They woke with curses and thunder, yelling back at Ishtar with earthquakes and whipping winds, but she was already on her way out. The moment she freed the last god from his prison, she turned her sword on the blue dome of the sky, smashing it open like a window to reveal the black void beyond.

"I hereby turn my back on this world," she announced in a ringing voice. "We offered you purpose and divine perfection, and you threw it back in our faces. Live then in the hell of your mistakes, and enjoy your miserable, meaningless deaths in the darkness without gods."

That last word was still ringing through the air when Ishtar's giant glowing form stepped through the hole she'd made in the sky and vanished into the torrent of time. The other gods quickly followed, fleeing into the void behind her. Their retreat was so bright that Bex had to hide her eyes, burying her face in Adrian's coat until every divine presence was gone, and the world fell into a stillness deeper than any she'd ever felt before.

"What is that?" she whispered when the quiet didn't stop.

"Peace," the Morrigan breathed, collapsing back into her human form as she leaned on the Old Wives' arms. "It's over. Gilgamesh is dead, and the gods are gone. There's no one left to rule over us now."

"Can we please go back to English?" Adrian asked desperately. "Because I don't speak Riverlander, and I have no idea what's going on."

"Well, *my* Riverlander is coming along splendidly," Boston said proudly as he jumped off of Bran, who'd been hiding them both on the other side of the tank's rim. "I was able to understand almost all of that, which is how *I* know that the Morrigan worked with the Blackwood to bind herself and all the other gods to the Great Cycles. By tying herself to the turning of this world, she forced the rest of her kind into a devil's choice: Stay here and grow old along with everything else or leave and keep their immortality. As you just saw, they all chose to go, which means we're *finally* out from under every pair of want-to-be-divine ruler's boots. Is that correct?"

"It is indeed," the Morrigan said, giving the cat an impressed smile. "Good work, little familiar."

Boston's chest puffed out so far that Bex was worried he'd pull something, but Adrian just looked floored.

"*That's* how all that forest got here!" he cried, getting so close to the new window the Morrigan had ripped in the floor that Bex grabbed his coat on instinct. "I thought there was a lot more tree coverage than quintessence-accelerated growth could account for."

"That's because the Morrigan added her own blood to your mix," his mother explained. "She bound herself to our coven, allowing the forest's roots to enter her heart, where they then spread into the magic shared by all the gods for the construction of Paradise."

Adrian frowned. "But I thought the Morrigan didn't contribute to Paradise?"

"Not willingly," the Morrigan said. "But as I'm sure you've noticed by now, my kind has never cared much for consent. They dragged me into their plans just as they did everything else in this world, and now that greed has become their downfall." Her pale face split into a grin. "Seems the gods and Gilgamesh had even more in common than they realized."

"All tyrants are the same," Muriel agreed. "But we should be grateful for that. Had Gilgamesh not sought total control, he never would've allowed Adrian into his Heaven and opened the crack that allowed all of this to happen."

"It could *only* have gone as it went," the Morrigan said. "It wouldn't have mattered if I'd tied the gods to mortality while they were still trapped in their coffins. They had to be up and about again in order to know what they'd lost and choose to leave. It was quite the needle to thread, but I had no doubt. My sweet Muriel has always been the best when it comes to these things."

The Witch of the Future dipped her wide-brimmed witch hat gracefully at the compliment, but Adrian just rubbed his temples with a sigh.

"Well," he said, "at least now I understand why you let Gilgamesh kidnap me."

"You were our Trojan horse into many things," his mother informed him with a wink. "Never underestimate the patience of witches."

"I think this goes beyond patience," Adrian argued, glaring at the Morrigan. "Just how long were you planning all of this for?"

"Since Gilgamesh conquered Paradise the first time," the goddess replied with a shrug. "That's when I had the original idea, though I didn't get serious until around a thousand years ago." She heaved a long sigh. "Even I can fall victim to the divine fallacy of infinite time, though I suppose I'm free of that now that I'm mortal."

"How long will you live?" Bex asked.

"Who knows?" the goddess said as her thin lips curved into a smile. "But I'm excited to find out. Having limited time is a new experience for me. It makes everything feel more important and exciting, especially since I've got a forest of my own now." She turned to Adrian. "Do you always feel everything crawling on you, or does that fade with time?"

"It doesn't fade, but you do get used to it," Adrian said. "But what do you mean *your* forest? All of this grew out of *my* heart tree."

"You should be grateful she's committed to taking it over," his mother chided. "Unless you want to be stuck in Paradise for the rest of your life?"

"Not particularly," Adrian admitted, rubbing the back of his neck. "Assuming I survived, I was actually planning to move everything back to Seattle the moment Gilgamesh was dead. Unless *you're* planning to stay, of course."

He'd been talking to his mother, so Bex didn't realize that last part was meant for her until Adrian turned around.

"I don't know what I'm doing," she confessed, glancing down at the new, inhospitable-looking forest. "I've always promised my people that I'd return them to Paradise, but I don't see any Rivers of Death down there."

"The rivers will never flow here again," the Morrigan informed her gravely. "The only reason they were in Paradise to begin with is because that's where the Wheel of Reincarnation forced them to flow. Now that the wheel is broken, they're back to flowing where they used to before the gods started meddling: into the great beyond."

"Well, that's going to be a problem," Bex said angrily. "We might not be Ishtar's tools anymore, but my people still need to eat. Without rivers full of souls to pull from, where are they supposed to get their sins?"

"How is that my problem?" the Morrigan snapped. "Gilgamesh broke the wheel, not me. You should be grateful to be free."

"I am grateful," Bex insisted, running her hands between her new horns. "It's just... Paradise is supposed to be our home. It's the land we always thought we'd come back to, but how can I tell my people to make a life in a place with no food?"

"Maybe you don't have to," Adrian said, reaching out to touch her shoulder. "I know Paradise was always the goal, but I've heard you talk to a lot of demons at this point, and the number one thing they've always said they wanted was for you to set them free, which you did. They're free from Gilgamesh *and* Ishtar thanks to what we did today! But just because this place is no longer the Paradise it used to be five thousand years ago doesn't mean you've failed. Quite the opposite. You've already led your people to a *new* paradise full of food where they can raise their families in peace and live exactly as they please."

He finished with a smile, but Bex still felt like she'd missed something important. "What are you talking about?"

"I'm talking about Earth," Adrian said, grinning wider. "It's the home of every human in existence. That's enough sin to feed your entire population a thousand times over, and thanks to the evacuation, your people are already there! They don't even have to worry about being named. Now that the gods have all left and taken their quintessence blood with them, Gilgamesh's warlocks are finished. They could know the name of every demon on the planet, but with no more quintessence coming down from Heaven, they won't have enough power to order one to tie their shoes."

His blue-gray eyes flashed as he moved closer. "You know what that means, right? Your people are free. Truly, one hundred percent completely at liberty in a land with tons of food, no threats, and no one who can tell them what to do. You don't have to take them back to Paradise. They're already there, and *you're* the one who made it possible."

It did sound incredible when he put it that way, but Bex was still shaking her head. Adrian didn't understand. Paradise was more than a place. It was their promised land, their sacred home. Even if it was isolated and covered in impenetrable jungle, she couldn't just let it—

Why couldn't you? Drox asked quietly in her mind. *When you confronted Ishtar and took her power, you said you were doing it to set your people free, and so you* have done. Paradise has been our rallying cry for a long time, but this place is not the Riverlands of Ishtar. That was a golden realm of plenty. This is a mosquito-infested hellscape.

"I can't believe you're okay with this," Bex muttered, staring at her ring. "We're talking about *Paradise*. Our *home*."

Homes change, Drox replied in a wistful voice. *Other than the Queen of Pride and the people of Wrath who were trapped in Limbo, none of the demons alive today are old enough to know what Paradise looked like, including yourself. Even those who do remember it wouldn't recognize it now. If you ask me, this jungle is worse than the Goddeath Wastes. At least Gilgamesh's desert didn't have predators.*

Bex did see some big shapes moving through the forest now that Drox pointed them out. Just thinking about that on top of everything else made her want to cry, but she couldn't give up on this. She'd never given up on anything when it came to her people, but—

You're not giving up, Drox said. *You're choosing the better path and the strategically stronger one. Nothing undermines a queen's stability like starvation and dissatisfaction. Even your faithful Lysanae would object if you asked them to live in a foodless jungle over a land of plenty like Seattle purely for the sake of tradition.*

He was right. Lys would hate the *crap* out of that jungle no matter what Bex called it, and funny enough, the image of their horrified face was what changed her mind. Lys was the one who'd been saying Bex would take them home to Paradise longer than anyone else. If even they wouldn't want to return to a place like this, then that was the end of it.

Wise choice, my queen, her sword said. *I'm sure your people will appreciate you bending on this matter.*

Bex was certain they would. Even pious old Zargrexa would balk if Bex told her she was moving the wrath demons, who'd already suffered so many years of starvation, to somewhere that didn't even have a river. In fact, she couldn't think of a single demon who'd call the jungle below them Paradise.

That made her feel better about her choice than anything else yet, and she turned to the Morrigan with a smile.

"If any of my people *really* want to return to our ancestral home, I hope you'll allow them into your jungle," she said. "In exchange, I'm willing to officially relinquish our claim on the former Riverlands of Paradise to the Witches of Blackwood. Is that acceptable?"

"Quite," the Morrigan said, giving Bex a sharp-toothed grin. "It's gratifying to know our victory won't be marred by an ugly territorial fight. If you give up your lands to the wilds peacefully, I promise to welcome all demons beneath my trees. Just be sure your people understand that permission to live here is not the same as guaranteeing their safety." Her grin grew wider. "The forest does not coddle the weak."

"I'll pass that along," Bex promised. "I don't think anyone will actually take me up on the offer, but I wanted to give them a choice. My demons have been forced to obey other people's whims for far too long. I want the decision of where to live to be in their hands, not mine. All I've ever wanted is for them to be free."

The words rolled so easily off her tongue that Bex didn't realize the full implication of what she'd just said until several seconds later.

Her people were free. Paradise might not be a paradise anymore, but that was just semantics. Whatever land the demons called home from this day forward, Gilgamesh was dead and the gods were gone. There'd be no more quintessence or divine edicts after today, nothing that could force her people to do or say or be anything they didn't want to. Until the other queens woke up, there was no one except Bex left who could make them bow, which meant…

"It's over," she whispered, staggering into Adrian so hard she almost knocked them both over. "The war is over. We won. We're *free*!"

She broke down totally after that, laughing and sobbing at the same time as she grabbed Adrian and spun him around in a fit of pure joy. She was so happy she felt sick and so relieved that she felt drunk. The heady combination pushed every other thought away, so Bex wasn't surprised when she finally emerged from her victory-induced delirium to discover it was just her and Adrian sitting alone on top of the Morrigan's invisible window above the forest.

"Hey," he said, pulling her tight against his side. "Have you finally come down?"

"I don't think I'll ever come down from this," Bex said, looking around the quintessence tank, which they were still technically sitting at the bottom of. "Where'd everybody go?"

"My family went back to the Blackwood to finish up Gilgamesh's army, the Morrigan is off inspecting her new forest, and Boston decided to go exploring with Bran," he informed her before his face fell into a scowl. "I should probably go check on those last two, actually. They've been gone for quite a while."

"I'm sure they're fine," Bex said, settling her head back against his shoulder with a sigh. "I'm sure everything's fine and nothing will ever be wrong again."

"You'll forgive me if I don't trust your addled judgement," Adrian said, adjusting her position slightly so that her horns wouldn't stab him in the face. Her *two* horns.

"Wait," Bex said, sitting back up as she jerked her hands to her head. "What happened to my horns?"

"I was going to talk to you about that when you were more coherent," Adrian said as he reached sheepishly into his coat. "But while you were busy processing all the emotions caused by nearly dying multiple times, the loss of your gods, and achieving the single driving ambition of all your lifetimes, they sort of… fell off."

"They *fell off*?" Bex repeated, gaping in horror as Adrian handed her the four long black horns he'd pulled out of his enchanted pockets.

"I don't… I can't… why did this happen?" Bex stuttered as she took them. "I've never heard of any demon's horns just falling off. What does it mean? Did I do something wrong?"

She was terrified it was because she'd given up their claim on Paradise. As always, though, Drox was there with the practical explanation.

They fell off because you kept your promise, her sword told her calmly. *You said it yourself: Your demons put that crown on your head so that you could defeat*

Gilgamesh, and you did. All the tyrants are gone and your people are free, which means there's no more need for you to keep weighing yourself down with such heavy burdens.

His black ring turned on her finger to bump against the four black horns Bex was clutching to her chest.

Your duty is completed, Bex of the Bonfire, Blade of Her People. Rest now from your labors and enjoy the peace your dedication has earned.

Drox's voice went silent then, leaving Bex alone in her head. She was still processing it all when Adrian leaned over to peek at her lowered face.

"You were just talking to your sword, right? What did he say?"

"He said I'm done," Bex whispered, moving the four shed horns to her left hand so she could reach up and touch the two she still had with her right.

It felt like stepping back in time. The two horns she hadn't lost were at her temples, in the exact same position as her original pair, but that wasn't where the similarities stopped. They had the same curve, the same ridges, even the same weight as the ones the Queen of War had ripped off her head. The only difference was that she didn't feel them pushing down when she thought the name *Rebexa*. These were still her new crown, Bex's horns. Otherwise, everything felt the same as it had the evening Adrian pulled her out of his bonfire. No fear-demon scales or war-demon bronze appeared on her arm when she clenched her fist, either, and Bex's lips curled into a smile.

"Huh," she said as she lowered her hand. "Looks like I'm back to being just the Queen of Wrath again."

"Is that a good thing?" Adrian asked nervously.

"It's fantastic," Bex assured him, handing her horns back to Adrian since the leggings she was wearing didn't have pockets. "All that power and responsibility was a pain in the neck, and my people deserve to make their own decisions for once. They just got free of Gilgamesh's warlocks. The last thing they need is a queen bossing them around."

"You deserve a break from them as well," Adrian said as his lips curved into a sly smile. "You know, if you're looking for something to do with all your new free time, I happen to be acquainted with a witch who'd love to take you on a very extensive, very leisurely tour of all the interesting things to do in Seattle."

Bex smiled back. "Do you, now?"

"He desperately needs your help," Adrian told her gravely. "He's terrible at doing fun things by himself. I mean, he's lived in Seattle all summer, and he's only visited one brewery, one tourist-trap restaurant, and one boba tea shop. That's pathetic."

"That just means he's got a lot left to explore," Bex said, scooting closer. "How soon would this witch like to start?"

"The moment you're ready," Adrian replied, offering her his hand with a flourish. "Just say the word, and I'll fly us to dinner right now."

Bex's stomach rumbled loudly at the mention of dinner. She couldn't actually remember the last time she'd eaten real food. She was so hungry right now that any edible substance sounded like heaven, especially if she got to eat it with Adrian, but...

"Are you sure we can?" she asked nervously. "What about the battle for the Blackwood?"

"What about it?" Adrian asked with a shrug. "The main grove's got the Three Old Wives, the bull of Ishtar, my entire coven, and half a million demons fighting against an army of coddled cowards who've just learned their god-king has been defeated and their magic's about to be toast. I'm pretty sure it can survive our absence. I, however, will perish right here on this spot if I don't take you out for pizza in the next five minutes."

"I definitely don't want you to die after all that trouble," Bex said, laughing as she grabbed his hand. "And I *love* pizza."

Adrian pulled her to her feet with a grin, pausing just long enough to kiss her on the cheek before whirling around to yell for Boston to come back so they could go get dinner.

Epilogue

Six weeks later.

"And that about wraps it up for us," said the old hate demon who ran the new demon community in Atlanta. "The Ponce Anchor Market finally collapsed last week due to lack of quintessence, but we'd already picked it down to the floorboards, so it wasn't a loss. Between those goods and the gold we stripped off Gilgamesh's palace, our budget's set for the foreseeable future."

"Good work," Bex said, holding her two remaining horns high as she smiled at the grid of horned, fanged faces that'd shown up for her weekly video call with demon leaders from the southern US. "Thank you, everyone. for your hard work and for keeping me informed. We'll do this again same time next week. If you have any problems before then, send a message to Lys, and we'll get right back to you."

"Great queen," the demons all said, bowing their horns before everyone switched off their cameras and left the video call, leaving Bex sitting alone at her desk in the new client-suite-turned-office-turned-smoking-crater-turned-back-to-office at the nose of their Winnebago.

Honestly, the repair was a *huge* improvement. Their old RV had been overdue for a renovation even before Heaven's attack on the Seattle Anchor pulverized it. She'd worried it couldn't be saved at all now that quintessence was rarer than sunshine in a Seattle January, but that was before Leander had stepped up and offered to help. Not only was he a kick-ass sorcerer, as the only surviving white-blooded prince, he was also the last remaining source of quintessence in the entire world.

That gave him the power and the skills to do a lot more than RV repair, but he'd still done an incredible job. He'd put their whole home back together and then some, adding more power to the engine and more space to the inside, including an office expansion that gave them enough room for Bex, Lys, and Iggs to all have their own desks.

They certainly needed them. Bex might not be the official Queen of All Demons anymore, but she was still the only one all the newly freed factions could agree to listen to. After the fall of Paradise and the defeat of Heaven's final army at the Blackwood, the demon population had scattered to the four winds. This was partially due to practical concerns—with no more access to the Rivers of Death, everyone had to eat emotions straight from humans, and too many demons feeding off one population quickly led to problems—but an equally big part of it was freedom.

Now that they were free to go anywhere, anywhere was where they went, scattering all over the globe in search of new food, new opportunities, and a chance to finally get away from each other after the horrific overcrowding of the Hells. There were still a few teams of former slaves who'd become trench buddies after centuries of working together under a warlock, but the vast majority of demonkind seemed to want to get as far from anything involving their old life as possible.

The diaspora made it harder to keep tabs on everyone, but Bex didn't care. That freedom was the entire reason she'd done this. She *wanted* her people to run off and enjoy their new lives, especially since modern technology made getting resources to demons who needed them easy even when they were on the other side of the planet. The number of video meetings was already decreasing as everyone settled into their new homes. Case in point, Bex didn't have anything on her schedule for the rest of the afternoon, which meant she was finally free to get out of this damn chair.

Rising with a stretch that didn't get anywhere near the office's new arched ceiling, Bex grabbed her new leather jacket—a present from Adrian, who'd made it himself—off the wall hook and made her way out the door. In the RV's old configuration, this would've put her in the hallway on the crew level, but Leander had expanded more than just the office. The lower floor of their RV had been completely gutted and redone into a hospital wing for the sleeping queens.

Nemini was with them as always, sitting in her new recliner with her eyes closed. She spent eight hours a day like that, searching through the darkness as she called out for their lost sisters, but her yellow eyes opened when Bex came over.

"Any luck?"

"Luck is just a projection of our personal wants upon the infinitely unpredictable cosmos," the Queen of Pride reminded her. "Our sisters have been lost in an infinite void for five thousand years. Even with their names returned, it would be extremely unlikely for me to find them so soon."

"I wish I could've saved their swords," Bex grumbled. "I found their hands when I searched Gilgamesh's workshop, but their rings had already been turned to ash." She heaved a furious sigh. "It's my fault. If I'd just remembered to go back sooner instead of having a joy-induced meltdown, I could've saved them and given you some help."

"It wouldn't have made a difference," Nemini assured her, reaching up to touch the nest of snakes snoozing on her head. "From what you've said about Gilgamesh's setup, he chose his fuel well. Once they get going, nothing can extinguish Enki's sparks of creation. Even if you'd removed the rings the moment you laid eyes on them, they still would've burned to ash."

So she kept saying, but that didn't stop Bex from feeling guilty as she turned to look at the only bed in the big new room that was separated from the others by a curtain.

It was Mara's bed, and Leander was sitting beside it as usual. The Queen of Sorrow still hadn't budged—she *never* moved except to breathe—but she was looking much better with her huge, downward-pointing crown of horns back on her head and her right hand reattached to her wrist. Bex was certain she would've looked even better with her ring, but the sight still gave her hope.

"They'll come back," she said, more for herself than Nemini. "And we'll be waiting. Even if it takes another five thousand years, we'll be here to welcome them home."

"Five thousand years is longer than you think," Nemini warned as her eyes slid closed again. "But I hope you're right."

Bex was certain she would be. She had no idea how long her life would last now that she was filled with the fires of life instead of Ishtar's wrath, but her flames were far from out. She'd hold on until her sisters found their way home, and then she'd explain to them in person exactly how things had ended up this way. After all they'd been through, it was the least she could do.

She just wished they were *all* there. Leander had designed it to look palatial, but the queens' recovery room still had only six beds. Bex and Nemini didn't need spots, of course, but despite promising that she'd look, the Morrigan had yet to turn up any sign of the Queen of War's body. Not that a traitor like her deserved to lie here with the rest of them, but Bex still felt bad about leaving her behind, especially given how terrifying the Morrigan's new jungle was becoming.

As Bex had predicted, *none* of her demons had wanted to move there. A few adventurous souls had visited the new Blackwood just for a chance to see Paradise with their own eyes, but every one of them had come racing back through the roots with stories about a nightmare jungle that sounded like a haunted version of the Amazon on steroids. Bex was happier than ever that she'd decided not to take her people back there, but she still felt bad about leaving War's body behind to rot. Still, her sister was strong and stubborn. She'd turn up eventually, Bex was sure of it.

Meanwhile, she had other, much more pleasant things to look forward to.

Speaking of which, it was getting close to dinnertime. Adrian had said something about getting sushi. Bex had never tried sushi, but he swore raw fish was the best fish, and her witch hadn't led her wrong yet when it came to food. He hadn't led her wrong, period, which was enough to make Bex grin as she left Nemini to her meditation and started toward the stairs. She'd just begun climbing up the steep spiral that led to the RV's main floor when a man's voice called her name.

"Queen of Wrath."

Bex looked back over her shoulder and saw Leander standing at the foot of the stairs. The prince was looking *much* better these days. Not that it'd be hard to look better than the skeleton he'd been when she'd pulled him out of the Lowest Hells, but the healthy man standing behind her was an improvement even over the gaunt prince he'd been when Bex had first seen him on the street behind Pike Place Market. He'd put on weight, cut his dark hair, even gotten himself some new clothes—boring, severe clothes that made him look like a lawyer, but still an enormous step up from the haunted man in dirty white pajamas who'd helped her and Adrian storm Gilgamesh's tower.

He insisted the changes were for Mara's sake, that a man seeking to woo a queen couldn't possibly do so while looking like a starved vagabond, but Bex suspected that Adrian had a great deal to with it. He'd been stuffing food into Leander like a worried grandmother from the moment his brother arrived in Seattle. She wasn't sure if it was brotherly affection or allowing anyone to be underfed in his presence went against Adrian's nature as a Witch of the Flesh, but Leander was looking much better for it. He was also looking impatient, so Bex turned all the way around and gave him her full attention.

"What's up?"

"I would like to ask a favor, if I may," the prince said, looking up at Bex with mirrored eyes that would never stop creeping her out.

"Name it," she told him. "We owe you big time for fixing our home."

"That is good to hear," the prince replied. "Because your home is what I wanted to talk to you about. I'm about to begin renovations on the topmost story, and I was wondering if you'd be willing to let me use the master suite."

"The master suite?" Bex repeated, crossing her arms over her chest. "You mean *my* master suite?"

"That would be why I'm asking you instead of someone else," the prince answered drily.

It made sense when he put it that way, but, "Didn't Adrian already build you a whole bedroom in his loft?"

"My youngest brother has been most hospitable," Leander acknowledged. "But while my new room is perfectly adequate, I find living in a witchwood to be... emotionally unpleasant. I'd much rather be here where I can't feel the forest, and where I'm closer to Mara."

As always when he said her name, Leander's face softened, making him look almost handsome. "I'd like to be as close as possible when she wakes up," he continued. "I'd also like a private bathroom, and since you never seem to spend the night in your own room anymore these days, I thought it'd be more practical if we switched."

By the time he finished, Bex's face was so hot, she was shocked she hadn't burst into flames. Embarrassment aside, though, Leander had a point. Since Adrian had brought her home after their victory in Heaven, he and Bex had gotten much closer. *So* close that she couldn't actually remember the last time she'd used her suite at the top of the RV. Her guitar, toiletries, and all her clothes had already migrated over to Adrian's. The only things left in her room at this point were the furniture and the first aid kit she no longer needed to use.

"I don't have a problem if you want to live in the RV," she said, rubbing the back of her neck in an attempt to hide how flushed her face still was. "You're here all the time anyway, so it's definitely more practical, but I should probably ask Adrian if he's okay with it first."

"I'm sure he won't mind," Leander replied with utmost confidence as he walked back to Mara's bedside. "I'll go ahead and start on the renovations tomorrow. Make sure you move anything you don't want crushed out of the way before then. Stretched space has a low tolerance for preserving obstacles."

"You could wait until I actually say 'yes' first," Bex called after him, but he was already making himself comfortable in his chair, so of course her complaint was ignored.

Muttering under her breath about arrogant princes, she turned around and stomped up the stairs, heading through the ground floor of the RV, which still looked pretty much the same as it had before. Leander hadn't cared about this level nearly as much as he had about the place where Mara would be, so he'd just repaired things back to the way they'd been originally. This included Norma, who was right back in her usual seat up in the driver's cab, humming off-key to herself as she happily read through the new road atlas Iggs had bought for her. She greeted Bex with a cheerful "Howdy!" as the queen walked by, but otherwise paid no attention as Bex opened the aluminum side door and stepped out into the forest.

Even after all these weeks, it felt amazingly good to be home. It was now full-on winter in Seattle, but all the rain and cold in the world couldn't make Adrian's Blackwood look anything less than magical. Even the drips building up on the branches over her head looked like crystal beads, and the air smelled of rain and woodsmoke. Bex found it all incredibly cozy, though the small group of demons shivering in a line on the new path that led up to the clearing didn't look like they agreed.

Since they all shared a portion of her divine presence, every demon in the world had felt it when Ishtar left. Bex had worried that would be a crushing problem, but while there were definitely a few crises of faith, Ishtar had always been a dead goddess to the vast majority of the demon population. Bex's wrath demons were the only ones who actually remembered a time when Ishtar was around acting like a goddess. They were taking the loss the hardest, but everyone else, *especially* the demons Bex had freed from the Hells, barely seemed to care. There were still a few who wanted divine guidance, though, and since Bex and her sisters were the closest things to gods that remained on Earth, most of those seekers ended up on Adrian's doorstep.

He'd been extremely understanding about the whole situation, even going so far as to make the pilgrims a safe path through his forest so they'd stop leaving offerings on the roadside where they could become a traffic hazard. All that worship still made Bex wildly uncomfortable, though. Fortunately for her, Lys had four hundred years of experience controlling access to the queen.

Her lust demon had jumped on the new worshipers before they could become a problem, taking their offerings, writing down prayers, and so forth. They'd even made Bex a schedule so she could meet with her new faithful during a controlled time window and tell them everything was going to be fine. That was all most of them wanted to hear anyway, and for once it wasn't even a lie. Compared to how things had been for her people before the fall of Gilgamesh, life was freaking fantastic.

Bex was more than happy to tell them so, though she wished they'd stop bringing her so much stuff. Even with the new wealth her demons were enjoying thanks to all the gold they'd stripped off Gilgamesh's palace, setting up new lives for an entire population was *expensive*. The pilgrims always looked especially threadbare, proof that they needed their gifts much more than Bex did. No matter how many times she told them to stop, they never did.

At least the line was shorter these days. Lys was in their normal position under the wooden shelter Adrian had built for them, but only a half dozen people were waiting in front of their desk when Bex walked over. They all bowed low when the queen approached, but Lys was too busy glaring at the tall blond fear demon leaning against one of the shelter's support beams to give Bex more than a nod.

"Hello, Your Majesty," Desh said with a lavish bow, dumping all the rain that had pooled on the hood of his rain jacket straight onto the middle of the plastic folding table Lys used as a desk.

"Could you *not*?" they growled, slinging the water back at him.

"Sorry," Desh replied, sounding like he meant it for once. "Just trying to pay my respects to the queen who saved us all."

The line of pious demons who'd come to see Bex nodded wildly, and Lys sighed.

"Yes, yes, we're all very respectful," they muttered, grabbing a towel off the back of their chair to wipe up the water they hadn't managed to sling at Desh. "Though I'd respect you a lot more if you got to the point."

"No need to be touchy," Desh chided, digging into his coat. "I just dropped by to say hello and to pass this on."

He handed Bex a heavy packet of thick, seemingly homemade paper wrapped in waxed cloth and tied with a black string.

"What's that?" she asked curiously. "It looks like a challenge letter."

"It's a bill, I'm afraid," Desh said sheepishly. "As I told you in my report last month, the Battle for the Blackwood was a total rout in our favor. Gilgamesh's army didn't even have a prince, just a bunch of

Heavenly pigs who hadn't left their troughs in eons. They were powerful sorcerers, but they were so used to living in Heaven that they had to guzzle quintessence like cheap beer just to stay upright. Enemy supplies were already running low before word even got back that Gilgamesh had died. As soon as they realized they no longer had a king in their corner *and* there'd be no more quintessence coming, the whole front folded like a cheap deck chair."

"If it was that easy, why are we getting a bill?" Lys growled.

"Because the sorcerers weren't the ones who did the most damage," Desh explained, keeping his orange eyes on Bex. "That honor went to Ishtar's bull. The battle-maddened bastard flattened ten hectares of old-growth forest on his way to the fight. He also flattened a bunch of sorcerers, so nobody's mad at him, but the damage still has to be covered, and since you're the one who sent him, the witches asked me to bring you the bad news once they finished healing me up from my heroic war wounds."

He pulled his dripping hood back to show Bex the new notch missing from one of his horns, and she smiled.

"I suppose that's only fair," she said, untying the packet of handmade paper to find a carefully itemized list of expenses that looked like it had been written by a very annoyed person using a feather quill. "I mostly sent the bull to the Blackwood to get him off my back, so I don't mind paying for the damages."

"*I* mind," Lys snapped, hauling themselves up with the cane they unfortunately had to use now, since even Adrian's witchcraft hadn't been enough to heal all the damage left by their fight with the prince. If having a cane slowed Lys down, though, Bex couldn't tell. They'd already snatched the papers out of her hands, their amber eyes going huge as they flipped through the seemingly endless list of numbers.

"Those greedy witches want seven figures!" they cried. "There's no way trees are that expensive."

"It's *really* okay," Bex insisted. "But I'll talk to Adrian about it if it makes you feel better."

"You'd better talk to him," Lys grumbled as they flopped back into their chair. "What's the point of shacking up with the head witch's son if it doesn't get us a discount? Do those witches understand how much it costs to find new housing for an entire population?"

"Sounds like the matter's settled, then," Desh said cheerfully as he stepped back out into the drizzling rain. "Lovely as always to see you both again, but I've got to get going. I left Streya with some old mates of ours from the Hells, but she's still got major separation anxiety. It'll be better for everybody if I get back quick-like, so I'm off. You know my number if you need me!"

"No one needs you," Lys told him, but their voice held no venom for once as they added, "Don't fall off the ferry."

Desh waved over his head and jogged off down the path, vanishing into the dripping forest the second he reached it like a deer into the mist.

Shaking her head at the seemingly obligatory fear-demon need to make a dramatic exit, Bex took a seat at the table next to Lys and spent a few minutes accepting prayers from the demons who'd come to see her. When they were all satisfied that their queen had heard them and were safely on their way out of the forest, Bex told Lys to go get some dinner and made her way at last to Adrian's cabin.

She still wasn't sure how the building had made it back here from the Holy City. The last time she'd seen it, the cabin had been sitting high in the branches of his giant tree. When they'd finally come back to his forest after pizza, though, the cozy witch hut had been right back where Adrian set it up the first day he'd come to Bainbridge.

That had seriously freaked her out. As with all the weird happenings in his forest, however, Adrian had taken it in stride. Or maybe he'd just been in a hurry to get her inside. That *had* been their first night back together and alone. Thinking back on it now still made Bex a little giddy, a feeling that was only amplified when she saw Adrian waiting for her.

He was right where he always was when she got off work: sitting in one of the two new wooden Adirondacks he'd made for his porch so they wouldn't have to sit on the stairs now that it was the rainy season. Not that Bex wouldn't have gladly sat on the ground if it meant being next to him, but the new chairs were insanely comfortable for something made from wood. Adrian was hard at work making something else out of wood right now, carving down a large stick of maple while Boston snoozed beside him next to the clay chiminea Adrian had set up on the porch to take the chill out of the wet air.

His whole face lit up when he spotted Bex walking over. He sprang out of his chair at once, setting his woodworking down on the armrest to give her a kiss that tasted faintly of sawdust.

"Hello," he whispered in a warm voice before giving her another kiss on the neck that made Bex's whole body shiver. "Your tea is on your chair."

"Thanks," Bex said as she staggered to her seat. She didn't know when Adrian's kisses would stop making her stomach feel like a swarm of butterflies, but so far, the answer seemed to be *never*.

Still blushing furiously, Bex groped for the tea he'd made for her, which was exactly where he'd said it'd be on the arm of the chair that he'd also made for her. He'd made her a whole ton of stuff now that he had time, including a hand-thrown pottery mug sized exactly to fit her hand with a leaf-shaped lid to keep her tea warm.

"Thanks," she said again, cupping the warm cup between her hands as she relaxed into the smooth, sturdy chair that put her at the perfect angle to look up at the forest's dripping canopy. "Can I talk to you about—"

"If this is about the bill, I'm on it," he said as he plopped back down in his own chair. "I already told the Old Wives I'd replace the trees last week, but my cousin Arachne is the coven's accountant, and she's a stickler for this sort of thing."

He picked up his woodworking project again with a sigh. "I'll go through the roots tomorrow and take a look at the damage myself. At the very least, you shouldn't have to pay what she's asking. Market value for the lumber is just ridiculous, especially since you're not even getting the wood."

"I really don't mind paying for damages I incurred," Bex insisted. Then she smiled. "But I don't want to spend the money if I can avoid it. We probably won't be getting another Heavenly palace to strip, and being queen isn't exactly raking in the cash. I need to make the funds we've got last, so thanks for looking out for us."

Adrian huffed as though he were insulted she thought he wouldn't, and Bex's smile grew wider.

"Did you want to talk about the scales, then?" he asked instead. "I read Iggs's report about the baby. It really looks like the spell that put scales in every human's eyes at birth ended with Gilgamesh. That doesn't affect the scales that are already in people's eyes, of course, but things are going to get very interesting in the next few years when all the babies who can see magic their scale-eyed parents can't get old enough to talk."

"Very interesting," Bex agreed. "But that wasn't what I wanted to talk about either."

"I'll stop guessing blindly, then," Adrian said, giving her a sheepish look as he put down his woodworking and turned to give her his full attention. "What's on your mind?"

It was actually much harder to broach the subject now that he was looking at her so intently, but Bex had faced princes, gods, and a god-king, and she managed this, too, eventually.

"It's about your brother, actually," she said, putting down her mug so she could give him her full attention as well. "Leander wants to move into the RV."

"That would be a relief," Adrian admitted. "Not that I mind hosting him, but he's not the most pleasant roommate. Also, three's a crowd."

He finished with a slow smile that made Bex blush to the roots of her hair, which was ridiculous considering what she was about to ask. Her shyness must've been truly baked in, though, because Bex couldn't stop nervously fidgeting with Drox's ring as she forced herself to continue.

"He asked me if he could have my room upstairs," she said, spinning the heavy black loop like a pinwheel on her finger. "Since, you know, I'm not in it much these days."

"Sounds sensible," Adrian replied with a beaming smile that told Bex he already knew where this was going. "But if he's taking your room, you're going to need somewhere else to live."

"Yeah," she said, letting go of her ring to tug on her black hair instead. "I was hoping, that is, if it's okay with you, maybe I could—"

"Move into my place?" he finished eagerly. "I thought you'd never ask. I would *love* for you to move in with me, Bex."

"*I'd* love for you to move in with him," Boston added lazily from his spot in front of the chiminea. "Maybe he'll actually be able to focus on work for once if he's not pining all day waiting for your return."

Adrian shot his cat an irritated look, but Bex just smiled. "Well, if you're both okay with it, I'm in. It won't even really be moving, since most of my stuff's already here." She flashed Adrian a nervous smile. "Thanks for letting me invade."

"Thanks for wanting to," he said, reaching out to grip her still-fidgeting hand. "Thank you for everything."

"That's my line," Bex said, blushing furiously but keeping her eyes on Adrian as he pulled her captured hand over to his chair. "I get to move into a custom house on an island. All you get are a bunch of demons knocking on your door at all hours."

"They were doing that anyway," he reminded her, leaning down to press a kiss against her knuckles that somehow managed to go straight through the rest of Bex as well. "But I've never minded the demons. I love being part of your team, and I love that you moving in means I'll get to see you even more. I love you in general, just in case you needed a reminder."

Bex didn't. Adrian said and showed that he loved her every day, but that didn't stop her from grinning like an idiot.

"I love you too," she whispered back, squeezing his fingers tight. "Thanks for sticking through everything with me."

"As if I'd ever let you go," he said, kissing her hand again before he pulled her up from her chair and guided her inside his cozy cottage, where dinner was already warming on top of the stove.

Thank you for reading

....

Thank you for reading *Tear Down Heaven*!

I hope you enjoyed the story and that you'll consider leaving a review. Reviews, good or bad, are vital to every author's career, and I'd be extremely grateful if you'd take a moment to write one for me.

With this book finished, we're at the end. It's one of the most epic conclusions I've ever put together and hope you enjoyed it.

Want to be the first to know when my next book comes out? Sign up for my **new release mailing list**! (rachelaaron.net) List members get first dibs on all my books and I only email when I've got something new, so there's zero spam. Signing up is free and easy, so come join the fun!

Again, thank you so much for giving my stuff a chance! Readers like you are why independent books exist. Thank you from the bottom of my heart.

Yours always and forever,
Rachel Aaron

WANT MORE BOOKS?

....

Tear Down Heaven is only the latest addition to the Rachel Aaron library. I have plenty more books of all sorts for you to enjoy, including five finished series! Keep paging to see my top picks for new readers or visit **rachelaaron.net** for the full list, and, as always, thank you for reading!

Fortune's Pawn

(written as Rachel Bach)

A propulsive space opera perfect for fans of *Firefly* and *Killjoys*!

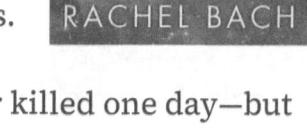

"Devi is hands-down one of the best sci-fi heroines I've read in a long time." **- RT Book Reviews**

Devi Morris isn't your average mercenary. She has plans. Big ones. And a ton of ambition. It's a combination that's going to get her killed one day—but not just yet.

That is, until she just gets a job on a tiny trade ship with a nasty reputation for surprises. *The Glorious Fool* isn't misnamed: it likes to get into trouble, so much so that one year of security work under its captain is equal to five years everywhere else. With odds like that, Devi knows she's found the perfect way to get the jump on the next part of her Plan. But the Fool doesn't give up its secrets without a fight, and one year on this ship might be more than even Devi can handle.

Powered armor and kissing, what more could you want?

Nice Dragons Finish Last

"Super fun, fast-paced urban fantasy full of heart, and plenty of magic, charm and humor to spare, this self-published gem was one of my favorite discoveries this year!" - **The Midnight Garden**

"A deliriously smart and funny beginning to a new urban fantasy series about dragons in the ruins of Detroit...inventive, uproariously clever, and completely un-put-down-able!" - **SF Signal**

As the smallest dragon in the Heartstriker clan, Julius survives by a simple code: stay quiet, don't cause trouble, and keep out of the way of bigger dragons. But this meek behavior doesn't cut it in a family of ambitious predators, and his mother, Bethesda the Heartstriker, has finally reached the end of her patience.

Now, sealed in human form and banished to the DFZ--a vertical metropolis built on the ruins of Old Detroit--Julius has one month to prove to his mother that he can be a ruthless dragon or lose his true shape forever. But in a city of modern mages and vengeful spirits where dragons are seen as monsters to be exterminated, he's going to need some serious help to survive this test.

He just hopes humans are more trustworthy than dragons.

The first and most popular DFZ series, complete at 5 books.

Minimum Wage Magic

"A catchy title, a plucky protagonist and a maximum effort by the author, honestly readers can't ask for more in the urban fantasy genre."- **Fantasy Book Critic**

The DFZ, the metropolis formerly known as Detroit, is the world's most magical city with a population of nine million and zero public safety laws. That's a lot of mages, cybernetically enhanced chrome heads, and mythical beasties who die, get into debt, and otherwise fail to pay their rent. When they can't pay their bills, their stuff gets sold to the highest bidder to cover the tab.

That's when they call me. My name is Opal Yong-ae, and I'm a Cleaner: a freelance mage with an art history degree who's employed by the DFZ to sort through the mountains of magical junk people leave behind. It's not a pretty job, or a safe one--there's a reason I wear bite-proof gloves--but when you're deep in debt in a lawless city where gods are real, dragons are traffic hazards, and buildings move around on their own, you don't get to be picky about where your money comes from. You just have to make it work, even when the only thing of value in your latest repossessed apartment is the dead body of the mage who used to live there.

A fun, standalone adventure set in the always-wild DFZ, complete at 3 books.

About the Author

Rachel Aaron is the author of twenty-plus novels both self-published and through Orbit Books. When she's not holed up in her writing cave, she lives a nerdy, bookish life in Colorado with her perpetual-motion son, long-suffering husband, and mountains of books. To learn more about Rachel and read samples of all her work, visit **rachelaaron.net**!

© 2026 by Rachel Aaron. All rights reserved.

Cover Illustration by *Luisa Preissler*
Cover Design by *Rachel Aaron*
Editing provided by *Red Adept Editing*

As ever, this book would not be as good without the amazing Linda Hall, the sharpest beta reader of all time. Thanks for all you do, Linda!

www.ingramcontent.com/pod-product-compliance
Lightning Source LLC
LaVergne TN
LVHW040035080526
838202LV00045B/3343